W9-DGB-854

SUSAN DICK is Associate Professor of English at Queen's University.

*To the Lighthouse* is thought by many to be Virginia Woolf's supreme achievement in fiction: with it, as she herself said, she became mistress of her medium. The novel exists in only two forms, the original holograph draft and the printed text. No intermediate versions have come to light. Susan Dick has transcribed the draft, page by page, and line by line, supplying references to the corresponding pages in the published editions of 1927.

A comparison between the draft and the final text tells us much about Virginia Woolf's way of working. We can follow the cutting of superfluous words and digressions, the enhancement of the energy and rhythmical flow of the prose, the changing emphasis on scenes, characters, and themes, and the intensification of significant images. The revisions testify to her remarkable understanding of language – an understanding won by hard work – and of the potentialities of the novel.

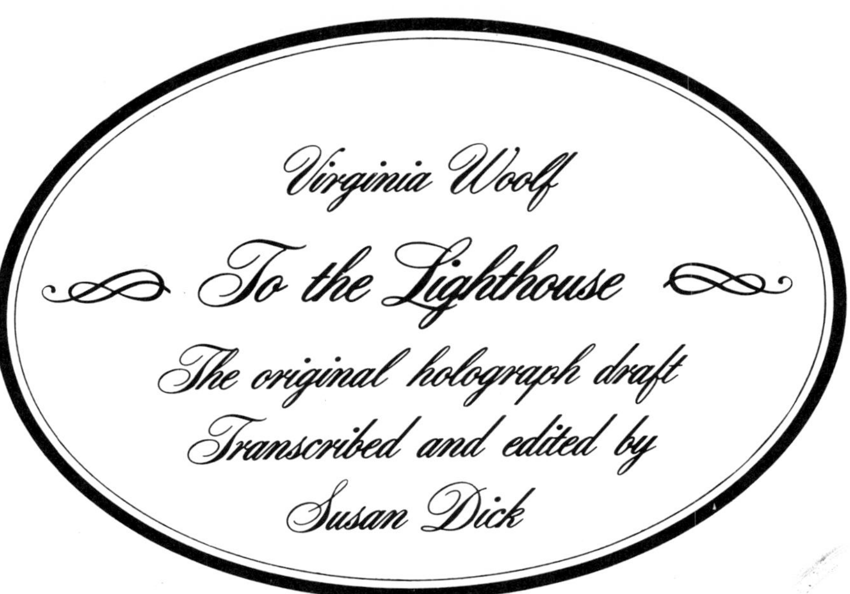




UNIVERSITY OF TORONTO PRESS
Toronto and Buffalo

Toronto Buffalo London
Printed in Canada
ISBN 0-8020-5524-9

---

**Canadian Cataloguing in Publication Data**

Woolf Virginia, 1882–1941.
To the lighthouse : the original holograph draft

ISBN 0-8020-5524-9

1. Woolf, Virginia, 1882–1941 – Manuscripts – Facsimiles. I. Dick, Susan, 1940– II. Title: To the lighthouse : the original holograph draft.

PR6045.072T6 1982 823'.912 C81–095139–8

---

# Contents

# Acknowledgments

For permission to transcribe and to publish the manuscript of *To the Lighthouse*, I wish to thank Quentin Bell and Angelica Garnett, administrators of the Author's Literary Estate, and the Henry W. and Albert A. Berg Collection, The New York Public Library, Astor, Lenox and Tilden Foundations. The Hogarth Press Ltd has kindly given me permission to quote from The Hogarth Press edition of *To the Lighthouse*, published in 1927. Excerpts from the Harcourt Brace Jovanovich edition of *To the Lighthouse* by Virginia Woolf are reprinted by permission of Harcourt Brace Jovanovich, Inc.

The research for this project was financed with the assistance of the Canada Council. This book has been published with the help of a grant from the Canadian Federation for the Humanities, using funds provided by the Social Sciences and Humanities Research Council of Canada, and a grant from the Publications Fund of the University of Toronto Press.

For help, encouragement, and advice, I wish also to thank Quentin Bell, Richard Ellmann, John Graham, A.C. Hamilton, S.P. Rosenbaum, Jon Stallworthy, John Stedmond, Leon Surette, Lola Szladits, and George Whalley. I owe special thanks to Jean C. Jamieson, Margaret Parker, and Prudence Tracy, editors at the University of Toronto Press. Continuing thanks go to my parents, Mr and Mrs James Dick.

Virginia Woolf
To the Lighthouse
The original holograph draft

# *Introduction*

## THE MANUSCRIPT

The manuscript of *To the Lighthouse* consists of three volumes. Volumes 1 and 2 are bound writing books, and volume 3 is a folder containing unbound pages.

Volume 1 has a shiny sea-green cover with a design drawn faintly in ink on the front which resembles the Hogarth Press logo. The first page is the title page, on which Virginia Woolf wrote 'To the Lighthouse, / Monks House, / begun (August 6th 1925) – Jan. 18th 1926 / finished March 16th 192~~6~~7.' The following two pages are taken up with notes for the novel, and the narrative begins on the fourth page. Each page has a heavy blue vertical line drawn down the left-hand side which marks off a wide margin. Here Virginia Woolf wrote words and passages which were to be incorporated into the narrative. The entire manuscript is written with a fine-point fountain pen in violet ink, probably the same kind she told Dorothy Brett about in 1923: 'The ink is Waterman's fountain pen ink. Cheap, violet, indelible.'[1] Practically all of the first writing book was used for *To the Lighthouse* (the narrative here covers 148 manuscript pages). The exceptions are the four pages on which Virginia Woolf sketched out portions of her essay on *Robinson Crusoe* and of her lecture 'How Should One Read a Book?' (MS 41–4) and two pages at the end of the book on which she wrote a segment of 'The Ghost of Sterne.'

Volume 2 has a dull blue cover but is otherwise similar to volume 1. On the cover Virginia Woolf drew a square in which she wrote '*To the Lighthouse* Vol. 2.' The manuscript takes up only twenty-seven pages of this book. The final page of the narrative is dated (in pencil) '29th March 1926,' and although the following page has 'To the' written at the top, the rest of the book is empty.

Volume 3 is a faded green folder with 'Miscellaneous' written on the cover (probably by Leonard Woolf). The manuscript pages contained here are all loose-leaf pages which appear to have been at one time in a notebook, for the holes are worn, though seldom torn. Two kinds of paper were used: paper on which Virginia Woolf drew the heavy blue marginal line and paper on which a thin red marginal line was printed. She began to use the second type of paper (which is otherwise like the first) with MS 283.

The pages of the writing books are unnumbered though frequently dated. The unbound pages are numbered and dated by Virginia Woolf. Volume 3 begins with her page 138. Since the manuscript covers 175 pages at this point, it is probable that 138 refers to the number of typed pages the manuscript now covered. According to Leonard Woolf, it was Virginia Woolf's habit to type in the afternoon what she had written in the morning.[2] Nothing seems to be missing from the manuscript, for volume 2 ends with the description of Mrs Ramsay leaving the dinner table and volume 3 opens with the account of her thoughts immediately after this. The scene is fragmentary, but then many scenes in the first draft are. Later in the manuscript Virginia Woolf again seems to key her pagination to a typescript. This occurs at MS 283, where she changed to the second kind of paper.[3] Just before this, she broke off her description of Lily's thoughts after Mr Ramsay, Cam, and James have left and wrote two portions of her lecture 'How Should One Read a Book?' The next page (MS 283) has 'To the Lighthouse' written in the centre at the top and 'type page 202' written in the right-hand corner (the date, 4 August 1926, is on the left). Her last page had been numbered 231. She now began to rework earlier passages found on her pages 216–25. My guess is that she had typed the narrative up to this point and now proceeded to revise it, again making the pagination follow that of her typescript. From this point on the pagination is continuous. She did not number the last thirteen pages.

All the evidence suggests that this is the complete first draft of the novel. I have been unable to locate any other drafts, any typescripts, or page proofs. The French translation of 'Time Passes,' published in *Commerce* in the winter of 1926, is the only transitional version I have found.[4] Aside from the comments made in her diary, the only notes for *To the Lighthouse* which appear to have survived (indeed, they may be the only ones she made) are those written in the notebook labelled 'Notes for Writing,' the outline of 'Time Passes,' and the few notes found in the manuscript itself.[5]

Virginia Woolf's handwriting is, on the whole, quite legible. At the beginning of the writing day, and at the top of each page, she wrote in a clear, small script. As she neared the bottom of the page, her letters grew larger and less well-defined, and the lines began to slant uphill. The manuscript pages are covered with cancellations and interlinear and marginal emendations. The interlinear emendations seem to have been written at the same time as the narrative, but the darker ink of many of the marginal emendations in all three volumes suggests that these may have been added later. Occasionally phrases are written in pencil, and these too were probably added later. From time to time a few notes are written on the verso pages, but these are infrequent and always brief.

The manuscript of *To the Lighthouse*, like her diary, shows that Virginia Woolf had by no means worked out every aspect of the novel before she began to write it, yet anyone reading the opening page, for example will be immediately struck by its similarity to the final text: '"If it's a fine day tomorrow" said Mrs. Ramsay. "But you'll have to be up with the lark," she added.' Throughout the first draft of the novel, Virginia Woolf's grasp of the direction the narrative would take, the relationships between the characters, and even the dominant image patterns and the main ideas she would explore, is firm. Each of the three sections has the shape in the first draft it would have in the final one. Though individual scenes caused her considerable trouble, the novel as a whole did not undergo the kind of complicated metamorphosis of which the manuscripts of earlier and later novels show evidence.[6] She used the word 'sketchy' to describe much of the first draft (D 117). In revising it – and sometimes she revised as she wrote, so one can watch some passages going through several stages in the manuscript – she turned this sketch into a richly textured work, but she did this without losing the freshness and energy of many of the original lines.

The manuscript also support Virginia Woolf's observations about the speed with which she wrote *To the Lighthouse*, but it demonstrates too that speed was not necessarily accompanied by an easy fluency. While reading through the manuscript, one has the impression of Virginia Woolf pushing herself as she wrote, forcing herself to say something even if it would later prove to be inadequate. In the manuscript she describes Mr Carmichael as a poet who waits patiently for inspiration: 'If words came they came. What good writing has ever been done in a hurry?... Did he not sometimes wait a whole winter for words to come to him' (MS 160). Virginia Woolf was not this kind of writer. She did her two pages a day whether words flew her way or not. Frequently they did, of course. Yet the manuscript also gives vivid evidence of the times when words would not obey her call and refused to shape themselves as she wanted them to. The contrast between sections which appear to have been written quite easily and those which had given her more trouble does not, so far as I can tell, reveal any clear pattern. I would guess that on the whole her fluency depended to a large extent upon her energy and that when she was feeling well and was not distracted by other responsibilities, her writing went quite well. Certain scenes did, as the reader will see, require more reworking than others, and some characters (Charles Tansley in particular) underwent a greater change during the revisions than did others.

Using the manuscript, comments from her diary, and Leonard Woolf's observations of her writing habits, one can speculate about how she actually composed. One of the first things that a reader of the manuscript notices is the great number of incomplete sentences in it. She appears to have begun each writing session by first reading over what she had last written. I suspect that this would not only jog her memory, but also help to start a particular rhythm in her mind. 'Style is a very simple matter,' she wrote to Vita Sackville-West while at work on *To the Lighthouse*, 'it is all rhythm.' She elaborated:

*Once you get that, you can't use the wrong words. But on the other hand here am I sitting after half the morning, crammed with ideas, and visions, and so on, and can't dislodge them, for lack of the right rhythm. Now this is very profound, what rhythm is, and goes far deeper than words. A sight, an emotion creates this wave in the mind, long before it makes words to fit it; and in writing [such is my present belief] one has to recapture this, and set this working [which has nothing apparently to do with words] and then, as it breaks and tumbles in the mind, it makes words to fit it.*[7]

The incomplete sentences found throughout the manuscript give the impression that she was often writing a kind of shorthand; when she could find the right rhythm, the words she put down would be directed by that and would probably enable her to find that rhythm again. When she was failing to recapture that 'wave in the mind' the sentence fragments may represent her attempt to overcome the barrier.

One also has the impression that at times her mind was working more swiftly than her pen and that she was able only to jot down fragments of her thoughts before these were crowded out by others. In *To the Lighthouse*, Lily's thoughts are said to move so rapidly that to follow them 'was like following a voice which speaks too quickly to be taken down with one's pencil' (40). When she wrote this passage in the manuscript, her handwriting changed noticeably, becoming larger and more hurried (MS 51). In his autobiography, Leonard Woolf has described what he calls his wife's 'genius' and he cites as evidence of this the way thoughts and images sometimes 'fountained up spontaneously, not directed and consciously controlled' in the midst of a conversation.[8] He also refers to her description in her diary of the way she seemed to 'stumble after' her own voice as she wrote the last pages of *The Waves*. 'Or almost,' she added, 'after some sort of speaker (as when I was mad) I was almost afraid, remembering the voices that used to fly ahead.'[9]

Though fragmentary in many ways, and for many reasons, the first draft of *To the Lighthouse* was, as the reader will see, firmly conceived. Once she had written the last words – 'But she had had her vision' – Virginia Woolf was ready to begin the second stage in the writing of her novel.

## SOME STYLISTIC AND BIOGRAPHICAL IMPLICATIONS

Since only the manuscript and the final version of the novel can be compared, one must speculate about the intermediary stages of the book. Without the typescripts, it is impossible to know how much revision was done during the first stage of typing. Presumably the major task of revision the novel began only after Virginia Woolf had completed the whole of the first draft. The patterns which emerge as one compares the manuscript with the final version suggest the method of revision that she must have used at each stage in the process. For purposes of discussion, the kinds of revisions she made may be grouped into several closely related categories: those that refined the style, those that altered the details, those that modified the shape of individual scenes and the characters within the scenes, and those that affected the emphasis placed on certain themes in the novel.

One of the most astonishing accomplishments of the revisions is the transformation of the fragmentary phrases, sentences, and paragraphs of the first draft into the poetic and syntactically complex prose of the final version. Sometimes the first and the final versions of a particular passage are quite similar, and revising these was primarily a matter of polishing the original prose. One example of this is one sentence from the second paragraph on the opening page (I quote the manuscript omitting most of the cancellations):

| | |
|---|---|
| *To her son these words conveyed* | *To her son these words conveyed* |
| *an extraordinary impression of* | *an extraordinary* |
| *joy. It seemed as if it were now* | *joy, as if it were* |
| *settled, & the expedition certain* | *settled, the expedition were bound* |
| *to take place, & the wonders to* | *to take place, and the wonder to* |
| *which he had looked forward* | *which he had looked forward* |
| *within touch* <with> *only a dazzling,* | *for years and years it seemed, was,* |
| *uneasy disquietude, & a nights,* | *after a night's darkness and* |
| <pains> *& then a day's sail,* | *a day's sail, within touch.* |
| *between.* | |

She noted on 9 March 1926, that she was writing 'oppositely from my other books: very loosely at first; not tight at first; & shall have to tighten finally, instead of loosening as always before' (MS 3). One can see her writing 'loosely' in the above passage, composed the previous August. In revising, she cut superfluous words and phrases, such as 'impression of,' 'It seemed,' and 'now,' and tightened the syntax by adding verbs and eliminating the awkward phrasing at the end of the sentence. The addition of 'for years and years it seemed' reinforces the connection between James and his mother (she also exaggerates), who are both members of that 'great clan' for whom a moment can be suddenly crystallized and transfixed. Other changes introduced into the whole paragraph illustrate Virginia Woolf's tendency to use words or phrases that balance one another in a rhythmical pattern. The pairs in the final version – a night's darkness and a day's sail, this feeling separate from that, joys and sorrows, crystallise and transfix, gloom or radiance – are for the most part present in the first draft, but the syntax does not accommodate them as it does in the final version. Another example of this can be seen in a later passage, where 'only a year or two ago <Cam & James> had been bundles of delight ... Now they squabbled' (MS 98) is transformed into the far more energetic sentence 'These two she would have liked to keep for ever just as they were, demons of wickedness, angels of delight' (89).

Besides using balanced words and phrases to increase the rhythm and energy of her prose, she introduced verb patterns into the narrative which are only suggested in the first draft. For instance, the sentence 'Mrs. Ramsay could not help smiling, and soon, sure enough, walking up and down, he hummed it, dropped it, fell silent' (52) began as 'Mrs. Ramsay could not but smile. & then, after a minute or two, some one had blundered petered out, <sank into nonentity> & Mr. Ramsay paced ~~the terrace in~~ <up & down up down> profound silence, thinking' (MS 63). The frequent references in the novel to up and down gestures of one kind or another, which contribute to its fluctuating rhythms, are present far less often in the manuscript. This is one of the patterns which Virginia Woolf must have seen emerging as she began to revise the book.

The central images in *To the Lighthouse* are present in the first draft, but often they are not developed in as varied and as subtle a way as they are in the final version. One example of this is the development of the symbolic use of light. In the final version of the novel, the many references to light make it into what E.K. Brown has called an 'expanding symbol.'[10] We cannot isolate any single emblematic meaning for light since it is used or suggested so frequently and in such varied contexts. A complex network of images and associations related to light develops as Mr Ramsay, Mrs Ramsay, and Lily are all linked with light in various ways, just as the rhythms of the novel are also expressed in part through images of light and darkness. While references to light are frequent in the first draft, Virginia Woolf saw many more opportunities to introduce or further exploit this resonant image as she revised the novel. One example of this is the scene with which chapter xiv of part I ends. Paul Rayley has just proposed to Minta Doyle. Awed by his courage he resolves to tell Mrs Ramsay what has happened as soon as he arrives at the house, for he is convinced that she is responsible for his action. 'She had made him feel all that, and directly they got back (he looked for the lights of the house above the bay) he would go to her and say, "I've done it, Mrs. Ramsay; thanks to you"' (119). The parenthetical aside obliquely connects Mrs Ramsay and the lights of the house. The word 'lights' then recurs eight times more in the next few lines, as Paul expresses his happiness in the chant 'Lights, lights, lights.' In the first version, Paul looks at the house where the lights burning in the bedroom windows tell him it must be late. 'Burn, he said; blaze; make a hole in the night, ~~brave lights;~~ & they were her eyes, ~~only~~ & her childrens, <eyes> ... which seemed to him ~~to~~ burning there, blazing there' (MS 128). This is both more explicit and more self-consciously poetic. The simple repetition of 'lights' in the final version leaves it to the reader to relate the many references to light in earlier scenes to this one.

Often one can watch an image develop as Virginia Woolf writes and rewrites particular passages. For instance, the image of the wave, used metaphorically to describe Lily's sense of life as something 'which bore one up with it and threw one down with it, there, with a dash on the beach' (73) is initially simply a rough simile. The manuscript gives the impression of Virginia Woolf discovering the potentialities of the image as she develops the passage, although she has not yet invested it with the rhythmical force it will have in the final version: 'Life broke like a wave on a rock ... & one could not retreat from it, {one was snatched} or keep ones head or ~~say~~ point out faults. ... {Grasped them up} ~~took~~ one up, ~~bent one out~~, & flung one ~~in~~ down, splash, in one wave. It was like a wave of the sea' (MS 85).

A more detailed example of the evolution of a particular image can be found in the passages in which she searches for a way to express Lily's discovery that instead of a great revelation, life offers only the 'little daily miracles, illuminations, matches struck unexpectedly in the dark' (240). This section is too long to quote in full here, but the reader who turns to it (MS 293–4) can see how Virginia Woolf worked toward the image she would finally use. The dominant images in the manuscript passage are initially those related to water and light. At first she seems uncertain about whether the image of the waves or that of light will serve her meaning best, though it seems clear that the two will not work together easily here. 'These moments ... were high waves' is cancelled and 'flashes of torches <light>' takes its place. Then she tries the image of the wave again because it suits the notion of days following one another in an even and uneventful sequence. But soon two new words grow insistent: 'flashes & jerks.' She is looking for a way to express the sudden perception of the extraordinary in the ordinary and she turns from the waves, which one observes as external to oneself, to images suggesting something felt: 'lights were pressed in one's eyes; & things flashed & jerked.' Next she experiments with a different terminology and says of one of these moments, 'And it could be held in the fingers, looked up & round; & never lost its endlessness ... Threw out like radium its ~~store~~ meaning ... {all things at once came together – like an organic compound}' Now light is accompanied by energy, for the compound might be stuck 'in a jar, if need be ... throwing out light heat colour.' 'Match' is used for the first time two pages later in the passage describing Lily's sense of the luminous past: '& it was due to her own intensity of feeling that the moment had filled itself with light, had glowed there all these years ... It was like a candle burning. She went back to it, stuck a match in, & ... lit up this & that.' In the final version this is condensed to: 'It was like a drop of silver in which one dipped and illumined the darkness of the past' (256). In refining the references to light in these passages, Virginia Woolf has sharpened the focus by removing images that she found excessive or distracting, and she has made the connection between Lily's discovery here and several earlier scenes (the moment when the candles are lit at dinner in particular) less obvious, though still implied.

Since the sentences in the manuscript are so often incomplete, one must be cautious when generalizing about the sentence forms she uses in it. In one of her manuscript notes, she says her aim is 'to find a unit for the sentence which shall be less emphatic & intense than that in Mrs. D.; an everyday sentence for carrying on the narrative easily' (MS 2). This intention may partly explain the relative flatness of the prose in the manuscript. When she revised the novel, she may have found her sentences too 'everyday,' for one frequently sees her reshaping sentences, or sentence fragments, into more varied and more energetic forms. She has, I think, introduced a greater variety of sentence forms into the narrative of *To the Lighthouse* than is found in *Mrs. Dalloway*, and she has in particular made greater use of short declarative sentences, of sentences in which the subject and verb are not inverted (as they often are in *Mrs. Dalloway*), and of simple questions. She does continue to use syntactically complex long sentences in which clauses are embedded within clauses, and these occur most often in passages reflecting Mrs Ramsay's thoughts, as in *Mrs. Dalloway* they express Mrs Dalloway's thoughts. It was apparently not until she had written *Orlando* that she felt she had finally succeeded in learning how to write 'a direct sentence' (D 203).

Changes in the kinds of details used in the narrative naturally affect the style of the novel. Once can find many examples of Virginia Woolf replacing explicit statements with oblique ones, a habit which increases the suggestiveness of the novel and is closely related to the poetic quality of her style. Often this obliquity is increased by the simple elimination of superfluous details. In the first draft Mr Ramsay names two men of genius (MS 66), Mrs Ramsay thinks of specific universities where her husband is in demand (MS 72), a partial recipe for *boeuf en daube* is given (MS 129), *The Antiquary* is named (MS 193), and so on. In other passages one can see Virginia Woolf attempting to express a particular feeling or idea, finding it difficult to locate the words she needs, and eventually abandoning the effort and replacing an explicit statement with an inexplicit one. In these instances she appears to use the difficulty itself rather than overcome it. One notes the recurrence in the final version of the word 'thing,' as in Mrs Ramsay's thoughts about marriage: 'Marriage needed – oh, all sorts of qualities ... one – she need not name it – that was essential; the thing she had with her husband' (93). In the manuscript she does try to name it, but has little success in doing so (MS 102). In the final version, Virginia Woolf takes advantage of the fairy tale (and this particular tale is not used in the first draft) to suggest obliquely what that 'thing' might be. The reader can find other examples of this tendency by comparing the passages on pages 172, 187, 192, and 197 of the manuscript to related passages in the published version. Related to these changes is her apparent indecision about how articulate Mrs Ramsay would be. On MS 57 she says that Mrs Ramsay could be eloquent, while on MS 106 Mrs Ramsay regrets that she does not have language at her command. She seems to have found a way to compromise these extremes by making Mrs Ramsay eloquent in her thoughts. The use of indirect interior monologue gives Virginia Woolf the freedom to shape Mrs Ramsay's thoughts more poetically than Mrs Ramsay might have done herself in speech.

Besides making the novel more suggestive, the elimination of some of the direct statements and specific details also made it less obviously biographical. In the first draft she included a number of additional details directly related to the lives of her parents which are not found in the final version. For example, Mrs Ramsay is said to have descended from a French family, as Julia Stephen did, while in the final version this has become an Italian family (although the recipe for *boeuf en daube* comes, Mr Bankes is told, from Mrs Ramsay's French grandmother). More time is spent describing Mrs Ramsay's grandmother's painter friends, a detail which recalls Julia Stephen's connections with the Prinsep family. When Mrs Ramsay looks sad she is remembering a young man's death, just as Julia Stephen would have remembered the death of her young husband. Mr Ramsay is associated more explicitly with the 'decay of religious belief' (MS 152), as Leslie Stephen, the author of *An Agnostic's Apology*, was, and James's memory of his father preaching 'There is no God' may be a reference to the talks Leslie Stephen gave to the Ethical Societies.

The inclusion of many specific details in the manuscript, like the use of clichés ('into the bargain' recurs), cumbersome phrases, simple similes, and the like, further illustrates what Virginia Woolf has called the looseness of the writing in the first draft. 'Tightening' involved not only refining the style but also pruning away or shaping anew the details which had seemed useful and important at first.

As she was nearing the completion of the first draft, Virginia Woolf observed, 'It is hopelessly undramatic. It is all in oratio obliqua. Not quite all; for I have a few direct sentences' (D 106). The manuscript gives one the impression that, though she planned the book with specific scenes in mind and developed it by moving from scene to scene, her interest was less in the dramatic content of a particular scene than in the development of the characters' inner lives, and through them the central ideas in the novel. When revising the book, one method she used to make it more dramatic was to refine the point of view in it. One of the most distinctive and subtle characteristics of *To the Lighthouse* is the shifting or multiple points of view from which the narrative is presented.[11] Virginia Woolf does move from the mind of one character to that of another in the first draft, but more often the narrative is told through the voice of the omniscient narrator. The marvellous interplay between characters observed and characters observing, which we enjoy because of the shifting points of view, is often not present in the first draft. As a result, many scenes seem expositive and undramatic as they were originally cast.

One can compare, for example, the first and last versions of the passage describing Mr Ramsay's dismay at Mr Carmichael's wish for a second plate of soup. As the scene begins in the first draft, it is shown through Mr Bankes's eyes, then soon shifts to the point of view of the omniscient narrator (MS 153). The narrator then moves into Mr Ramsay's mind, and the tension is quickly dissipated as Mr

Ramsay thinks about Mr Carmichael's unhappy life and his strange adventures in India. Next we seem to leave Mr Ramsay's thoughts as we learn more about Mr Carmichael's life and his friendship with Andrew. It is only several pages later that Mrs Ramsay, seeing the children grown restive, asks them to light the candles. By eliminating the digression on Mr Carmichael's career in the final version and by dramatizing the scene as Mrs Ramsay sees it, Virginia Woolf makes the command 'Light the candles' much more forceful and the change in atmosphere felt by Lily far more suggestive.

Besides redirecting the point of view throughout the novel, she added many small details to the final version which remind the reader that the characters are acting as well as thinking, as when she added to an early scene that the family was 'at table' (MS 8), or to another that Mrs Ramsay was standing by the window (MS 15). Virginia Woolf has expressed her impatience with 'this appalling narrative business of the realist: getting on from lunch to dinner' (D 209), and the manuscript shows that as she wrote she was clearly most preoccupied with the development of the internal drama of her characters, a preoccupation which reflects her assumption that the recognition of 'reality' depends more upon the disposition of the mind than it does upon the appearances of the external world. She was not ready to abandon the 'realist's' concern with external action when she wrote *To the Lighthouse*, but after keeping, as she put it, 'the realities at bay' in *Orlando* (D 203), she moved on to develop her own form of realism in *The Waves*. One can see further evidence of this evolution in her work in the manuscript of *To the Lighthouse*.

Several ideas are developed in the manuscript which, while present in the final version, are less a part of the foreground there. In her first note on the novel she refers to the 'great cleavages in to which the human race is split, through the Ramsays not liking Mr. Tansley ... How much more important divisions between people are than between countries. The source of all evil.'[12] This notion is explored in some detail in passages where Charles Tansley plays an important role. At times he comes to resemble Leonard Bast, who is used by Forster in *Howards End* to dramatize a similar theme. The differences between people become less a matter of class in the final version and more a matter of instinctual sympathies or antipathies joining or dividing people. As this theme was refined during the process of revision, Charles Tansley became a less insistent presence in the novel.

References to religious ideas are generally oblique in the final version, but in the manuscript Virginia Woolf presents these in a more direct and, I find, curious way. At first Lily appears to be a quite conventional Christian. She worships God (MS 34) and goes to church on Sunday (MS 35), a habit Mr Bankes admires though he cannot share her piety. As everyone sits around the dinner table, Mr Bankes gives some thought to the decay of religious belief, and he observes that such thoughts always make one turn to Mr Ramsay (MS 152). Lily thinks of Mr Ramsay as someone she could go to in a crisis, if, for instance, she were thinking of becoming a Roman Catholic (MS 110). None of these details is present in the final version, where only the religious attitudes of Mr and Mrs Ramsay play a part in the wider question Lily asks specifically and the novel as a whole poses: 'What does it mean, then, what can it all mean?' (217).

The issue of the usefulness of art is explored more directly in the manuscript. And the recognition of the insincerity which lies at the heart of so much action is developed in considerably more detail here than in the final version. These themes remain important elements in *To the Lighthouse*, but they are presented in the finished novel with greater subtlety and indirection.

All the revisions – whether they resulted in the refinement of the style, the enrichment and extension of image patterns, the replacement of direct statements with oblique ones, the redirecting of point of view, or the clarification, compression, or amplification of individual scenes – illustrate Virginia Woolf's remarkable understanding of language and of the potentialities of prose and of the novel. Though she called the process of revision a 'drudgery,' she must nonetheless have been pleased to find that the design, characters, images, and language of the first draft were leading her on to the rediscovery, and undoubtedly the reshaping, of her original vision, the vision which must, as Lily says, 'be perpetually remade' (270).

It is possible to reconstruct a fairly detailed chronology of the period during which Virginia Woolf planned and wrote *To the Lighthouse*.[13] She later claimed that the idea for it came to her in what Lily might call a vision:

> *Then one day walking round Tavistock Square I made up, as I sometimes make up my books,* To the Lighthouse*; in a great, apparently involuntary, rush. One thing burst into another. Blowing bubbles out of a pipe gives the feeling of the rapid crowd of ideas and scenes which blew out of my mind, so that my lips seemed syllabling of their own accord as I walked. What blew the bubbles? Why then? I have no notion. But I wrote the book very quickly; and when it was written, I ceased to be obsessed by my mother.*[14]

This may have occurred in March 1952, when she wrote the first notes for the novel. These show that she had already decided upon using the tripartite structure – 'two blocks joined by a corridor' – and that she foresaw some of the details of part I.[15] The first reference in her diary to *To the Lighthouse* comes on 14 May 1925 (the day on which *Mrs Dalloway* was published), when she noted simply that she was eager to get on with it. On 14 June she remarked, 'I've ... thought out, perhaps too clearly, To the Lighthouse.' The phrase 'perhaps too clearly' is interesting, for it suggests that she may have feared that the completeness of her idea of the book would hinder her spontaneity once she began to write it. She may also have been anticipating an encounter with the 'demons' Lily so dreads once she began to make that difficult passage from conception to work. Throughout June and July, she explored in her diary the themes, scope, and details of the novel. As we learn from her diary, she was 'vacillating' between focusing sharply on her father's character and writing a 'far wider, slower book' (D 27). Her diary comments on her novels, and on this one in particular, are briefer and less detailed than the discussions Henry James carried on with himself in his notebooks, but like James's notes they show that she planned the general design of her book carefully before she began to write. They also show that hers was essentially a scenic approach, for in her diary comments and in her notes she sees the novel evolving through specific scenes which present themselves to her almost as tableaux. Indeed, the manuscript shows, as we have seen, that her 'liability to scenes,' as she later called it,[16] made the first draft of the novel far less dramatic than the final draft would be.

The wider, slower book had, one suspects, won out by 6 August 1925, when she drew up a plan of the book on the second page of the manuscript. In describing part I, she outlined the action and then noted, 'But this is all to be filled up as richly and variously as possible.' Most important, this plan shows that her central interest had now shifted from Mr Ramsay to Mrs Ramsay: 'The theme of the 1st part shall *really* contribute to Mrs. R's character; at least Mrs. R's character shall be displayed, but finally in conjunction with his, so that one gets an impression of their relationship.' She concluded by noting: 'Whether this will be long or short, I do not know. The dominating impression is to be of Mrs. R's character' (MS 2).

Two dates follow the word 'begun' on the title page of the manuscript: 6 August 1925 and 18 January 1926. Only one other date, 3 September, appears on the early pages of the manuscript (MS 31). The next date given is 15 January 1926, when she noted back on the third page, 'The idea has grown in the interval since I wrote the beginning.' The second date found on the title page, 18 January, also appears on MS 46.

This second start was caused, not surprisingly, by Virginia Woolf's health. Ten days after she first began to write *To the Lighthouse*, she collapsed at Charleston. Another bout of ill health had begun, and she did not recover fully from it, according to Quentin Bell, until the spring of 1926.[17] Yet, in spite of illness, she continued to write the opening pages of her new novel. By 3 September she had covered thirty pages in the manuscript book, and one can see that, ill or not, she was indeed making a 'flourishing attack' on the novel, as she noted in her diary on 5 September.[18] The spirited reference to her new book in this entry follows, however, the description of her collapse at Charleston: 'And why couldn't I see or feel that all this time I was getting a little used up & riding on a flat tyre?' Though she was pleased with her 'flourishing attack,' she was forced to add, 'I am still crawling & easily enfeebled.' Evidently she was able to 'get up steam again' for a little while longer (probably until around 13 September) and to complete thirty-seven pages (covering roughly the first thirty-three pages of the final version). On 16 September, she complained of her illness in a letter to Roger Fry, saying 'Cant write (with a whole novel in my head too – its damnable).'[19] And on 2 October she told Saxon Sydney-Turner that writing had become 'a frivolity and a weariness,' though she also noted that she had managed to write him a four-page letter in fifteen minutes.[20]

Although she stopped writing *To the Lighthouse* now, she apparently felt well enough to sketch out (on MS 41–4) some of the ideas she would develop in her essay on *Robinson Crusoe* and in her lecture 'How Should One Read a Book?' These pages were probably written in mid-September, for in a letter to Janet Case dated the 18th she explores some of the ideas found in these fragments.[21]

When she began writing her novel again in January of 1926, she apparently read over what she had written earlier and then decided to develop in more detail the scene in which Lily and Mr Bankes look out at the bay and discuss Mr Ramsay. This section is sketchy in the earlier version and interrupts the account of Mrs Ramsay and Charles Tansley going into the village. When she returned to it again, she was much surer of her material, as a comparison of these pages with the final version shows, for the first draft is remarkably similar to the final version at this point.

After 18 January she set a steady pace in her writing, as the dates on the manuscript indicate. On 26 January she told Vita Sackville-West that she had written twenty pages. 'To tell you the truth,' she added, 'I have been very excited, writing. I have never written so fast ... I think I can write now, never before – an illusion which attends me always for 50 pages. But its true I write quick – all in a spash; then feel, thank God, thats over.'[22] The dates on the manuscript, along with the convention she adopted on 27 February of beginning each day on a new page, often make it possible to infer how much she wrote at a single sitting and where a new day's writing begins (D 62). On the average, she appears to have written two to two and a half pages a day. In September, when she was nearing the completion of the novel, she referred in her diary to writing every morning until 12.30 and thus doing her two pages, and this seems to be the pace she set herself throughout the composition of the novel (D 106).

She wrote steadily from January to September with many minor but only one major interruption. Minor interruptions were caused by the many domestic matters which always impinged upon Virginia Woolf's daily routine. Though she and Leonard were based in London, where they looked after the running of the Hogarth Press, they made frequent trips to Rodmell, and in April they took a brief holiday in Devon. The 'change of perspective' she complained of in a letter to Vita Sackville-West must have been caused not only by the constant shifting of her attention from her novel to the ordinary life around her, but also by these frequent changes of scene.[23] The major interruption came in July, when she had 'a whole nervous breakdown in miniature' (D 103). I would guess that she stopped writing in the second week of July. On 21 June she was writing the descriptions of Lily's first attempts at her painting and of Mr Ramsay, Cam, and James in the boat. She was dealing with difficult material, and she was clearly having some trouble finding the best way to express Lily's thoughts about love and art. On the last page of this section of the manuscript (MS 282) she cancelled the four lines which complete the sentence on the previous page; these are then followed by two numbered fragments of the lecture 'How Should One Read a Book?' As before when ill health forced her to stop work on her novel, the manuscript itself gives evidence of her distraction.

By the end of July she appears to have been working her way out of this breakdown, for it was during this period that she wrote the fascinating series of notes entitled 'Rodmell, 1926' (D 102–5). The echoes in these notes of ideas she was about to develop in *To the Lighthouse* (compare for instance, 'Suppose one could catch them [one's thoughts] before they became "works of art"?' to Lily's desire to get 'the thing itself before it has been made anything' (287)) make one view her illness as almost necessary to the completion of the novel. In February of 1930 she wrote, 'If I could stay in bed another fortnight ... I believe I could see the whole of The Waves' (D 286). Her illness and her art were always, as she recognized, closely intertwined.

On 4 August she began to write the novel again. By 17 August she had finished reworking some earlier passages and had begun to move steadily forward in the narrative. The final date given in the manuscript is 15 September, which appears on the penultimate page. The manuscript and her diary both show that, as usual, the final stages of the novel were causing her considerable anxiety. She had some trouble deciding how to end it, and she found especially difficult the dramatization of James's changing feelings for his father. Her diary contains an entry dated 15 September and entitled 'A State of Mind,' which is eloquent of her anxious conviction of complete failure.[24] In 1934 she looked back in her diary and noted that after *To the Lighthouse* 'I was, I remember, nearer suicide, seriously, than since 1913.'[25] She was still feeling depressed on 30 September, though in that entry one sees that there may be a double-edge to this 'profound gloom,' a 'mystical side of this solitude,' for, like Lily's sense of unreality, it is frightening, but exciting too.

She began to revise the novel, 'some parts three times over,' on 25 October (D 123). By 23 November she was 're-doing six pages of *Lighthouse* daily,' and on 29 December she told Vanessa, who was to design the cover, that she was 'in a hideous rush putting the last touches to my novel.'[26] On 14 January 1927 she was able to record in her diary: 'This moment I have finished the final drudgery.' It was now ready for Leonard to read. Nine days later she had his judgment: 'It is a "masterpiece"' (D 123). She now went through the familiar period of small worries and minor revisions. The novel was set in type in February, when she then read it 'straight through in print ... for the first time.' She wanted to 'read largely & freely once: then to niggle over details' (D 127). On 18 February, while correcting two sets of proofs, she wrote to Vita Sackville-West that she did not know whether the book was good or bad. 'I'm dazed, I'm bored, I'm sick to death: I go on crossing out commas and putting in semi-colons in a state of marmoreal despair.'[27] The niggling over details resulted in a surprising number of changes,[28] but the process of revision must have come to an end on 16 March, for this is the date given on the title page of the manuscript after 'finished.' When she read the novel again on 21 March she was very pleased with it, for she wrote in her diary: 'Dear me, how lovely some parts of The Lighthouse are! Soft & pliable, & I think deep, & never a word wrong for a page at a time. This I feel about the dinner party, & the children in the boat; but not of Lily on the lawn. That I do not much like. But I like the end' (D 132).

The day of publication, 5 May (also her mother's death-day), and the first reviews brought with them the usual period of doubt. She was especially worried about 'Time Passes,' which she felt Roger Fry had not liked, and she thought the whole book might be 'pronounced soft, shallow, insipid, sentimental' (D 134). The only early review she commented on is the one that appeared in the *Times Literary Supplement*, for it darkened her mood, she said, like 'the shadow' of a 'damp cloud.'[29] But on the whole, the reviews were favourable, and her family and her friends were filled with praise.[30]

## EDITORIAL CONVENTIONS

The manuscript of *To the Lighthouse* has been transcribed *literatim*, page for page and line for line. In the case of lines which exceed the type-measure, the concluding words are indented and placed directly beneath the line of which they are a part, preceded by a bracket.

*Pagination.* I have numbered the recto pages of the manuscript consecutively from beginning to end: these numbers appear in the running heads. Virginia Woolf occasionally wrote notes or marginal emendations on the verso pages. When a verso page appears in the transcription it is given the same number as the previous page and designated a verso page.

As an aid to readers who might wish to compare sections of the transcription with the manuscript, the pagination supplied by the Berg Collection is given within parentheses in the bottom right-hand corner of each page (volume followed by page). The Berg Collection has numbered each volume of the manuscript anew and has numbered both the verso and the recto sides of each page.

The numbers which appear beneath the rule in the upper right-hand corner of the page, beginning with MS186, indicate Virginia Woolf's own pagination of the manuscript.

*Marginalia and interlineations*. Marginal additions and emendations begin where they begin in the manuscript. These are single-spaced and in smaller type. Interlineations also begin where they begin in the manuscript except where minor adjustments have had to be made to keep them from running together. Occasionally Virginia Woolf used carets and lines to indicate where the marginalia and interlineations should go. All such carets and lines have been included.

*Cancellations*. Virginia Woolf used both horizontal and vertical lines to cancel words or passages. These, along with all other marks made by her, have been reproduced as they appear on the manuscript.

*Signs*.

† Daggers in the left-hand margin refer the reader to footnotes indicating corresponding pages (often approximate) in the first British (B) edition (Hogarth Press 1927) and the first American (A) edition (Harcourt, Brace and World, Inc. 1927). The correspondences are between scenes or, in some cases, phrases.

[ ] Square brackets have been reserved for editorial comments. Virginia Woolf used these rarely, and when they appear on the manuscript they have been drawn in. Square brackets are used to indicate the following:

[home?] A doubtful reading. Occasionally two readings seem equally possible. These are indicated as follows: [senseless?/surely?].

[?] An illegible word.

* Asterisks refer the reader to footnotes. These are placed:

at the beginning of a passage that has been reworked elsewhere in the manuscript (the footnote refers the reader to these related pages);

at the ending of a passage or word for which the footnote provides some other kind of information: these notes refer to related material in the introduction and appendices; describe a particular characteristic of the manuscript (eg, a word written in pencil); note misspellings when these are of special interest or could cause confusion; or identify quotations that appear in the manuscript.

*Appendices*. Four appendices follow the transcription. The first three contain manuscript material directly related to the first holograph draft. The fourth is a chronology of the writing of *To the Lighthouse*.

## NOTES

Unless otherwise indicated, page numbers in parentheses after quotations refer to the edition of *To the Lighthouse* published by Harcourt, Brace and World, Inc. (1927, 1955).

Other page references given within the text are to:

D *The Diary of Virginia Woolf*, volume III: 1925–1930, ed Anne Olivier Bell (London, Hogarth Press 1980);

MS the manuscript of *To the Lighthouse* (Henry W. and Albert A. Berg Collection of English and American Literature of The New York Public Library, Astor, Lenox and Tilden Foundations). Page numbers refer to the continuous pagination I have supplied in the running heads.

The following signs are used in the quotations from the manuscript:

<> word(s) within pointed brackets are interlinear additions or emendations;

{ } word(s) within braces are marginal additions or emendations.

1. *A Change of Perspective: The Letters of Virginia Woolf: 1923–1928*, volume III, ed Nigel Nicolson (London, Hogarth Press 1977), p 18 (hereafter cited as *Letters* III)
2. Leonard Woolf, *Beginning Again* (London, Hogarth Press 1964, 1972), p 232
3. This follows the 'whole nervous breakdown in miniature' referred to below (p 28).
4. The version Virginia Woolf gave Charles Mauron to translate for *Commerce* has passages in it which are found in the manuscript but not in the final version. For a discussion of the relationship of these three versions, see S. Dick, 'The Restless Searcher: A Discussion of the Evolution of "Time Passes" in *To the Lighthouse*,' *English Studies in Canada*, V, 3 (Fall 1979), 311–29.
5. See appendices A and B and MS 2 and 3.
6. See, for example, Charles G. Hoffman, 'From Short

Story to Novel: The Manuscript Revisions of Virginia Woolf's *Mrs. Dalloway*,' *Modern Fiction Studies*, XIV, 2 (Summer 1968), 171–86; 'From Lunch to Dinner: Virginia Woolf's Apprenticeship,' *Texas Studies in Literature and Language*, X (Winter 1969), 609–27; 'Fact and Fantasy in *Orlando*: Virginia Woolf's Manuscript Revisions,' *Texas Studies in Literature and Language*, X (Fall 1968), 435–44; 'Virginia Woolf's Manuscript Revisions of *The Years*,' PMLA, LXXXIV (1969), 79–89; John W. Graham, 'Editing a Manuscript: Virginia Woolf's *The Waves*,' in *Editing Twentieth Century Texts*, ed Francess G. Halpenny (Toronto, University of Toronto Press 1972), pp 77–92; and John W. Graham, ed, *The Waves: The Two Holograph Drafts* (Toronto, University of Toronto Press 1976).

7. *Letters* III, 247. For other comments on rhythm see *The Diary of Virginia Woolf*, volume II: 1920–24, ed Anne Olivier Bell (London: Hogarth Press 1978) 322; *A Reflection of the Other Person: The Letters of Virginia Woolf: 1929–1931*, volume IV, ed Nigel Nicolson (London, Hogarth Press 1978), pp 204 and 303.

8. *Beginning Again*, p 31

9. *A Writer's Diary*, ed Leonard Woolf (London, Hogarth Press 1953, 1972), p 169

10. E.K. Brown, *Rhythm in the Novel* (Toronto, University of Toronto Press 1963), pp 33–59

11. Mitchell Leaska has written a full-length study of point of view in this novel: *Virginia Woolf's Lighthouse: A Study in Critical Method* (London, Hogarth Press 1970).

12. See 'Notes for Writing,' appendix A.

13. See appendix D for a chronological outline.

14. 'A Sketch of the Past,' in *Moments of Being: Unpublished Autobiographical Writings of Virginia Woolf*, ed Jeanne Schulkind (Sussex, The University of Sussex Press 1976), p 81 (hereafter cited as MB)

15. See 'Notes for Writing,' appendix A.

16. MB 122. Virginia Woolf calls scene-making her natural way of marking the past. In a passage reminiscent of Lily's discoveries she describes 'the sensation that we are sealed vessels afloat on what it is convenient to call reality; and at some moments, the sealing matter cracks; in floods reality; that is, these scenes – for why do they survive undamaged year after year unless they are made of something compara-

tively permanent? Is this liability to scenes the origin of my writing impulse?'

17. Quentin Bell, *Virginia Woolf: A Biography* (London, Hogarth Press 1972), II, 114

18. D 39. She says here that she has written '22 pages straight off in less than a fortnight,' a comment which suggests that she wrote more after her illness at Charleston than before it.

19. *Letters* III, 208

20. Ibid, 212

21. Ibid, 211. See appendix C.

22. *Letters* III, 232

23. Ibid, 244

24. 'Woke up perhaps at 3. Oh its beginning its coming – the horror – physically like a painful wave swelling about the heart – tossing me up. I'm unhappy unhappy! Down – God, I wish I were dead. Pause. But why am I feeling this? Let me watch the wave rise. I watch. Vanessa. Children. Failure. Yes; I detect that. Failure failure. (The wave rises)' (D 110).

25. *A Writer's Diary*, p 229

26. *Letters* III, 311

27. Ibid, 333

28. For a discussion of the variants in the two first editions of *To the Lighthouse* see J.A. Lavin, 'The First Editions of Virginia Woolf's *To the Lighthouse*,' *Proof*, ed Joseph Katz (Columbia, S.C., (University of South Carolina Press 1972), II, 185–211. On 12 February, Virginia Woolf noted in her diary that 'the first symptoms of Lighthouse are unfavourable.' 'But,' she added, 'these opinions refer to the rough copy, unrevised' (D 127). One of the two sets of proofs which she told Vita Sackville-West she was correcting must have been the set which she sent to Harcourt Brace in February to be used as setting copy (Lavin, 188). On 1 March, she sent Harcourt further revisions to five pages (Lavin, 188). Anne Olivier Bell speculates that 'Virginia Woolf made emendations on her proof which were effected by Clarks [the English printers] but not transmitted to America' (D n128). This may be true, but Lavin's research indicates that she also made emendations to the American edition which were not made to the first or later English editions. Lavin presents a nine-page table in which he records the 180 sub-

stantive and semi-substantive variations between the two first editions. These follow a pattern which leads me to agree with Lavin's view that the first American edition embodies Virginia Woolf's final revisions of that time. Lavin also records in a separate table the ten new substantive revisions Virginia Woolf made in the second English edition (Everyman 1938). It is curious that Virginia Woolf never incorporated the revisions made in the American edition into the later English edition. The English and American editions continue to be significantly different.

29. D 134. The reviewer was not enthusiastic about her method of creating characters and he thought 'Time Passes' not the novel's 'strongest part.' Otherwise, he praised the novel.

30. She was especially pleased with Vanessa's response. Her letter is reprinted in *Letters* III, 572–3.

To the Lighthouse

"If its a fine day tomorrow" said Mrs Ramsay. "But you'll
have to be up with the lark," she added.
To her son ~~these~~ ~~her~~ these words conveyed an extraordinary impression of
joy. It seemed ~~indeed~~ as if it were now settled, & the expedition
~~to which he~~ ~~with all its~~ certain to take place, & the
the wonders to which he had looked forward ~~the~~ for brought within touch
~~to~~ near – only a night & a sail with only a dazzling, unclouded
disquietude, a ~~glittering~~ a night, & then a day's sail, between.
Since he belonged to ~~the~~ even at the age of six to that great
clan which cannot keep its emotions within separate
compartments, but must let future prospects, & their
joy or sorrow, colour ~~the~~ what is ~~[illegible]~~ ~~for~~ actually on hand,
~~[illegible], further, so alter the ~ let them~~ since to such
people, even in earliest childhood, ~~the~~ a joy or a sorrow
~~[illegible]~~ pleasure, laughter, whatever it may be, has the
power to crystallise or transfix any moment upon which its
gloom or radiance alights, James Ramsay, sitting on the
floor, cutting out pictures from the Catalogue of the Army &
Navy Stores, ~~endowed~~ entranced ~~a~~ ~~[illegible]~~ ~~refrigerat~~ the picture of a
refrigerator as his mother spoke, with heavenly tenderness.
bliss. ~~already~~ ~~[illegible] with such [illegible]~~, ~~already~~ cupboards,
The wheelbarrow, the lawn mower, pictures, leaves whitening
~~sounds~~, ~~[illegible]~~ the sound of the poplar trees, dresses,
before rain, rooks cawing, ~~&~~ brooms knocking,
all ~~these~~ ~~already~~ ~~each of the sounds of the daily~~ domestic
~~&~~ rustling – already ~~[illegible]~~ distinguished
life, ~~were only~~ were already so coloured &
in his mind; ~~&~~ ~~he~~ they had already his private code
~~of~~ his ~~language which is~~ own language, & though
~~it would have been~~ to look at, ~~in his~~ he appeared
the ~~[illegible]~~ picture of stark & uncompromising severity.
so that his mother imagined him playing a man's part in

Page 4: The first page of narrative

351

as if ~~he~~ ~~probably~~, she.

Something had moved while she ~~was~~ had been turned ~~away~~ aside; & she must look to see what ~~it is~~ or, ~~perhaps~~, she had ~~there had~~ an idea had come to her.

It was only a trifle – It was one of those pictures that would be hung in the bedrooms, & then in the attics, it would be destroyed. Very likely, she thought, but it did not matter – what was the difference two pins? Two straws? –

She ~~stooped~~ took up her brush. She looked at her sketch, ~~which was~~ looked at the window & so, & the wall; & saw, as she had known that she would see, precisely what was needed.

~~That was it.~~ ~~A line~~ That (she drew a line) which solved her problem.

Mr Carmichael was standing at her elbow.

He looked at the canvas – He looked at the steps.

He watched her make the ~~line~~ mark which noted for her own eye the solution of the problem.

But what did that matter? She ~~looked at the~~ canvas. She looked at the steps. She drew a line, there, in the centre. She had solved her problem. ~~Not Mr Carmichael stood, letting his~~

It was ~~finished~~ over, that vision. Mr Carmichael, looking over her shoulder, at the canvas, at the ~~steps~~. There! ~~It was done~~. It was over. It was over! But she had had her vision. But she had had her vision.

Exactly as if something had happened in her absence,

The white shape stood perfectly still.

Page 366: The final page of the manuscript

The original dust jacket, designed by Vanessa Bell

To the Lighthouse

Monks House,

begun (August 6th 1925) – Jan. 18th 1926

finished March 16th 1920̸7

<u>August 6th 1925</u>

The plan of this book is roughly that it shall consist of three parts: one, Mrs. Ramsay (?) sitting at the window: while Mr. R. walks up & down in the dusk: the idea being that there shall be curves of conversation or reflection or description or in fact anything, modulated by his appearance & disappearance at the window: gradually it shall grow later; the child shall go to bed; the engaged couple shall appear: But this is all to be filled up as richly and variously as possible. My aim being to find a unit ~~wh~~ for the sentence which shall be less emphatic & intense than that in Mrs. D: an everyday sentence for carrying on the narrative easily. The theme of the 1st part shall <u>really</u> contribute to Mrs. R's character; at least Mrs. R's character shall be displayed, but finally ~~with~~ in conjunction with his, so that one gets an impression of their relationship: To precipitate feeling, there should be a sense of waiting, of expectation: the child waiting to go to the Lighthouse: the woman awaiting the return of the couple.

2.) The passing of time. I am not sure how this is to be given: an interesting experiment, ~~showi~~ giving the sense of 10 years passing.

3.) This is the voyage to the Lighthouse.

Several characters can be brought in: the young atheist, the old gentleman: the lovers: Episodes can be written on woman's beauty; on truth: but these should be greater & less knobbly then those in Mrs. D: making a more harmonious whole.

There need be no specification of date.

Whether this will be long or short, I do not know. The dominating [impression is to be of Mrs. R's character.

~~To the Lighthouse~~

Names to be used.

| | |
|---|---|
| David Ramsay | [Windle?] Simpson |
| Lucy Ramsay | Knighton. Seton. |
| Mr. Clutterbuck | Benjamin Prentice. Briscoe. Toomer. |
| Patience – Priscilla. | Fiske. Manning. Caffin. Sergeant. |
| Martin. Samson | Tombs. Grimes. Tabor. Silling |
| Samuel. Sara. Peregrine. | Doyle. Brooks. Faith. Redditch. |
| Tansy. Peaclock. James. | Abel. Miles. Lisle. Holcroft. |
| James Ramsay. Patcham. | Mildred. Holroyd. Silas |
| Sara Bridget. Warmbush. | Winbolt. Araminta. |

January 15th 1926 ~~This~~ The idea has grown in the interval since I wrote the beginning. ~~It~~ The presence of the 8 children; undifferentiated, should be important to bring out the sense of life in opposition to fate – i.e. waves, lighthouse. Then there is to be some ~~specif~~ movement as the evening passes: a great dinner scene, all the family, & after this I think, Minta & Charles go out to become engaged Also a scene in Mrs. Rs. bedroom, with children choosing jewels while the birds rise & fall outside; a scene of her descending the stairs, smelling burning fat; but all is to draw in towards the end, & leave the two alone: she expecting the return of the young couple. That poetry should be used in quotations to give the character.

March 9th 1926

I observe today that I am writing exactly oppositely from my other books: very loosely at first; not tight at first; & shall have to tighten finally, instead of loosening as always before. Also at perhaps 3 times the speed

## To the Lighthouse.

† "If it's a fine day tomorrow" said Mrs. Ramsay. "But you'll
have to be up with the lark," she added.
~~her~~ these
To her son ~~these~~ ^ words conveyed an extraordinary impression of
joy. It seemed ~~indeed~~ as if it were now settled, & the expedition
~~to which he~~ ~~with all its~~ certain to take place, & ~~the~~
the wonders to which he had looked forward ~~the for brought~~ within
with [touch
~~so near only a night & a sail~~ only a dazzling, uneasy
[pains?]
disquietude, a ~~glittering~~ a nights, & then a day's sail, between.
Since he belonged ~~to the~~ even at the age of six to that great
clan which cannot keep its emotions within separate
compartments, but must let future prospects, & their
joy or sorrow, colour ~~th~~ what is ~~bee~~ ~~go~~ actually on hand,
~~must, further, so alter the let them~~ since to such
people, even in earliest childhood, ~~the~~ a joy or a sorrow
[~~exp~~?] pleasure, laughter, whatever it may be, has the
power to crystallise or transfix any moment upon which its
gloom or radiance alights, James Ramsay, sitting on the
floor, cutting out pictures from the Catalogue of the Army &
embalmed
Navy Stores, ~~endowed a phot refrigerat~~ the picture of a
refrigerator, as his mother spoke, with heavenly ~~tenderness~~.
bliss. ~~Already~~ ~~Ringed with such hues~~, ~~already~~
cupboards
† the wheelbarrow, the lawn mower, pictures, leaves whitening
before rain, rooks cawing, ~~a~~ broom knocking, dresses
all these
~~w~~ rustling – al~~ready each of the sounds of the daily domest~~ic
~~life, wer was~~ were already so coloured & ~~dist~~ distinguished
that
in his mind; ~~& he~~ had already his private code
~~of~~ his ~~language which is~~ own language, & though
~~it would have been~~ to look at, ~~in his~~ he appeared
the ~~im~~ picture of stark & uncompromising severity.
so that his mother imagined him playing a man's part in

† B 11, A 9; B 12, A 10

* some crisis of public affairs he was at the moment expanding & contracting, contracting & expanding like the mainspring of a watch with joy.

"But" said Mr. Ramsay, stopping in front of the window, it won't be fine."

If there had been a knife handy, or any sharp implement
there & then
which could have gashed his father's breast & ~~let~~ killed him where he
stood, James would have seized it. ~~He hated him, loathed him~~
such
~~from the depths of his heart.~~ Mr. Ramsay excited extremes of
for / but then
emotion, ~~he spoke the truth; h~~ / he said what was disagreeable; he
† ~~said what was true, His~~ but it was true ~~what he said.~~ He was
incapable of ~~altering the~~ tampering with any fact, of altering
any~~thing which~~ truth, to suit the pleasure or convenience of
any mortal being, least of all his own children, of the male sex in
[particular,
who should be ~~impervious to such~~ from childhood made aware
~~of the~~ that life is hard, ~~life is~~ truth uncompromising, & the
passage to that fabled land, where according to Mr. Ramsay,
our brightest hopes are extinguished, & our little barks
is
founder in the darkness, / one that needs, above all, ~~courage,~~ fortitude
truth
~~& strength~~, & the power to endure.

"But it may be fine" said Mrs. Ramsay, ~~turning some~~
making some little adjustment of the stocking she was knitting.
&
~~w~~ which, ~~was~~ if she finished it, if they went to the Lighthouse
lighthouse
tomorrow, was to be ~~put in the b~~ given to the men. who ~~They~~
were to have, too, a whole pile of old magazines; & some
tobacco; & a pound of tea, & whatever she could find at the
last moment – lying about, not really wanted, & the very thing to
give those poor fellows, who must be bored to extinction
sitting there all day with nothing to do but polish the lamp,
& trim the wicks & ~~d~~ rake about in their scrap of
up on the rock garden, ~~a little pleasure~~. just a moments pleasure.
† For how would you like to be shut up for a whole
month at a time, & possibly more in stormy weather, upon a
rock the size of the tennis lawn, she would ask?

(1.11)

* Marginal lines written in pencil
† B 13, A 11; B 14, A 12

to have no / & seeing their wives & children

~~without a~~ letters or newspapers; ~~without a~~ doctor if they ~~ill~~ were ill; ~~without any~~ or any sort of amusement? How would you like to see the same dreary waves breaking all day long? & it would be much worse in winter, when ~~there were~~ storms, & sea birds dashed against the window, & the ~~lit~~ little tower was covered with spray, & the wind was so high that they couldn't even put their noses out of doors without being blown ~~away?~~ off into the sea?

Putting up his hand,

now

~~"Now~~ The wind ~~has changed to the~~ is ~~almost~~ due West" said the Atheist Tansy who was sharing Mr. Ramsay's evening walk.

it blew / very / for landing at the lighthouse wh could only be done on the calmest days

~~It blew~~ that is to say ^ from the worst direction ~~in a as~~ for ~~far as the lighthouse~~. & made landing at the lighthouse out of the ~~question~~ when the wind was due north. ~~Without Dan Mr Ramsay'~~s The little atheist was without Mr. Ramsay's power. & everybody in the house made mock of him except ~~the~~ Mr. & Mrs.

~~landing at~~

certainly / but / truthful.

Ramsay for being ~~so~~ disagreeable, ~~& yet~~ by no means impeccably ~~true above suspicion~~. Lucy mocked at him; ~~for~~

† ~~being the two~~ William, & Herbert & Roger mocked at him; Miss Doyle, Mr. Nolcroft mocked at him; Patcham & Mildred, & Silas, ~~all~~ mocked at him; even old Badger without a

† tooth in his jaw bit him; for being (as Lucy put it) the hundred & tenth young man to chase them all the way to the

without an idea in his head

Hebrides & ~~talk~~ when nobody wanted him. for no reason whatever.

But this was ~~being simply rude, &~~ simple silliness, said Mrs. Ramsay.

Sara Ramsay could be far too severe.

† B 15; A 13

(~~about~~ a hundred & ten when which implied that they were wh never alone ~~& that~~ happened to be which was true)

† For, apart from the fact that they ~~were in the~~ were not in the Hebrides, but in the Isles of Skye, apart from the exaggeration ^ Mrs. Ramsay much ~~particularly~~ disliked incivility to her guests ~~on if they were~~ if they were, as she called it, ~~poverty stricken~~ unappreciated particularly if they were rather humble rather ~~unattractive~~ young like this ~~Mr.~~ Charles Tansley men, on the part of her daughter. All young men, ~~according to~~ had claims upon her. It might be said indeed that she had taken the whole of the opposite sex under her protection; ~~& that~~ for reasons which she was incapable of explaining or realising, for reasons which had ~~no~~ their birth not in her own lifetime, but in her mothers, & even her grandmothers; ~~so that for reasons which were apart from Apart from these reasons, they~~ for their chivalry & poetry & valour; for the fact that they negotiated treaties, ruled India, & controlled created the Bank of England. ~~Nobody could deny them those achievements; & the it is But~~ all ~~this gave them a claim upon her~~ for an attitude towards herself which surely ~~any needed no~~ anyone ~~nobody~~ could ~~understand~~ ~~deny~~ ~~a simple trustful attitude,~~ or fail to find most sympathetic, ~~&~~ something ~~trustful~~ trusting, something childlike. something which ~~had~~ an old woman could take from a young man without loss of dignity, & woe betide the girl who did not feel it, & respect it this to the marrow of her bone / — So

† ~~that when Lucy or Priscilla or Magdalen, suddenly~~ ~~she was severe with too severe~~ she turned too hard with severity upon ~~this~~ the ~~frivolous~~ & frivolous speech; & heartless way of talking the speech which exaggerated.

Charles Tansley ~~had not chased them~~ had not chased them he had been asked to come. ~~Instantly before she could even finish the action which~~ ~~Moreover it could not be denied that there were other reasons.~~ Moreover, there was her husband. ~~She felt that~~

Her daughters might find a way out ~~of thi~~ perhaps. might find a way ~~of~~ which she had, almost without knowing it lost; ~~so that~~ some perhaps simpler, less

† A 13; B 16 (1.15)

† laborious ~~way of life~~ method; but ~~she would never seek~~ – was not her hair
grey at fifty, & her cheeks sunk? – but for her own part she would
never think worth considering any ~~timid, half-hearted way of life~~, or
evasion ~~any~~ or failure, ~~or~~ to fulfil duties; – & here the severity of her face,
increased; to ~~a such a degree that~~ She was then formidable to
behold; & it was only in silence that her daughters – Rose, Lucy, Prue –
could sport with those infidel ideas ~~of~~ which certainly they had
brewed for themselves, of a life far lonelier than hers, & less
strict, of a life, Prue thought, on an island among sea birds, or
Rose thought, not on an island, but in Paris with painters; &
Lucy being the youngest, ~~& scarcely~~ with print petticoats scarcely
below her knee, thought just a life a / new life – but in all their
minds was the same constant questioning of all this beautiful,
manly-womanly relationship, its deference & chivalry,
humility charity, Bank of England & Empire of India elements,
~~which were~~ its flowing skirts & white hands though to them all
there was something even in this of the essence of beauty; something
which called out to the masculine element in all their girlish
hearts & made them, as they sat beneath their mothers
eyes, worship her strange severity, her ~~sim~~ exaggerated
nobility, her extreme & lovely courtesy, ~~as of a~~ like a Queen's,
† ~~to th who holds out her foot to be~~ washes a beggar's foot,
to the ~~atheist Tansley Moreover, there was~~
this wretched little man who had chased them, speaking
accurately to the Isles of Skye.

For there could be no two opinions: he was surely

† A 14; B 17

† For there could not be two opinions about Charles Tansley: he was a
miserable specimen. When he took his coat off to play cricket he
was all humps & hollows; ~~but what he liked best was & he joked so~~
Then one could hear him he walked ever
joked sarcastically ~~stiffly~~, & he poked & shuffled; what he ~~liked best~~ / was forever walking
forever & [up &
down with Mr. Ramsay, saying who had won this & that, who was
~~the~~ a 'first rate man' ~~at this or~~ that, who was 'brilliant but
fundamentally unsound' who, was the ablest ~~the~~ fellow in
tho ~~g~~ such generosity was alien to him Balliol, who had buried his light temporarily, at Bristol or
Bedford, but was bound to be heard of later when ~~some~~
pages
with profound ~~delight inter~~ interest his Prolegomena, of which Mr. Tansley had read the first ~~chapters~~ in
branch of
proof, ~~saw the light~~ were ~~finally delivered~~ – to some mathematical
wh. was respected, or philosophical or economical branch of science saw the light of
for (~~but~~ he was not naturally generous) day. ~~His most serious shortcoming~~, ~~however~~, It might be true
that the great universities of England & Scotland were ~~institutions~~
lamps ~~of~~ which in all ages had attracted to themselves the
finest spirits, plants of light, ~~which~~ like the wax white
of clarity & elegantly
bell shaped flowers in the ~~gard~~ garden, luminous, stately, when all
was thorn & thistle round them. Nobody had a word to say
or universities in the abstract
against learning ^ as such. Mr. Ramsay himself always
you you &
impressed, however he might annoy, by a purity, ~~an~~ integrity
which was that of ivory or bone from which all superfluity ~~or~~
the daily dropping fine
had been eaten away by ~~the~~ some / caustic; ~~dropped day by day,~~
no:
But Charles Tansley, ~~was not that~~; ~~Charles Tansley~~, ~~having~~
~~learnt all the parrot phrases of learning~~, ~~its repeated~~
could
simply what ~~he had picked up~~; ~~He might~~
repeat; ~~word for word, all the sad disillu authoritative~~
* ~~denunciations~~ ~~m of~~ he could deny; he could correct; he
could purse his lips up when Mrs. Ramsay who was herself given to
† picturesque exaggerations, spoke of waves "mountains high"
& of everyone "drenched to the skin, & say certainly it had been
saying something off his own bat a little rough, & his overcoat was wet but not right through;
but when it came to adding something, to giving himself away, so to
speak, to being not merely a repetition – but there, whoever it

* MS 11
† A 15; B18

(1.19)

was of Mrs. Ramsay's seven children that was trying to explain what was lacking in Charles Tansley, petered out dismally & fell an easy prey to whoever now wanted to talk about something else.

She fell an easy prey, for how could one ~~give~~ ~~find~~ reasonably explain that when she said she detested him, something ~~almost~~ so remote as to be almost ungetatable, so irrational as to be ridiculous could one get at it came to her mind, or rather presented itself before her in a series of ~~litt actions~~ – things he did – ~~judgments~~, or judgments upon subjects of wh he pressed which she knew nothing, like architecture or cookery, which so offended her that had she been either cook or architect ~~had~~ she practised any art which fell beneath his notice, there would have been such deathly chillness such an antipathy would have risen between them, ~~nothing~~ ~~for~~ the it but fight. ~~Such souls were damned~~; ~~cut~~ off, in this indescribable way by something not much more emphatic than a cough, or a mannerism, from all share in ~~natural~~ human life, condemned forever to remain, like these ~~at brilli~~ able Jones' brilliant but ~~fundamentally unsound~~ Smiths, college dons, ~~teachers, vociferators, men who could never~~ be admitted to ~~little men~~, a little miseries; & yet it was perfectly true, what William said, that he got on very well with Mr. Ramsay ~~He~~ ~~Nobody said he was stupid; it~~ He was no fool. ~~&~~ But why Mrs. Ramsay ~~so w~~ was so annoyed if they laughed at him, just because ~~he~~ Mr. Ramsay liked talking to him? But what reason was that?

(his shufflings his [grunts?] his

It was strange:

He was cut

† *Then he could ~~li~~ lift his eyebrows & sneer; he could "suspect a
& all the rest of it
little sentimental humbug" ~~with the best~~ of them. When Mrs.
Ramsay, herself inclined to exaggeration, spoke of waves as mountains
high" of everyone "drenched to the skin", he would say
"certainly it had been a little rough", & his overcoat was "damp, but
not wet through". – He would change his socks – that was all.
But when it came to explaining how it was not <u>this</u> that one
objected to ~~in~~ t~~he little atheist~~, ~~how~~ one did not mind certain sorts of
didn't how behaved one was not saying
~~ugliness &~~ care ~~a straw~~ about peoples' manners & obviously the
wild things
little wretch was clever – (~~engaging~~ correcting those ~~wrong estimates~~
that were often made of the population of foreign countries, or
what were
explaining ~~very~~ obviously accurately the ~~reason the policy of Lord~~
whigs & tories) when ~~it came to consolidating those~~
senti~~ments which~~ but objected to ~~his ugliness~~, something
all over
diffused ~~& universal~~ in him – his essence in short – then it
became more difficult, &, short of allowing the conversation to be
changed, it was necessary to lodge a more definite complaint –
for example was ~~what one called~~ simply
to the effect ~~for example~~ that he ~~protested~~ was a prig.
was
But a prig? – ~~what is~~ that? ~~Give him~~ Someone who had no
of his own then anyhow
~~natural easy~~ feelings, ~~but had~~ ~~to fake them~~. Observe him when
they talked about anything interesting – not facts, or history, of
course, for there he was in his element. But ~~suppose~~
pictures or poetry; or whether it was not ~~so~~ the loveliest
in the world seen
evening there had ever been? Then, ~~how~~ no crab on dry
arid
land showed more angular & ~~uneasy~~ & until he had thought of
~~which did not~~ something to say which had no bearing upon
the subject, but if you examined into it, merely asserted his own
virtue &
~~virtue, for he~~ ~~Claim right to his~~ ~~his right to~~ be ~~a plain man~~,
~~someone who did not like mere [ lean? ]~~ (that he ~~was~~ for the [ rare? ] [ ? ]
rather liked books to have a meaning, pictures to be like something;
& was very ~~plain and~~ that you could not expect ~~him~~ working
admire &
people to enjoy beauty until they were certain of a nights lodging)
he was ~~very like a little crab, blind, discomfited.~~
Until he had given the conversation a little flick, & made it

[Left margin:]
that he
was
stupid
for a moment

his

because he had
the welfare of
mankind at
heart,

& it might be
a beautiful
night, but
it was rain this [even?]

* MS 9
† A 15

(1.23)

† ~~somehow~~ bear witness to the struggles which he had been through the sense he had of ~~suffering~~, disorder, & social injustice, [himself, & which no fine evenings or fine ~~ph~~ phrases could remedy, he was, like a crab, ~~puzzled, irritated, out of~~ set on a table, turning this way & that angry, ~~puzzled~~ alarmed, bewildered.

† A 16

† * Strife, division, difference of opinion, ~~impossible barriers~~, prejudices ~~rooted in the very~~ twisted into the very fibre of being, barriers that for all accident might do to disregard them, bringing ~~Mr.~~ Charles Tansley ~~into collision~~ [to the same table for an entire week] with the Ramsays, would assert themselves indomitably, & so ~~work~~ contrive that he was cut by ~~R~~ William Ramsay six years later, to save trouble on both sides – ~~there were~~ there they were, in ~~these~~ ~~this~~ [this] vague pre-natal state, ~~in these discomforts, in these antagonisms, in which could only be hints, in their first stage of~~ like the shadows ~~phantoms of~~ of trees which ~~w~~ ~~dawn has~~ are so transparent in the early ~~morning~~ [dawn] that it seems possible to walk through them; only the rising sun reveals their hardness – already Rose could not get on with Charles; he was known generally [throughout the household] ~~with a certain degree of contempt~~ as "the atheist".

suspected glanced at,

Strife, division, differences of opinion, disagreements ~~as to~~ like this [as to whether] about books – should they have a message? – ~~were~~ [cry out] they not ~~instruments~~ [to] [people] teach? – or about ~~the~~ things so intangible that it seemed poor-spirited to notice them – ~~his~~ colours flowers, how the rooms looked, & the ~~change~~ amazing effect of a bust of Venus stood against the hedge – none of which he his complete indifference to ~~ev~~ all ~~beauty &~~ sensuality, in short; ~~might~~ were they [such differences] between people after all negligible? Could you dismiss them, in comparison with the Indian Mutiny ~~or~~ the ~~sinking crime~~ Charge of the Light Brigade, or the Industrial Revolution, as of no account when in fact such differences preceded those catastrophes, & brought the world to ~~su~~ the miserable condition in which it was to day?

his very precarious seat on the back of life,

& his constant though perhaps unconscious protest that he lacked nothing of the sort;

† For ~~they,~~ ~~jumpin~~ ~~stealing~~ disappearing as stealthily as stags, ~~from vanishing in a forest,~~ ~~all those~~ from the dining room table the eight sons & daughters of Mr.

* See 'Notes for Writing,' appendix A.
† A 17, B 19; A 16, B 18

(1.27)

& Mrs. Ramsay sought their bedrooms, their fastnesses in a house
where there was no privacy, to debate the misery of the world;
† to question; ~~to~~ while the sun, pouring into those attics & corners,
which a plank ~~of~~ alone separated from each other, as often as not,
so that the ~~tramp~~ of ~~the~~ every footstep could be plainly
heard, or the moan of the Swiss ~~gr~~ girl whose father was
dying of cancer sounded night after night, lit up ~~the~~
books while it drew
~~usual litter of~~ ~~bays~~ bats, flannel shirts, straw hats, & long
a peculiar ~~weedish~~ smell in ~~sat~~ weeds & sea;
frilled sea weeds which ~~hung were~~ nailed to the door. ~~That~~
little man was a prig: ~~hate had sown its seeds: infinite~~ & the danger
complexity
~~the complexity~~ & difficulty ~~& danger~~ of life ~~was~~ now

Mrs. Ramsay thought it all so silly.

ink pots, paint pots, beetles, the skulls of small birds, which was in the towels, too, sandy from bathing.

† Mrs. Ramsay thought it all pure nonsense. She walked from
the dinner table holding James by the hand, but, since he wanted to
go with the others, she let him. It seemed to her pure nonsense,
these
inventing ~~making out~~ differences. ~~Either she was a very simple woman~~, when,
only
differ / too vastly, ~~as people very well know~~, it was kinder ~~& better~~, not &
these
people as it is, here she dwelt upon ~~those~~ ~~that~~ those divisions
~~rank, wh~~ into higher & lower
of ~~rank & we~~ ~~higher & lower~~, rich~~er~~ & poor~~er~~, which ~~were~~
much
were ~~of~~ ~~was con~~stantly in her mind, & the great in birth
receiving from her a simple, feudal, ~~half~~ romantic respect, which
a
Loire ~~Cl~~ermont, arose partly from her own descent, from ~~the~~ French house of
the little thread of gold being dipped & sunk,
~~Clareville~~, & the obscurity which had befallen that race, so
that people ~~ignored her~~ took her simply for an English parson's
daughter ~~fo~~ – ~~& this was~~ ~~w~~ when her worldliness & her wit ~~&~~
straight from the
came from ~~France~~, ~~ran~~ ~~thus~~ those ~~ambitious scheming~~ warm blooded
whom she loved † French ~~people~~, ~~& then too~~, ~~curbing~~ but, ~~far~~ equally she ~~was~~
the &
ruminated, ~~that~~ problem ~~which~~ of poverty ~~which~~ ~~day by day~~
~~filled her desk with letters~~ & ~~had~~ ~~these~~ disastrous ~~results~~. ~~She knew~~
~~of homes where~~ consequences which she ~~knew~~ ~~by~~ ~~&~~ ~~in all~~
when she visited
~~their~~ saw, weekly, daily, making her ~~excursions~~ to this widow, that
struggling wife, in person – ~~long, exhausting excursions~~ with a
with which she
† bag on arm, & a note book & pencil ~~in case~~ believing, ~~that~~
wrote down
could ~~did one write it all down~~ & ~~reduce~~ ~~the~~ wages & spendings ~~in~~
~~to averages, something~~ & facts about employment &
in [separate?] trade, ~~hoping thus to~~ elevate her private charities to the
[?] ~~rank of an enquiry & to~~ some ~~& thus~~ in the hope
[usual?] woman
that thus she would cease to be a private unattached individual,
~~woman~~, & ~~become of use to the~~ ~~throw light upon the~~
~~& become~~ & whose charity was half a sop to her own
indignation, half a relief to ~~the~~ her own discomfort, &
become, what with her untrained mind she greatly admired, an
elucidating
investigator, ~~throwing light upon~~ a problem.

So this carping & criticising annoyed her. ~~True she~~
~~loved it~~. ~~For there~~ ~~It seemed to her~~ Her daughters

† "Would it bore you ~~entirely~~ utterly ~~& unutterably~~ unspeakably entirely to come with me?" she said to ~~Mr.~~ Charles Tansley, when all her eight children withdrew like stags to their fastnesses, & ~~Mr~~. Charles Tansley, who was after all their guest, was left standing ~~in~~ investigating with the tip of his finger, very self-consciously, some marvellous construction of Williams – a ~~boat that~~ a steamer ~~with a me~~ that ~~would~~ was intended to cross the pond under its own power, – left on the table. Her children were all gone: Lily Doyle & Mr. Holcroft too; Mr. Carmichael, her husband – As for herself, she had a very dull job in the town, if he like to escort her. And she would write one note, & ~~then~~ put on her hat – an incongruous hat, it seemed rather, but there she was, ten minutes later, with her basket & her parasol, ~~rather merry ready equipped~~, giving out a sense of readiness, & anticipation, & ~~going~~ on a jaunt, which she must however, interrupt a moment in order to see if Mr. Carmichael who was ~~asleep~~ basking with his his strange cats eyes in an almost livid face ajar, so that, like in cats, they seemed to reflect the ~~brandes~~ branches moving or the clouds passing, but to give no inkling of inner thoughts or any emotion [whatsoever wanted anything – stamps, writing paper, tobacco?

they were all gone.

flat, unsupported, [vaguely?] feathery

being set

as they passed the tennis lawn

For they were making ~~a~~ the great expedition, she said. The poor man had taken opium for years she told Mr. Tansley The cats eyes having blinked, the hand clasped themselves over his capacious paunch, ~~for all the world~~ as if he would like to reply kindly to these blandishments, but could not move, sunk as he was in a grey-green somnolence, ~~in a vast & benevolent lethargy~~ which embraced them all in a vast & benevolent lethargy; all the house; all the world; all the people in it, he having lunched well & then slipped into his

† glass a few drops of something which accounted, her children thought, for the vivid streak of canary yellow in moustaches – beard that were otherwise milk white. ~~That~~ Without these he ~~was a~~

should have been * a great philosopher, ~~Mrs. Ramsay~~ & only missed it because of an unfortunate marriage, & this habit which was the result of it, Mrs. Ramsay believed; & being

* MS 39 (1.33)

† B 21; B 22

~~baulked of that~~ so walking down ~~the to~~ to the fishing village with Mr. Tansley carrying her basket ~~& she~~ holding her parasol / very erect above her [head

† she told him how this wonderful career had been cut short & without blaming the poor little untaught creature who had married him, conveyed to Mr. Tansley ~~a~~ the assurance, – conviction which he found soothing, consolatory, as balm to the wounds ~~he carried~~ inflicted by William, Lucy, Roger & the no one could ~~others~~ that of course without unless being he was a man helped & believed in & had ~~having~~ the sordid worries of life ~~discharged for them~~, taken off him, ~~no philosopher or poet could he could not~~

(there need be no harshness, but certainly there need be no ~~questioning~~ doubt)

The impression that the blame must fall on her, ~~not on him;~~ that no devotion could be too complete ~~on a~~ from wife's part; that it was ~~indeed a great~~ their privilege; that no great work could be done without it; that the greatness of man's intellect had her most humble & enthusiastic veneration; all of which assuaged Mr. Tansley's own feelings, & ~~yet~~ had into the bargain ~~a~~ so ~~conciliatory~~ an effect ~~that he~~ on him (after what he had been through) that he felt beginning conciliatory effect upon him, though, as Mrs. Ramsay talked ~~he felt that~~ this ~~rash~~ generous woman, with all her enthusiasm, with her ~~light~~ directness, her lightness, & some of the power which she was beginning to exert unmistakably upon him, put upon the whole of the opposite sex an enormous responsibility.

That this gorged alligator who lay on her lawn *capable only of doing sums in his head & offering to teach Roger hindustanee was her doing

which one could not really call helpful, to teach the boys Hindustanee, for

He began to notice**

* MS 39, 45

** Written in pencil

† A 20

affected him strangely unaccustomed as he was to strangeness: ~~It~~ she moved made him envious of wishing to do something gallant, to pay some [him little sum on her behalf; ~~or~~ & yet puzzled him; for though she appeared so confident & even sparkling flattering as she talked to him he could not help feeling ~~doubtful~~ ~~both~~ that this kindness to him in particular was ~~a~~ an depended upon incident on the surface of some wide ~~general~~ & deeper more capacious feeling, ~~what~~ which for all her exaggerations, lent her words a gravity, ~~which was odd~~ & then & sometimes she was inattentive this ~~easy~~ ready admission concession to his sex of every virtue put while ~~made~~ in him it certainly an flattered [him, enormous responsibility, ~~on~~ them while ~~it~~ at the same time – a little uneasy; well ~~there was Mr. Ramsay, there was Mr. Carmichael &~~ when he thought of Mr. Ramsay, & then of Mr. Carmichael, it didn't at all mean that she [?] he ~~& Mrs. Ramsay in complete control of them both~~. did she not control them ~~all~~ when he then not claim for her own sex, stupendous power lea' to i sex? If so, it was by some ~~for~~ & did she mean that ~~they~~ all men depended utterly [on her: if they ~~failed, as~~ married ~~some unl~~ the wrong wife, then, they took opium & sat on the lawn: her ~~Did she not hold herself res~~ponsible that ~~both~~ failure & success, the triumph of great poets, the works of senior wranglers, depended equally ~~upon~~ on them?

(& it was true; Mrs. Ramsay was very sorry for this youth)

his own brain was

(he felt capable of anything)*

seemed a little as if ~~his~~ they did perhaps a little lack

(& he thought of Mr. Ramsay & he thought of Mr. Carmichael)

Now, it was ~~all very~~ probably instinctive. Stopping suddenly, she ~~gazed at a her head thrown back, her lips parted~~, at a exclaimed

† what was there to please her so in that sight? – A man on a ladder pasting an enormous bill against a ~~dead~~ wall? With every deft shove of his brush, the vast flapping ~~highly coloured~~ sheet flattened itself out & ~~stu~~ adhered, beautifully

† smoothed, & glistening with reds & blues, ~~&~~ revealing, with each fresh dab, ~~more~~ fresh legs & hoops & horses, until ~~the whole scene of a~~ until ~~the great~~ half the wall was covered with that enormous advertisement of Hengless Circus, ~~&~~ its ~~miraculous~~ hundred horsemen, its ~~miraculous~~ performing seals, its lions & tigers? Mrs. Ramsay looked.

She stopped & gazed ~~while~~–

The man who was pasting had only one arm. The other ~~had been cut off~~** she said had been cut off by an accident

* Written in pencil

** Cancelled in pencil

† B 23; A 21

(1.37)

with a reaping machine two years ago: Still she looked.

Her attention was attracted equally by the man's skill, In ~~Yet~~ she said, what a dangerous job ~~to have given~~ for a one armed man? & the absurd yet undeniably attractive prospect of ~~going~~ taking going, as she said, in a ~~large~~ bunch, "taking the children, & the servants ~~taking~~ & buy them a box" ~~she said~~, tomorrow night, ~~& seeing the~~ to the circus" – a prospect which had no lure whatever for Mr. Tansley, until she put it so, & then being destitute of natural spirits, & very much cramped by ~~his~~ the strenuous intellectual toil which had been, as Mrs. Ramsay guessed, absolutely necessary, for he was the son of very poor parents, & ~~his fat~~ now it was his turn to help them – only she would have liked him better if he had not told her this & been ~~so~~ conscious of it & dwelt upon his poverty – ~~but~~ when Mrs. Ramsay said this, he suddenly wanted to be sportive & frisky; & to feel that it really was good fun, this circus, though why the Ramsays he found it very difficult to understand the matter. The Ramsays enjoyed the highest culture.

with

so often contemplated with approval,

& could not tick off 15 pages in his little book,

things that waved & beckoned

upon his own conception of himself,

Mr. Tansley was all screwed up in a ball by this talk of going to the Circus, servants – children all in a bunch

~~&~~ to feel, naturally, that it was fun to spend an evening at the Circus. But it was not easy all in a moment to destroy, cheerfully, ~~those~~ the so the divisions of his day; to sacrifice fifteen pages of Sorel ~~& the appropriate~~ adequate annotation to Hengless' Circus; ~~& the curiously pure~~ to obliterate ~~stoical~~ vision of himself ~~going to bed~~ at midnight, ~~dogged~~, a little rose round the eyes, advanced one more rocky stage on his journey & rightly complacent to ~~the~~ another, ~~quite different: a~~ of a man who had wanted a whole evening, & lost a stage of his journey looking at the legs of women in tights, & pretending ~~a~~ merriment at the antics of ~~bumpkins:~~ horses ~~Mr. Ramsay would think~~ ~~For~~ But it was the Ramsays who did it, people, that is, who ~~represented for him~~ were at the summit ~~of all he would like to be.~~ of human existence (save for the fact that Mr. Ramsay having means of his own, had ~~not~~ been able to disregard professorships, lectureships, wardenships, masterships & all the other splendours, which beckoned to Tansley himself, of an academic career) ~~He~~ And thinking of the odd inconsistency ~~which~~ feeling the unpleasant assault, wishing for gifts which were not his, but doggedly ~~returning to ass~~ asserting that his ~~plain~~ duty was plain – for once he was he was all right, quite gratified

† learned & self-supporting he was / not going to hoard it; he would teach; ~~&~~ poor men, working men, men like himself who had had to fight every inch of the way; ~~&~~ he would remedy some of that monstrous injustice; when Mrs.

~~Here Mrs. Ramsay,~~

Ramsay ~~touched his arm, & called his attention to the~~

† ~~view of the bay, the view~~ Oh it was so beautiful!

It was considered extremely beautiful. ~~Indeed,~~ ~~after leav~~ ~~They had~~ ~~Indeed~~ And here was Mr. ~~Talboys~~

† Bearley painting it; Mr. Bearley in his panama hat & white tennis shoes; painting, with a circle of boys another of those pictures of the lovely bay which since the Mr. Paunceforte came there & invented a

The bay she meant. The ~~th~~ great plateful of sparkling blue water with the hoary lighthouse in the centre, &

† A 22, B 24; A 23, B 25; B 26

& all round it, fading & falling, low, desolate ~~grey like~~ with sand dunes & green with ~~g~~ wild flowing grasses which even across the water seemed to be running away into silence into wildness, into some eternal communion of their own, eternal ~~with silent~~ unimparted, with the sky & sea. It was this view ∧ she said that her husband loved; & now, ~~she said~~, artists had come, & there indeed, only a few paces out, for they had reached the harbour, ~~sat~~ stood Mr. Archer ~~the usual painter~~ in panama hat & red tennis shoes, ~~painting~~ seriously softly, absorbedly, with an air of profound content on his round weather beaten face, ~~dipping~~ – gazing, & then when he had gazed, dipping; His picture, like almost all ~~that~~ painted ~~there~~ in the island; ~~was a little spectral.~~ Since the visit of Mr. Pauncefort three years ago, was a ~~little~~ green & grey with a lemon coloured boat & a pink lady; but Mrs. Ramsay ~~who~~ was at / a distant remove from pictures, who she criticised art almost entirely ~~from the point of v~~ as she supposed her grandmother's friends would have criticised it, & could tell ~~yo~~ many a tale of the difficulty these great men had had in keeping their colours damp.

flickering merriment which was also wild & heartless

the tip imbuing his brush ~~with~~ in in some soft mound pink or grey now. †

had imposed a method, or point of view,

First, she told Mr. Tansley, there was the business of grinding the paints; next they had to be soaked in salad oil. For among her grandmothers friends, there were many who mixed their own colours, ~~It was a fact that seemed,~~ to first ground them, then soaked them in salad oil; & it was this attitude which had, was ~~not~~ very critical of this school, & Mr. Tansley was impressed by the extreme derision with which she pronounced against Mr. Bearley's lighthouse, directly they were out of hearing.

† A 24

It was often a matter of considerable difficulty. ~~As~~ It had been her privilege to help sometimes in these studios. Thus she unveiled slightly [the treasure chamber of her past, which Mr. Tansley felt certain was such a [past as he most coveted full of interesting ~~people~~ — cultivated people; with an & the highest standards infallible tastes in art & literature. With her sanction ~~With Mrs. Ramsay's sanction~~, he too dismissed the Paunceforte school of ~~mod~~ painting, ~~with its~~ & ~~satirised~~ ~~the~~ Mr. Archer dismissed, with a smile, these pictures of grey sands & ~~green wa~~ pink ladies which had ~~none of the qualities~~ obvious defects, since the painters ~~scamped their work~~, & did not as Mrs. Ramsay remembered her grandmother's friends doing, grind their colours for themselves, & keep them moist.

~~With all~~ But her this infallibility in these matters was ~~only~~ what he ~~was~~ began to expect of her for she stirred ~~him~~ in him the strangest feelings, so † that when they stopped at a door in a back street, & she went in, ~~&~~ he ~~was left outside, he felt~~ upstairs, & he was asked to wait in the usual mahogany crowded room with mats & glass cases ~~downstairs~~; the sound of her voice in the room above invalid's bedroom ~~ro~~ above, & her † ~~light~~ quick step coming out, & her ~~beautiful~~ cheerful & private & [?] yet so on the landing sympathetic voice saying ~~whatever~~ something about coming ~~soon~~ again, & being sure to keep the windows open, & ~~(for~~ the woman with all the ~~young children was dying~~ of cancer) ~~& then~~ ~~the change from gaiety to almost rigid~~ Then re- her appearance among the mats & [horsehair?], quiet, firm, & sad again, with ~~an~~ its added firmness & quietude, ~~no~~ for she told him the ~~poor~~ woman with four young children was dying of cancer, ~~suddenly~~ all suddenly fanned up ~~in him~~; what ~~for~~ had been hitherto ~~a grudging timid flame~~ into one flame of this astounding certainty — ~~of~~ her beauty. ~~It was astonishing as she stood~~ She ~~too~~ stood against the picture of Queen Victoria in ~~her~~ widows robes wearing the ribbon of the garter. ~~Now, as they left~~ ~~More~~ Like a figure that had ~~been~~ dredged the depths of the sea of bitterness & sorrow & had come to the surface to life again with eyes pearl encrusted with ~~the~~ ~~tears~~ tears, & brows starred with immortality; tears & ~~stars, the mourning &~~ immortality & ~~sorrow~~, the ~~image of~~ like

he thought of nothing but her; & when he heard ~~her~~

laughing back some thanks &

a stone figure; a statue set on a height always to look the depths of the
night in the face; ~~like a~~ with stars in her eyes & purple veils about her
hair; this ~~with wild hyacinths, & grey, & white & steadfast,~~
some
~~by virtue of her~~ ~~superior knowledge~~ steadfast ~~where all~~
when ~~every~~ the cyclamens & the hyacinths, the asphodels &
[before?]
the wild violets waiting & ~~floating~~ flowing, ~~bowing to the flail of~~ the wind &
abasing themselves at her feet; the ~~figure who~~ mourner ~~the~~
by the grave of the unwedded girl; ~~the~~ Helen passing before
the eyes of the old men; taking to her breast the first
fallen in
buds, & the lambs ~~who have fallen;~~ the ~~vir~~ mother whose
~~arm hollow~~ a arm is security – Mr. Tansley did
not wish to make a fool of himself, & gush over a woman's
beauty, ~~moreover~~ Mrs. Ramsay was a woman fifty into the
bargain, & had eight children. Still it did come over
how extraordinary it was [he to?]
him at the moment; & take his breath away. And he noticed how,
as they walked down the street, he carrying her basket, & she
again holding the black parasol erect, people ~~just~~ looked
† out as she passed, looked at her as if they were startled & then
looked down, poor men, who were hawking fish, or leaning against
the wall in the sunshine, looked at her, with the same odd
stare; ~~which~~ of which Mrs. Ramsay seemed perfectly unconscious.

† B 28

† Perhaps you will wake up & find the sun shining & the birds singing,
Said Mrs. Ramsay, half mechanically, smoothing the little boys
hair, ~~& in order to~~ for her husband had completely dashed his
~~pleasure, she happ~~ spirits, she could see: 'going to the lighthouse'
~~having been his~~ being ~~his~~ a passion of his, which, perhaps foolishly
she had let him think would be gratified tomorrow. But now – it
said that it would rain;
was very annoying – her husband threw cold water on it; & then
still further ily
† Mr. Tansley went & rubbed it in, ~~which was~~ quite unnecessary for
at
James was quick enough ~~to~~ understanding, & all she could do now
was to admire the refrigerator which he had cut out, & to
turn the pages of the list in the hope that she might find
something very difficult – like a mowing machine – which with its
need
long handles would ~~want~~ extraordinary ~~skll~~ skill. All
these young men parodied her husband, she reflected. If <u>he</u> said it was
going to rain, <u>they</u> said it would be a positive tornado.

But her ~~ser~~ search for mowing machines was ~~momentarily~~
The
interrupted. ~~That~~ gruff murmur ~~the terse question~~; the ~~s~~hort
by
~~answer,~~ which often unnaturally broken ~~into~~ by ~~the~~
bay
puffs at their pipes, represented to her, sitting in the / window,
which opened onto the terrace, the men talking; the sound which
had now lasted half an hour & taken its place in her scale of
perception with the tap of balls upon cricket bats, the
sharp sudden bark now & then "Hows that?"* & the
~~& the~~ regular monotonous thud of the waves on the beach, – ~~of the~~
~~that sound~~ which on a still night became almost ominous in its
one
† thunder its persistency & made ~~one~~ think of the destruction
engulfing final engulf
of this ~~si~~ island & its absorption finally into the sea,
to
† & often beat the most measured & soothing tattoo to her
[~~from~~?]
thoughts, & sometimes seemed to her consolingly that
~~nothing~~ as if it repeated over & over again a
the words of some old cradle song, murmured by nature,
who, in her cosmogony, had long supplanted for
reasons she could scarcely name, the hierarchy of Heaven,

* See 'Notes for Writing,' appendix A. (1.49)
† A 26; B 29; A 28, B 30; A 27

your support
– "~~we are~~ I am guarding you – I am ~~at hand~~ nature then seemed to say,
more frequent such
but at other times, & these perhaps were ~~commoner~~, had no kindly
meaning but like a ghostly roll of drums ~~remorsll~~ remorselessly,
† ~~inexorably~~ beat the measure of life, & warned her whose
as
days seemed to fly so ~~fast & to be~~ such a phantasmagoria –
[these?]
helter skelter of events which she had scarcely time to
realise, of the fleetingness of all this, of the quick passage of
[how?]
~~her~~ of rainbow ∧ waterfall – such it seemed to her – into the
abyss, & the shattered race of risen waters afterwards. That she
might die first – that was her urgent desire: ~~And she~~ With this
wish in her mind, she ~~shut~~ looked up, & startled from her
round startled, composing half a dozen thoughts together, ~~by~~ because
the sound of voices had ceased
one of the sounds – the sound of voices had stopped. That she
might die first. ~~In that~~ ~~It was~~ So she looked at her
husband.

He was now alone. Falling in one second from the instinctive
clutch & tension ~~of this~~ which had gripped her to the extreme,
after expense of
which, as if to recoup her unnecessary emotion ~~with a~~
was cool as ~~an ice~~ amused, even faintly malicious,
Charles
she concluded that poor ~~Mr.~~ Tansley had been shed. That was
of little account to her: ~~compared with her husbands stat~~e of
[?]
mind. If he required sacrifices, & she ~~there was no~~
often
~~doubt that~~ he did, ~~require sacrifices~~ she cheerfully
offered up Charles Tansley.

† A 28

~~She ascertained~~, ~~She ascertained~~ ~~w~~ W ith the speed of practise that she assured herself

† all was well:] &, so bending down again began looking for mowing machines, or many bladed knives, ~~while from the garden~~ for her son to cut out soothed by the assurance which reached her, ~~suddenly~~ now loudly ~~now & then as her~~ now faintly, as her husband ~~reached the~~ appeared at the window & passed it, ~~&~~ & again appeared & passed, it that he was content:

clenching his hands & throwing his head back & reciting words which came at her in gusts & faded away,

Stormed at by shot & shell
Boldly they rode & well —*

so long as he declaimed ~~that to~~ like that, & shook his magnificent head & clenched his fists,

Stormed at by shot & shell
Boldly they rode & well —

~~It~~ The words ~~came~~ rang out, he tossed his head back & clenched his that all was well.

~~Yet it~~ was a sight that never failed to rouse wonder in those unfamiliar with it. The familiar sight, ~~the soothing sound,~~ the assurance she at once received, of happiness, for ~~she had the they suited each other, had the~~ his eccentricities ~~drew at~~ coincided with her normalities, & again, where he was ~~sane &~~ when she, ~~perhaps~~ owing to her foreign blood, / perhaps was romantic & extreme; ~~never failed to rouse surprise in those who but familiar as~~ ~~it~~ ~~they were was to her soothed~~ her; but ~~to~~ upon casual visitors or servants unused to his ways had precisely the opposite effect. They thought it very strange — ~~Mr.~~ Cooks or & housemaids peering into the study & seeing the litter ~~there~~ of papers, the accumulation of books ~~which~~ of an unintelligible kind which Mr. Ramsay dragged from one end of the British Isles to the other, ~~& could not~~ noting too

gave her a sense of well being & ~~right~~ comfort

---

* A. Tennyson, 'The Charge of the Light Brigade.' Also quoted on MS 52, 60, 63. (1.53)

† B 31; A 29

the extraordinary number of disabilities which seemed to affect him in daily life – his ~~incapacity~~ ~~to~~ inability to find things; to tie up parcels, to ~~remember his~~ tie up things ~~tie,~~ ~~or~~ whether he had put his tie on, or ~~changed his coat~~, concluded quite simply that here was a case of ~~bok~~ book learning ~~& greatness~~ ~~& which~~ in the extreme; something ~~at once pitiable & venerable:~~ which the casual visitor ~~who~~ who was pressed a little further ~~& asked others~~, ~~also who were~~ & took counsel with other similarly puzzled debated this problem about Mr. Ramsay: how ~~the~~ one man ~~who was reason personified could also~~ – & ~~they added instances of his~~ could combine such extremes of reason & oddity; could be at once so formidable & so childish; denude the world of every marsh & flower, & ~~yet revel in the emotions~~ ~~simplest sentiments~~, ~~the~~ which befitted a girl of fifteen.

his tempers
his

could
cherish illusions

a phantom

did

as if ~~an~~ claiming kinship then, being the

Here he was [?] ~~coldly~~ predicting rain; next, charging at the head of an army, & receiving ~~into his body a dozen spears, &~~ wounds of which he died gloriously on the heights of ~~Bla~~ Balaclava. Did one extreme account for the ~~give rise~~ to another – & was his ~~did he balance his~~ balancing & ~~this~~ his present indulgence in the simplest of schoolboy emotions by a majesterial severity at table? where no one was quicker than he to ~~pluck the stigmatise the~~ folly, of ~~man & the~~ & riddle sentiment with ridicule? ~~And th~~en this his
He was the fi
Then there was this passion for views. He liked them to be wild & bare; he endless liked to wave his hand at some barren moor or waste of water; & ~~he would~~ sit on the point of a rock jutting out into the Atlantic & gaze ~~at the water. No~~ & gaze at the & gaze at the flood Now easy, ~~these~~ ~~Nothing could be easier,~~ than the to exalt him almost above human stature; ~~&~~ as Charles Tansley did, & others of his sort; ~~but how then account for the~~ ~~the imita~~ but watching the spare scholars figure crouched there, ~~with~~ he was shabby & wild & uncouth, yet exquisitely finished too, ethereal, to exalt him above human stature & feel as Charles Tansley did, that here was the philosopher whose search for truth had led him, alone, through the desert, & identify him with truth & purity; ~~& other~~ high & exalted ~~qualities, to~~ feel that but no sooner had you settled into the riddle of that belief – & ~~women could~~ then he threw you. People said, in short, that he loved

But Mr. ~~Ramsay had~~ They might gaze & speculate; Mr. Ramsay was charging at the head of the Light Brigade & as was immense. He was exalted. He was in fact crying ~~&~~ vociferously, freely, like a ~~sch~~ schoolboy after a heat, one

~~Did one always,~~ ~~indeed,~~ ~~At any rate,~~

† *Such labours as his ~~must~~ were be indeed ~~something that the~~ so inconceivable that ~~of~~ Miss Sophie Briscoe, ~~that~~ a kindly rosy ~~& well covered~~ lady who ~~had~~ spent much of her life sketching, ~~rather~~ was rather fluttered when, in his turnings & pacings he approached her end of the terrace. ~~where~~ ~~No, one couldn't conceive how~~ She felt as if she, ~~being only a mortal~~, had need of a telescope, with which to communicate with him; ~~as if anyone~~ so low as she was in the scale of intelligence; ~~had need~~ ~~of a~~ he & might, conceivably, speak to her. Happily, he ~~said~~ nothing passed ~~seemed~~ unaware of her presence. But the mere thought of the things that were in that man's head made her grave in ~~the~~ an ~~pouting~~ irresponsible ~~way of~~ ~~way of an~~ old maids ~~ish~~ ~~maids way~~, ~~who, secure~~ (for, ~~though she had~~ had her offers of marriage ~~she was glad, at 55, to think she had refused the~~ ~~refused them all~~ having refused all offers & kept retained her right to view male eccentricity from a distance –) ~~Her brain~~ ~~tried for a She tried~~ to make her brain prod a little way along that path – He wrote about books about metaphysics. ~~He was always thinking~~

She could not conceive what he thought about.

When he was quite silent ~~at dinner~~ he was thinking of something which, she was afraid, she could not grasp even if he explained it to her. It was something philosophic. without any shape, which did not ~~really~~ matter to anyone in the least, but to be able to ~~understand this thing was~~, she had been told, ~~this~~ only one man in a thousand, could even understand what this thing was; & Mr. Ramsay ~~was~~ ~~one of~~ ~~not~~ ~~could~~ ~~never~~ spent all his time thinking about it. Now such things. She always ~~illustrated his occupation~~ by ~~seeing~~ in her mind's eye a table; when she considered what ~~was~~ Mr. ~~& trying to make herself~~ ~~all~~ ~~the question was~~ about a table & whether it existed or not for ~~her~~ she had ~~heard~~ read enough of his books once to Ramsay was thinking about. She believed ~~he~~ ~~could~~ that

* MS 31, 49
† A 29, B 32

a table played a great part in his arguments. Sophie Briscoe was glad that her own ~~gifts were~~ tastes were for ~~nice~~ hedgerows, cottages, (especially the thatched cottage of the south) ~~& fiction~~, ~~sunny garden~~ 'bits', like this of the ~~pampas~~ jacmanna grass against the sky which she was now painting, & fiction: but she did nevertheless often think, as she sat sketching ~~of how~~ about ~~the~~ ~~elder~~ Ramsays; ~~& his~~ being ~~so~~ such an [?] extraordinary, man; & there was a ~~bit~~ part of her, she seriously thought quite left out, since she could not understand a word ~~of his great book on The Meaning~~ ~~what~~ [?] he wrote.

"But nobody can." said ~~Char~~ Mr. ~~Stenner~~ Pritchard.

~~What~~ ~~he~~ H meant was, he ~~proceeded to~~ explained, that to understand "The ~~Meaning~~ of Reality" one must have a certain knowledge of mathematics. He ~~knew~~ / ~~enough~~ only had ~~himself merely to~~

"Ah, said Miss Briscoe.

And they watched Mr. Ramsay receding with his hands ~~for~~ flung out as he went.

Both

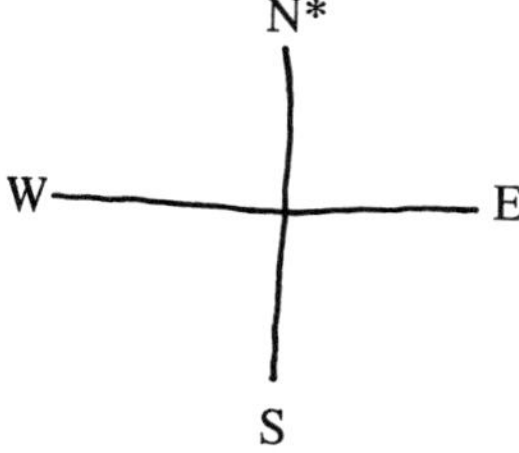


* Drawn near the top of the page (1.62)

Sept. 3rd.

*Mr. Ramsay's pacing ground was bounded on the ~~west~~ northwest by a hedge; on the south east by ~~Miss~~ Lily Briscoe ~~& William Bankes~~ who was painting & by ~~M~~ William Bankes who was watching her. Miss Briscoe was not afraid that Mr. Ramsay would knock her ~~down~~ over nor did she expect him to stop & speak to her; but as he marched, flinging out his hand, as he ~~died~~ rode ~~gloriously~~ ~~valiantly~~ or rather at the head of his [troops

† Stormed at by shot & shell

& died gloriously on the heights of Balaclava,

† ~~She~~ Miss Briscoe had no fears for her easel, no fears that the astonishing man would ~~speak~~ stop to her, but only such a mixture of feeling so ~~profound~~ that her whole being quivered slightly & / like ~~liquid in~~ liquid in a glass with ~~the laughter, the tears, the~~ amusement, gratitude & anguish, & reverence, ~~something ple~~ & all sorts of feelings which staying with the Ramsays & the autumn evening, the whole & him reciting & Mrs. Ramsay sitting there in the window thing in short bred in her, & ~~seemed~~ sitting painting to make the ~~little~~

& glowed wanly

† spray of purple jacmanna against the white washed wall ~~also quiver~~ too. ~~What did he think about?~~ He was the oddest mixture – ~~It was all very well for the~~ How one human being could combine such extremes ~~of reason~~ & childishness, ~~could~~ frighten one to death just by one word, & then behave worse than – baby – Lily Briscoe (Mrs. Ramsay tried) but did not know, & then, at once, ~~with that~~ with the humility of the uneducated (& she had no education, & ~~no profession,~~ yet was 33 & would never marry, though Mrs. Ramsay said "Nonsense. but added at once "the unmarried are just as good") humble & liberal as she was she supposed that if you spent your time thinking of the kind of things Mr. Ramsay thought about – ~~which were~~ truth, good, things subject & object. Meaning. The Nature of Reality (here Lily repeated words she had seen in one of Mr. Ramsay's books, purloined to read, but utterly unintelligible) then, after that, well, it was probably impossible to behave like other people.

the violet blue against the dazzling white inextricably for ever / associated with this moment)

† Mr. Bankes she had rooms in the village.

---

* MS 29, 49

† B 31; B 32; A 30; B 33

(1.63)

This little distinction ~~& its the need it~~ the walk to & fro, the opportunity they gave for summing up a talk, or for ~~some comment information~~, adding a few words of explanation, ~~had~~ – as for ~~instance~~ that perhaps, not ~~one~~ more than ten men in England did understand [^ood] ~~what~~ Mr. Ramsay ~~wrote~~ [^books] – or ~~that~~ Mrs. Ramsay ~~as a girl had been something quite surprising~~ – ~~had looked beautiful, but ah but twenty years ago!~~ – beauty was "of the ~~k~~ rare kind that improves. But she looks ~~sometimes~~ terribly worn," this little distinction had drawn the two together, ~~so that~~ & their relation, in view of Mr. Bankes' age, & ~~his~~ [^[he?]] being a widower ~~had a something~~ & a great botanist into the bargain had something filial, paternal, ~~colourless~~, cool, colourless, & to Lily Briscoe singularly congenial, for she found Mr. Bankes quite [^an extraordinary restful person to be with: like a [guest?] so wise;] easy to talk to; she did not mind in the least if he sat & watched her painting. He told her, too, the most fascinating things ~~about plants. She found him a great standby; & now~~ And she ~~could~~ didn't mind telling him that she ~~supposed something was left out in her, but she could not understand~~ [^she had failed utterly to understand a word] a word [^that] of Mr. Ramsay's ~~wrote~~ book.

'~~But~~ [^But] some knowledge of mathematics is necessary" said Mr. Bankes.

~~He would tell~~ [^He had] her ~~little~~ stories about 'Ramsay' as he called him: how the first time he saw him he was breaking the ice in his bath with a poker. ~~Lily observed that they scarcely spoke to each other.~~ so he told her incongruously, watching Ramsay; his tall, ~~watching him, sm~~ half smiling: Yes, he had these oddities, Mr. Bankes seemed to say: But how could one ~~not~~ [^fail to] feel the ~~extraordinary~~ respect which Mr. Bankes felt for Mr. Ramsay?

"Without a stitch of clothing on" he said.

"I daresay the window was open into the bargain."
The scrupulous exactitude with which Mr. Bankes spoke, so always which lent his sayings ~~speech~~, however unimportant, ~~even about~~ nothing whatever however unimportant an indescribable charm of ~~wa~~ his own shirts cuffs, & socks of his own aroma of
† propriety, cleanliness & calm, delighted Lily Briscoe. & the way he raised his eyeglass & let it fall, & the astonishing simplicity & directness with which he spoke – she felt him & ~~his~~ his way of saying "yes" to himself, at the end of a sentence; ~~But~~ So thinking she painted;

† A 31

† Indeed, there could be no doubt about it; she was in love. But with the [not with one] world, not one person: with the world that this garden held; ~~its people, its~~ [~~light, its~~] ~~& all that Mr. Bankes said~~ & thus Mr. Bankes had only to recollect to refer to the past, to mention anything connected with the Ramsay's ~~&~~ [to] ~~Lily saw felt~~ that saying seemed to Lily like a silver cord attached to a ~~glowing &~~ [soaring universe] balloon – ~~another world that is~~ [a world], infinitely superior to her own [world] trodden underfoot, trodden dirty, familiar, dull, ~~which was~~ upon which (she lived off the Brompton Road) the gothic towers of the Natural History Museum & the florid solidity of Harrods seemed to weigh, ~~down The Ramsays world, Mr. Bankes words were attached~~ a world ~~of~~ from which, rightly, she did not question it, she was forever excluded. ~~but~~ And yet, ~~though she felt this~~, it was [as much] part of her ~~charm, & of the~~ & [indeed] constituted ~~the~~ [her] charm ~~of her~~, ~~that & value~~ & idiosyncracy, that ~~she th~~ she did not abase herself ~~in the least~~; kept her independence; & could view the Ramsay world ~~shrewdly enough~~ from her own corner, where, (~~& to this she was unal~~terably ~~attached) she had her~~ she worshipped God.

person

an inhabitant,
~~as~~ as familiar,
haunt it
though she might.

And that fact made a great deal of difference.

"And ~~the~~ I daresay the window was open into the bargain" said Mr. Bankes, following Mr. Ramsay, ~~&~~ to the end of the terrace, ~~with~~

But Lily Briscoe could not help observing ~~first that~~ a ~~kind of~~ sort of apology, in or deprecation uneasiness, on Mr. Bankes' part; a ~~desire which she could not gratify, as the to explain to~~ as if he ~~understood~~ ~~hoped~~ ~~that Lily~~ feared that Lily might be led to disparage ~~the~~ Mr. Ramsay because there were, & he did not deny it, ~~weaknesses~~, little weaknesses, little eccentricities; ~~in that~~ but no: Mr. Bankes ~~was~~ ~~had~~ ~~rather~~ credited the

† girl with too much sense. He had observed with pleasure the excellence of her shoes; which ~~without being clumsy~~ allowed the toes their natural expansion, & yet ~~should~~ ~~f~~ fitted ~~the~~ what was an unusually he well shaped foot; Further, ~~William Bankes~~ he had noticed ~~how~~ that without the least protestation, she went off to Church ⋀ which, ~~wit~~ in spite of his own view, ~~festered~~ & a lifetime spent in investigation ~~which~~ that ~~tended~~ to the opposite conclusions some~~how~~ made him think ~~the~~ all the better of a woman, or ~~though she had not~~ even if she did so any ~~special~~ ~~attractiveness~~ ~~did not strike the eye like Minta Doyle~~ ~~No, no:~~ But he could trust Miss Briscoe to ~~take a see what was obviously~~ ~~judge Ramsay~~ ~~come to~~ a

(who could with that ~~so~~ sing song going on before them?)

but [marching?] going on, that singing,

on Sunday

even if she did somewhat, though not unpleasantly, lack some of the more obvious attractions of her sex.

† "A stroll?" he said, feeling in the some slight ~~first place~~ ~~that~~ a chilliness about his ankles, which warned him, ~~fastidious~~ as he was & inclined to view his own health pessimistically, so that, however much Mrs. Ramsay might press him, he preferred to lunch & to dine in his own room, where his servant could be trusted to prepare vegetables in such a way as to preserve the natural salt, ~~of That~~ a that the island breezes in mid-September have a ~~bite~~ in them, and Lily was really glad to put her brushes down; ~~for~~

† A 31, B 33; A 31, B 34

~~She saw the jacmanna, the white wall. The sky, so~~

Lily Briscoe agreed with alacrity.

The jacmanna was bright violet; the wall was glaring white.

† She would not have considered it honest to tamper with<br>
of nature, since it bright<br>
the brightness ~~of nature~~, ~~th what~~ she saw, fashionable though it was,<br>
since Mr. Paunceforte's visit, to make everything pale, ~~half~~<br>
lemon, pink, silver. So she got up – gladly, leaving for<br>
a moment ~~that was fa~~ struggle which ~~so~~ often brought her<br>
this<br>
to the ~~very threshold~~ to the verge of tears; that struggle to<br>
the<br>
maintain her integrity: that struggle to face imperturbably<br>
[~~to~~ lamely?]<br>
† without breaking down & sobbing on Mrs. Ramsays knee – after all,<br>
looked so worn – everyone confided in her<br>
Mrs. Ramsay had enough of her own to bear – the appalling tragedy<br>
of her life. Not to be educated, ~~to~~ not to be beautiful, (~~only to have~~<br>
her only good points were ~~her~~ feet & figure) ~~not~~ to be therefore as<br>
obviously superfluous as a human being could be, &<br>
yet how could it have been otherwise? – left motherless as she was<br>
& the eldest, with ~~an~~ younger sisters (they had married) & a<br>
father who ~~could not~~ wanted her. No, she could not see<br>
how things could have been different, & her ~~only~~ plain duty was<br>
to<br>
to ~~be~~ look ~~clean~~ & tidy, & never to ~~let anybody guess~~ not to cry,<br>
though, for some reason, when she came to stay with the Ramsays<br>
&<br>
& saw them so happy, so free, ~~& it became, at moments,~~<br>
~~intolerable~~. with all sorts of chances she had never had, & a<br>
father & mother, like that, the pain, ~~sometimes~~, was scarcely ~~to be~~<br>
~~born~~. ~~Mr. Bankes~~ But with Mr. Bankes it was<br>
somehow easy & comfortable, & she felt mildly ~~that~~ successful with him,<br>
side by side in the box<br>
& so, ~~putting~~ laying down her brushes with alacrity, she<br>
~~did~~ agreed, it ~~was~~ got suddenly cold:

† "The sun seems to give less heat" she said,<br>
for it was bright enough, the grass bright soft green; the

[Left margin:]<br>
to ~~see th~~ paint things bright if she saw them bright;<br>
nodded her (She ~~used~~ to head at each item<br>
to keep cheerful;<br>
bearable

† A 32; B 35; A 33

(1.73)

the shadows sharp; the house starred with purple passion flowers –

However, off they went, to stroll ~~about~~ down the garden which in the usual direction; to that break in the thick hedge ~~where~~ through which one saw the Bay.

Guarded by red hot pokers which burst their clear red coal against the
blue, through which they saw the bay.

† ~~It brought them back to look at i~~t regularly, ~~morning~~s & evenings,
The moving bay brought them back to it regularly ~~with~~ a to
stand & look at it, as if indeed ~~this~~ the water ~~took~~ floated off, &
on dry land.
set sailing feelings, thoughts, which ~~as they~~ anchored in them & stagnated
[?]
as they sat talking ~~on dry land~~ ~~& reduced~~ them to rigidity. ~~&~~
~~fixedness on dry land~~. First, ~~it was~~ the ~~changing colour~~; ~~the~~
with blue
one could watch the pulse of colour, flood the bay ~~intermittently~~,
now
~~capriciously~~; ~~its it was now stained~~ blue: ~~now~~ & ~~all~~ the heart
expanded with it in ~~dep deep & exquisite delight~~; ~~we~~ as the
~~so~~ as ~~if~~ next moment ~~blue spread,~~ & the body ~~seemed~~
swam; ~~basking~~, only next instant, to be ~~ruffled~~ & checked & chilled by
the breeze, which made ruffled the water in to black flakes
suddenly a ~~spurt~~ of white spray would spurt up behind the rocks:
thin, lovelily & lazily the little waves would slip & fall.

† * It was this: Mr. Carmichael was one of the most brilliant young men of his time; that was in the sixties; he had a genius, a positive genius for mathematics. "And then you know," said Mrs. Ramsay, speaking as if of course Mr. Tansley knew what she ~~knew~~, ~~&~~ & all ~~y~~ men & women of mature age knew, there was a ~~gir~~ girl, I think at an Inn, where they stayed when they were reading together – a whole party of young men, my husband was one of them. ~~He~~ I ~~didn't~~ don't suppose there [was

any harm in her – She was like Annie – ~~my~~ the housemaid: ~~just in a nice country girl~~." ~~Nevertheless it~~ {but somehow it was conveyed to Mr. – a kind of Tansley that she was just this like her – a very commonplace girl, & how that Mr. Carmichael was a very remarkable man & ~~furth what was still~~ he married her, & his career was ruined & it was the wife's fault & of course nothing could be expected, nothing at all, ~~of a~~ when a / man who & of course when a marries it is his wife who is responsible, ~~men being~~ – How could it be otherwise, given this fatal beginning; by regular stages Mr. Carmichael had descended; he did take this drug;

done his best; now they let him be;

everybody knew it; her husband had ~~tried~~; to so there he lay, – he came to them indeed every summer, / there he lay, / on the lawn,

as Mr. Tansley saw

like that, half asleep, yet said Mrs. Ramsay, with ~~her~~ a intent & ~~direct~~ childlike [warmth?] in childlike simple sincerity of belief which ~~instantly assuaged~~ mollified Tansley, ~~after the way the young Tan~~ & gave him self-confidence & made him feel more ~~& more~~ very odd, unusual, pleased, "he has ~~the kindest heart~~ – ~~he~~ still

All that one can make [as might?] of course

** he does the most ~~wonder~~ difficult problems in his head, & offers to teach the boys Hindustanee – ~~which is not very~~ useful" she ~~said~~ laughed – ~~Perplexing woman~~! – with For really, not that there is any use in that'. she reflected. ~~But~~ She conceded to the other sex every merit. Tansley felt that one of these days he he would like her to see him, gowned & hooded walking in a procession; he felt capable of anything & yet ~~there were~~ that was ~~by no means~~ the end of it. No: He would say she had a will of her own. There was Mr. Ramsay: well: ~~he was not~~ who really ran things, of the two of them? ~~Who~~ And Carmichael asleep – the lawn; &, – quickened excited, by whatever it was in her,

* MS 16 (1.79)
** MS 17, 45
† A 20, B 22

something that he had discovered & would explain to friends, Tansley [wished for a chance that she would give him a chance to show what

a desire to take her ~~bag~~ – [but?] ~~he ha~~ ~~she~~ parasol, but she wouldn't, † ~~exer~~ exacerbating his self conceit

Tansley felt a delicious sense of ease steal through his veins, bringing with it courage, & self confidence, & healing ~~lit~~ those pricks & scratches which, without knowing whence they came, he had felt ~~in his~~ the last few days, staying with the Ramsays, this exaltation of ~~his~~ own sex was partly the cause of it ~~So great it was in Mrs. Ramsay's eyes~~; & He too belonged to the race of the great the brilliant the distinguished the eminent; who

lay on the lawn;

translated ~~b~~ proverbs from the Persia; ~~& lay~~ he shared their rightful exemption from petty criticism. Only ~~some~~ about Mrs. Ramsay there was some ~~air of authority~~, some briskness, ~~air~~ some air of authority which did ~~not mate brought before him~~, made him see her in control of things, not docile by any means, not subservient – no; did they not, in fact, seem rather to depend on her, Mr. Ramsay, Mr. Carmichael?*

---

* Pages 41–4 contain portions of Virginia Woolf's essay 'Robinson Crusoe' and her lecture 'How Should One Read a Book?' See appendix C. (1.81)

† B 23

† astonishing, ~~sen~~ self-confidence, & a desire to die for her, – yes, he to whom sixpence counted would have ~~run~~ charged a battery

† for her, & much regretted that she would not part with her bag, ~~her he having felt~~ during the last day or two ~~rasped~~, ~~snubbed,~~ having rasped him, ~~snub~~ snubbed him – ~~Yes~~ *"Yet, said Mrs. Ramsay "he solves the most difficult problems in his head. He has offered to teach the boys Hindustanee." He wished, ~~she~~ if she would not give him her bag, she would at least

her daughter

* MS 17, 39

† A 20, B 22; B 23

Jan. 18th
1926

† ~~That loveliness~~ So Lily Briscoe & William Bankes standing there felt in spite of their differences, a common hilarity, ~~for a expressed~~ excited by the swift cutting skating movement of a ~~b b~~ sailing boat which, having sliced a curve in the bay, stopped shivered, lets its sails fall; & then, ~~Mr. Bankes,~~ with a natural instinct, ~~wh which led them to~~ after this swift movement, both of them looked at the dunes, far away, & instead of merriment felt come over them som~~ething like~~ sadness. Yet why? ~~Was~~ It was ~~grey green~~ partly the grey green colour, & then the distan~~ce; &~~ the everlasting look of distant views

† which seem to outlast by a million years the gazer; to be already communing with a sky which ~~look~~ beholds an earth entirely at rest. Only, William Bankes, who had been talking of Ramsay, thought of him; thought of him, of course, long long ago, desolate & austere on a mountain road somewhere in Westmoreland, advancing by himself ~~into the heart of th~~ that solitude which seemed to be his natural ~~to him~~ [air]; ~~only~~ which was suddenly interrupted (& this must actually have happened) by a hen, advancing down a path, straggling her wings out in protection of a whole covy of little chicks upon which Ramsay had pointed his stick & said "Pretty – pretty" – an odd illumination into his heart, Bankes thought it; & somehow it seemed to him as if their friendship had ceased at a certain spot on the mountain road. After that Ramsay had married. After that, what with one thing or another, the pulp had gone out of their intimacy. Whose fault it was, he could not say, only, after a point, ~~some~~ repetition had taken the place of ~~freshness~~ [newness] & though

hung round
with

for showing him
tender & simple, &
with that
love of ~~humb~~ the
humble, the
genuine, wh. was

† A 34, B 36; B 37

~~they met still,~~ It was to repeat, that they met – William Bankes
however maintained in this instantaneous dumb colloquy
that his affection for Ramsay had no way diminished
& there, conserved like a ~~fossil~~ the body of a young man
preserved in peat for a century, fresh with the red on
the lips, was his friendship, in its acuteness & reality,
† ~~kep~~ alive again when he looked across the bay at
the sand dunes.

† B 38

(1.95)

~~So that~~ He was anxious ~~to~~ [~~brin~~?] ~~for~~ ~~to convey~~ for the sake of this friendship, & also, perhaps, in order to clear himself in his own mind from the imputation of having ~~himself~~ dried & shrunk, for Ramsay lived in a welter of children, whereas Bankes was childless & a widower, – he was anxious that Lily Briscoe should not ~~fall into the error o~~f disparage Ramsay; ~~&~~ ~~yet~~ yet should understand how things stood between them. Begun long ago, their friendship had petered out on a Westmoreland road, ~~after which he~~ there had ~~come to pass this curious fact~~ – & th~~en, Ramsay having married~~, † after which Ramsay having married, & their paths lying different ways, there had been certainly, for no ones fault, ~~&~~ some tendency when they met mainly to repeat. ~~yes.~~

where the hen was

Rose
Lucy
Prue
Cam
Andrew
James
Jasper

And so turning from the view, as if it had pained him, Mr. Bankes was ~~so~~ all alive to little things ~~in this~~ which would not have struck him, had not ~~that~~ those sandhills revealed to him the body of his anci~~ent~~ friendship; ~~& stopped as~~ they walked ~~up the~~ for instance ~~P~~ Cam, the little girl. Ramsays little girl. She was picking Sweet Alice. She was wild & fierce. ~~But~~ She would not "~~Sti~~ give a flower to the gentleman" as Mildred, the nursemaid, bade her. ~~And~~ & the Ramsays were not rich; they had all these children.

No no no &
No. ~~Ramsay~~

† ~~"Eight children" said Mr. Bankes~~, & it was a wonder how they contrived it managed at all. And there was another child, Jasper this time, strolling nonchalantly ~~b~~ by to have a shot at a bird, he said, swinging Lilys hand like a pump handle as he passed, which caused Mr. Bankes to say that she was a favourite; And there was their education to be considered, let alone the daily wear of shoes & † stockings which those 'great fellows', all well grown

Mr. Bankes was [?] & made him feel himself somehow put in the wrong. He had

† A 36; B 39; A 37

vigorous, angular, ruthless youngsters, must require. As for being sure which was which, that was beyond him, he confessed, or how they ordered themselves; [more;] but Rose would have beauty he thought; Andrew brains – ~~for the rest,~~ And while he thus commented to Lily Briscoe [& she] upon ~~the~~ this & that little trait which he had observed, he r~~espected Ramsay~~; [who had intimate knowledge of all these boys & girls)] at once commiserated Ramsay, envied him, as if he had
† seen him divest himself of all those glories of isolation & solitude to cumber himself definitely with fluttering wings & clacking domesticities; which while they had given him something – William Bankes acknowledge that – ~~had yet~~ (it would have been pleasant if Cam had stuck a flower in his coat, or ~~climbed,~~ [craned] as he had seen her, to look at pictures, over her fathers shoulder) ~~It~~ had also in [his old friends, by] Mr. Bankes opinion, destroyed something: For ~~what~~ [what wd. a stranger think] could one help noticing that habits grew on him? Eccentricities, moods? He was, well, touchy. And it was sometimes astonishing how a man of his intellect could stoop as low as he did, frankly it was beneath him, to pick up complements. ~~Silly brainless pretty girls~~ – ~~a bad review~~ – to require encouragement.

† * "~~Well~~ But, said Lily Briscoe, think of his work." As always on these occasions, that phantom kitchen table swam before her, lodged in the fork of a pear tree (for they had reached the orchard, the strawberry beds, the
† vegetable garden.) And with a painful effort of imagination she conscientiously focused her mind, not upon the silver bossed bark of the tree, or its fish like leaves, but upon a mind so differently constituted from her own that it saw only a kitchen table which was not there.

* MS 29–31

† B 40; A 38; B 41

(1.99)

One of those scrubbed board tables, [grained & knotted] ~~which~~ the essence of integrity & ~~austerity.~~ cleanliness. ~~It was a feat of almost unimaginable~~ which hung there. Naturally if ones days passed in this supreme effort, this seeing of angular essences, this reducing of lovely evenings, with the ~~sa most~~ all the movement of the clouds. & the blue & the pear trees, to that – a four legged table – naturally, one could not be judged ~~as~~ like ordinary people.

so lovely behind the pear tree

† Mr. Bankes liked [approved of] her all the better for thinking of Mr. Ramsays work. He thought of it, more accurately. The exact nature of that ~~t~~ little forward movement – for it was on the whole not unreasonable to think that Ramsay had made a definite contribution – in a slim book, written when he was thirty – to thought; ~~though what he had done for~~ the last five & twenty years was ~~more or less a repetition – an expansion~~ – he amplified & expanded – was known to him. Exquisitely judicial, scrupulously exact, giving out to every one of Lily's senses ~~the~~ an aroma of fairness ~~he~~ William Bankes paused, on the edge of the strawberry bed, & looking at him Lily could not help ~~comparing the two men~~, saying to herself, There is a severity about him which ~~I adore: he~~ is most satisfactory: I respect this in every atom, throughout; he is not vain; he is impersonal; he has neither wife nor child; he lives for science (incongruously, potato parings rose before her eyes) & Praise would be an insult to this man. But then she remembered how

wh. for

& rather unnecessarily [teased?] &

Her soul seemed to flow up in an incense of adoration

† ~~his~~ he ~~required~~ brought a valet, all the way up here; objected to dogs on the chairs, & would prose on for hours (Mr. Ramsay could not stand it) about salt in vegetables. ~~He & Mrs. Ramsay would talk cookery by the hour.~~ '~~The iniquity~~ of English cookery". How then did one know what one thought of people? How

† A 39; A 40

How, in this extraordinary profusion of contradictory impressions, this mixture of good & bad

then did one come to any conclusion whatsoever? ~~For it was all so~~ How then did one approve of any one absolutely; & ~~how then~~ with these –. How difficult it was then, how agitating, how extraordinarily part of staying with the Ramsays – to feel ~~shoved~~ taken up out of ones backwater & made to feel the enormous importance of everything; & how, for no reason whatever, suddenly, standing with Mr. Bankes by the strawberry bed, she seemed to see into the things, ~~into the~~ & how Mr. Bankes had this quality of manly impersonal strength, which no one reverenced (Lily Briscoe was so besieged by impressions that even the
† thinking was like following a voice which speaks too quickly to be taken down by ones pencil; & yet this voice says the most terrifically important things, once & for ever) He has that sort of greatness: & Mr. Ramsay had none of it. ~~He~~ but was is vain & selfish & egotistical & spoilt; but he had, what Mr. Bankes had not, a fiery unworldliness & austerity, ~~& he~~ knows nothing about vegetables & salt; & he loves dogs; & ~~altogether life which~~ & his children, & not caring a straw – did he not put ~~his~~ two coats on the other night? – & meanwhile the whole swarm of her
† feelings seemed to be ~~roll~~ dancing up & down as the pear tree boughs & would be there forever;

where hung the phantom kitchen table

in a moment of such intensity that Lily Briscoe was positively released, uprooted when Mr. Bankes which held it like a that it when Mr. Bankes turned. When a shot went off, & flying as it were out of her thought wh. had
† exploded of its own intensity came flocks of starlings. Their wings

† B 43; A 41; B 44

"Jasper" said Mr. Bankes, & they turned the way the starlings flew, over the terrace. ~~So great~~ Following the scatter of swift-flying birds in the sky, they stepped through the gap in the high hedge straight into Mr. Ramsay who ~~cried~~ boomed tragically

"Someone had blundered"*

His eyes ~~rest meeting theirs for a moment~~, glazed with emotion, & ~~heroi~~ defiant tragic intensity, met theirs for a second; then ~~half~~ raising his hand which seemed to tremble halfway to his face ~~he seemed~~ to brushed off in an agony of peevish shame — as if he had exposed in some private indignity their normal gaze; ~~t~~ as if begging them to withold for a moment long~~er their~~ what he knew to be inevitable, ~~to as if they had done wh~~ making them feel the discomfort ~~of having outraged decency~~, taken him at a disadvantage, opened the door on him in his ~~shirt~~ sitting on a bed, in his shirt dishevelled~~; & received in return the~~ childish spite ~~of one thus interrupted~~, who ~~strives~~ even in the ~~strives~~ has determined moment of discovery not to be routed utterly, to hold fast to something ~~of this of what~~ of this delicious emotion, this impure rhapsody ∧ which was his own private affair not anybody elses, he turned abruptly & ~~they~~ looking up into the sky, Lily Briscoe & Mr. Bankes observed that the flock of starlings, which Jasper had routed with his gun, had settled ~~on the~~ on the tops of the elm trees.

to avert daylight

& he resented impressing on them

of which he was ashamed †

---

* 'The Charge of the Light Brigade,' MS 26, 60, 63 (1.105)

† A 42

## III*

Jan. 21st

'Even if it isn't fine tomorrow, it will be ~~another day~~", said Mrs.
† Ramsay; raising her eyes to glance at William Bankes, & Lily Briscoe, ~~thinking~~ "another day". ~~And~~ [And] ~~Stand up~~" she ~~sai~~ ~~told the little boy,~~ said, thinking how Chinese [in her little sallow face,] Lilies eyes were, & that was not everbodies taste ^ "I want to measure ~~your~~ ~~these~~ this stocking" For if they did [go] after all ~~go~~ to the lighthouse tomorrow she must finish ~~the W little W~~ill Sorleys stocking – he was about ~~Jam~~ the same height as James – "And [Well it might happen] they might marry" she thought, watching the backs of Lily & William Bankes walk in together – & her ~~face~~ eyes filled with that sudden direct amusement which seemed to be the natural ~~out~~ [outcome] expression of ~~some~~ her wiser capacity. ~~for some~~ genius ~~of~~ [in] action. Ideas struck her – why shouldn't those two marry? – an admirable plan – &, ~~knowing her own~~ her singleness, her simplicity made her ~~smile~~ [laugh] Thus, And smiling she took the heather mixture stocking with the crisscross of steel knitting needles at the mouth of it & measured it against James's leg "My dear, stand still she said. ~~not~~ But, not liking to be treated as a measuring block for the lighthouse keeper's
† little boy, James protested. And how could she see whether it was too short still?

stand up

your legs

a sort of piquancy she had – not beauty

* VW has omitted II.

† A 42, B 45; A 43

"Hold your leg straight" she bade him, for he persisted in ~~bed~~ bending his knee. so that ~~holding~~ stretching the stocking, she looked up to see what mischief possessed him, her youngest, her most cherished. She looked up, & ~~then~~ ~~cast~~ her ~~own~~ head was cut out ~~against~~ in profile against one of those large brown ~~pictures~~ photographs of authenticated masterpieces (Michael Angelo, Titian) which, rigged in a cheap frame stood upon an easel. ~~For~~ Much luxury could not be
† achieved – Arm chairs were sufficient but the covers faded; sofas whose en~~trails~~ springs buldged protruded must positively be mended next year; ~~& so~~ as for carpets & so on, what point would there be in ~~bringing~~ leaving anything that could be spoilt to spoil in the long wet island winter, when the house, visited weekly by an old woman, only dripped with wet? (Mrs. Ramsay said) But then, since they only came for the summer & the rent was precisely twopence halfpenny a year, & the children loved it, & it did her husband good to be three thousand ~~or~~ three hundred, ~~then if~~ miles then from his library & his lectures & ~~all~~ his disciples, it was worth the some discomfort was inevitable. journey. And they could all get in. ~~And~~ There were even spare rooms. There were Mats, camp beds, crazy ghosts of of chairs & tables whose London life of service was done, – they would do well [enough; photographs, some of them, she recollected once ~~hanging~~ in her grandmother's house & bearing the signatures of great men whose colours had to kept moist with under damp cloths; & books, oh always books, there was ~~no lack of books~~, ~~brought~~ left by people who stayed there, given by young authors, ~~gi~~ sent by the great who had been ~~happy~~ with her – & yet, she thought, glancing to ~~re~~ spent happy days with her whose wishes have to be obliged 'with the happier Helen our days'

[Left margin: or if she must be accurate]

[Left margin: then there were the old & she ~~had~~ nailed up those]

She looked, half remembering words of ~~kindn~~ gratitude & praise, & how she had never found time to read her Crooms translation of the sagas, or Jones on Mind

Old Jones had written a about the face that launched a thousand ships

at the shelf, which against her declaration that one room at least should be free from books had already crowded a white wood case,

but was there anything, she wondered, that she could [would do to] send to the lighthouse? She doubted it. She wished that her † children could be taught to wipe their shoes. – They brought in the whole beach with them. Anything in reason – a crab for example, if Andrew really wished to study crabs; & ~~would see to its~~ would keep it properly – she did not ~~object to~~ [~~se~~ mind]; or sea weed, if kept out of doors, ~~for the smell of it drying~~ since Jasper believed that a delicious soup could be made of it; or Roses objects – flowers shells – But the ~~effect upon a [?], she concluded,~~ whole ~~effect~~ ~~aspect~~ effect, she concluded was becoming summer by summer ~~more~~ shabby[ier] & [shabbier;] & paler ~~& paler~~, the bamboo bleaching, in the mat, which had been ~~green~~ green, ~~now was~~ now ~~almost~~ for ~~a~~ whole breadths (unfortunately, it faded unevenly) pale yellow. ~~while, up in the corner~~, As for the honeysuckle [in the wallpaper] which had been so ~~pretty only~~ ~~bright~~, next year the eye of faith only would believe, what ~~was~~ nevertheless [was] properly true – that the design was by Huckle & Bennet – cost she was ashamed to remember, [how much] pounds, pound Still if every ~~window~~ [door] in a house is left perpetually open, & no locksmith in the whole of Scotland ~~can~~ can apparently [be trust] ~~mend a~~ ~~repair~~ [mend] a bolt, ~~for she could~~ as usual ~~the~~ [her] drawing room door was open; & The hall door was open, & presumably the kitchen door was open, & it sounded to her as if the bedroom doors were open; & certainly the window on the landing was open, for that she opened herself, ~~it~~ – of course things faded, & it was little use pinning up a green cashmere shawl, for that too would fade; &

† A 44, B 47

And yet her maids could not understand that ~~she~~ to open a door was one thing, to open a w

for that she did insist upon – though maids / it made [humans?] [?], who left doors open,

† never opened their windows an inch, ~~except that for~~ with the exception of that poor little thing, Marthe, the Swiss girl who, [~~C~~?] she was glad to

† find, agreed with her entirely that it is ~~worse~~ better to have no bath than to sleep with one's windows shut, & then at home there were the beautiful mountains to look at;" & there, ~~alas~~, her father was dying of cancer of the throat, & ~~what~~ leaving us fatherless, madame" she had said. For there is no escape.

† B 48; A 45

grieved
~~agreed~~
"None whatever" Mrs. Ramsay ~~said.~~ And that was all she would
say; her eloquence – & she could run up phrases when she
chose & decorate incidents, could exaggerate & demonstrate &
scold, as over this this matter of doors, windows, ~~until~~
in a voice full of emphasis, with ~~a~~ hands expanding instinctively
expanding ~~instinctively~~ or clutching themselves – ~~a~~ the ~~ceased~~ all
folded itself close about her, as after a flight from
tree to tree the wings of a bird fold themselves, ~~& the ver~~
quietly, & the very colour of its plumage seems to
flash
change in a second from [steel blue] to softness: ~~& She no,~~
She would say nothing whatever about ~~All~~ the truth she knew.
All she would prove when the girl spoke thus, with
tears in her eyes, of what Mrs. Ramsay knew for herself to be
But
~~a fact.~~ the truth. She would say nothing whatever about it.
~~that.~~ Only, with a spasm of irritation, speaking sharply,
she told James "not to be tiresome": & he at once ~~stood~~
straightened his leg, aware that her severity was just; &
rebuked it were
The stockings ~~that what~~ his triviality deserved ~~And It was~~ too
probability
† short by an inch, allowing for the ~~fact~~ that Will Sorley
~~had thinner legs th~~ was less well grown than James –
another
† ~~so~~ that ~~She thought~~ was the fact; & ~~one more of these~~
~~salt,~~ ~~dark~~ bitter, sharp,
~~bitter~~ tears, which seemed from ~~time to time~~ to formed
~~deep~~ within her ~~with~~ in darkness ~~& silence~~, fell ~~& all~~
the waters swayed this way & that, received it, & were at
Certainly
rest ~~again~~. Never did anybody look so sad.
whether was
But ~~was~~ it true that years ago somebody whom she
was to marry had blown his brains out ~~&~~ or had
died, ~~less dramatically~~ in India? ~~or~~ There had been
could say
~~something; but~~ Nobody knew. Mrs. Ramsay ~~never~~ made
no
~~a~~ sigh. Nothing – no moment in a girls life,
her engagement for example, no parting, not one

of those solitary & heart gnawing tragedies in ~~w~~ of love, ~~or~~

*to the relief of words*

thwarted, ambition foiled, which were told her ~~or~~ & helped by her

surprised her ~~for a~~ into revelation, easily though she

*however it had happened*

might have then said then, without reproach, how she too –

whatever it was – had been ruined. But ~~sh~~ no.

She knew, then, without having learnt. Her simplicity

*& diffused*

fathomed what clever ~~women~~ people falsified & [denied?] might have failed to

reach; (she was not clever); her singleness of mind, that

~~whole of her seeming to have some~~ [?] unity which

made her drop plumb ~~like~~ as a stone, alight

exact ~~lik~~ as a bird, ~~to~~ gave her ~~this~~ this

a ~~sweep & fellness which~~ swoop & fall of the

spirit on the truth which delighted, eased, sustained; &

"Noble" was the obvious word; ~~&~~ stern, ~~&~~ pure;

all of course coming more readily ~~&~~ to the lips

because there really they seemed, flocking together in their

*& not, after all so rare –*

disembodied shapes, ~~qualities m~~erely th~~at you o~~ne

might meet with ~~so~~ in many people – nobility

truth, purity, combined with a certain strictness &

fire are not rare – seemed in her to have dipped themselves

† in flesh & so assembling, like a ring of graces

*in combination in*

joining hands ~~&~~ in meadows of asphodel to have ~~made to~~ combined together

her face. ~~There it was, like~~ If sadness ~~is the~~

were the general effect, ~~that might be attributed to~~

beauty ~~itself which,~~ in one in ~~its~~ one of its forms at least – (her's

was notably Greek) has ~~that look~~ always of the truth

seeming to preside, or to seem look out, ~~&~~ over a great space; to

await ~~something coming, not to disdain, so much as to~~

*in youth at any rate*

~~overlook, &~~ & ~~if~~ as this beauty ages, while it loses its

~~roundness~~ something of its suppleness & roundness, it

~~it takes on~~ saddens; ~~it~~ sharpens. But what she had

looked for, & ~~what seen,~~ or whether it were not

mere accident that hollowed & chiselled, made the

eyes & the nostrils & the lips, – ~~no~~ or whether she

† B 50, A 47

(1.117)

had in youth actually seen something so stern, for
instance a skeleton on a white horse which had
had given fixity to her softness, severity to her
charm, & thus made her impatient when people
trifled with the truth of things or exploited the thin
miseries of frivolity & heartlessness ~~over the,~~ & threw veils
plausibility & optimism over what was sheer as a
cliff & black as the sea beneath it, – [depth night]
people argued. no one knew. They saw one thing; they
said another ~~thing~~. ~~And~~ Certainly, one fact was teasing;
rather tantalised tickling: how the background – for
20 Forum 20 Todd 20 Eliot 15 Nation 8 Lecture 83* instance the soul, draped in a shawl had always
~~one~~ [a] element, ~~if not more,~~ ~~that was~~ [of the] cheap, ridiculous
incongruous. ~~or it~~ (So ~~she sat.~~ / [now] Or she took off a
nail in the hall an old deerstalkers cap, clapped it
on her head; or ~~So that to make up the~~ & went
foraging for slugs; grapsed a ~~cloak~~ man's umbrella;
put galoshes on her narrow feet;) [which] making it always
necessary to recompose her, should one look at her
aesthetically; or endow her, if it was a character
tame this crudity fuse it, into rest ✓ † one considered her, with ~~the~~ [endow] some latent desire to
doff her royalty of form, & be [dig her nails into clay] as other people; as if her
† Her ~~beauty gave her no plea~~sure. beauty &
all that could be said & must continue to be said
about her beauty bored her. So now she knitted a
reddish brown stocking against the cheap easel & the
brown Michael Angelo.

* This may be a tabulation of VW's income from articles published in periodicals: *Forum, Vogue* (ed Miss Todd), *Criterion* (ed T.S. Eliot), *Nation*. The lecture may be 'How Should One Read a Book?' which she delivered on 30 January 1926, at Hayes Common. See appendix C. (1.119)

† B 51; A 48

IV.

1926
Sunday
Jan 24th

† But ~~Rhoderick had~~ what had happened?

"Some one had blundered."*

~~That~~ ~~Her husbands words echoed in her mind~~, &, Starting from her musing, she ~~ch~~ ~~recalled~~ – suddenly gave meaning to words which she had held meaningless in her mind for some stretch of time. Her husband He was now coming towards her; & ~~being shortsighted, she~~ fixing her short sighted eyes on him she gazed steadily until his closeness revealed to her ~~this~~ – ~~that something had~~ from the look on his face that something had happened ~~annoyed~~ him.

the jingle (song ran in her head "some one had blundered"

† And she could not for the life of her think what.

Yet ~~But it was intolerable.~~ He ha~~d died upon the heights of Balaclava~~ – Stormed at by shot & shell

† boldly we rode & well – flashed through the valley of death – volleyed & thundered. & Suddenly ran headlong one met Bankes & Lily Briscoe. ~~And all that ride of his~~ & it was shattered ~~somehow had~~ ~~some~~ Worse ~~Worse~~ he ~~had no right~~ to must have been talking aloud, & what he imagined hidden, ~~was~~ had been heard, & his vanity – for he ~~did himself ride at the head of his men &~~ had a genuine pride in his fierce splendid appearance, fell ~~fierce~~ as a thunderbolt, ~~fell~~ as a hawk, all was shattered. all petered out into distant day light. ~~He was Rho~~derick Ramsay on a terrace. ~~Only~~ ~~But~~ Not for the world would she have spoken to him, realizing from ~~the~~ familiar signs, his eyes averted & some curious gathering together of his ~~be~~ person as if he wrapped himself about & ~~requ~~ ~~demanded privacy~~ that ~~in~~ he needed privacy in which to regain his equilibrium, ~~once~~ for some reason in ~~shattered~~. ~~In passing on to her son the action intended for her husband,~~ ~~smoothing~~ stroking the little boys head, she ~~superintended~~ ~~the~~ watched him chalk yellow the dress shirt of a gentleman ~~of~~ in the Army, Navy Stores catalogue. ~~Whether~~

Ah! – he shivered – [In?]

riding at the head of his men, with flying cloak & d

& hunched himself together

fragments.

transfering her solicitude to him,

* 'The Charge of the Light Brigade,' MS 26, 52, 63 (1.121)

† A 48; B 52; A 49

Indeed,

& why should he not!

† It would be delightful if James turned out to be a great artist. And so, looking up, as ~~Rhod~~ her husband again passed her, she was relieved to find the ruin already veiled; domesticity prevailing; custom ~~casting its~~ crooning humming its soothing rhythm; so

† that when, drawing up by the window, he bent quizzically & whimsically down to tickle James' ~~ca~~ bare calf with a spray of something it was all quite ~~righ~~ right now & perfect peace was established;

twitted him with despatching

had she thought it worth while she would have twitted him with his discomposure, but only asked [?] coaxing whether ~~murmured~~ instead

† had he despatched that poor young man?

Oh Tansly had to write his dissertation.

"James will have to write his dissertation one of these days," he proceeded,

Hating his father, James flicked away the tickling spray with which, in a manner peculiar to him, he teased his youngest son's bare leg.

compound of severity & humour,

~~And, Mr. Ramsay proceeded~~

She was had to get these finishing stockings finished for Sorleys little boy, Mrs. Ramsay said.

But there wasn't the slightest possible chance that they could get to the Lighthouse tomorrow," Mr. Ramsay snapped out rebuked her.

"How ~~did he~~ do you know? The wind often changed." she ~~said~~ replied.

The extraordinary irrationality of her remark enraged him.

When he told her what he happened to know, she should believe him. He stamped his ~~foot~~ in his eyes on the step. For he had ridden through the valley of death; been interrupted, & ~~now to fly in the face of facts~~ now She flew in the face of facts; made James hope what was impossible.

& run into Bankes,

† A 49; B 53; A 50

& Her optimism, her irrationality enraged him.

The toe of his boot scraping on the rough step set her teeth on edge; & He stamped his on the step.

~~But neither said a word~~. ~~She thought him in some~~

† ~~respects the most~~ [But] And what had she said? Simply that it might be fine tomorrow. So it might.

But not with the barometer falling & the wind due west.

† If she wished for actual proof he would walk over to the coast ~~guard~~ station. He would ~~fetch his~~ [look at their] instrument ~~The mind~~ [To] ~~that could~~ pursue truth with such astonishing lack of consideration for peoples feelings ~~amazed her~~ seemed to her so ~~horrible~~, [that] ~~& she~~ without replying she bent her head, as if ~~to~~ though nothing would ~~temp~~ to let the pelt of jagged hail storm the shower of dirty water bathe her bespatter her ~~bent~~ bowed shoulders.

horrible an outrage ~~upon~~ human upon decency the tearing up of all the writs of human civilisation

He said he would step over & ask the coast guards if she liked.

~~And~~ There was nobody whom she reverenced as she did reverenced him.

She would take his word for it, she said. [Then] She would not trouble to cut sandwiches or anything.

There was nobody who so made her feel ~~so~~ safe. ~~so.~~

They came to her, naturally, since she was a woman, all day long with this that & the other; unhappy love affairs; one wanted this, another that; the children were growing up; she often felt she was nothing but an old sponge ~~sopp~~ sopped up with human emotion. [Then] ~~And Rhoderick~~ said ~~This is the truth~~. ~~He said~~ It must rain. ~~He made her feel~~ – [The] Or he said

† It [will] would not rain. Heaven opened before her.

If it were a question of sitting down in the mud & pulling off his boots she would do it instantly.

† B 54; A 51; B 55 (1.125)

Already ashamed of that petulance of that gesticulation of the hands

when he ed [which he

† had made charging at the head of his troops, Mr. Ramsay rather sheepishly

once more

prodded his tickled his son's legs, then with a movement which oddly reminded

throwing his his head flinging himself

his wife of the great sea lion at the Zoo, turning backwards with the

water after crunching his fishing fish, div & walloping off into

where [for?] [?]

water which is at once rocks with waves from his

he

impetus, Mr. dived again into the fading evening

air it was al

already growing thinner air water dimming slightly & taking away the substance of leaves, hedges,

but letting here a rose, there a geranium burn softly & bloomingly

bloom with a the softness of a unseen by day

but as if in return restoring to roses & sweet williams

a a

of yellow & purple the lustre, the bloom, which they had not by day. And now,

Someone had blundered.*

"In June he gets

out of tune,**

But how extraordinarily his note had changed! as if he were now trying over, feathering about, tentatively seeking some new phrase for a new mood, &, having only this at hand, used it, incongruously & ridiculously, without any conviction, so that hearing him, Mrs. Ramsay could not but smile.

† And then, he did & then, after a minute or two, some one had

sank into nonentity up & down up down

blundered petered out, & Mr. Ramsay paced the terrace, in

profound silence, thinking.

It was past, all that gesticulation & excitability, thanks &

He restored to privacy, rendered somehow secure, by the sight which he took in once in one moment's revelation (he

[staring?]

looked at his wife & son for a second; as he turned,

at his wife & son

without their seeing it – indeed they were now bent over

The The

a book together.) The sight of them together, like a hedgeside or barn, a cluster of horses on a hill, a moat, sheep, seen from the window of an express train as one looks up from some absorbing page, which seems to

† illustrate the poem, to be a particular & to enf illus

& to enforce it – Robbed of all detail, there, motherhood

---

* 'The Charge of the Light Brigade,' MS 26, 52, 60 (1.127)

** From the nursery rhyme 'To the Cuckoo'; 'In June I change my tune' (*The Oxford Nursery Rhyme Book*, assembled by Iona and Peter Opie, Oxford 1955, p 74)

† A 52; B 56; A 53

& childhood seemed to him ~~to~~ displayed, & home, & peace, & privacy, & innocence, & what he held most precious, & defenceless, so that while he could not hold himself guiltless of needing protection, some sort of soothing & ~~car~~ing at the hands of this divinity, yet it stimulated him too & concentrated this effort of his to arrive at a more perfectly clear conception of the problem which now engaged his splendid mind

in the window, bent over the pages of the book which & consecrated
& made him feel secure & protected, this effort of his to arrive at a perfectly clear conception
of the problem which engaged the energies of his splendid ~~brain~~
intellect.

The splendid intellect had no sort of difficulty, supposing
thought to be like the keyboard of a piano divided into so
one by one / one after another many notes, or like ~~the letters of~~ the alphabet ranged
in twenty six separate letters, in ~~sepa~~ running over those letters,
firmly in order till ~~say~~ it reached perhaps Q. ~~Mr. Ramsay~~
He reached Q. ~~(And it was there that~~ here stopping by the
He stone urn which held geraniums; he opened his eyes again.
stopped saw ~~through a veil~~ at a great distance ~~that vision of~~
mother & child which, ~~seen without any~~ detail, ~~was so~~
~~like without connection~~ like ~~unconscious~~ children playing
on the ~~sh verge of an ocean which they disregard~~
far far away unconscious, indifferent, like children
picking up shells, ~~on the an like~~ he ~~saw them, &~~
deaf to the thunder, & ~~innocent or~~ & innocent –
ignorant & divinely occupied with the trifles ~~of their~~
† the immediate present ~~things.~~ ~~To~~ ~~And now what~~ But after Q? after
Q what comes? ~~He~~ then? After Q there are a
number of letters the last of which is ~~of course~~ Z.
Bu~~t now to reach Z~~ after Q, ~~after Q – to make~~
Mr. Ramsay went back to the beginning; ~~& made~~
qu~~ite sure o~~f ~~again~~ to A: to B: to C: & so on:
† until there he was at Q again, at Q, he made
sure of it, ~~plated his~~ dug his heels in, ~~felt~~
summoned the resources of his heroic determination, &
attempted R. If Q is really Q then R –
~~He~~ Here halting he knocked his pipe out, with

† B 57; A 54

three resonant taps on the ~~rams~~ earthenware ram's head, &
proceeded: Then R.

Qualities that ~~had~~ would have saved a ships company exposed
on a broiling sea with six biscuits & a flask of water –
endurance & justice, ~~so~~ foresight devotion – came to his help &
nerved him for the attack – on R is then –

A shutter, like the leathern eyelid of ~~some~~ a lizard, flickered over
the fierce intensity of his gaze: obliterating shut out the sight of R.
In wh. flicker of a second he ~~had~~ knew the
People said him ~~he was~~ a failure. They said that it was praised him
~~was~~ immensely ~~to his credi~~t it was immensely to his credit to
~~have~~ reached Q: but they said – Bankes said, or at any rate
~~felt, for it was obvious that~~ made clear it felt by what he didnt
~~omitted~~ to say – that R was already beyond him. ~~They praised him~~
Still, ~~he wanted~~ But still – still –

Qualities that in any desolate expedition across the
icy solitudes of the North Pole would have made him the
leader, the last to drop, ~~the last to fail, the~~ the physician the of the men, the
† ~~the~~ & that firm temper which is neither hopeful with
despondency but surveys with equanimity whatever ~~is~~
~~m~~ is to be – were his, ~~are in~~ again now, in this
further assault. R –

~~There are~~ But ~~the qualities that~~ R is not
But ~~in the assault on R~~ ~~what is needed is one~~
Those who reach ~~storm~~ R ~~(as he knew~~ the leathern ~~eye~~lid
flickered across his vision again) ~~either~~ only do so
† either by ~~repe~~ superhuman strength & the power to
repeat the whole alphabet in order – all 26 letters;
or ~~there is~~ they reach Z ~~s~~ that way (as Clark reached it)
& they reach ~~seem~~ (this is the more puzzling way) ~~to~~ as [Kingdom?]
reached it, by somehow contriving, to make all those
divisions disappear. Men of genius – & the
flickering eyelid brought before him with distracting
vividness a man of genius, throwing sticks into the

† B 58; A 55

marvellous
Serpentine. He had\had a power of ~~making the most~~ scientific
demonstration. He ~~explained~~ would explain to a picnic party why
the laws of refraction – with his oar dropped in the water –
~~But~~ R – R.

He had not that power: he had not the synthetic imagination: he
then
† had not genius. Who /has 'genius'? In a century, one man only
thousand
perhaps: ~~in a population that is to say of~~ among many millions
the name
only ~~one; & even that man~~ one has the gift; & ~~that one man is~~
of that man lasts for two thousand years: ~~&~~ what are
two thousand years?

And there was only tobacco enough for another pipe –
As for fame, he would be a cur to complain.

† B 59

The way of genius.
He had not ~~that sort of~~ genius; he laid no claim to it: but h~~e ha~~d,
or might have had, the power to repeat every letter of the
from A to Z alphabet accurately in order. He might have had it.
Bankes & other men of worth agreed with him there.
~~Powers that~~ ~~Qualities that would~~
† ~~Sensations that would~~ Feelings that would not have disgraced a
~~le the~~ a leader, ~~of a~~ who, now that the snow has begun to fall, &
the mountain top is covered in mist, knows that he must
lay himself down & die before morning comes, stole upon him,
paling ~~reaching~~ ~~his~~ the light in his eyes, ~~somehow~~ giving him ~~a~~
even in the two minutes of his turn on the terrace ~~faded~~ bleached ~~perished~~ ashen look of ~~extreme~~ withered old age ~~as though his body had~~
Yet he would not die lying down; he would find some
† crag of rock & there ~~standing wit~~h his eyes fixed on the
storm, trying to the end to pierce the mist, he would
die standing. He would never reach R.
But how many men in a thousand million men
† ~~press on to~~ reach Z? One perhaps. And his fame
lasts how long? Perhaps two thousand years.
And what are two thousand years ~~in the long~~ in the
roll of the ages? ~~And~~ What indeed? The very stones one
kicks with the toe of ones boot ~~have~~ will outlast~~ed Plato.~~
Shakespeare. His little light would shine, not very
brightly for a year or two, & then be ~~seen no more, &~~
merged in some bigger light, & that in a bigger still –
Roam on. The light ~~is~~ we sought is
Shining still. I wandered till I died.*
And after all, who could blame the leader of that
forlorn party, if, ~~before~~ before death stiffened his
limbs ~~l~~ beyond all movement, he does, a little

---

* Matthew Arnold, 'Thyrsis'; not used in the final version (1.137)
† B 58; B 59; A 56

† consciously, ~~take on~~ ^[strike] an attitude ~~of her~~ raise his numbed fingers
to his brow, ~~st~~ square his shoulders, so that when his
rescuers come they shall perceive that he died at his post, the
fine figure of a soldier?

I wandered till I died

~~Roam on. The Light~~ we sought is shining still,

Mr. Ramsay murmured between clenched teeth.

† Further, who shall blame that heroic man, if
having adventured to the utmost, & used his strength,
wholly to the last ounce, he falls asleep, ~~& wakes~~
not much caring whether he wakes or not, ~~but~~ & then
perceives by the pricking of his toes that he is alive; &
does not on the whole object, but requires sympathy &
attention, a glass of hot whisky & some one to tell ~~him~~ the
story of his sufferings ~~at~~ ^[to] once? Who shall blame
human nature? Who shall require of men that they
be ~~gods~~ ^[as] gods in strength & ^[in] endurance? Who ~~shall~~ will not
secretly rejoice ~~at the~~ when the hero puts off his armour &
~~descends~~? ~~And~~ halting by the window, gazing now with
ascertaining ~~with~~ that there they are – wife & child – the
holiest heart of life – ( & her divine worn beauty
~~almost~~ with the boy ~~in~~ ^[on] her knee, her ~~chin~~ ^[lips] resting
~~very~~ lightly on his head, her arm encircling him, &
such an expression of tenderness on her
that she looked like the profound spirit brooding over the waters of life,
~~does homage to the~~ restoring peace to perplexity &
simplicity to the worn heart of men,
† does homage ~~the~~ ^[to] the heart of the world

[margin: all his ~~ardour~~ [with?] about him,]

V.

James hated him.

James hated him.
felt the vibration in the air
felt the emotion
a bad emotion?
All emotion is bad to ~~chi~~
Felt his mothers emotion –
What her emotion was
The fatal male sterility
Must have sympathy
Plunges his great beak in
She is pouring forth life
radium from every [cch.?]
A prodigal waste of feeling.
J. does not feel any emotion to his father*

* Entire page written in pencil

31st Jan.

V

His son hated him. He hated him for coming up to them, &
† stopping, & looking down on them; he hated him for interrupting
them; he hated him for the exaltation & sublimity of his
gesture & the magnificence of his head, & the atmosphere of
tenderness & aloofness & exactingness & egotism – (for
there he stood commanding them to attend to him) ~~which he~~
~~brought with him~~ – Most of all he hated the vibration in
the air, the twang & twitter, ~~which~~ of his father's ~~emotions~~ emotion,
~~made~~ & ~~the way in which~~ ~~for it seemed to him~~ ~~fo~~ which his
~~fathers presence wrought in the ease & simplicity of the~~
which disturbed the perfect simplicity & the complete good sense of his
relations with his mother. ~~Then he~~ ~~Taking no notice~~
By looking fixedly at the page, he hoped t~~hat the~~ to make him move on avoid
him; he ~~longed desperately for his father to move on; he~~
~~held the book open, when~~ by pointing putting his finger ~~hand~~ ~~in the~~ at a word
~~page~~ he hoped to recall his mothers attention, which, he felt
~~the very second his father stopped, seemed to~~ go wavering
~~Indeed he could feel, without any change of position~~,
But no. nothing would make Mr. Ramsay go. There he
stood demanding sympathy.

† A 58

Sympathy – sympathy

~~It was as if~~ Mrs. Ramsay, who had been sitting loosely folding her son
[in
her arm, ~~now~~ braced herself, & half turning, seemed to raise herself,
& at once to
with an effort, to ~~pour out in~~ ~~big cit in~~ begin ~~p~~
† pouring out a rain of energy, a fountain of life, a column of
a spray ~~a~~ compound of her mind her emotion & some thing so
vital to herself that then in that instant she seemed to
fusing
be herself, alive to the core & spending all her energy in one
into &
blaze; ~~it was into~~ this ~~blaze of~~ fecundity ~~that~~
that the fatal sterility of the male plunged itself.
Mr. Ramsay steeped himself again & again in it.
~~His~~ He fell, James felt, like an eagle upon them;
required He was not a
Mr. Ramsay ~~demanded~~ to be assured that he was
she assured him But
not a failure; & more than that ~~that he was~~ to have
then to be taken within
† was desired & treasured & within the circle of life & not
outside it, perched like snow on a mountain top; he
required that his barrenness should be made fertile, &
his senses restored to him; & his functions restored, that
he should be made whole, & that this immense strength of his
~~should~~ be made fruitful, ~~brought into alliance with~~
He wanted the room to be full of life, & behind the room, the
kitchen, above the kitchen, the bedroom, the nurseries; all
to be full of life, in which he could steep his
barrenness.

like a beak of brass, like something which is barren, has in it neither warmth or life but only concentration

There was
~~Had she not asked~~ Charles Tansley ~~down,~~ ~~on purpose~~
~~that he might~~ & did ~~he not~~ who thought him so
Mrs. Ramsay, ~~still~~ pouring out gaily, with laughter –
† indeed, flashing her needles to & fro, gallantly
created the whole world, & James standing still
between her knees, ~~know~~ felt that all the strength was
flaring up to be gashed & drunk & devoured
by the ~~br~~ beak of brass, the arid scimitar of the male
smote
which ~~swooped~~ ~~on~~ her, again, again, again,
demanding sympathy

† B 62; A 59; B 63

† Flicking her needles, she blew the words back at him, ~~on the with~~ on the crest of one of those waves, which ~~now that she~~ seemed to run through her, making ~~of her~~ her being bound & ~~roll~~ leap forward while it remained perfectly controlled. He was not a failure. Charles Tansley thought him the greatest philosopher of the age.

But he must have more than that. ~~He must~~ He must have sympathy. ~~He must be~~ Charles Tansley, yes, well enough; but ~~Tansley was~~ a both a young man, a solitary, & after all, somehow a meagre young man ~~young man~~ Well then, the University of Leeds of Manchester, of Liverpool, Universities all over the world in short (but notably Mrs. Ramsay ~~no~~ did not exaggerate; she spoke soundly & [?] ~~to obvious~~ wellknown facts) ~~wished~~ implored him to ~~lecture;~~ just to come there. The Americans would give him, she did not know what sum, merely to live among them. But he wanted sympathy. his senses must be restored to him; he must be assured, somehow, that he lived in the heart of things, was no forlorn speculator tangling his feet in cobwebs.

But it was Look at all this then all his; ~~&~~ Flashing her needles, looking once over her shoulder, once into the garden, Mrs. Ramsay assured him her husband, by her vitality, her competency, her complete self-assurance, – & the lovely energetic poise of her body so upright & proper poised in her chair, how the house was full; & the garden full, & behind the drawing room was the kitchen; & above the kitchen the bedrooms; how life came pouring in a spate round them, &

& a word or two of the children of the [mar?]

- He wants women to be dumb
- Relies upon the ability to bend the truth

wherever he went, whether he crossed the hall & went to his study, or rambled through the garden, or chose, for a change to sit beside her in his own arm chair, ~~he was within the~~ ~~elastic~~ he was surrounded by life ~~precisely what he wanted,~~ & had only to go on, working thinking, & nothing, she promised him, should hurt him, nor for a single second should he find himself solitary. So, boasting almost save that in her singlemindedness & sincerity she had ~~no~~ almost ~~thought of~~ had forgotten ~~that~~ that she herself was the fount of ~~all~~ ~~this~~ these words, ~~she spent herself~~, curved herself & flared, as James felt standing stiff between her knees, into or an a [bowl?] of [rare?] & juicy fruit innumerably petalled rosy flower, into which the beak of brass, plunged the arid scimitar of ~~the~~ his father egotis~~tical~~ ~~m~~an smote again & again ~~& again~~ demanding sympathy.

that there was scarcely any shell of herself left for her to know herself by all was poured & spent

† Then he would take a turn & see how the cricket was going. And immediately sinking down, one petal ~~falli~~ folding into another – the whole fabric, falling in ~~from~~ exhaustion, upon itself, Mrs. Ramsay seemed to – all [fume?] ~~fade out~~ & fold herself together, & ~~let her hands,~~ & to have only strength enough to move her finger, in exquisite abandonment to exhaustion, & ~~relief at the splendid flowering of her being~~ across the page of Grimms fairy story, while there throbbed through her like the pulse in a spring which has been expanded to its full width & now gently to beat ceases, the exquisite ~~pleasure~~ rapture of ~~cre~~ ~~satisfaction~~ ~~of~~ creation.

satisfaction of having created.

~~Yet, she~~ ~~Very well then;~~ Now they must hurry up & finish the story of the three dwarfs;* for it was almost bedtime. And, taking James again on her knee, she read about ~~that~~ ~~those~~ the three dwarfs,

(The strain of having told lies)**

* Probably 'The Three Dwarfs in the Forest.' See MS 96, 101, 103, 104. In the final version Mrs Ramsay reads 'The Fisherman and His Wife.' (Both tales are in Grimm.) (1.147)

** Written in pencil

† B 64

Every throb of this pulse seemed to enclose her & her husband, to hold them together, to give to each that solace which, as

unite them too

different notes, one high one low, sound together in the air, seems to envelope them too. Yet as the resonance died away, & Mrs. Ramsay felt ~~the~~ some exhaustion of body, the pulse no longer carried so far, & then crept in some ~~little~~ dissatisfaction jar, some faintly disagreeable sensation. Not that reading aloud the story of the Three Dwarfs, she ~~asked herself~~ knew pricisely what it came from; nor did she let herself put into words ~~the~~ her

† dissatisfaction, ~~since it was, she knew, this~~: when she realized, as she did before she turned the page, ~~how she did~~ that it ~~came from being so much m finer than he was~~, & ~~not quite liking to be always giving~~; came not quite being sure of the entire truth of what she said. ~~Universities she made no~~ They did want him – these universities – & lectures, she had no doubt, believed implicitly, [?] which made him known

† to the young mattered supremely, but in their relation, in her having to give always so much, in his being always so

so dependent

incapable ~~of control~~ there ~~was~~ were was ~~the~~ seeds of ~~falsehood~~, discomfort, [misfit?] falsehood & ~~if~~ when people said, He depended ~~so~~ on ~~his~~ her

then she was indignant – he they must see how utterly he out-shone her in every way.

wife, where upon she was enraged ~~she~~ which, knowing him to be in ~~every~~ most ways, so great, so good incensed her. ~~And they~~ But not to be able to tell him the truth – ~~to be afraid of the this or that, to be~~ to fear his knowing that it was expensive, ~~med~~ mending the greenhouse roof, to fear his guessing it was not a failure, precisely, his ~~last book, but not a great~~ but ~~people~~ Mr. Bankes was not, she knew, enthusiastic quite sure about it, & to have to hide things ~~from~~ him, – ~~not that they were big things~~, un only small daily things – ~~she must do it; but~~ she did hide, – this ~~somehow just~~ diminished the joy perhaps, of that great joy, that entire joy, being making able to – Well, she

† B 65; A 62 (1.149)

also to free each other in different ways

the air the sky the rooks

did not speak of what it was that she did; knowing so well, all the structure of life she bore on her; ~~&~~ its rooms, its ~~ceil~~ ceilings; its everything, from top to toe; & besides, that that great venture which ~~she~~ now she must brace herself to put forth – her eight children, her four sons, four daughters – that too

all to be ~~floated~~ flung from her own hands

In all that, naturally, ~~how~~ could ~~he help~~? he could not help: how could looked at [he? ~~Naturally she must~~

She turned the page:

† ~~But James~~ It was ~~now~~ old Mr. Carmichael standing there. Precisely now at this very moment when ~~telling~~ his ~~to~~ – ~~not~~ she was feeling, oh at her worst. And

† B 66

(1.151)

of the inadequacies of human relationships. That the most perfect was flawed & could not bear the examination which she, ~~in~~ ~~with her~~ with her love of him loving truth instinctively, turned upon it, & thus that she herself was convicted of unworthiness – some knowledge of this kind ~~may have been~~ ~~was the~~ fretted her, ignobly; ~~sad~~ ~~egotistically~~, & fretted thus & then, she could not help ~~saying to M~~r. calling out to Mr. Carmichael, as he shuffled past, ~~& making him stop something friendly.~~

[Margin: was ~~impeded~~, & made uneasy, & impeded in her proper function † lies, exaggeration,]

"Going indoors Mr. Carmichael?"

~~she said~~.

VI

He took opium. The children said ~~that~~ he had stained his beard yellow with it; ~~or~~ ~~but~~ what was obvious ~~to her~~ was that the poor man suffered; was unhappy; came to them as an escape, & (~~for all his learning, his prodigious learning, was awkward to have about the house~~.) ~~was~~ ~~yet~~ always feared her. She said to him, "I am going to the town – do you want stamps, tobacco?" & she felt him ~~absolutely~~ shrink from her ~~away from her~~. ~~Of course~~, ~~There was~~ ~~The horror of it was, as she had seen once~~, ~~that~~ ~~this~~ wife, a ~~vulgar woman, was~~ as she ~~had seen once~~, going to ~~call on~~ them in St. John's Wood, she had seen once ~~And~~ ~~as~~ his wife had made ~~that~~ him do, ~~by an~~ iniquity of ~~behaviour~~ which ~~would~~ had ~~made her~~, Mrs. Ramsay, turn to steel & adamant there in the horrid little ~~dining~~ room in St. John' Wood ~~where~~ when ~~she had seen~~, with her own eyes, ~~that odious woman~~ she had seen poor Mr. Carmichael turned out of the room snubbed. ~~of course~~ He was unkempt, ~~dropping the~~ he dropped ~~the soup~~ things on his coat; & ~~no doubt~~ had all the tiresomeness of an old man, who neglects himself; but

[Margin: came to them for weeks; And; visit †; (how odius* vulgar [?]); wh was his wifes doing; & that iniquity of hers toward him, which had made]

* VW's misspelling
† A 63; B 67

† to be turned from the room – "Mrs. Ramsay & I want to have a little
talk together." & done in a way which made Mrs. Ramsay feel how
what innumerable ~~insults lay behind it,~~ miseries for him
lay behind it; – as if he were ~~not~~ not fit to be there – ~~as if he~~
poor old man ~~were~~ And always now he shrank from her. But
what more could she have done? There was ~~the~~ a sunny
room given up to him. Never did she show him the least
sign of not wanting him. ~~Yet~~ She went out of her way, indeed,
to be kind, to be friendly – And after all – after all,
† Mrs. Ramsay felt, she had not ~~to~~ generally any difficulty in
happy with her making her friends – Mr. Manning, George Wallace – feel
~~at their ease~~. She ~~had did indeed know in her~~
She bore about with her, she carried erect into any
room she entered, ~~that~~ ~~the~~ ~~beauty, that flame which was~~
~~the~~ the torch of her beauty; & after all, after all –
† veil it as she might & even shrink from the
monotony of bearing it imposed on her –
~~always to be admired was fool~~ish to h~~er thinking~~,
Still she had been admired. She had been loved. She
had entered rooms where mourners sat ~~solitary.~~ Tears,
had flown in her presence. Men, & women too, letting go
~~of all that little silly~~ the multiplicity of things – ~~the~~
fuss, & the ceremony, & all that fetters ~~& frets,~~ –
[distorts?] – had allowed themselves with her that
~~extraordinary~~ [the?] relief of simplicity. It now injured her
that Mr. Carmichael should shrink. It hurt her.
And yet, not cleanly, rightly. ~~No~~. ~~She had~~
That was what she minded – coming as it did on top of her
discontent with her husband – ~~she minded~~ the
sense she had now when Mr. Carmichael shuffled
past with the Spectator beneath his arm, in
his old flapping wide awake, that she was

suspected; & that all this giving of hers was a form of vanity. For her own self satisfaction was it, that she wished so instinctively always to help & give – that they might say of her, oh Mrs. Ramsay, ~~there is no one like you.~~ Mrs. Ramsay, Mrs. Ramsay – should call for her, need her, ask her for this ~~& that,~~ ~~to~~ to help them ~~to~~ advise them – did she not

† secretly desire all this, & therefore feel, when Mr. Carmichael shrank away from her, not only the horror of his ~~wounds~~, his wincing & flinching, & making off, away, alone, to some corner where he did acrostics endlessly ~~endlessly~~, but also, humiliated? A petty minded

† woman ~~she~~ was (& ~~oddly~~ shabby & worn & not presumably a

much of a sight ~~for~~ now for anyone to kindle at) & she had better ~~put her mind~~

think about the ~~read~~ ~~into~~ the story of the Three Dwarfs, & so ~~put~~ & pacify that bundle of sensitiveness – her son James.

† felt ~~that~~ exhilarated by the ~~mere~~ force & clarity of the phrases which the youth of Cardiff seemed to be shaping in his brain; which as he made them they seemed to be applauding; so that to Mr. Ramsay, walking on his terrace, ~~the~~ Hume became momentarily more & more visible.

† A 67, B 70

nodded : he approved;
† However he did not stop ~~long~~; he looked, he ~~acquiesced~~ he returned,
slipped
he slid, seeing the yew hedge before him which had over & over again
rounded some pause, & the urns with the geraniums in them –
he which had decorated moments of waking. ~~he returned again~~
mood ~~wh.~~ speculation
† he slipped into that ~~mood~~ something in The Times had put into his head,
~~of asking~~ about Shakespeare – & Shakespeare's position in the world:
Whether that is to say if Shakespeare had never existed the world would
have differed very much from what it is today – whether, then, the
progress of civilisation depends upon great men; whether
the lot of the average human being is ~~much~~ better now than it
was in the time of the Pharohs? & again, what ~~exact~~ relation the
arts bear to human life – are they ~~whether they are the expression of~~ the
an or do they
~~they the~~ expression ~~do they~~ express it, or merely serve to decorate it?
~~Fishermen~~, However all this may be, [~~Mr. Ramsay was~~
far
the ~~ultimate problems remain as~~ ~~beyond the reach of human~~ reason
~~as ever~~] & Mr. Ramsay ~~liked~~ explored ~~these ideas such~~
~~put an immense~~ had at his command considerable knowledge, &
a familiarity with the avenues & lanes of this world,
[to him?]
† ~~which~~ [ful?] ~~which made~~ his progress rather like that of a man
who reaches from his horse to pick a branch of nuts, or
stuff his pockets with wild roses as he ambles at his
ease through the lanes & fields of a country which is
fam
~~not only~~ known to him from boyhood, & loved, ~~&~~ – however all
this may be, now comes, – & here Mr. Ramsay having reached
~~the~~ some ~~fa~~ turn on the road, where many a time, in the
falling light, or by the pallor of the stars, he had
dismounted, tied his horse to a tree, & ~~gone on~~ proceeded on foot
† alone ~~to a little spit of land, surrounded by the sea,~~
~~once~~ again, dismounted – ~~however all this may be,~~
face
& proceeded to ~~ask himself~~ ~~put to himse~~lf that
other ~~question~~ fact – which is that the problem of human
our ignorance is complete,
existence remains insoluble: we know nothing; ~~we never~~
shall know anything & no solution of the We know
nothing, said

whether the average human being.
civilisation can take into account the
shd. be
lot of the average human being,
or by that of his exceptional [person?]:
the problem of equality –

Mr. Ramsay

† A 66, B 69, B 70; A 67; A 68, B 71; B 72 (1.161)

all* diversions & excursions having been made

we have to face the fact of our ignorance;
fact which he was used to meeting, ~~which he~~ of human ignorance
& our powerlessness in the face of the greatest problems of life.
we come out on to a spit of land which the sea is slowly eating
away & there ~~we~~ stand ~~each~~ alone, ~~contemplating~~
And there, ~~indeed~~, he stood. It was his gift ~~or~~ his peculiarity,
thus suddenly to shed ~~all~~ all superfluities; to shrink ~~into a~~
[~~yet?~~] ~~without~~ & diminish, ~~even physically~~, so that he looked
barer & sparer, ~~yet to~~ even physically, yet lost none of his
~~alertness~~ & intensity of mind; & so to stand on his
~~spit of~~ little ledge ~~watching~~ facing the fact of human
~~impotence~~ We know nothing. ~~We Human life & We shall~~
~~never know~~ We We can never ignorance, & how we know
† nothing; & ~~how~~ the sea eats away the ~~lan~~ ground ~~beneath us; is~~
how we too must we stand on. ~~Here he was Mr.~~ And

all gestures &

~~As for~~ And having dismounted from his horse, having
thrown away with his coat, ~~& other encumbrances~~, those
trophies of roses & nuts, ~~he~~ having & shrunk so that he
forgot perhaps ~~even~~ his own name, yet kept ~~the~~ even ~~in~~

even in that desolation

~~this desolate outpost~~ ~~the~~ a vigilance ~~of a terrier which~~
~~kept the~~ which spared no phantom, & luxuriated in no vision,
in this guise, of ~~entire probity & truth~~, he inspired in
his wife, & William Bankes, & Lily Briscoe, & Charles
Tansley a mixture of reverence & pity. ~~w such as the~~ Like
~~a lonely~~ as a stake driven into the bed of a channel, to mark
~~upon which~~ the ~~pass~~ upon which the gulls perch & the
waves beat, wh sometimes almost submerged, at others
erect & bare, a landmark, a guide, ~~there he~~
had his station, he seems to have taken upon itself
a duty towards the rest of mankind, & to have
advanced upon its behalf into the sea of
~~human~~ perplexity; where, now almost submerged, now
bare & erect, it remains to & to be lonely & to be
& to be venerable.

* 'All' written in pencil

† A 69

inspires in those who behold it, so l~~onely, so~~ faithful, ~~sad~~ now almost submerged, ~~now high~~ bare ~~& prominent~~ ~~a sentiment~~ a feeling of gratitude for thus having taken upon it a duty to mankind

for thus marking the ~~chan~~ channel for sailors. for thus advancing ~~on~~ into the [curious?]†
sea

But the father of eight children has little choice. With some such phrase as this Mr. Ramsay was apt to sum it all up, to stop, to sigh, to ~~fil~~ fill his pipe, to seek out his wife, to ~~tick~~ tease his little boy James, to turn away from the sight of human ignorance, & the dark dealing of human kind, which, had he been in a position to contemplate it fixedly might have absorbed him; & to find consolation in something ~~so~~ ~~in itself~~ so slight mean, despicable compared with the august theme of human ~~ignorance~~ fate that he was ~~not~~ disposed to slur over his relief, to dissemble his joy, & ~~thus~~ to thus, disposed to slur it over & blind himself & deprecate his natural appetite for pleasure. Thus Locke, Hume, & Bishop Berkely, & the fact that he had promised in very little over six weeks time – the engagement was fixed for the middle of October – to talk some ~~lecture~~ nonsense to the young men of Cardiff upon the English philosophers, – ~~all this had~~ ~~these~~ this, & the pleasure he took in it all – the pleasure he took in the compliment, in the greetings, in the ~~appla~~ phrases he made, in the applause with which these phrases were greeted, in the ardour of youth, in the beauty of his wife, in the atmosphere of recognition & admiration which surrounded him in Cardiff, Swansea; Exeter, Southampton & Kidderminster when he lectured upon the English philosophers, all this had to be ~~veiled in some~~ deprecated, & veiled made little of, – ~~in~~ ~~&~~ & if it ~~had not been~~ ~~because it is not~~ ~~it was not somehow~~ & concealed under the ~~apparent~~ appearance of dejection. "Talking nonsense to the young

† the figures of ~~in a curious~~ as if to be caught happy in a world of misery was ~~a crime~~ for an honest man the most despicable of crimes.

(1.167)*

* Manuscript misnumbered : 165 omitted

† B 73; A 70

that this is hopeful

men of Cardiff", it was a phrase, a disguise; & pitiable rather, it
† to those ~~who~~ like William Bankes, ~~or~~ & Lily Briscoe, who
wondered why such subterfuges should be required; why ~~a~~ so
~~Mr. Ramsay had need of such little convenien~~ brave a man was
should be so ~~at the same time~~ ~~so~~ timid; ~~why &~~ unless, indeed, – (~~here was~~
preaching & teaching The ~~career of teacher~~ is beyond human power; exaltation must
be paid for by abasement; & the private lives
of all who arise ~~out of~~ ~~discov~~er, ~~exhibit~~ ~~show, when it comes to~~
out in advance of the human race; exhibit the same kind of
lamentable decrepitude, [miserable?] in practice;
prove that the makers of rules are the rule makers are ~~decrepitude~~, uncertainty; ~~vacillation~~; as if ~~it soon~~
~~they were peculiarly liable, having~~ ~~were~~ always the most
liable to be trapped by ~~their own~~ instincts. In Mr.
† Bankes' opinion the young had ceased to be influenced by
Carlyle because of the for this very reason. A surly old
shall no [only?]
who grumbler, – how ~~should~~ he preach to us was what Mr.
that the young people said nowadays.
Bankes understood them to say. But Lily Briscoe,
thought that ~~this being~~ human like the rest of us –
being ~~even~~ specially human in a silly babyish way, like Mr.
~~Ramsay & Carlyle~~, of wanting praise, & having no self control,
† & thinking if one's little finger ached ~~that the whole~~ world
was going to come to an end this, though not good in itself,
had at any rate one advantage, looked at from an ordinary
~~point of view~~: if Mr. Ramsay had been ~~a~~ [~~Cart~~?] great all through
consistent, perhaps one would not have liked him. Besides –
that one liked him better for it. ~~No he~~ Only There was one
things in order to be [contradict?]
thing she did not like – saying one thing when you meant
a bit
another. Being a hypocrite? Mr. Bankes suggested.
But who could call Mr. Ramsay a hypocrite? They
could not
looked at him; & no: you ~~cannot~~ call a man like that a
hypocrite; anything but a hypocrite: so shabby, so
distinguished; so What indeed could they call
him to his face? Lily Briscoe had to look
down at her brushes, which she was putting away

† B 74; A 71, B 75; A 72 (1.169)

& to concentrate upon the idea of Mr. Ramsay in absence, before she could put to herself, not to Mr. Bankes, her theory that

† he asked too much of his wife (but that was largely her own fault) & for her own part there was ~~something~~ a side of things – typified she looked at the jacmanna, the wall, the starlings – ~~& that was~~ something spontaneous – [very?] immediate [?] which these teachers, of whom of course she was unworthy to speak, these great men who saw kitchen tables in pear trees & lectured, worked & exhibited – of that there could be no doubt in Mr. Ramsays case, the most perfect [austerity?] in private life – there was a side of things which they neglected. Now take Mr. Ramsay –

Ah, said Mr. Bankes,

† A 71, B 74

† But this had to be to advanced with her eyes turned away. Directly she looked up &

~~Now, take~~" Mrs. Ramsay –

Mrs. Ramsay, ~~Ah~~ said Mr. Bankes.

But of course he was not going to discuss her.

he — But this had to be advanced with her eyes turned down away.

[walking?] [?] — Directly she looked up & saw them, she became ~~involved in~~ involved in it all again, them ~~a part of~~ their lives, received a station & had a part allotted to her, & then of course ~~she could no more trace~~

could not retrace — these diagrams ~~than~~ ~~because of~~ Mr. Ramsay & Mrs. Ramsays ~~became~~ ~~his~~ characters became inundated with feelings which she could not confine at all within in the marks she had made, Then, ~~far from be~~ ~~something else~~ she was ~~at once~~ aware ~~how~~ of a million million things; which

& had her, in part allotted to her, & — ~~that~~ they both man walking, that woman sitting were; ~~how~~ of they were house & trees & ~~t~~ sky & garden; yes, & part of herself too; ~~It was odd indeed that~~ how ~~one felt~~ that was the delight of staying with them –

one was snapped up — ~~that they did~~ ~~how~~ that every now & then – ~~when one~~

† sat ~~down to dinner, fifteen~~ ~~life~~ life broke like a wave on a rock. ~~Then, it was not~~ & one could not ~~be sure~~ ~~whether one was~~ ~~what one was~~, ~~what any one was~~ –

one was snatched — retreat from it, or keep ones head or ~~say~~ point out faults. ~~Some~~ anymore.

Grasped them up ~~took~~ one up, ~~bent one out~~, & flung one ~~in~~ down, splash, in one wave. It was like a wave of the sea

~~In all this,~~ It was Mrs. Ramsay ~~was the prime force~~ that was the prime force in all this; no doubt.

Now Mrs. Ramsay – Lily Briscoe was

† A 72, B 76; A 73

~~inclined to~~ rather ~~thought she had~~ wished ~~to tell Mr. Bankes~~ rather thought ~~she h~~ had, looking up & looking down, ~~arrived~~ she had something to say about her; but before she had said it – ~~& it was nothing very something~~ Mr. Bankes had ~~all~~ put it out of her head entirely by his rapture. For
† such it was, considering his age was turned sixty & he had both the asperity & the cleanliness of a scientist spiritually again wore, ~~almost~~ spiritually, a white coat & smelt of disinfectants. ~~For this elderly &~~ For him to gaze at Mrs. Ramsay like that was a rapture equivalent, Lily Briscoe felt, to the loves of dozens of young men; ~~but it was dis~~ it was love distilled & filtered; it was love that had never attempted to clutch its object, ~~but had~~ but &, like the love
† ~~of the~~ which mathematicians bear their ~~f~~ symbols, & ~~arti~~ writers ~~bear~~ their visions, ~~it~~ it was ~~intense &~~ both intense & ~~quite~~ impersonal: The world should have shared it, had it been in his power; ~~he~~ ~~but it was not in~~ Mr. Bankes power to say why that woman so pleased him. Why the sight of her, reading fairy stories to her child in the window, had upon him precisely the same effect as ~~a~~ the beautiful ~~solution of~~ ~~piece of work~~ ~~demonstration in~~ solution of a scientific problem, so that he rested in contemplation of it, & felt (as if he had proved something about the digestive system of plants) ~~how~~ that the reign of chaos ~~had~~ was ~~been~~ subdued.

was meant to be spread over the world & made part of the universal inheritance.

Such a rapture – for by what word was one to call it? – made Lily Briscoe forget entirely what she had been about to say. It was nothing of importance; something about Mrs. Ramsay. ~~Yet,~~ It paled beside this 'rapture' (an intense, impersonal, silent stare) of Mr. Bankes', for which she worshipped him; for she felt that

† B 77; A 74

† nothing so solaced her ~~of the~~ in the conflict of life, so eased her of the [sense
of futility, & miraculously raised all the trivial worry from
her shoulders, as this solemn power. & one no more disturbed it, or
interrupted it then, broke the sunlight lying straight upon
the ~~matting~~. floor.

That people should love ~~other people~~ their kind, in this way,
was
that Mr. Bankes should feel this for Mrs. Ramsay, ~~seemed to~~ her
it was
~~so satisfactory~~, ~~to~~ beautiful, satisfactory, helpful, exalting
~~under the~~ She wiped first one brush, then another, ~~upon~~ ~~tht~~
† with a piece of old rag. ~~Some~~ ~~As a woman, too~~, she
took shelter beneath ~~the~~ ~~a~~ reverence which covered all
herself too
women. ~~She~~ felt praised. But, when she considered the
~~beginning of~~ her picture – & she could not help taking a
look at it, after her ~~afternoon's work~~, walk round the
garden, her picture of the hedge, the wall, & the jacmanna,
~~She~~ she ~~could~~ ~~have wept.~~ ~~was discomforted.~~ It was so bad.
Mr. Paunceforte would have seen it ~~all~~ half transparent, in
greys & silver, with spots of green & rose. She saw it
~~directly~~ ~~entirely differently~~; ~~& her picture was already hal~~
heavy & clumsy, – ~~Still if~~ ~~She saw it~~ glaring, staring
to go on painting; in greens & blues. ~~And~~ it would never be hung anywhere;
& it was waste of time; & Mr. Tansley ~~was always~~ said
possibly Now
~~saying~~ that no woman could ^paint; She recollected
~~then~~ what she had been going to say about Mrs. Ramsay,
when Mr. Bankes ~~inter~~ put it out of her mind, looking as he did;
that
† she had been going ~~to say~~ ~~how~~ ~~Mrs. Ramsay always~~
~~seemed to her~~ a led the conversation somehow towards ~~the~~
her funniness. That ~~there was the solemn side, everybody~~
to the funniness of
knew; but did Mrs. Ramsay ~~& her being~~ as she was
not sheltered by this sort of worship; (for ~~two women~~
~~were~~ it was impossible for two women to
for no ~~two~~ women could not ~~shelter each other~~
worship each other ~~but as~~ could ~~not~~ only seek shelter

† B 78; A 75; B 79

under the shade which men like Mr. Bankes extended over them; she
could not look at Mrs. Ramsay quite in that light, though she did
† think her ~~und~~ undoubtedly ~~the most~~ much the loveliest of
people; & the best, perhaps; but also ~~she was odd~~, ~~she was~~
~~so queer;~~ she was no more like ~~th~~ what people thought her
than ~~she was~~ than – no comparison came to Lilys mind,
& she wiped ~~her~~ another brush; & began to scrape the
palette of all those mounds of blue & brown which she
knew she would never make do what she wanted,
& yet she would never give up trying to make them do
what she wanted; She was the very opposite of     whate~~ver~~ she
all that – ~~heroic~~ submissive, devoted, sublime – She was like a
bird for speed; ~~or~~ like an arrow for decision – She was wilful &
commanding. She ~~brooked~~ stood no contradiction. ~~She~~
(of course, Lily reminded herself, I am ~~speaking~~ thinking of her
relations with women – with a woman who is much
younger than she is) – ~~she was thinking~~, ~~for example~~, of
† ~~Mrs. Ramsay~~ open~~ing~~ed all the bedroom windows; of
~~Mrs. Ramsay making up matches; of Mrs. Ramsay~~
of her determination to m~~arry~~ ~~one off; of~~
make ~~one a~~ ~~woman marry a~~ men & women marry;
her fixed single & simple belief that no career
she dictated all the doings of the day. Arriving late
at night, with a light tap on the door of one's bedroom,
wrapped in an old fur coat, how ~~eloque~~ ~~dele~~ ~~vehemently~~
~~&~~ how she would ~~recount the~~ run over the tale of
things sayings, doings, observations & ~~oddities~~ of the days –
& ~~infallibly~~ adroitly shape them; & how she would insist, or
even not think it worth ~~that~~ the trouble, that Lily ~~would~~
† must ~~of course~~ marry; 'must', since in the whole
world whatever laurels might be tossed her, or
triumphs won by her, there could be no disputing this:
that an unmarried woman ~~was~~ ~~obviously~~ ~~miserable.~~
had missed the ~~greatest~~ ~~of~~ best of life.

† A 76; B 80; A 77

† But ~~Lil~~ Lily would protest, she could not leave her home;
her father; her ~~sisters;~~ brothers; she would even dare, ~~to~~ as the
white
night drew on, & ~~between the~~ ~~pale~~ light parted the
bedroom curtains, to ~~proclaim the fact~~ ~~her~~ deny for
herself ~~at least the~~ the necessity of marriage; would
her own exemption on the law — urge that Mrs. Ramsay's law did not apply to her; & so
the a
have to meet ~~that~~ ~~serious~~, ~~intent, almost~~ exasperating
stare, ~~w~~ from eyes ~~which~~ ~~with~~ ~~all their beauty~~
of unparalleled depth; ~~& the~~ to ~~front the~~ confront
Mrs. Ramsays ~~perfectly~~ simple ~~ex~~ conviction, Mrs. Ramsays
~~inscrutable~~ – ~~entire~~ ~~&~~ unshakable certainty, that she was a
fool. Then, Lily ~~remembered~~, it was ~~hop~~ impossible; then she
lap one must
remembered, one had to lay one's head on her knee; & laugh –
until
laugh – laugh & Mrs. Ramsay said [?]
the thought of her
to laugh & laugh at Mrs. Ramsay, presiding so ~~sternly so~~
with simple misunderstanding — beautifully so unquestioningly ov~~er~~ yet somehow so
women
mistakenly over the destinies of others. But into what
sanctuary had one penetrated? Lily Briscoe had
~~made herself~~ looked up at last; & there was Mrs. Ramsay
unwitting entirely what caused her laughter, still presiding
~~serene~~; ~~but~~ ~~on~~ but now with every trace ~~of the~~ ~~tyrant, of the~~
wilfulness abolished; & in its place the calm of tropic
a place
seas where the halcyon hovers; ~~the~~ something soft as the
night & ~~as pure as~~ ~~childhood;~~ which the clouds,
having trailed ~~&~~ ~~&~~ & flowed, at last uncover – ~~one~~
~~had the sense of looking up into something~~
† One looked up at length into that little space of sky
which is quite steadfast, near the moon.

† B 81; B 82

Was it ~~tiredness~~ wisdom? Was it knowledge? Was ~~there~~ it ~~again~~ again the deceptiveness of beauty, or did she lock up in her own person that final knowledge ~~of~~ which certainly Lily Briscoe believed that some people must have; for it was not possible that all ~~people~~ of ~~us~~ should be as ~~little~~ helter skelter as she was, ~~living from hand to mouth~~, some must know. But if they knew, could they give share, what they knew could they ~~communicate~~? Sitting on the floor, with her arms round Mrs. ~~B~~ Ramsay's knees, ~~she~~ close as she could get, she imagined how in the chambers of the mind & heart ~~of that other~~ the woman who was, physically touching her, (& she hugged [her knees were ~~displayed~~ stood, like the treasures in the tombs of kings, ~~sacred~~ tablets bearing sacred inscriptions, which, if one penetrated to those chambers one could spell out; but they would never be offered, ~~presented~~ opened or never, made public. [Could one guess her secrets by pressing close to her? Was there any way yet devised ~~by passion or cunning~~ for the] One might press close to her. ~~One might even take~~ in ~~the~~ a ~~childish way which touch &~~ These tablets engraved with sacred inscriptions had been written very slowly year by year; & then sealed; & then locked up, for] what art was there, known to love or cunning, by which one [prised?] ~~those~~ secret chambers? ~~Who~~ Did closeness bring one nearer? She held the fingers of Mrs. Ramsays hand; & Could one ask? Could one What device for sharing, became ~~less~~ like waters poured into one jar, inextricably the same? ~~Did nearness of the body achieve~~ Could the body achieve it — ~~mingling its~~ essences, fearlessly & wholly? or ~~could~~ the mind, ~~brilli su~~ subtly mingling in the intricate passages of the brain? or could the heart? which ~~desired~~ in ~~its own way could seem to make of her & of~~ Mrs. Ramsay ~~but one~~ for the moment, at least,

or the word did not exist;

† A 79

~~as~~ she sat there ~~in the early dawn, seemed to~~

not knowledge but unity;

† Could loving her, as people called it, make them one – & so impart ~~to~~ – for it was that, perhaps, unity & ~~onene~~ that was knowledge – not inscriptions on tablets, nothing that could be written out in any language known to man, it ~~was~~ [but] is; ~~to~~ [for] intimacy, that is knowledge, she had thought, still leaning her head against Mrs. Ramsays knee; &

~~Which is im~~ [And it is not] possible, she had decided; & how did she know that it was not an illusion – her sense of ~~the~~ knowledge & wisdom, of of wisdom, ~~of something~~ stored up in ~~Mrs.~~ the chambers of Mrs. Ramsays heart, & was it not due to her beauty – to the How did one know one thing or another, about people, sealed as they were? ~~but only~~ [Only] like a bee drawn by an instinct,

† drawn by some sharpness or sweetness in the air, intangible to touch or taste, one haunted the domelike hive, ranged the air ~~widely alone, & then with~~ the countries of the world widely alone, & then haunted those hives, so full of mysterious murmurs, even of signals & beckonings, which were / [other] people; which ~~Mrs.~~ were Mrs. Ramsay. ~~And getting up & [stret?]~~ Then she got up: & Mrs. Ramsay got up; & for days ~~afterwards Lily Briscoe had~~ there had hung about her – ~~as v~~ more vividly than anything she said, ~~like a~~ a sound of [soft] murmuring. She had seen her sitting in a wicker arm chair in her drawing room like a dome.

~~That~~ [That it was all] Things are / [very] odd, she ~~might~~ [was about to say] have said, as she finished scraping her palette; ~~only but~~ But while she had been looking down into her paint box, ~~on~~ & ~~arranging~~ making ready to ~~[ha f?]~~ pack up,

† Mr. Bankes had, unknown to her, put on his spectacles ~~to look~~ [& stood considering] at her picture. He had raised his hand. He

† B 83; A 80; B 84

VIII*

~~was whether it would not be better without the corner of the wall~~

[?] [?] stiffen slightly ~~raise~~ her head

He was examining ~~Lilys~~ her picture with detachment. ~~She~~ He was standing saw him ~~Al~~ She winced like a ~~whipped~~ a dog. who sees a hand raised to strike it. ~~Here was~~ She wanted to snatch her picture off the easel & throw it, face ~~downwards,~~ on its in the grass.

280
04
1100
1680
17,900

But as a soldier has to brace himself to ~~rise~~ stand up ~~from he against the~~ bullets, so she, too, resolved to abide this awful trial: that Mr. Bankes was looking at her picture. ~~She had exposed to the~~ world something ~~which~~ that another person should see what she had stated there, & pronounce had concocted ~~& stated~~; what ~~was~~

† had been in her mind as a baby, ~~&~~ what was the residue of ~~all~~ her thirty three years; the deposit of each day, ~~the~~ something mysterious

But He was puzzled by the triangular shadow on the left, he said. That was Mrs. Ramsay reading to James, she said. She had foreseen the objection. ~~about~~ – that ~~it was~~ there was no attempt at a likeness of them. It was for the

† sake of the composition ~~that she wis~~hed to ~~ha a shadow~~ she explained. ~~Mr. Bankes had not~~ ~~And~~ B Mr. Bankes outraged as he was – for mother & child were to him ~~the most~~ objects of veneration – ~~showed~~ patiently stood there ~~(she felt~~ ~~patiently~~ & ~~an extraordinary~~ gratitude to him, & relief ~~relief, for here was~~ & ~~Freedom~~ s~~tealing over her~~, & sudden exaltation at being able to discuss the matter impersonally, wi~~thout question of sex~~, ~~&~~ for he was not going to say to her No woman can paint; he was like a priest in his scientist) & she ~~said to him~~ told him how she felt that with that line there, you must have a shadow there.

lack of the [?] sexual passion; vindictiveness.

† He ~~was~~ was interested in the idea that mother & children might be reduced to shadows in a picture without irreverence. ~~He was~~ ~~All his~~ ~~All~~ His interests it is true, were on the opposite side. At his house in Knightsbridge the picture he remembered best was a

* VW has omitted VII.

† A 81; B 85; A 82

(1.187)

a very careful water colour of a ~~hou~~ village on the Kennet where he had spent his honeymoon. Lily felt that there was nothing that he would not give up in the cause of truth. It interested him, &

† he would ~~stand~~ give his best mind to the question ~~of~~ which

absorbed ~~vexed~~ her of ~~this~~ the relations between one part of her picture

& ~~to~~ another part of her picture. So that she put herself again into position; again considered the thing as a whole. Was the triangular purple perhaps too heavy, so that the ~~light sky~~ sky became too light? ~~How should one~~ &

† ~~link up~~ ~~bridge the~~ ~~connect the~~ two chief blocks of matter ~~so that~~ must somehow be joined together –

the obsequious dejected [deplorable?]

Ah well, she broke off returning again, apologetically to the extreme modesty of ~~spinsters' art.~~ ~~a painting~~ uneducated womanhood; & took it off the easel

[But her picture had been looked at; her picture had been cut from her; & had taken its place on the other side ~~of that deep &~~ of that horrid little ditch, ~~where~~ which ~~that~~ men like Charles Tansley cut so indefatigably round women who wanted to do anything,]

it had been placed

But here was somebody who made it seem possible to paint a picture; &, returning to the normal relationship again; not of women & trees, but of women & human beings, she ~~would~~ was ~~have thanked him for~~ ~~not~~ by his extraordinary magnanimity, ~~would have~~ which was so rare, ~~so~~ in her experience, & ~~how odd it was, sometimes~~ ~~to~~ be which lightened the whole of her horizon – for here was a man, & one of the most brilliant too (she had heard Mr. Ramsay ~~desc~~ call him the most brilliant botanist in Europe) who ~~did not~~ would let one talk to him. That was the sort of thing

† that did happen, if one stayed with the Ramsays – one lived for 30 years believing this to be true; suddenly here

was Mr. Bankes – & one cd. talk about painting. ~~Now with~~ his ~~trained mind~~, And Lily Briscoe ~~put~~ [~~strai?~~] nicked the tin paint box ~~too~~ to, with a vivid & amazing scene, which wd. be for ever

† B86; A 83; B 87

to connected with a tin paint box; & the ~~extraord~~ sudden impact of that
wild villain, Cam.

IX

For Cam grazed the easel by an inch; she would not stop for
he [~~ou~~?] held out his hand
Mr. Bankes & Lily Briscoe; though Mr. Bankes would have liked her to
† stop: she would not stop for her father whom also she grazed
by an inch; nor for her mother, who called Cam! as she
dashed past, — ~~For~~ She ~~was off~~ ~~For she wanted~~
or
She was off — She ~~was~~ like a bird, a ~~pu~~ bullet an arrow,
~~im impelled by~~ But impelled by what desire, who had shot her,
at what she was directed, who could say? ~~A vision, a~~
It might have been a sudden vision: of a ~~leaf~~ ~~shadow~~ ~~flower~~
wheel barrow, ~~a shadow,~~ a nothing whatever. raising her hand to

But when Mrs. Ramsay called Cam! a second time;
dropped to the earth, Cam
~~Cam~~ stopped, ~~shot~~ dead in mid career, & trotted ~~back to the~~
by the
dra~~wing~~ came lagging back, pulling a leaf ~~on~~ ~~her~~ way,
ba~~ck~~ to her mother.

thinking of something different.
The little girls mind was completely ~~vacant,~~ as Mrs.
Ramsay saw; & the message which Cam was to take to
Andrew &
Mildred in the [~~guestroom~~?] kitchen. — Have Miss Doyle & Mr. Rayley
[come back? —
had to be repeated twice, to be dropped into ~~that~~ those ~~extraord~~
those ~~extraordinary depths, at once~~ so that well, where if the
waters were clear they were also so extraordinarily distorting
simple words about
that, even as the ~~words~~ descended, one saw them twisting: ~~from side to~~
to the cook [~~side~~
What message ~~Cam~~ would Cam deliver, Mrs. Ramsay wondered?
† And indeed it was only by ~~a~~ the use of parrot like instinct
which reproduced her mothers words accurately ~~without any~~
deprived of all meaning in a ~~kind~~ an absent minded singsong
that Cam asked, ~~looking at~~ staring at Mrs. McLeod,
who ~~was on a visit, & had~~ had come to ask for blankets, &
wore bugles, Have Andrew, Miss Doyle & Mr. Rayley
come back? & not considering ~~th~~ So that ~~when~~ the answer to Mrs.
[Ramsays
~~question~~ was that a very old woman was in the kitchen who
wore bugles.

[Left margin notes:]

The idea
appeared

~~the li~~
the ~~wild~~ bullet
the projectile

to make heaven
knew
what
[pattern?]
& lying in the
strangest order
upon the floor

& ~~not~~ not
listening to Mildreds
reply — No —
they have not
come back — Ellen
has cleared away
tea —

† A 84; B 88; A 85

Mrs. McLeod had come to get her blankets, Mrs. Ramsay divined, – ~~She~~ [for her
~~whose~~ mother ^who was dying of cancer – but as for the message,
about Andrew & the others, ~~that that could~~ the answer to that
~~could only be~~ was only to be reached by waiting patiently for
Cam to repeat, like a sleep walker, "No they haven't, & I've
told Ellen to clear away tea."

Minta Doyle & Paul Rayley had not come back. And
~~what did that mean~~? Then It could only mean, Mrs. Ramsay thought,
that something had happened–that she had made up her
mind that there was an end of all those hesitations which
while they did her honour, could not be go on ~~prolonged without~~ indefinitely
forever. [& yet?] ~~Either~~ she must accept a man him, or she must refuse
him. And this going off after luncheon for a walk
eventhough Andrew was with them, – what could it mean?
~~one did not~~ except that ~~after~~ she had decided, rightly,
Mrs. Ramsay thought, to accept Paul Rayley who was
obviously entirely devoted to her, a good fellow, ~~&~~ one
of the nicest yng fellows ~~young men~~ she knew – which was not saying
of course that he was brilliant, for that he was not, but
it would be a very happy marriage, Mrs. Ramsay thought, &
~~they would have very lovely babies~~, & he would do well enough
but that did not matter for he had prospects, &
~~& there would be lovely children, & in short Minta would be~~
She She ~~tried to soon~~ saw them going off after lunch,
down the path to the gate, & tried to see Minta, ~~with~~
the expression on Minta's face ~~& to~~ the thought of which
for how could Minta, now, say that she would not have him?
† Not if she let ~~herself~~ agreed to spend whole afternoons
trapesing about the country practically alone –
for ~~Adre~~ Andrew would be off after his crabs –
practically alone – Mrs. Ramsay thought, & saw them,

were quite right, of course, for nothing needed more care, †

& she was very very fond of Minta

she had no doubt

before they went
† looking at the sky, wondering about wet or fine, which she knew was
to push them off [only
to cover their being shy; & so she had said that there wasn't a
cloud anywhere within miles; though as she knew, ~~she~~
~~damaged her reputation~~ with good little Charles Tansley ~~every~~
~~time she~~ thought her a perfect imbecile for the way she talked.
are absolutely
she didnt mind But ~~then~~ perfect imbeciles are, she thought, ~~need~~ necessary
sometimes – & it did not matter a fig –

~~However~~ – ~~Those~~

Here James ~~pointed~~ drew her attention to the
had just time
story of the Woodman's daughter, which they could possibly
to finish before bed~~time~~ if Cam would only decide whether she
sit still
wanted to play in the garden, or to hear about the little
girl who ~~wanted to~~ had tea with the bears in the
middle of the forest.*

And so they had gone off, Mrs. Ramsay remembered,
she had seen as she found her place, down the drive, & she rather thought
Nancy ~~had~~ join~~ed~~ them, so there would be four of them, &
who knows whether, in the ~~cir~~ circumstances, anything would
But
say something † happen? ~~And~~ if not, she would have to ~~speak~~ to Minta – not
was
severely (& how It ~~is~~ not fair to him – & to go trapesing over
the country, even with the children there, must make
people, even blind bats like ~~that little~~ Charles Tansley – repeat; &
those excellent people for Mrs. Ramsay always thought of them [?] as a poker & a stuffed owl – a stuffed owl admirable oh yes – [?] oh yes – but ~~oh~~ highly admirable people they were, the ~~moment~~ how difficult it is to stop talk, once it
begins, she knew; & here, at the ends of the earth as they
were, she was responsible to Minta's parents, if
Minta could be said to have parents, which Mrs.
Ramsay doubted: you could scarcely call ~~that starched~~
a man with a chin like that. & But had Nancy gone?
he w

XIV**

† Yes, Nancy had gone, dropping her mallet, for, as Mrs. Ramsay

* 'The Story of the Three Bears.' See MS 73, 101, 103, 104. (1.195)

** VW may have meant this to be X, though it looks like XI or XIV.

† B 90; A 87, B 91; A 112, B 116

Feb. 18th

† could not possibly have seen, ~~for~~ with with her shortsighted eyes, she was shortsighted, & engaged too in distracting the attention of ~~that~~ Charles Tansley, Minta Doyle had implored her to come, not in words; Minta was dumb; but in speechless language which roused in Nancy's heart a an extraordinary ~~ecstasy.~~ elation ~~For having no character to speak of~~, being fifteen & being one of eight children, & being anonymous & amorphous as a jelly which floats hither & thither secretly absorbing nourishment, ~~but~~ & yet has been once or twice near enough the top of the wave to see a buoy, a steamer, a cloud, boatload of tourists, & then sink to the depths again, suddenly a ray light fell on her, she felt herself singled out & made from [?] & flew into that dazzling & intricate affair – a grown up for the first time in her life responsible in ~~the vast world of human beings which awaited her — a world where~~ for the conduct of human affairs. Minta Doyle had ~~no need to say anything~~. done nothing but say "Nancy must come", & Nancy instantly dropped her mallet & losing the all that ecstasy of tapping balls [?] accurately & exactly skilfully which had absorbed her, came to catch crabs too.

† A 112, B 116

X Once a woman had accused her of
robbing her of her daughter's affections

& indeed she resented it, &
~~owed a grudge~~ possibly
~~may have~~ & she put it down to
her being like that to
look at;

† Although it ~~amused her to indulge~~ she enjoyed phrase-making in
private
He wore a wig in the House of Commons, & she ably assisted him
at the head of the stairs. Between them they had produced among
other children this perfectly incongruous creature, with this
passion for the open air & a hole, it seemed to Mrs. Ramsay,

perpetually

~~always~~ in the heel of her stocking. Seeing her there in that
as believed
portentious atmosphere where, ~~it seemed~~ to Mrs. Ramsay, a maid
was always removing in a dust pan the sand which the parrot had
scattered, & conversation was almost entirely reduced to ~~that~~ the
† interesting but after all limited ~~topic~~ – ~~the topic~~ the exploits
of that bird, Mrs. Ramsay had asked her to lunch, to dinner, to tea, to
stay with them finally – which had resulted in some friction with her
[mother,
only to be appeased by more calling, more conversation more gravel;
~~with~~ Mrs. Doyle for some reason suspected, her. Indeed, Mrs.
upon which
Ramsay divined that here was another ~~occasion~~ occasion ~~of~~
&
~~misunderstanding~~. She was accused of dominating, ~~of~~ interfering, ~~of~~
making people do her will rather than their own – a perfectly
genuinely believed;
baseless accusation; Mrs. Ramsay thought, & yet if she had had

Mrs. Ramsay
had no passionate
love for the ~~parrot~~
bird
was not
naturally
attached to parrots

† time & wealth, she would have liked to ~~give give expression to a~~
small
take one or two things in hand, certainly; to get a ~~really good~~
for one thing
hospital built up in these islands; that was a matter she had set
on foot. ~~& would see or~~ & do something to ~~impro~~ make ~~it~~
the sale of
~~illegal to sell~~ dirty milk – & often milk was delivered at her
† in a state which was possible dangerous to healthy, illegal; to
found a model dairy near London. When the children
were older, she would have time ~~for~~ perhaps for doing more –
ah, but she never wanted them to grow a day older!
They were adorable, just as they were; it made her
miserable to see them growing into long legged monsters –
when Cam & James
like James & Cam ~~who~~ only a year or two ago had been
~~like more~~ bundles of delight – & she had been able to
carry them about with her now. Now they squabbled.

of first rate
importance, &
one she intended
to carry
through
somehow:

† A 88, B 91; B 92; A 89, B 93 (1.199)

Prue

Andrew

Nancy

Roger

Rose

dreadfully – sometimes it was Cam's fault, sometimes it was James'es,
but ~~they were~~ it was Cam's fault mostly, because she was older, & a
a perfect angel of goodness to the others – & the only one who was really beautiful; a little girl, & sisters ought to control their brothers, not
fight with them. Still, without being vain, she hoped
were full of promise; a perfect angel
† the children ~~did~~, on the whole, do her credit; there was Prue – she
was beautiful; Andrew – her husband thought he had an
extraordinary gift for mathematics; then Nancy & Roger – at
he was one of those boys who care for the things that aren't taught at school the moment they cared for nothing but cricket & football, but
Nancy was fond of reading too, & Roger, she believed, had a
real feeling for architecture. They went to see the city churches together;
St. Bartholomew; probably he was so bad at lessons for that
reason, which was one schoolmasters made no allowance for,
the things that interested him were not the things that people
her nose was much too big [?]
he ~~liked~~ knew all the city churches by heart; were expected to know; Then Rose – she would never be a
beauty; because her nose was too big; but she had an extraordinary
it was Rose who invented all the
gift with her hands; if they had charades, ~~she made~~ ~~wonderful~~ clothes –
head dresses out of nothing. ~~she~~ ~~Alas,~~ none of her children
had inherited any sense of tidiness, ~~&~~ & none of them had her own
grown much too fast love of music, unless it was Timothy – but Timothy, ~~like~~ had
all little boys of twelve was ~~half~~ a perfect baby &
But it must ~~was~~ most unfair to Timothy.
unfair of
did nothing but try to make steamers (~~Her hus~~band ~~said he~~
to call him Which
mess about in the pond. ~~was~~ the fool of the family. But it was nonsense. None
only
of her children were fools. ~~But~~ she ~~did~~ wish that ~~some~~
oh no – what she wished
† ~~the little one would~~ never grow up. She ~~wanted~~ always
wanted a baby ~~with~~ about the house – ~~to~~ not too heavy for
her to carry, & go to school, & come home, grown out of all
knowledge. She wanted there to be always a baby; ~~a~~
Even James was too big now for her to carry him about;
& – she could not help feeling, though her husband
~~he~~ it was foolish to think this – he ~~had~~ would never ~~be so~~
as he was now
power of being in all his life be so happy ~~as he wa~~ again: – ~~f~~ their lives
y
~~were~~ happ~~iness~~ was almost unbelievable.

† A 90; B 94

A child's power of happiness was something indescribable. Came could still be happy for days with a tenpenny tea set. It seemed to Mrs. ~~Ramsay that~~ They began early in the morning. ~~A ch sound of~~ shouting & stamping began over her head in the nursery about seven o'clock. Then they came ~~burs~~ bustling along the passages, & then the door sprang open & in they came, James royally seated in Susie's arms; Cam, plucking at her apron, ~~both so sure as if it~~

† both ~~g~~ [staring] wide awake, as if this coming into the dining room after breakfast were a positive event to them – & so on all day long; till she went up to say good night, & found them netted into their cots, like birds among cherries & strawberries, ~~still crowing & shouting with~~ flushed & mischievous, & still so ~~happy that, as she~~ entirely &

[margin: having lived one day & being about to live another that,]

† absolutely happy, that as she said to her husband, she could not bear to think they must grow up & lose it all. He ~~was could not~~ did not like her to [say that] take what he called "a gloomy view of life". ~~He With all~~ His [own] ~~apparent 'gloom'~~ for ~~all its apparent violence, was far less~~ view of life, for all the violence of his sayings, was really more cheerful than her own; more [& perhaps] robust perhaps, not that she did despair, even of some sort of final arrangement, by which the tragedies & sorrows should be made ~~up~~, good: it was only that if one did not accept the usual beliefs & if one had lived, as she had, fifty years, if ~~one saw, on the whole,~~ [had seen] something of the suffering that went on – for instance among the poor; & ~~in one had tried~~ could not altogether overcome certain, ~~well~~ Early impressions, (& now she did revisit, ~~either~~ that ~~pra~~ particular event – ~~it was nothing but a~~ young man's death; but she had which ~~with the~~ [with] in ~~the~~ her curious single mindedness she ~~had neither~~ [had] made neither into a ~~beautiful~~ beauty nor into habit: but had ~~kept it~~ [worn] sharp & uncompromising, at ~~the~~ her heart, like a hair shirt)

[margin: anyhow, making phrases was a great alleviation to him & she wished she had the power; but]

[margin: about wh people debated – had it any real existence or not? – it happened to be in [?])*]

Then, how could one be thoughtlessly,

† A 91; B 95 (1.203)

* Written in pencil

completely, rapturously happy, like those heavenly children, who
must ~~would~~ grow up & lose it all? If she could have her way ~~arrange it~~, James &
Cam should always remain like this – sitting beside her, listening to
† the story of the woodman's daughter.* ~~Indeed~~, She would like always
to have a baby: though indeed she had no right to have had
eight, considering that how much it meant ~~it meant a good deal of~~ anxiety – ~~how to~~ g
† giving all the boys a proper education – & there was the
greenhouse roof that wanted mending; & it meant that he
had to make some money every ~~year to supplement their income~~;
though she was resolved that he should never ~~desert his~~
however hard they were pressed ~~have~~ to give up his own ~~special~~ work, his philosophy – ~~that~~
pursuit of the letter Z ~~which still escaped him~~ – ~~As for~~
~~herself, she~~ For that was the most important of all things
& she could manage somehow.

† Anyhow, Minta Doyle would miss the best thing in the
whole world if she had no children. Of that Mrs. Ramsay was
positive. Argument was ~~so~~ silly – how could she ~~you~~ argue?
~~Sometimes she~~ Anyone wilfully missing or putting aside for
any reason the chance of motherhood that side of life was so ~~pita~~ profoundly to be pitied
that Mrs. Ramsay for one almost thought that the State
should make some arrangement by which every woman had
† ~~at least~~ the opportunity – ~~Only~~ But ~~sh~~ there remained
of course something else – ~~that~~ relationship of man & woman
~~which~~ of the husband & wife. Minta was perfectly right to think it over.
Nothing would induce Mrs. Ramsay to hurry her: she must
remind herself, she must curb herself, she must, whatever
happened, check that masterfulness which, she admitted
was in her, ~~here~~; ~~she must~~ ~~for once sh~~e had made a
match, & she had regretted it. It was one of the things she blamed
herself ~~for~~ was in her & had led her to make some ~~very~~ horrid [mistakes?] For instance the Parry Jacksons; ~~it~~ it had
been an unhappy marriage; & she had helped, certainly, to
make it. ~~Lily~~ Nor could she altogether acquit herself of
worldliness. He was so rich – had a great home in Somerset.
~~Could she have~~ It was in her, that vice too: not
very profoundly; but she did enjoy undoubtedly, a sense
of wordly grandeur, at moments. 'But not – thank God – not

* MS 97, 103, 104

† A 90, B 94; A 92, B 96; A 93; B 97

But there remained, of course, something else, & Minta was perfectly right to take time & Mrs. Ramsay anxiously assured made sure herself that she had not pressed her; for she was aware of her own masterfulness; & how it had led ~~her once~~ once, in the case of Alice ~~M~~ Owen, to ~~an~~ a marraige ~~results which she had nev never ceased regretting an unhappy marriage~~ — ~~w~~ — a most unhappy marriage — which was partly her doing — & she never forgave herself for it — ~~The relation of husband & wife~~ — ~~that was what the It was the taking~~ — The relationship between husband & wife — that remained. That it should be perfectly how should she put it to herself? — ~~serious~~: ~~not frivolous.~~ not momentary, not frivolous; & ~~that~~ there should ~~be respect between them~~; ~~integrity~~ on both sides; ~~for something she meant~~, ~~in the relationship which the sort of thing~~ what she had for her husband; only ~~&~~ both sides should feel ~~how for such an after all it was much~~ is the most important of human relationships - ~~so that~~ & failure there, on either side, is this was something of what she meant, so that of course Minta was perfectly right, if she had any sort of doubt, ~~on~~ not ~~account~~ to marry either for the sake of being marriages ed children, or of having home or anything, except that union, which alone, Mrs. Ramsay thought, reviewing her eight childbirths, & the worries, & the illnesses, & the boots & shoes & stockings & ~~men~~ & the greenhouse wanting mending & all the effort ~~&~~ & all the anxiety it all was; Still ~~survived, & made it even without~~ did survive (~~Everyday~~ & she never did let people staying or household bothers prevent just some half hour alone with him everyday) Still & made it seem worth while

for she had certainly influenced Alice,

For ~~that~~ there remained

respect not

but he was in many ways exceptional — one cd. not expect him to of course one could not say everything which

~~And it~~ But why had they not come back? ~~There might have been an accident~~. She saw them gathering about the front door; ~~then~~ & then there was Andrew always so set on getting what he wanted. ~~He was the~~ It was crabs — most obstinate boy He would climb out on to some rock: & then he would be cut off; ~~& then~~ or there would be one of those dangerous paths on the very edge of the cliff, which she was always terrified of. One of them would slip. For it was ever so late for them to be out, &

people might say what they liked — a man like that could not be bothered with small worries — it was not fair [on her?] †

& So, she read, without allowing her voice to change,

† A 94; B 98

| | |
|---:|---:|
| 50 | 40 |
| 4 | 4 |
| 200 | 160 |
| £10 | £8 |

~~all the bears came to the wedding, &~~
~~So~~ the little girl was carried up to bed, & fell fast asleep ~~until she~~
& dreamed of ~~the forest.~~ all night of the bears in the forest.*
And thats the end, she said, shutting the book. ~~&~~
X She must ~~face~~ get up & find out ~~about~~ ~~whether~~
The children were not anxious – Even as she ~~could hardly~~ sit still
possessed by that sudden fear, that picture of disaster, of somebody
falling, & ~~ask~~ find out; but they were not anxious <u>in the least</u>,
~~&~~ they were quite absorbed, still, by the story; both of them sitting
perfectly still & ~~looking~~ then she saw what was it? – something
extraordinarily beautiful; a sort of wonder in their faces; an
a look of awe, of rapture, as if both of them ~~had~~ they had
~~been~~ there had mingled with the dying strains of the fairy story
some new astonishing pleasure. It was the lighthouse. Yes, they
the lighthouse had been lit, & they could see it rather pale at first, in the
making its three strokes across the bay: the ~~long~~ slow one first; then the
two quick ones. But James would begin to ~~think about his~~
† ~~disappointment;~~ they were not going there, his father said;
Happily here was Mildred, come to take them to bed: before he
remembered. Off they trotted, for nobody could carry
James any~~more.~~ & Theres the lighthouse she said, ~~loo~~
Yes, it was beginning; rather pale still in the halflight; like ~~a~~
indeed it looked almost like very ~~pale~~ sun ~~beams, & it only~~ Still,
just touching the waves.

Where is he? thought Mrs. Ramsay – she looked for
her husband.

---

* MS 97, 101, 104

† A 95

(1.209)

Feb. 22nd

X

† The children were not anxious. They were absorbed still by the story. One could almost see them both pondering those last words about the little girl dreaming of the bears;* & then, as that ~~story~~ faded, ~~suddenly~~ Mrs. Ramsay saw ~~them both~~ come into their eyes some new wonder – Oh [it was] the lighthouse! Yes, they had lit the lighthouse. That – Turning she looked across the ~~B~~ bay; & there, sure enough, was that pale light, which, at the moment, one might [almost] mistake for sun[light]shine; ~~but it came & went, over the sea: first~~ only it came & went, ~~a first~~ two quick strokes & then one long steady stroke, silvering the waves faintly, for it was still light.

something pale, ecstatic

James would ~~think about~~ [begin to ask whether they were] going to the lighthouse: ~~his~~

† & they were not going to the Lighthouse: his father said it was impossible out ~~of the question~~: But happily, here was Mildred to [take in?] [off] them to bed; but ~~Cam~~ & then, she trusted [~~he~~ he wd. think eternally] he would forget all about going to the Lighthouse. But she doubted it. Children never forgot anything.

† No, t~~hey forget nothin~~g she thought, putting together some ~~of the bits of paper that were strewn about the floor~~ [pictures he had cut out], – the refrigerator, the gentleman in the yellow shirt front, the mowing machine, – & taking her knitting. They forget nothing. She sighed. [But] It was a great relief when they did go to bed. For now she ~~was~~ need not think about anybody for a moment. She could be herself, by herself; & that was what now she had ~~come~~ often felt the need of – to think, well, not even to think. ~~What then was it~~? To be alone. And as it happened that she was more often left alone in the evening, ~~the~~ it was familiar to her to [be] ~~w~~atching that lighthouse, as she was ~~sewing~~ knitt[ed]~~ing;~~ ~~& it was~~ [& it] the two quick strokes & then the long [still] stroke. ~~The~~ ~~And~~ Of the three strokes it was the ~~third~~

† really felt in sympathy with. The third stroke was

knitting, looking up from her knitting at

* MS 97, 101, 103 (1.211)

† A 94; A 95; B 99; A 96

that ~~with~~ which ~~seemed~~ to her the real one; if it could be said that one thing was more real than another thing It was

† like that – ~~quite ruthless~~, ~~quite direct~~ – ~~And~~ For she had a sense of ~~their~~ there ~~being~~ something in one, in her at least, more real most real; herself? ~~or~~ no: not the self that went about doing things; ~~& not~~ ~~but~~ not ever the self here, now, in this room; ~~yes~~, & when there was no one to be nice to; no children; no husband; for that Then ~~was~~ one was rather awful, she thought, Or was it life? but [did not, that ruthless direct stroke, that third stroke, ~~which~~ was ~~what~~

the one she was so tired of;

† the real one, & ~~as~~ one ~~did not~~ could not escape. Children never forget. What we have done, we have done. but the self which was at the beck & call – could one deny it? – of – She ~~did not know~~ never had a word for it, she was singularly dumb; she thought of it as that – there – the long third stroke ~~direct~~ ~~ruthless stroke~~ Children never forget; she knew that perfectly well; & the lighthouse had nothing to teach her about that; No. for example: she was growing old; for example: ~~&~~ they would die, & it would all be over. And ~~who was going to deny~~ Well? that? She looked over ~~the~~ her knitting. When she said to her husband, how at the back of her mind she did not despair, there was that, just that.

[enough?]

She woke up in the night & saw it stroking ~~crossing~~ the floor

Merely, she supposed, every rational person in the course of life achieves what is after all only common sense: they said

† (her mother said) We are in the hands of the Lord; She never ~~had~~ had the least inclination to say that. We are in the hands of the Lord – How could any Lord create a world of such ~~suffering~~ pain, such horrible injustice? But the Lighthouse was a ~~little~~ different. It was ~~perfectly~~ quite ruthless; ~~but it was~~ nobody had any ~~illusion~~ doubt about that; ~~but~~ it came; it went; & ~~somehow~~, as ~~one grew~~ &, flowing ~~older one learnt felt that very~~ thing ~~in ones bones~~. itself was in ones bones. It had her own expression. Her eyes she felt were full of it: ~~that~~ She was like it. It drew her to it.

For ~~when she was quite alone~~, it ~~was~~ is odd, being alone, how surprisingly strong ~~the~~ one finds ~~some~~ those almost forgotten & the perfectly foolish feelings – &

† A 96, B 100; A 97; B 101, A 98 (1.213)

† community with things which have no bearing upon one's life at all.
Flowers, yes; & some lonely places, where ~~she, who was hardly ever~~
in alone
alone, went down to drink, ~~laying aside her clothes at the river's edge,~~
ones there ones
putting off ~~the greenhouse~~ clothes, laying side clothes.
That was what she would consider, when they were all grown up; & she
how it [?]
had time. ~~Then~~ She would get it straight. She would find out what it
how there is
was, ~~to~~ this twofold nature; ~~of the other relationship; not~~
between herself
the other relationship, of mind ~~&~~ what did one call it? She

how there is one relation: James & her husband: another, herself &

† ~~held~~ stopped knitting. She gazed again, with some irony in her
interrogation, at that ~~lovely~~ cryptic light: that silent light; ~~that~~
which was silvering the waves a little more brightly, as daylight faded.
She had for it some irrational tenderness; it gave her, as it gave her
children, some queer ecstasy; ~~some &~~ the sight of ~~that~~
those lights, the two quick lights & then the long light, which
say what you like (& as for her husband, he would say, quite tenderly,
gave her
that it was nonsense) such happiness as almost transcended
worry & loss: how they had not come back: & might be killed.
† For ~~if the~~ there was no treachery too base for the world ~~not~~ to
commit: of that she was well aware. All she replied to
the worlds treachery was, (& she ~~grasped her stock~~ knitted
with her firm composure, & a little pressure of the lips)
~~But she made no reply~~. She watched the lighthouse for a
minute or two. There was no reply. For in asking this or that of
life, in praying questioning, ~~mo~~ one must have at one's command
made
language, which she had not; one must be altogether ~~made~~ differently;
[for
~~in her~~ for she never saw things, or formulated things; but
only opposed to fate, what she [~~was~~?], that she did not
by any means give way; & was able ~~to understand~~ without moving
from her chair to

† A 97; A 99, B 103; A 98, B 102 (1.215)

- not believing in inherent structure → control we are in the hands of the

of the three strokes.

† The third stroke was her stroke; but what did she mean by that? She was singularly dumb. She found herself sitting & looking, sitting & looking, until she almost became the thing she looked at. And she said to herself; Children never forget, she was growing old; I am ~~we are~~ in the hands of the Lord. it will all have to end. — But no she never said that ~~though she used those words she~~ did not mean them at all; ~~but~~ No. She was ~~much~~ felt much more in sympathy with the long third stroke, ~~which~~ she saw bent, half on the bed, half on the floor, when she woke up at night. She ~~looked up over her knitting~~. How ~~could any Lord have made a world~~ like ~~this~~? ~~And~~ ~~precise~~ly. And She looked up over her knitting, meeting the third stroke which ~~somehow~~ seemed to her like her own eyes meeting her own eyes; & ~~yet of course~~ / ~~or~~ It was odd how when one was alone, ~~some~~ one felt these leanings towards things which had no bearing in ones own life; that they expressed things in one, became part of one, ~~so that one attributed~~ how one felt ~~that~~ irrational tenderness; how one felt (~~that~~ just sitting here alone knitting) as if inside, far down, there rose up like a wraith, like a mist curling off water, some ghost, ~~some~~ bride, rising to meet the lover. She was ~~Indeed what happened was simply~~ ~~When~~ ~~She~~ She would try to get it all straight one of these days, when they were all grown up; — For ~~certainly~~ ~~there was a~~ when the children went to bed, & she sat knitting, alone; like this ~~then~~ & ~~then~~ she ~~liked~~ to be ~~sure that there was something there~~: ~~what~~ found this thing ~~in her~~; ~~she found herself~~ & as she was sitting here, she connected it naturally with the lighthouse; & ~~Often~~ things in her: & looking at the lighthouse, she ~~connected~~ it she had that queer association; no doubt some people had it, but with the light, which ~~was so~~ as it came & went, seemed to have her just seemed to her — what could she ask it? — ~~For~~ B how could any Lord have made this world? How indeed? with its vice, its torture. ~~No;~~ They had not come back. They might be killed. There was no treachery too base for the world to commit. Of that she

And the light ~~went~~ came ~~& w~~ & went; it was ruthless; it had no pity; & it ~~part~~ had become part of her thoughts †

*but the futility of the words seemed to*

& it was not that. †

for a tree, for a stream, for anything; as for oneself,

†

a lake

why one felt anything like that

s word
f oneself,
& the lover —
n between
t — &

with [?] times so
or;

She devoted great part of creating 86 life to creating She positions she thinks are just reasonable and ordered

---

* Written in pencil

† A 97, B 101; A 98; A 97; B 102

(1.217)

† ~~was aware.~~ No baseness too despicable even in men & women.
~~And their~~ [No] happiness ~~was not lasting~~ [that lasted]. ~~And they~~
She ~~turned her~~ She knitted with firm composure, slightly ~~p~~
pursing her lips, so that when Mr. Ramsay passed her, ~~he~~
though he was thinking ~~of Hume~~ & how Hume having grown
enormously [fat] stout, stuck [on] in a bog, he could not help ~~t at~~
making a note of that severity, which was part of her beauty, –
There was her [stroke] ~~light again, the third stroke~~. It was ~~the~~ long
third stroke, direct, & im – ~~And~~ she thought with a
sort of carelessness which ~~in the~~ ~~she could~~ was entirely
No ~~happiness~~ And they must die. [she thought] [Nothing she minded for herself,] For herself she
quite reckless. ~~That indeed was~~ one ~~of~~ thing that struck her –
probably if it were not for the children, she was
reckless: ~~rather~~ unscrupulous, as in this matter of arranging
marriages; ~~& rather~~ intolerant of restriction ~~If she had been rich~~
If she had had more money – if she had been for example, Lady So & [So –
† She stopped knitting. She gazed with some irony in her
interrogation, some veiling of the eye, at that ~~cry~~ steady
light, that remorseless light, ~~which however was so~~
~~searching, so pure & its~~ which was so much her; ~~And yet~~
& so little her at the same ~~time~~; had her at its beck & call,
perhaps; but for all that she ~~was extremely conscious~~ – she
thought watching it [~~I dont~~] silvering the waves a little more she did not find it [easy to give in – watching it
brightly as daylight faded – she ~~never~~ could ~~not~~
~~a~~ abdicate ~~her own power, as some people could, she~~
she never did submit: ~~her own~~ she ~~was not~~ did not find it
easy to give way – & ~~her~~ it came & rolling ~~pur~~
† waves of pure lemon, lovely & ethereal, upon the beach.
~~For~~ ~~And yet~~ [For they] it distressed ~~him,~~ Mr. Ramsay, passing again –
~~not her she~~ not that her temperament ~~was~~ ~~should~~ had part in
~~among oth with all its simple~~ [in] he ~~found tinged with~~ [it] [that severity] melancholy
But he felt that he would** not like to interrupt her: there
are moments of ~~great~~ estrangement: the ~~fits of~~ irritability

[Margin: the soul of it, the flame. Yet it distressed him.]

[Margin: how reckless she cd. [have?] [been?]]

[Margin: she did not scorn envy*]

---

* Written in pencil (1.219)

** 'Could' appears to have been changed to 'would.' Cf line 3, MS 109.

† A 98; A 99, B 103; A 100, B 104

beauty in her mind but

It awed him; it saddened him; he was

& all its beauty ~~was~~ burnt in her, as in her childrens eyes; such ecstasy
~~there was for her & such irra~~tional joy. of joy, or from wonder at beauty
† between them. She passed sometimes out of his reach. He[w] could not
like to interrupt her For him, there was something awful, suddenly, in
Nor could ~~he reach~~ her, nor save her, nor protect her even from the
negation of his own miserable importunities: his demands; his
irritability. Hume stuck in a bog & an old woman ~~only~~
† rescued him on condition he said the Lords Prayer.
He snorted out his sudden laugh as he passed her He was not sure
how far that story would go down at Cardiff. He would ask ~~his wife~~ her.
But he would ~~take her hand~~ & put it to his lips, with his
extraordinary charm, his extreme sympathy, ~~asking her, to~~
fo~~rgive him, saying to her~~ his directness which disarmed her always,
& ~~that~~ what could he putting his lips to her hand, he
whether she thought that Mrs. Bowley ~~was~~ would be shocked
(For they were staying with the Bowleys at Cardiff)

"Hume grew to be very fat, &

† A 98, B 102; A 111, B 116

† It distressed him; it saddened him, Mr. Ramsay thought, passing a second time. He could not save her; he could not protect her not even from his own miserable irritability. He \had\ been ~~annoyed~~ foolishly irritated about the Lighthouse.

[margin: the spasms of]

† But then if his house was made absolutely intolerable to him by the presence of Bankes & that young woman, Lily Briscoe, at every corner, ~~But it~~ He became absorbed in his own thoughts. He had ~~this these~~ his lectures to write. "And Hume, grown very fat stuck in a bog & an old woman rescued him on condition he said the Lord's Prayer" – He drew up, & snorting a queer snort of laughter, beside the window, wanting ~~He wanted~~ to ask ~~her~~ his wife if he could tell that story at Cardiff. ~~But~~ But – as even Lily Briscoe allowed, in ~~her w~~ those moments of violent irritation with Mr. Ramsay which, occurring at breakfast for example, when he behaved with more than usual blindness to the feelings of others, when he was more than usually bleak, cutting & disagreeable – so that her egg spoon trembled in her hand, & she flushed with anger – ~~if she, &~~ even she, at that moment had to admit (~~if~~ directly she looked up) that ~~he was~~ there was a scrupulosity about him: he never ~~devoured you~~; overcame your privacy: but on the contrary, had some [sort of ~~even in~~ perfect manners; not politeness; but ~~integrity~~, ~~breeding~~ (only it was difficult to find words for what she meant, sure that she could have gone to him ~~for~~ in a crisis – say, if she wished to become a Roman Catholic ~~2~~ & he would have respected her personality –) so now, ~~but,~~ ~~though~~

[margin: he cd. not help showing it]

† though he wished to speak to ~~her,~~ his wife he did not like to interrupt her. He could not protect her, alas. And it was Mrs. Ramsay who looked at him; Mrs. Ramsay whose lips parted; as she resumed her knitting & Mrs. Ramsay who returned ~~, &~~ to him, & resumed intercourse with him

† A 98, B 102; A 99; A 111, B 116; A 100, B 104 (1.223)

of her own free will, oh yes; for he was wanting her to come out into the garden with him, wanting her, but would not ~~for an instant~~ break in upon her solitude; if she ~~would not claim anything~~; & had been a little irritable, about ~~the Light~~ going to the Lighthouse.

knew that he could not protect her,

XI

To save going upstairs she pulled the green shawl off the easel, &, wrapping it round her, took his arm for a stroll. It was a question what she meant to do about the flowers next year – & whether ~~to employ that~~ go on employing Kennedy, the whose beauty was great, but whose industry was /she feared getting smaller & smaller And it was a question ~~too~~ about the dear ~~[illegible]~~ Rowleys at Cardiff, whether they would be shocked if he ~~r~~ stayed at an Inn; ~~for when he~~ & ~~not with them~~, to avoid the intolerable boredom of their ~~evening parties~~ domestic evenings; ~~& also~~ it was a question whether it was ~~safe~~ ~~were~~ good to let Timothy have an air gun. ~~It was a horrible instinct, but Mr. Ramsay said, he~~ Mr. Ramsay said; he had rather not forbid a boy; he had rather he found out ~~for himself~~. humaner ways for himself. ~~Then~~ Was William Bankes planted on them for ever? Then Poor Carmichael seemed tolerably cheerful, though it might be better not to enquire the causes of his cheerfulness. Opium, said Mrs. Ramsay, would have been her refuge had she married Mrs. Carmichael; if not worse. Then there was poor Tansley. The children had a nickname for him – "the atheist". It was ~~fairly obvious that he was not popular~~. ~~but for what reason~~? ~~She had him a little on her conscience~~, ~~Mrs. Ramsay said~~. The Atheist – the little atheist – He was not a polished specimen, said Mr. Ramsay: She supposed it was all right.

† gardener

better ways of employing himself

for some unknown reason.

† B 105, A 101

said, Mrs. Ramsay, leaving him to his own devices? He had his dissertation to write, said Mrs. Ramsay. She ~~had heard~~ [knew about that] a good deal about <u>that</u>, [said] Mrs. Ramsay, said. rather significantly; But then, said Mr. Ramsay, it was all he had to count on. At any rate, Prue would not marry him If she did, he would disinherit her tomorrow, said Mr. Ramsay, but added that there was no harm in the youth: he was not prepossessing. ~~But~~ [&] as he was the only young man [about] who ~~was so~~ was so deluded as to read [admire] his – Mr. Ramsays – books. But it was a question of Kennedy, the gardener – She could never be sure that he planted the bulbs she sent him. Resolved not to ~~worry~~ [bother] her with his own affairs again, ~~Mr. R~~ & priding himself for his forbearance, Mr. Ramsay observed that the hot pokers seemed creditable. But then Mrs. Ramsay had planted the hot pokers with her own hands. If she stood over him with a spade all day long he occasionally did do something. She was teaching her daughters to exaggerate, ~~he said.~~ Mr. Ramsay said. Mrs. Ramsay ~~owned that she had~~ said that ~~it~~ her ~~great~~ Aunt Camilla was far worse than she was. But nobody ever held up / [her] Aunt Camilla as a model of virtue, said Mr. Ramsay. ~~Well~~, she was the most beautiful woman of her time, said Mrs. Ramsay. ~~Nonsense~~ [Nonsense] Her daughter would be far more beautiful than she was, said Mrs. Ramsay. He could see no trace of that ~~whatever~~, said Mr. Ramsay. ~~Andrew is~~ How proud they would be when Andrew was senior wrangler, said Mrs. Ramsay. She had better not fix her ~~heart~~ thoughts upon that said Mr. Ramsay (But it was he who dreamt of it all night long) she [not] ~~thought examinations so silly~~ – she thought examining boys ~~simply~~ idiotic. ~~But~~ [only that she] presumably ~~if you~~ [when] had universities, [[was?] for] you had to do it.

Margin notes:

† said Mrs. Ramsay stopping to consider her dahlias.

† He should look at Prue tonight then, said Mrs. Ramsay.

† A 102; B 106; A 103, B107

Her folly really passed belief, said Mr. Ramsay. If Andrew got a scholarship, either at Balloil or at Trinity it would be something to be proud of. The idea of being proud of him because he got a scholarship! – she was proud of him ~~just~~ as he was.

Did he not think it very late – rather late – for ~~those~~ them
still ~~young~~ ~~people~~ to be out? ~~She w~~ she asked. ~~Might~~
pained ~~Might he~~ He was a little ~~saddened~~ worried. It was not reasonable of her to be so anxious. And he wished to tell her, when he was walking on the terrace ~~he thought she looked so sad~~.

† he did not like to see her looking – so – sad

~~Oh~~ I was half asleep – wool gathering, she said.

& standing in the gap between the hot pokers they looked at the Bay

† A 104, B 108

She refuses to say "I love you"



he began again—

~~how~~ it had pained him — just now on the terrace — that she should look [~~so~~ sad ~~sad;~~ But she was only woolgathering she said flushing a little, after reading fairy tales to the children. He did not like her so She should not look sad; he repeated; but not that he meant quite that he did not mean sad; & she knew that he did not mean sad: ~~quite what he said~~, but ~~that he could not~~ She had not been exactly sad. Had she known that he was looking at her, she thought, she would never have been thinking about such things —

how did he ~~know~~ explain why she should not do it why it pained him;

There was the Lighthouse again, for they had reached the gap between the red hot pokers, ~~whose~~ There was the Bay & the There were the sandhills. And there, on the left the ~~little fishing town was~~ lights of the town ~~were lit~~ — ~~here & there,~~ rippling & running, as if they were water in a wind. drops of silver water which were held firm. ~~above the roofs~~ up almost And all the torture, all the vice, Mrs. Ramsay thought, looking at the town & thinking of the old woman dying there, had turned to silver lights; & there was nothing to mark all that ~~she knew of~~ the poverty ~~&~~ the vice & the hardness of their lives — but those lights which, rising into the air, & suspended above the houses, ~~marked~~ seemed like ~~the net of a city~~ soul the a symbol, ~~a~~ phantom; the thing which rises from the ~~body, & is as~~ like a ~~net floating~~ a starry net floating there to mark the position of the little town.

the little streets; the hot bedrooms;

There was no reason whatever to be anxious, said † Mr. Ramsay. At Andrews age, he used to walk all day with nothing but a biscuit in his pocket. Mrs. Ramsay said that she could ~~quite~~ believe him capable of any such absurdity. He was still capable of almost any absurdity. ~~He had~~ ~~But she~~ knew that he was growing old. ~~He~~ & he knew it, ~~&~~ but would not allow it. He would not ~~But~~ He ~~was~~ was nettled at the thought that he was growing old. He ~~would~~ could put a biscuit in his pocket, walk all day still he said. But he knew that he would never do that again: & it annoyed him; it angered him; that

† A 105, B 109

for wet boots &

never a human being to interrupt you all day long. Where you could

~~There~~ was the ~~sea, breaking~~ little sandy beach where ~~in even~~ no one had been since the beginning of the world

She did not even contradict him. for She knew it would never do it. She prevented him; she restrained him. For years ago ~~he had been~~ before he married, he had been reckless. Had he cared then whether he sat down soaked to his bread & cheese? Had he cared ~~for~~ how ~~long he~~ [had far he went, or ~~how~~ whether he worked all night or not? There, on the far side of the bay, dwindling away into darkness, where the sandhills. There was the lonely country he loved best. ~~Those h~~ with never a house or a signpost or a village; nothing ~~but tracks over the hills, & so that you~~ walk a whole day without meeting a soul. ~~And suddenly,~~ We know nothing, he ~~sai~~ automatically murmured to himself, ~~for~~ & & seemed to be standing again on the familiar [?] spit of land of the which the sea eats away. We are a stand on the edge of a precipice ~~looking into the abyss~~. he murmured; ~~but~~ in his abstraction without meaning it, he ~~could~~ whispered said the last words "the edge of a precipice" above his breath; & instantly repented. He had no right. She was there. The parents of eight

† children, he ~~recalled~~ recollected; of eight sons & daughters – & ~~had no~~ have no choice. They would see to it, he thought; meaning that they at least – his Andrew & his Prue & all the rest of them, not least that obstinate little beggar James ~~with his~~ would somehow put off the day of reckoning would ~~stave~~ stem the flood a bit; ~~would~~ were the best token he could give – they could give – his wife & himself – that they did not damn the poor little universe entirely; this poor speck of matter; this little crag, ~~with~~ girt by floods; for one reason why he loved ~~Finlay was that~~ these remote islands was that ~~this poor little island~~. ~~Indeed he could be~~ ~~It~~ They had a pathetic smallness, on an evening like this. The little island seemed ~~vanish~~ swallowed up in the sea. "Poor little town," he murmured looking at the village,

"On the edge of a precipice", Mr. Ramsay thought. He said the most melancholy things & ~~always~~ ~~he~~, she noticed, directly he had said them, he was always particularly cheerful. ~~He seemed always to be playing a game~~ – It was like a game to him But she ~~liked~~ enjoyed his games ~~– she~~ & she believed in them odd as they were; she believed that he was And after all they agreed on the most important points. ~~Al~~ All this

† A 106, B 110

phrase making, for if ~~she had said what he~~ he had believed what he said, he should have shot himself long ago. ~~But he~~ as it was, he seemed to become more cheerful. He ought to be ashamed of himself, she said, ~~It was a~~ to stan~~d there, on a night like this~~, ~~to complain on a night like this~~, to talk of precipices on a night like this, & all the children well; & so good; & so full of promise.

† They turned away from the view, & began to walk up the ~~drive, w~~ path ~~which~~ was ~~bordered with silvery green thick leaved plants,~~
by the flower beds where there green ~~clumps~~ of spear like plants,
with
& soft ~~bones of~~ footstools of dull purple ~~flowering~~ between
them; ~~& behind on the top of the bank~~ & on the top of the grassy
particularly sparely branched [gently?] [round?]
ill-kempt bank, tall ~~rather~~ wind-scourged trees their lean [?]
~~He had not~~ ~~She should not listen to him, he said irritably~~.
that she should
He did not mind her overhear~~ing~~ him; ~~for~~ should
guessed
She had ~~retrieved~~ his thought, & answered it;
did He wd. be an ungrateful brute if he did,
He was not complaining of his lot: he said. On the whole the world he said.
had treated him very well. ~~He~~ He had married her.

~~They~~ He did not despair, so long as there was any fight left in him.

He ~~might be~~ might be p~~ast some things; he thought~~, but he
had still a lot of fight left in him. he could still use his brains,
& he ~~held~~ & straightened his stoop,
as for the matter of that his fists very ~~sa~~ efficiently; &
as they walked by the bank up the tennis lawn, Mrs.
felt how muscular his arm was;
Ramsay ~~felt~~ thought how young he was still: how
he was
untamed; ~~how~~ optimistic, though that was the last word
people would have used of him; how exhilarated by the prospect of
these lectures, & a hard winter's work; how c~~ontroversy delighted him~~,
seemed to
& how to ~~do p~~ be convinced of all the things of which he
was convinced – ~~the~~ about God, about Hell, & ~~about~~ ignorance
~~fol~~ human idiocy – k~~ept him extr~~ did not depress him, as
but rather enlivened him.
one might have expected. Was it not odd she reflected; yes, he
other pe
often seemed to her made differently from ~~anyone else~~; born
blind & deaf & dumb to half the things most people cared for.
on ~~the other hand~~, did he notice the flowers? No. Did he
notice the view? No. Did he ~~notice~~ even ~~care for~~
notice
notice his ~~da~~ own daughter's beauty, or whether it was
fine or wet? ~~was he not always absorbed in his some~~
He would sit at table with them all round him & ~~not~~ seem to
talk to him
~~say things to himse~~lf. The habit was growing on him, she feared –
& she must make a point, though it annoyed him, of

The things wished to
pretended
When he ~~wished~~ that he had not said
answering what he said. ~~But with it all~~, It was all distinctly
† uncomfortable sometimes – But then Mrs. Ramsay thought, intimating
by pressing his arm, that she ~~wished~~ must stop for a moment
were
to see whether those ~~horrid moles were~~ fresh molehills on the
bank – then, she thought, ~~he~~ gr~~eat minds are must be~~
a ~~man with~~ a great mind like his, must be different. ~~He was~~
Her husband was a great man, she thought. ~~But~~ It might be a
if he
~~Kn~~ Kennedy must put up netting.
rabbit that had got in; & he would destroy all her plants, &
of ~~his greatness, she had not the least doubt; nor of the~~
He was a great man, & therefore must be different. All
All the great men she had ever known were like that.
~~She could remember~~ any ~~And~~ one could not expect
man
~~little~~ And he was great. And though she ~~had a~~ sometimes laughed,
import
Oxford & Cambridge were very serious things, she knew: & she
su~~ppose~~d degrees did matter, ~~of~~ course; & though she sometimes
grudged these journeys to Cardiff & places, yet she knew,
there
was good for the young men merely to see a man like her
to lecture
husband; to ~~see anybody~~ & ~~that he~~ ~~should~~ hear ~~him to~~
about
~~his views on~~ Locke, Berkeley & Hume – It was right; it was
good. Without shooting rabbits, how was one to keep
them down? she wondered. And observed above the thin
trees the exquisite silver moon; ~~which~~ but she said
nothing about it to her husband. for one thing because
she could not describe the pleasure it gave her –
& then again, it would not give him pleasure, to look at
cd. not resist showing
He might begin to talk about death.
the moon; He But she would have him notice the
Evening Primroses; "Very fine" he said, abstractedly, but
to please her, stopp~~ed & fingered one~~; & pretended to look at them
~~one of them~~; as he would pretend sometimes that he had liked a
dress of hers, or had noticed some arrangement in the house.
† Ah, but he was a great man; & that was William Bankes
walking ~~Here was~~ up & ~~down~~ the lawn with Lily Briscoe,
she made out, focussing her shortsighted eyes upon the
backs of the retreating couple. I ~~think there is~~ She foretold
this ~~a~~ marriage.
It would be a most
admirable arrangement

Hume & the old lady*

XIII**

* Written in pencil (1.239)

** VW corrects her misnumbering on the next page.

† A 108, B 112; A 109, B 113

XII.

Mr. Bankes was saying that he had been to Amsterdam. He had seen the Rembrandts. He had been to Madrid. Unfortunately, it was Good Friday, & he had not seen the Prado. He had been to Rome. Had Miss Briscoe never been to Rome? Oh she should try to go to Rome. It would be a wonderful experience for her – the Sistine Chapel; Michael Angelo: & Siena, with its ~~car~~ Giottos. His wife having been a ~~great invalid, &~~ in bad health for so many years, their sightseeing had been on a modest scale; ~~but~~ She had been to Brussels; she had been to Paris; but only for a flying visit; she had been to Dresden, said Lily.

one so depressed with one's own work

† But perhaps it was better not to see pictures, she said. They made ~~it seem~~ one's own pictures seem so foolish. But Mr. Bankes thought one might carry that point of view to excess.

† We cannot all be Darwins or Titians. On the other hand your Darwin ~~is~~ depends to some extent upon your ~~little~~ nonentity who has done the spade work for him. Whether that applied to art, Mr. Bankes could not say. Lily ~~thought that~~ said that anyhow ~~it made no difference~~ – one could always go on painting. Mr. Bankes was about to ask her whether she had ~~much~~ difficulty in finding subjects in London – when they reached the end of the lawn, & turned, & saw the Ramsays.

"~~Well~~, said Lily, observing the Ramsays, "in the winter one ~~either did can~~ do sketches –"

Mrs. Ramsay was wearing ~~that~~ a green shawl; & ~~she was~~ holding it her husbands arm ~~up with one~~ hand, ~~so that it fell in folds, which being quite accidental,~~ ~~she~~ it ~~fell in folds~~; ~~& was somehow~~ the whole group (they had paused to look at ~~Prue & Jasper, tossing catches~~) wore for a second some pair of them, coming slowly up the drive, arm in arm,

gently talking; stopping here to look at some flower, ~~& had~~
suddenly took on in Lily's eyes ~~that~~ the majesty which ~~suddenly~~, for
† no reason, ~~human beings~~ sometimes in a the lift of a tube,
sometimes pausing to open a door, one knows not when or why,
descends on people, magnifying them, solemning them, & endowing
the relation in which they stand at the moment, rising in the
life, opening the door or stopping as the Ramsays now stopped
to watch Prue & Timothy throwing catches, with all the
~~meaning of~~ ~~meaning of all~~ ~~all the~~ a ~~giant~~ gigantic ~~meaning~~ stature –
Crucified, & transcendent, ~~blessing the world~~, or
with ~~gestures of blessing a~~ with symbolical meaning.

stand

† with ~~some~~ symbolical majesty. It was now the ~~st~~ married state: the being husband & wife; which rising [& encircling] from them, made them so solemn, & so in their unconsciousness – for they were looking at Prue throwing catches – so awe inspiring & moving to the emotions, so that Lily thought how she saw now what Mrs. Ramsay meant about marriage; it was just that attitude of a woman & man looking together at ~~catches~~ a girl throwing a ball: [who] & suddenly the symbolical figure sank back [retreat [within?]] into them; & they became, as they reached them, Mr. & Mrs. Ramsay again – ~~Mr. Ramsay~~, ~~too, quite openly~~ Mr. & Mrs. Ramsay watching the children, who had finished their cricket, throwing catches. And if Mrs. Ramsay was amused, as Lily guessed, & came to her own inevitable conclusion, about her & William Bankes, still the ~~evening~~ [moment] was extraordinarily ~~random~~ random & irresponsible – with the ball soaring up, them all following it with their eyes, & at the same time seeing that one star, & ~~then~~ ~~the a~~ & the bare branched trees. ~~A~~ In the failing light they looked ~~pale &~~ aetherial, & sharpedged; they looked ~~as if~~ spectral; the swallows swooped low; & now with a dull thud, some ~~door~~ dor beetle struck the net which enclosed the lawn; or ~~whz~~ whizzed past her cheek. Nothing mattered in the least. And ~~if this lovely~~ [in] irresponsible beauty [moment] could ~~be induced to~~ stay, with its moths & its evening primroses its tennis balls & girls & boys staggering back looking upward, ~~its~~ sudden sharp ~~cries, its thuds, & whizzes~~, & its vast spaces between one figure & another, ~~then~~ for they seemed all far removed from each other, then nothing would matter ever again – [everything seemed possible – nothing mattered –] ~~The wildness the~~ ~~It was wild; it was impulsive~~; ~~However~~ [And], Prue ~~caught the ball, brilliantly; & running~~ ran full tilt at them & caught the ball brilliantly, ~~&~~ in one hand; & her mother ~~said~~, asked her,

"Haven't they come back yet?"

† Did Nancy go with them?" her mother asked.

[Left margin notes:]

the encircling haze ~~so~~ shot itself up in them

(I have triumphed tonight" said Mrs. Ramsay meaning that William Bankes had agreed to dine with them)

I have triumphed

& all the natural world with its [ ? ], light had lapsed had relinquished its grasp: one had come

## XIII

(Certainly Nancy had gone with them, since Minta Doyle had asked it, in ~~words~~ ~~which~~ with her dumb look, ~~gazing~~ which sounded so strangely in Nancy's heart; so she had dropped her mallet & gone, feeling [~~?~~] ten years older, the companion of grown ~~up~~ people. & so had trudged along the road, up onto the cliff; & Minta had kept on ~~snat~~ taking her hand. Then she would let it go. Then she would take it again. But what did she want, Nancy wondered; & felt the whole world spread out beneath her; as, from ~~a mist~~ mist, some strange city, say Constantinople, rises beneath one,

† & one asks, is that Santa Sofia? – so ~~she~~ Nancy asked, ~~is that~~ when Minta took her hand & let it go, so quickened her vision so that her life seemed to lie before her – What does she want? – & here & there, emerg~~ing~~ed from the mist of her own future a ~~tower~~ a pinnacle, a dome; ~~was it~~ ~~something~~ ominous ~~which~~ & she

† when they ran down the hill side, the pinnacle, the dome disappeared again, in the mist & only ~~a disquiet~~ some disquiet ~~emotion~~ remained a roughness with

was it that? ~~wh~~ & what was that?

She was a fine walker, unimpeded by skirts. ~~She wore~~ Minta would ~~wade~~ stride into the middle of a stream; but while her rashness endeared her to Andrew, ~~he could~~ see that it would not ~~always~~ he cd. see do. She would kill herself one of these days. But the way she dressed was awfully sensible – ~~And~~ if one wanted an image for her, what could be better than the little yellow gorse flower, ~~with its~~ smooth & warm – silky with its nut like smell? She was silky, ~~somehow~~ & warm; audacious; & nutty; & had no sort of fear, ~~Had she not~~ ~~Either for bulls~~, except ~~for~~ of bulls. She ran at the sight of one, but as for minding owning up to it, she did not in the least Or to tears; or to enthusiasm; or to the desire which would

† come upon her, as now on the cliff, to sing. ~~It was~~ a wailing ~~unhappy~~ song she sang when they were all four ~~dangling~~ sitting on the cliff, watching the ships out at sea.

a comic loud [some?] song,

~~Paul Rayley had lit his pipe.~~ She wanted them all

† B 117; A 113; B 118

to join in – ~~to~~ but they could not sing, & Paul Rayley was smoking – &
† they must not dawdle too long, or the tide would be in, which was fatal.

"Fatal?" said ~~Na~~ Minta.

"~~Quite~~ fatal" said Paul Rayley, who had a better grasp than she had of the possibilities of ~~catching marine crabs~~ & making a good bag of ~~those~~ crabs & so on; "the marine curiosities for which these islands are justly celebrated" as the guide book had it.

So they pulled her up; & Andrew

† A 114 (1.249)

who was always capping Andrews quotations from the guide book ~~about~~
to the Hebrides – "these islands are justly celebrated for their park
like effects, & for ~~the~~ while ~~the marine curiosities are equally~~
~~they are remarkable for~~ the for the extent & variety of their
marine curiosities". So ~~quoting the guide book, & in~~
~~the highest spirits which roused Andrew's suspicions slightly,~~
~~for there it would not do, to this rout of shoutings~~
But it would not do altogether, this shouting & damning your eyes;
Andrew felt: picking his way down the path in front of them;
~~the~~ & the sudden friendliness, the clapping him on the back, the
calling him old fellow, the laughing too easily, all this would not
altogether do, was the worst of taking Rayley & Minta Doyle,
on
in an expedition together. So indeed, they separated;
it came about somehow. They said they were going to explore
the caves; but as 'the marine curiosities for which these
islands are justly celebrated are found only ~~out~~ on rocks
~~which the sea comes~~ ~~exposed to the~~ covered at high tide,
he was not going in to the caves; but taking off his socks he
out on to
rolled them up in his boots & set off barefoot; ~~over~~ the pope's nose
~~rocks~~. Nancy ~~would follow; but she but first she~~ wanted ~~to~~ first to
find shells; pointed shells ~~with green~~ lights in them to
~~stick on boxes;~~ or glass; or veined stones; or cowries, perhaps,
for Cam's collection. ~~but she scrambled~~ too, to ~~Andrews~~
the ~~big rock~~, w Then, if Andrew did the Popes Nose, she would
do the Devil's hoof ~~–~~ so they called it; ~~&~~ for
then she searched too into the deep ~~little~~ rock pools,
where the sea anemones flowered, the red & the yellow,
† streaming their tentacles in the ~~deep~~ current of the deep inland
sea, ~~when~~ where swam the whales & the sharks, she thought,
converting the pool into the depths of the ocean;
covering its sky with her hand so as to bring disaster –
† desolation, ~~to its~~ & then uncovering it to let the sun
beat down. She ~~But there~~ Once on the top of the

† B 119; A 115 (1.251)

Dobreé

Doyle

Vita

Bea Howe

V.W.

Mew

Siegfried*

* Bonamy Dobrée, Camilla Doyle, Vita Sackville-West, Bea Howe, (1.252) Virginia Woolf, Charlotte Mew, Siegfried Sassoon. The first five names (written in pencil) are those of writers whose works were published by or considered for publication by the Hogarth Press. 'Doyle' could refer to John Doyle, the pseudonym under which Robert Graves published *The Marmosite's Miscellany* (Hogarth Press 1925). VW met Charlotte Mew and Siegfried Sassoon in 1924, but the press did not publish their works. (See *Letters* III and *A Checklist of the Hogarth Press* (Hogarth Press, 1976).)

~~something extraordinary appeared,~~ wonderful [marlins?] appeared – she [shouted
for Andrew. He told her to mark the place; he would come over in
their highstepping legs, their fringes, their gauntlets, their [purple?] half a jiffy. But they slid into crevices & scaled [marlins?]
all fresh & glowing with their extravagant eccentricity &
shrank silently
~~charm, something~~ fantastic & high stepping – they retreated, ~~in~~ &
Nancy marking the crevice where he had disappeared,
watched from her rock that slightly irregular line of the
[?]
horizon: the wavering the stems ~~which~~ were the smoke of steamers; & so
being was overcome with the power of the waves, & their sullenness &
~~their indifference~~. ~~As they she thought, nobody had ever been~~
~~been~~ breaking round her. As she thought, this would go on;
go on for ever & ever; the waves breaking, & ~~swirling into the~~
booming in the caves. Filled with scorn & the
sweeping savagely up & then inevitably withdrawing.
As she thought, this would go on, go on for ever & ever. ~~What~~

Andrew shouted to her to get back to the beach, as
the sea was coming in. So she took off her shoes &
stockings took off the shoes & stockings of this negligible &
phantom,
evanescent spirit; & as she rolled the stockings & put
them in the shoes, she felt the sea in her heart; the content of
in her mind / in her veins; &
the sea; & ~~its~~ the power of the sea; & the nothingness ~~of life; & her own~~
power to ~~ride the bestride the universe~~; of the terror of life; & the
horror of life; & the life; & so stepped through the water on ~~the~~ to
† the shingle; & there – there they ~~we behind the rock~~ kissing behind
Paul Rayley & Minta Doyle were kissing. And Andrew
spot
[shouted?], had she marked her ~~rock~~? & they went out
He had seen it too: & seen enough. They shared the horror in silence. again to look for the fringed gauntletted, high stepping fish:
It must have been some sort of crayfish he said. He had
But too
some He had seen it too – people kissing – & so, ~~letting~~
~~after~~ as the fish would not come out, & they both felt
† awkward, & silent, & the waves seemed to Nancy sullener than ever,
more tremendous. And ~~she had~~ against the waves she had the
pitted the ferocity of man; the lust & the warmth;
the ravening & the cruelty: nothing
beautiful remained ~~of it~~ of it.

---

† B 120; A 116 (1.253)

Raw & protruberent the domes & pinnacles of life pricked through the [mist. And yet the waves splashed in; only the force wh. had been in them, was now divided against them; there was doom, & there was effort. She was on the side of the sea

~~But what with~~ It was not ~~late so late when they got up again on to the cliff~~; but until they got up again onto the cliff that Minta discovered how she had lost her grandmother's brooch. – Her grandmother's brooch – the sole ornament she possessed. ~~It was~~ a pearl brooch, oblong, set round a weeping willow landscape & her grandmother had always worn it to fasten her little lace cap. And she had lost it. Tears streamed from her eyes. They all went back. Paul Rayley searched desperate, ~~serious~~, determined, where they had been sitting. All this tension & seriousness about a pearl brooch, did not do at all, Andrew thought, compelled to ~~be~~ † search thoroughly "between that point & this ~~point~~" as Paul Rayley said making a ~~serious~~ perfect pother about it; And the sea was coming in would be in, over the place where they had sat, would cover the whole rock; "We shall be cut off" said Minta suddenly cried terrified; – as if there were any danger of that; ~~But as Andrew~~ as Andrew thought. ~~Then~~ & The men took counsel together, (Andrew became excessively manly) & decided they would plant Paul's stick a stick on the spot; then & come back at dawn. ~~So Minta was told~~, & still she [?] wept for the loss of her brooch & wept, ~~Nancy~~ & for some other loss ~~she wept;~~ as Nancy felt; – & † Paul comforted her; saying that he would be ~~up at dawn~~, – ~~would~~ tell the police about it, & be up at dawn, & this so ~~comfo~~ by degrees cheered Minta, & ~~certainly~~ it † cheered Paul, ~~who~~ & slowly he began fingering some ~~those~~ astonishing possessions – life, & being loved, & telling people about it. & its being declared to the world; & all he would do for her; & being married; & then children, & everything everything always together – ~~so he went on~~, until he had no

[Left margin notes:]
always till the day she died

She burst into tears. She implored them† to find it;

& Yet it was half pleasure, Nancy felt; she [liked?] [losing] that [brooch?] wh. was half pleasant There was not the least danger of that, Now it was [useless trying long?]

& always had found things,

notion what was happening to them exactly, or that the world could contain such feelings as his. To be believed in – & to be made one of: ~~to fin~~ he vowed he would be up at three & find her brooch, & put it on her plate; & take the boat to Edinburgh & buy another; ~~or somehow~~ prove to her what he could do for her. ~~And there~~ And this mingled with the ~~sudden~~ sprinkled lights coming out on the edge of the bay; bright, ~~clear sparkling~~, ~~rippling~~ with divine laughter & constant joy – this mingled with that, & light again he thought, as the some they came out on the road ~~of the~~ where it was lonely & brown-shaded, how awful the retreat was into themselves, into solitude, & bare existence together, ~~man~~ two human beings alone; ~~passing~~ walking along this road. But he would protect her; he would be up at dawn & † find her brooch; & the one person he ~~would~~ would tell was Mrs. Ramsay. Yes, Mrs. Ramsay. ~~He would go straight~~ to her. Telling her was his reward, for it had been positively awful – asking Minta to marry him: far the worst ~~thing he had ever~~ done in his life: it was far worse than any examination: ~~&~~ but he had won. And / ~~he would tell~~ Mrs. Ramsay. Tears rose in his eyes. He knew why Minta had cried. ~~It is~~ half pain, he noted; this ~~extreme~~ happiness is the most serious thing in the whole † world [but happy in?] Was it not through It was all Mrs. Ramsay that all this had come to him? ~~She had~~ It is Mrs. Ramsay who ~~was the~~ had taught him how feelings – how one may have feelings – She ~~had them~~ – these queer feelings – she had them, he knew; & He had felt her eyes on him all day long: ~~she was the presiding saint~~ her eyes One had saints. ~~But~~ Could one tell her what she had done for him – a ~~stubborn~~ an odious little ~~ass, of n thinking no end of himself,~~ man & no one caring a straw for him, until she took him up – All that was good in both of them they owed – Minta owed it too. And

[Left margin notes:]

of the town on the sea.

with ~~great~~ high ~~bushe~~ hedges

walking on & on ~~& on~~ alone along the road

Minta had not been crying for her brooch [if he?] knew.

following him; resting on him.

he cd. [himself?]

† B 123; A 119

so they reached the lane up to Finlay. ~~It~~ was awfully late, probably. One could tell that by the lights in the bedroom windows. & it must be late, with the lights in the windows. Burn, he said; blaze; make a hole in the the night, ~~brave lights;~~ & they were her eyes, ~~only~~ & her childrens, eyes ~~burning in in all their chambers;~~ & † which seemed to him ~~to~~ burning there, blazing there. But goodness knew, he didn't want to make a fool of himself.

† B 124

March 5th*

XIV**

† Well, then, ~~she supposed~~ [~~Mrs. Ramsay~~], Nancy had gone with them; Mrs. Ramsay supposed, wondering, as she ~~surv~~ ~~considered~~ which put down a brush, took up a comb, & said 'Come in' to ~~the little~~ a tap at the door, (Timothy & Rose came in) whether the fact that Nancy was with them made it less likely that anything would happen: somehow it was ~~not less~~ [less] likely that four people would be [drowned ~~at once~~ than three

Timothy & Rose said Mildred wanted to know whether she should wait dinner.

"Not for the Queen of England" said Mrs. Ramsay emphatically.

† "Not for the Emperor of Mexico" she added.

And if Timothy liked, while Rose took the message, he might choose which jewel she was to wear; for after all, where there are fifteen people sitting down to dinner, it is ~~quite~~ out of the question waiting – keeping things hot is tiresome enough. And it seemed to Mrs. Ramsay, now that she was active, that these people were only inconsiderate, not tragic, thinking † ~~nothing mattered~~ [it did not matter how late they were,], though, in fact, she particularly wished dinner to be nice, with ~~Mr~~. William Bankes dining with them; & to show him she did know how to cook vegetables, she was ~~having one course entirely~~ having ~~special~~ vegetables specially done for him, & [~~a~~ too] Boeuf ~~a la~~ [a la] au Daube, which had been been weighing on Mildred's spirits all day. You stand it in water for twenty four hours: you ~~add~~ stir continuously; you add a little bay leaf, & then a dash of sherry: the whole ~~being~~ never ~~been~~ being allowed, of course, to come to the boil. If they kept dinner waiting after all that, it would be most unfair upon Mildred. And then, tonight of all nights, they

* Written in pencil
** Written in blue pencil
† A 120; B 125; A 121

(1.261)

late.

offered / an opal

Timothy ~~would have liked~~ her to wear a gold necklace: Rose

an gold

~~wanted her opal~~ necklace; Which did look best against her black dress? Which did indeed, said Mrs. Ramsay absent mindedly,

† allowing her children to rummage among her things, while she looked at a sight which always amused her, the rooks

to decide

trying which tree to settle on; Everytime they changed their minds, & rose into the air again, ~~whether~~ because, she thought, the old

~~trouble~~

rook, the old father rook, was of ~~an unsettled disposition~~. troublesome

† Look, she said laughing. Weren't the old birds actually

fighting?

~~quarrelling~~? Anyhow up they all went again; & the air was cut into exquisite scimitar shapes; the movement of the wings ~~was~~ beating out, out, out, was one of the ~~sights~~ loveliest of all sights: ~~she~~ to her, in the pale sky

But which was it to be? They had all the trays of her old jewel case open; the gold, which was Italian:

† the opal, which Uncle James gave her; or should she wear her ~~old~~ amythysts? She let the children choose; she let Rose try this that & the other, Rose who was so horribly bad at her sums, Mrs. Ramsay said; but this little ceremony of choosing jewels was, Mrs. Ramsay half suspected, ~~only~~ perhaps not even half, for there were, in her relations with her children, always hidden pockets of emotion, ~~which~~ which she never examined,

a consolation to Rose;

this choosing jewels was ~~rather a serious~~ to ~~poor~~ that

woolgathering

~~dear tri scatterbrained~~, silent child, who, wished, passionately that her mother shd. wear the gold necklace, that she should fasten it, & should thus have one

~~&~~

She ~~loved the colours, seeing how things went, you 'white~~

The a ceremony to Rose; something she liked for

but / were / standing to let her change the necklace,

hidden reasons, what reasons, Mrs. Ramsay wondered, ~~thinking~~

Fondly of ~~her~~ all the things one could not know. ~~Was she~~

but a love, so natural as [must?] [not?] [question?] it;

divining, through her own past ~~the~~ some deep, some

but / not

buried, some [anguished?] love, & ~~not~~ thinking of it as love for –

love of herself

herself; nor was it perhaps, ~~but for to Rose but~~ for

was rather love of a voice, love of a face, love of a principle, almost, of motherhood holding its children maternally, & womanhood, in its valiancy, & ~~the of the~~ desire, passionate beyond telling,
to attract ~~to he one~~ herself ~~one~~ glance, one caress, or the [a glance] ~~tenderness~~ approval ~~& underst~~ of eyes which suddenly, in the strangest way, could bestow upon Rose heavenly bliss. ~~During~~ Now

~~Pt~~ XV

† "~~But~~ What have I done with my life?" ~~said~~ [thought] Mrs. Ramsay taking her place at the head of the long table. "William sit by me," she said. Lily there . . ." ~~For some reason she could not~~ ~~They had~~ ~~the a~~ ~~For it was all over.~~ They had ~~their moment~~. The This: [an] infinitely long, narrow, white table; with empty places; [& a heap of] plates: At the far end was her husband. ~~that who might say nothing from start to finish.~~ sitting down with a [that shake of the head, a] sigh. She had felt a great deal of emotion: she now felt none whatever; nothing but ~~that~~ [a] curious sense of being borne on, because things were stronger than oneself; [she was] They had 'that'; ~~lost~~ ~~what w~~ 'that' which finally landed one in long tables, & piles of plates. ~~A most curious sensation; to be~~ & that would change presumably to this. And for a moment she had a curious sense of being past everything, through everything; out of everything; as they handed the soupplates; so that, ~~having the~~ being ~~relieved of her burden~~ she ~~could~~ say, ~~Well then what have I done with my life?~~ ~~But of course~~, what have I done, she would ask; ~~for as it was certain that she had~~

† & wait (while they came in, one after another, Charles Tansley, Mr. Carmichael,) wait, passively, for somebody or other to ~~give her~~ an answer; ~~for~~ [or for] something ~~or other~~ to happen. ~~Only~~ But ~~this was not being sad.~~ And ~~if they knew what~~ But this is not a thing, she thought, ladling out another plate for someone, ~~to tell~~ that one says;

~~Lily, she thought to herself would have been an admirable old maid.~~ ~~One does not say it to Lily, she thought.~~ And smiling ironically at ~~her own~~ the discrepancy – that was what she was thinking & this was what she was doing – [ladling out] helping soup:

† she felt begin in her, like a ~~stream or a [?]~~ like the pulse of some machine which stopped for a moment begins inexplicably to work, the old familiar life again: & ~~soon~~ so on; she thought,

remembering how long people lived & how much they enjoyed it, & so
so on, she repeated, ironically, cautiously sheltering this still feeble [on; &] pulse,
which she must encourage, for form's sake; or how should she get
through dinner. ~~The truth of it is of course, she thought~~, And so on
she said, very nearly aloud this time, addressing herself to William Bankes,
who had been through it all; Dear William Bankes: poor William
Bankes, for after all it must be better dining up here than alone in
† lodgings! And at that moment, cautiously in her pity for him, &
a ~~new~~ life began; & she noticed it, not without weariness, though
anything else would have been intolerable; noticed it, as the sailor sees his
sail fill out; & ~~we~~ knows himself off now: & with this wind in her
sails, Mrs. Ramsay too ~~in one second would be off~~ was off –
And yet the strangeness remained;

† like an [outcast?] ; ~~like the~~ as if a shade had fallen, & robbed of colour, she saw things truly; & then, not of her own willing, but independently like the pulse of a machine, which, inexplicably stopped, inexplicably begins again, the old familiar life began ~~beating~~. And so on & so on, she thought, mechanically, ~~as if she too~~ thinking how long peoples lives are & how much on the whole they seem to enjoy them). And so on & so on, she repeated, cautiously

one, two, three, irrationally.

† sheltering & [fostering] furthering the still feeble pulse, ~~so~~ as one might guard a weak flame with a newspaper. And so on, she concluded, ~~finding the life in her now almost~~ strong enough. addressing herself, by bending slightly in his direction, to William Bankes, – poor man! ~~He~~ [who] had no wife, no children,

† & in pity for him, life being now strongly [to bear her on again] enough established, she ~~said~~ began again, all this ~~being~~ business, ~~as a sailor~~ sees ~~the wind~~ not without weariness, as a sailor sees the wind fill his sail, & yet hardly wants to be off again; thinks ~~for a moment how the boat~~ [how the boat] had it sunk, ~~might have the boat~~ might have ~~plunged~~ him to the depths of the sea.

~~taken~~ – whirled him down & down ~~w~~ to the depths of the sea.

"~~Well~~, ~~she said; to William~~, Did ~~they~~ you find your letters. [She said] I told them to put them in the hall for you."

Lily Briscoe noticed it – her drifting into that ~~odd~~ strange no man's land, where following is impossible, ~~& only~~

† ~~some~~ & ~~one resents the~~ & ~~as some~~ & yet to let them ~~go &~~ leave us is intolerable; ~~so~~ so that Lily thought, seeing Mrs. Ramsay ladling out soup, ~~that she loo~~ked [how old she] ~~older than she should look, & then, for & more~~ how old she looked; how worn she looked; how stern; & then, when she turned to William Bankes, Lily thought, with ~~some~~ amusement, why does she pity him? For that was the impression she gave, when she told him about his letters; ~~that~~ Poor William Bankes, she seemed to be saying.

(resenting it)

† A 126, B 130; B 131; A 127; B 132

as if her own weariness which was so visible came from pity; & the
† life in her were stirred by pity. And it was not true, Lily thought.
~~But then~~ Mr. Bankes was perfectly happy she was sure. He
had his work. ~~But then~~ Lily felt ~~every~~ that ~~everyone was~~
very sure: Lily felt, ~~The wonderful thing about life is this:~~
~~how~~ one [may] ~~thinks its like this: when, as a matter of fact,~~
~~it is not like this~~: I ~~now know where~~ I shall put the ~~light there~~
tree rather further ~~over; & so~~ to the middle: Then I shall
avoid that break, which is ~~I'm sure now~~, what was puzzling me. sure
She would do that first thing next morning. And
† ~~How seldom~~ one [never] gets anything by the post ~~that is~~
really worth having ~~said Mr. Bankes~~. ~~Yet~~ Yet one always
wants ~~lett~~ one's letters, said Mr. Bankes.
~~He Wat But~~ What rot they [that is] talked, what rot,
thought Charles Tansley ~~who had~~ laying down his spoon
in the middle of his plate precisely, having ~~eaten swept~~ [cleaned] it
perfectly bare. as if, Lily thought, (he was precisely
opposite her) he ~~was made~~ [was determined to make] sure of his meals; ~~as if~~ he
had not an ounce of generosity [of any sort] over, There he would sit,
in his pepper & salt coat of grey flannel trousers, eating his
way through the meal like a [all] cockchafer; bristly, ~~packing.~~ [& [?] all which]
† And Mrs. Ramsay would pity him: [now;] she pitied men, always;
never women. ~~Still~~ Poor Charles Tansley – that was
precisely what Mrs. Ramsay was thinking. ~~Poor litt little man~~
~~For~~ He was not a gentleman: ~~No~~. Charles Tansley was
thinking how he could never say thing ~~about~~ like that
~~He was uneasy.~~ [No. He had ~~no conv~~ nothing to say.] What could she say to make him feel easy?
~~Well~~ [But], he would not be made easy; [Did you notice the lovely light] ~~he would not talk~~
~~nonsense~~, ~~Charles Tansley thought.~~ He would not talk nonsense.
For having finished the second volume of Sorel's history of the
French Revolution, & sandwiched in a chapter of Meredith,
(this was more than he had bargained for, too) Charles
Tansley was rather up in his [in the [world?]] own estimation; had
not envious ~~of~~ [that] lacking small talk was
any drawback.

† A 128; B 133; A 129

† come down stairs on the stroke of eight; & ~~from that~~ here they were, two silly women making men talk ~~rot~~. He despised women; not in the foolish way of a boy; but as men despise them. ~~He~~ If it were not for women, the world would have been civilised centuries ago. In every age they are the great hindrance to free thought, & ~~responsible~~ proper life. Some ages have idealised them. Now vaunting themselves the equals of men they will now have to face frank criticism. ~~Unfortunately~~ But, with minds of wax, they will never face anything. There ~~was little~~ is no chance of going to the lighthouse, ~~he was afraid~~, Charles Tansley said. ~~Were the~~ Why, then, did one mind what he

turning in his chair

† said, Lily Briscoe wondered. ~~for~~ ~~being so~~ insignificant as he was! O it's Shakespeare, she corrected herself – as a forgetful person entering ~~Hyde Park~~, Regents Park, ~~might wonder why~~ & seeing the Park keeper was coming towards her menacingly; ~~they make on dogs must be on a lead~~; might exclaim Oh I of course remember dogs must be on a lead! So Lily Briscoe remembered that ~~everyon~~ ~~man~~ has Shakespeare ~~behind him;~~ & women have not. ~~We are not nearly so clever as they are, she thought, & therefore I must~~ What then could she say? ~~to~~ inferior as she was; & was it not much easier to be inferior after all? – That is the whole secret of art, she thought to herself. To care for the thing: not for oneself what does it matter whether I succeed or not? And joyous as she was tonight, about her picture, she ~~abused h~~ was very very nice, to Charles Tansley. She was, a very charming creature, Lily; her Lily; Mrs. Ramsay thought Without any striking charm, without any of the glow that made one notice Minta directly she came in ~~into a room~~. Lily had qualities that would

how men have that behind them; & women nothing.

& did she mind being inferior, did she feel, on the whole inferior? –

he could ot give harles ansley hat he anted.*

(1.275)

* Written in pencil
† B 134; A 130

† But did one not always like people when one looked at them? She must admit that his eyes were good: he had grey-blue honest eyes.

† "Do you write many letters, Mr. Tansley?" said Mrs. Ramsay pitying him too, Lily supposed; for that was true of Mrs. Ramsay: she pitied men always as if they lacked something; ~~nev not~~ & never ~~she did~~ not pity women, never as if they had something. Yet it was the other way round; women had nothing; men everything – ~~considered~~ from the material point of view, power office, money, education~~; & so on~~. ~~men had all that instantly~~. ~~It all~~, But it was very like it was part of Mrs. Ramsay

~~everything~~ were so much easier for men

He wrote to his mother; but otherwise he did not write to anybody, Mr. Tansley said

For he was not going to talk the sort of rot these people wanted him to talk. Having finished ~~his ch vo~~ vol two of Sorel before dinner, he had wedged in a chapter of Harry Richmond & was not going to be condescended to by these upper middle class women; whom he despised. ~~What~~

† ~~did they know of anything~~? "One never gets anything worth having by the post" – he shd. [?] in that was true. They never got anything worth having from one years end to another. They ~~exist~~ lived the most useless of lives; ~~& His own mother did more They did not know the meaning of work~~. talk, talk, talk; other women waiting on them; & ~~they despised~~ (It was women who made civilisation impossible. He despised women more & more.)

"No going to the Lighthouse tomorrow, Mrs. Ramsay" he said, half turning in his chair, as if to confirm his ~~weath~~ forecast. ~~of the weather.~~

† He was really, Lily Briscoe thought, the most uncharming human being she had ever met. ~~And so~~ Why, then, did one mind what he said? Oh, she remembered, Shakespeare – that is to say, she had momentarily forgotten in ~~in her own elation~~, ~~how wo~~ about women not being creative, & men being creative; & Charles Tansley therefore being quite within his rights when he ~~told~~ maintained that to talk down to her; to say what was the use of her paints?

† A 128; A 129, B 133; B 134; A 130 (1.277)

They could not paint or write or do anything ever: so that, being a man one had to respect him. ~~All~~ She had clean forgotten. Now, she said to herself; ~~lets have~~ now it over; meaning that ~~now~~ she would now [looking at him, descend to the ~~caves~~ bottom of despair & let the dark waves of humility break; ~~&~~ Then ~~she would~~ come up cringing. Down she went; horror & despair; annihilation; nonentity; sure enough, they arched crashed over her; ~~stooping form~~; & yet – & yet. Opening her eyes in the pale world of daylight again, she was aware of some ~~profound~~ small trophy retrieved ~~down~~ there; some talisman she would sew to the inside of her dress (how ~~the it is~~ things themselves matter) ~~not are enduring, indeed ever lasting~~; ~~how how~~ nothing else matters;) & opening her eyes ~~she~~ was so elated joyous in her freedom & did not the position of the salt cellar mark something important? – that she said to Mr. Tansley (whom she [wished?] (supposed she would continue to reverence, for she had no militancy in her, ~~did~~ & could not bear to be be called, as she might have been called had she come out with her views a feminist, for ~~she thought~~ it was safer, easier, less agitating threatening to a accept things: ~~like that~~) & she ~~could not bear to be~~ & after all, ~~half one's feelings were different~~ one never could say ~~quite what one meant~~) ~~she~~ & one always did accept things: it was too difficult to say know quite what one meant ) about all this). she said to him When ~~was the lighthouse built~~? She ~~had~~ was longing to go to the Lighthouse: did he really think it would be too rough?

their backs &

not success, not

& did not everything always happen when one stayed with the Ramsays

~~Certainly, said Mr. Ramsay, it would be far too rough~~

Charles Tansley turned in his chair again. He had a

~~It would be far too rough, he said;~~

Complete contempt for women. They have been always In every age they have been the great enemies of progress; ~~& reason & freedom~~ Without women, life wd be tolerable [?] some sort of civilisation might be possible. They never let us alone, he thought. ~~It is foolish to say that a young man has any~~ ~~And his~~ Mrs. Ramsay

had ruined Ramsays work. What did a philosopher want with eight [children?
He should have married a working class woman – for it irked him,
here he was staying with them; & he had no change of clothes for
the evening. He ~~to~~ did not know the sort of things they talked about –
like this "one never gets anything worth having by the post."
But one had to do it – & that was what Lily Briscoe felt:

they had to do it ~~come over her too. her but she did not want to feel it: how~~

a physical [?] a [mutual?] ~~the~~ a horror of m masculinity: ~~how but~~ came on her Oh but she was not a
feminist! That was a silly thing to say. Think of Shakespeare.
They must get on in the world, she supposed; like Mr. Tansley.
They had their scholarships & their fellowships & their
dissertations, & it was all very well for her, with two hundred a
year safe forever, to moon about with her painting; ~~they~~

But for A strong young man – here she was again, ~~just~~ saying
things she did not believe in the least: but she did mean to
go on saying them; for she would not be called a feminist, &
she knew for a fact that she could not understand things
that were plain as daylight to ~~M~~ Charles Tansley.
The rate of exchange was one of them.

Now he had to ~~tell~~ lay down laws for this silly creature that she could not go to
the Lighthouse.

~~Last night he had~~ They buzzed about one with questions;
but they never listened to what you told them. ~~If~~ He had never
known a woman who cared for truth in the [?]. All they wanted
was flirtation in one form or another. And Charles
& What could ~~she say to put him~~ at his ~~ease.~~
Tansley was quite ready to give them all that sort of thing:
but he was not ready to let them spoil his work.

† "Yes. Take it away" said Mrs. Ramsay, briefly.

~~For~~ It must have been twenty years ago ~~that~~ or almost, that she had stayed with the Careys; & William Bankes had actually heard from her: & she ~~had~~ was still living at Brimpton; & everything was still [?] the same? Oh she could remember it as if it were yesterday. She could remember a picnic on a bank. It was one of those chilly April days when most people prefer to stay in doors. The Careys, however, once they made a

† plan, stuck to it. There ~~was~~ It was very very cold. ~~Hebe Ch~~ Ellen was then alive. ~~And~~ – Yes, she could remember everything; & ~~it seemed to~~ Mrs. Ramsay ~~seemed to glide~~ stole like a ghost in between the chairs & tables of that ~~ho~~ drawing room on the banks of the Thames; where Ellen who had been her friend,

~~with~~ her sat – ~~what was she doing~~? doing something for she seemed to be ~~laughing~~; silent, ~~frie~~ friendly, yet [?] of a certain malice malicious; a ghost they could not see; & perhaps in the flesh they would never meet again; or ~~perhaps they would meet again; but still~~ but ~~once it was a~~ the ~~luxury~~ ~~& a~~ the ~~solace of growing old that the~~ but to visit ~~the~~ like this, was the delight of growing old: to talk of people one had known; & things one had done; & ~~sentimental perhaps. That is to say,~~ ~~when~~ it to know

She walked again what had become of them all. [ ? ] ~~& tende~~ with tenderness mixing in h Her amusement ~~was~~ tempered with tenderness: ~~for~~ what reason? ~~She~~ But as William Bankes had actually heard from Anne Carey himself, ~~he what~~ he felt he felt ~~noth~~ none of this ~~ch~~ oddity about them. ~~Why~~ "They ~~were~~ are building a new boat house" he said. ~~He did not~~ feel, as ~~Mrs. Ramsay felt, that it was impossible t~~hat That seemed to Mrs. Ramsay almost out of the question. How could they ~~be actually~~ were building a boat house? ~~Who would use it~~?

~~After all, Mr. Bankes said~~, It seemed to her so odd.

And William would actually see ~~Ellen~~ Anne Carey?

He was arranging to stay with them in October, said William Bankes.

† A 131, B 136, A 132; B 137

Would ~~Mrs. Ramsay~~ she yet like to see them?

No, no, said Mrs. Ramsay; ~~remembering~~ thinking that she had ~~not~~ whatever nothing to say to Mrs. Carey. in the flesh.

How strange – they were alive. For Mrs. Ramsay ~~con~~ found it very difficult to think that the Careys would have been living all † this time, without her thinking of them. How full, how eventful, her own life had been, these last ~~twenty years~~, fifteen years: ~~It seemed to her quite impossible that~~ ~~empty~~ Mrs. Carey ~~had~~ not ~~heard a word of it~~. must have heard of it: but no:

Had they never thought of her,

"People soon drop out" said William Bankes humorously; guessing Mrs. Ramsays thought. He ~~did a~~ could not help † feeling a little gratified Here was he, knowing them both; he stayed with the Ramsays: he stayed with the Careys. That seemed to show that he moved in more circles than one. ~~That seemed to show that he had kept~~ M He was a little amused; & gratified too; for did he not know both the Ramsays & the Careys? ~~He knew them both~~. did ~~it not seem to give him a superiority — &, he reflected~~, ~~D He wa~~ & made a point moved in more circles than one, he thought, approvingly; ~~laying down his spoon. He h y~~ nobody could say that he had got into groove; & thus ~~fortified he~~

Considered openly, what is human life?*

* Written in pencil

† A 133; B 138

(1.285)

† He was not going to talk the rot these people wanted him to talk. "One never gets anything worth having by the post" – unless the he ~~got his~~

† Except that he liked her rather, Mrs. Ramsay. But what did they want [of him. Small talk?

No going to the Lighthouse tomorrow, I'm afraid, Mrs. Ramsay" he [said.

† & that nothing she [much matters?]

Joyous in the elation wh this thought gave her,

† What did they want of him then? Tansley asked himself. turning in What did Ram –

~~Yes~~ He wanted (he cld) to say ~~something~~ the right sort of things to Miss Briscoe: something not quite serious: not merely straight out in so (~~It will~~) many words "It will be rough": something ~~more~~ He wanted to say the sort of thing ~~Charles~~ –

~~Pa~~ Rayley said to women. He was quite willing to flirt with women.

He wd have liked to be given a chance to show what he could do –

† A 129, B 133; B 134; A 130; A 131 (1.287)

[~~fa~~?]

† amused that Mrs. Ramsay should be so astonished at Mrs. Careys continued existence, gratified that he was the link between them. ~~He knew~~ them both; he had not drifted apart, he thought, laying down his spoon & wiping his clean shaved lips punctiliously, But perhaps he was rather unusual ~~in this~~ he thought, in this, that he never let himself get into a groove. He ~~never~~ had friends in all circles – ~~But~~ the ~~nat~~ reason why he preferred dining alone was to avoid the kind of wait which was ~~inevitable~~ unavoidable in a [big] ~~family~~ party. They kept one waiting while they changed the plates. Mrs. Ramsay had to break off & tell the maid something. At home he never spent more than twenty minutes dining. For say what one will, work is the great pleasure in life: ~~the great excitement: The poets talk of life being~~ short. work is the great excitement; Indeed, all these things waste time. Well, thought Mr. Bankes, preserving a demeanuor* of ~~the~~ exquisite courtesy, & merely spreading the fingers of his left hand on the tablecloth, as a mechanic examines a tool which is beautifully polished & ready for work in an interval of leisure; such ~~are the~~ little sacrifices [one] which one's friends demand of one. ~~And~~ He gave up ~~an~~ [his] evening's work ~~readily~~ [gladly]. Yet ~~he knew that~~ if he spoke the truth he knew that it was not worth it; not for him. His social appetite was soon satisfied. He would not ~~do it again~~ [But]. It was not worth it, for him. No, he thought, & thinking how Mrs. Ramsay had been astonished to hear of Mrs. Carey's existence; & whether [it is not worth it] he was unusually cold-blooded, or ~~whether he~~ the pursuit of silence is ~~so exacting that~~ it for ~~human people drift apart~~ except for ~~one or two~~ one or two people; silence is more satisfactory: the difficulties of After all, one sees people; one talks to people; but what solid he

makes willingly to friendship.

* VW's misspelling

† A 133, B 138

(1.289)

~~supposed that~~ reflected how ~~much of a broken & fleeting it all~~ it is is; how unsatisfactory: how, very little ~~did one dare say so, very~~ but then he was only speaking for himself: how very little ~~human re~~ one's friends matter compared with one's work. ~~And here was a little~~

all a little

† ~~And to~~ Looking at his hand, he could not help thinking ~~of the waste of~~ [~~time.~~

After He spent 20 minutes spent over dinner, ~~at home~~. Then he was free to ~~work~~. had he been alone, he would then have been free to work.

† Yes, he thought, it is a terrible waste of time. [Why, some of the children are not down yet – Nor could ~~they~~ they begin again where they broke off, when Mrs. Ramsay was ready to ~~talk~~ attend again; & the terrible "I wish one of you would run up to Roger's room" Mrs. Ramsay was saying –] ~~only~~ & ~~yet~~ he respected & admired the Ramsays, & yet, he thought, even so, ~~how pale this is~~, how trifling this is – ~~as a~~ how boring this is – for had he been free, he would have ~~done nothing but~~ read – But how could he think of his work now? – ~~with~~ sitting beside Mrs. Ramsay? ~~All~~ He admired them; he was ~~very~~ by way of being an old friend, all that: but Mrs. Ramsay was thinking of something else. And in the shade of her presence, which prevented him of course from fixing his mind upon any regrets of his own, he ~~thought with~~ compared the excitement & the pleasure & the sense of being part of eternity (for in working time seemed to have no existence) ~~& he~~ which he would have had had he been alone, he compared that intensity that excitement which he had foregone, with this – this miserable putting away suspension of all activity; ~~this & then~~ this sitting about drumming ones fingers on the table. This cynicism – yes, for what ~~did~~ do human relationships amount to then? There are the ~~Careys & the Ram~~says. I am by way of being ~~a great~~ devoted to her, he thought. Yet Mrs. Ramsay meant nothing to him, nothing, he thought, stared ~~glaring from his blue eyes~~ ~~so hopelessly~~ ~~that~~ blankly:

& yet she was only two feet away from him.

Indeed it was his conviction that

The ~~passion~~ ~~Preserved as he was by~~ He seldom thought about ~~the~~ such things: he was not a poet, not a novelist; his interest in life was purely scientific. Just every now & then – if he was put out by
† something – he asked himself questions like this: What should we say if we were honest? Is human life a good thing, or it is it a bad thing? Why do we desire the continuance of the human race upon earth? What do we live for? Such questions never occurred to him at other times. ~~He was~~

† "I ~~must~~ am so sorry" said Mrs. Ramsay; who had been giving instructions of some sort.

For

† A 135; B 140

† Yet

She is one of my oldest friends: I am by way of being devoted to her he thought. ~~And yet~~ But her presence meant nothing to him, her beauty meant nothing to him; he wished only to be ~~alone~~ by himself; & so relieved from the disagreeable necessity of realising that he had no feeling whatever for his friends: His work was what he wanted. ~~In default of~~ work ~~being impossible~~, ~~there.~~ But he must sit here, drumming his fingers on the table, & feeling uncomfortable because of this treachery – that he was not ~~enjoying himself~~, able to feel anything: ~~that it was all tasteless & insipid;~~ that he felt nothing for his friends. He did not enjoy family life. And it was in this sort of state that one asked oneself those ~~such questions as~~ – What do we live for? Why / do we desire the continuance of the human race? – questions † which never occurred ~~normally~~; ~~but were One never thought about it~~, if one was occupied. But ~~sometimes~~ one could not escape that sort of thing; especially when, as now, the frailty of the whole human relationship was 'brought' home to one; ~~Mrs. Ramsay~~ ~~that~~ Mrs. Ramsay had forgotten Mrs. Carey; ~~that~~ he ~~himself felt nothing for Mrs. Ramsay – sitting though he was a few inches from her, &~~ sat a few inches off Mrs. Ramsay, & was indifferent to her.

to be alone & able to work:

one asked oneself,

Is human life good on the whole? or bad?

† "I am so sorry" said Mrs. Ramsay who had been giving instructions of [some sort.

Rigid & barren as he felt himself, like a pair of boots which had been soaked & gone dry so that you can scarcely force your feet into them Mr. Bankes ~~bent~~ ~~inclined~~ bent his head. ~~That~~ Unless he was careful She would ~~now~~ discover his treachery: ~~unless he were careful; &~~ & that ~~would~~ be ~~very~~ painful, very painful.

How you must regret dining in this bear garden said Mrs. Ramsay:

† A 134, B 139; A 135; B 140 (1.295)

She had a social manner ~~sometimes,~~ /when she was a little distracted.
as, ~~in~~ when there is a strife of tongues at some meeting, the chairman,
in order to ~~unify the~~ obtain unity, ~~drops into French.~~
suggests that everyone shall speak French. Perhaps it is bad French;
† French may not contain the words necessary for the speaker's
thoughts; ~~nevertheless~~, but speaking French ~~nevertheless,~~
imposes some order, some uniformity. Replying to her in
the same language, Mr. Bankes said ~~that~~ "Not at all. ~~Not at all~~"
And
Mr. Tansley who had no understanding of this language, ~~even~~
from wh they read, as life goes on, to their friends
spoken thus, ~~we~~ / even in ~~one~~ words of one syllable. ~~He thought that~~
~~He was~~ added in that book which young people carry
with them on visits outside their own homes, "~~It is~~ ~~An intolerable visit~~ –
They never say what they think . . ." ~~But~~ & so / perhaps it would
shape itself for him, in years to come; a dinner party where
who had proved himself honest, incorruptible & so on.
people talked ~~in~~ such a fantastic [?] lingo that he / had no
notion what they were driving at; & so had determined with
~~that he~~ him ~~to~~ ~~that such~~ society was not for him, & so
go into that society again,
had made him resolve –. but at present, being actually
† at the Ramsays table, the scene had not shaped itself; & he
~~was curio desired more than anything to assert himself.~~
had not determined anything, & all he wished was, that he
could somehow impress himself ~~But~~ on the others.
If anybody could give him the chance, ~~there were~~
~~lots of things he could~~ say. he could tell them all about
† the fishing industry in the North of Scotland. if they asked him.
on the other side of the table was surveying him:
Miss Briscoe was ~~being~~ & waiting; was reflecting malicious Could she not
see, even as in a scientific photograph, the ribbs* &
thigh bones of Mr. Tansleys vanity: lying dark in the
mist of his flesh: the thin mist which convention
laid over his immense desire to assert himself.
† But she thought, why should I help h be nice to him?
He ~~wishes to assert~~ But And it seemed to her that perhaps this was
her duty: to help men to expose & so relieve their

* VW's misspelling (1.297)

† A 136; B 141; A 137; B 142

the thigh bone, the ribs, of their ~~childish~~ appalling vanity, their desire to assert themselves, as it is their duty to help us, she reflected; to ~~hel~~ stand in Tubes; to offer us security. But suppose she thought, suppose the Tube were to burst into flames & [put?] ~~[?]~~ [surely?] * ~~we~~ neither of us discharges these duties?

in accidents: with her invincible fairness.

~~R~~ You would be terribly seasick, Lily, said Mrs. You're not ~~pretending to~~ planning to go to the Lighthouse ~~Brisco~~ Ramsay; you would be terribly sea-sick. Often, even on the calmest days they have ~~to tack for hours~~ before they can land. It is a ~~terrible exhibition~~ expedition. ~~Some of the best~~ † There was Mr. Langley last year. He ~~had~~ has sailed in every part of the world crossed the Atlantic ~~twenty times at least, without a qualm. But when he~~ but he ~~had~~ never suffered as he did when my husband took him there, – Are you a ~~good sailor~~ seasick, Mr. Tansley?" she asked.

I shd certainly expect Mr. Tansley to show me the way out

~~So Lily in her~~ Indeed he was: but in his desire to make out ~~that he was~~ himself out remarkable, to cleave with a hammer the impalpable impediments ~~of this~~ Mr. Tansley said [?] he [?] could not imagine what it felt like – (~~yet~~ And Then he wd say his that would lead to † his grandfather being a fisherman; to his being self-taught; to his being the first of his family to obtain a university education; to his being glad of it; to his being Charles Tansley in short – ~~who was not even realised in this room~~ – & which nobody in this room seemed to realise. ~~And yet in he felt~~ Everybody here ~~will be glad to say~~ that they know me in ten years time, he thought, & felt almost pity; for as a grain of dynamite laid beneath bales of wool & barrels of comfortable [apples & hid?] clothing & food, might pity the ignorance ~~of~~ & the comfort – For he would blow them all sky high. ~~He was~~ He wd make going ~~to leave~~ his mark on the world. ~~Lily~~ "~~We~~ Will you take me, Mr. Tansley, said Lily in her arch rather kittenish way? for of course if Mrs. Ramsay said to her, as in effect she did, "I am drowning, my dear, in seas of fire. Unless you will apply a some balm to the anguish of ~~that~~ the horror, ~~He~~ life will run upon the rocks & indeed there is only just time to avert the collision. I hear the grating & the scrunching & my nerves are tight as

* Written in pencil

† A 138; B 143

(1.299)

† fiddle strings already. Another touch & they will snap – when Mrs.
[Ramsay
said all ~~do~~ this, as her tone said it, of course, for the fiftieth time, Lily
Briscoe had to renounce that experiment – ~~of how~~ what happens if
being
~~one is~~ not nice to men – & be nice. And he was relieved of his
~~burden of ego~~tism; & he ~~was~~ started ~~telling her talking to her about~~
~~himself; & then about Lighthouse, which~~ & told her how he had ~~da~~
† been thrown out of a boat when he was three; to teach him to swim;
& fished out again with a boat hook; & lighthouses were
set up about the year – he would look it up; he could not be
positive; ~~they the~~ The system is carefully arranged.

'my grandfather was an ordinary fisherman'

& Lily Briscoe thought, feeling Mrs. Ramsays relief, But what
haven't I paid to get it you? A sort of sincerity, she meant, has
† been lost. And ~~she thought~~ her eye caught the salt cellar &
she remembered with a shock of exquisite relief how ~~that~~
~~signified to her that~~ next morning she would move the
tree in her picture slightly to the right. How could she
gave
turn the conversation to painting? She ~~had given~~ him
every credit for knowing so much. No woman knew all
that about Lighthouses.

† "But how long do they leave ~~a man~~ men alone on a lighthouse?" she asked.

Mrs. Ramsay wished to talk about the Careys again; to enter that dreamland, that unreal land, where the trees stood stock still, & there was no haste – & no anxiety; & a sort of humour where everything had ~~already~~ already happened; ~~there was no~~ & pity from knowing what had happened; there was no future; ~~w for, now~~ & all the worries that had assailed her then were solved; & life which now poured terrifyingly over an abyss into unknown lands was sealed up ~~safe &~~ ran its course ~~safe between banks.~~ equally evenly between banks. She wished to talk of all that; ~~but~~ to re-enter all that it had left her. The opportunity had ~~floated away~~. ~~gone~~; the island floated away. ~~Like so many other things; but it was~~ It was unapproachable;

280 twitched away. ~~She knew it.~~ but ~~no: it~~ had floated from her.

114 ~~The mood had gone.~~ ~~Mr.~~ William Bankes was not in the mood. But ~~then~~ he sh~~ould be in the mood. But what was~~ it that she ~~did~~?

† "The children are ~~quite~~ disgraceful" she said.

~~But one must not be too~~ He replied something about punctuality being one of the ~~vir~~ minor virtues which we do not acquire until later in life.

Mrs. Ramsay knew quite well, & Mr. Bankes knew quite well ~~that here was a horrid affair:~~ that they were at loggerheads.

† "If at all" said Mrs. Ramsay, merely to fill up space. And conscious of his treachery, conscious of her desire for some ~~more~~ thing else from ~~intimate talk~~, ~~This~~ these perfunctory words if at all, ~~seemed seemed vain~~ & made Mr. Bankes ~~a~~ feel [profoundly?] that he pity her; & ~~then~~ But what was he to do? What were they to say? What were other people saying? ~~W~~ Surely one

catch some line thrown from the other end of the table? Lily & Mr. Tansley were talking about the fishing industry; ~~They were~~ & ~~emigration~~ & ~~They were~~ talking about emigration. ~~All that,~~ & that was all so admirable – that ~~the~~ facts should be discussed & injustice exposed; that the failure of some men to ~~bring in~~ make enough to live on this year should be deplored, & the pressure which drove them to America should be denounced; but honestly what was lacking? ~~in~~ ~~Why~~ ~~Some~~ ~~The usual thing~~ Already bored, Lily Bankes knew that something was lacking; William Bankes catching on to Tansleys last words "one of the most scandalous acts of the present government" knew that something was lacking. ~~And~~ Only ~~this: that no~~ ~~Some~~ The usual profound unreality had

† mixed itself in; & bending themselves to listen to the tale of suffering & injustice, what they felt was, pray Heaven that the inside of my mind may never be exposed to view not be seen for I am ~~fo~~ lying. ~~They~~ They would give money, ~~interest,~~ ~~attent~~ time, attention; but who of all those Always they had all felt this: when it came to the suffering of the poor: to the vast waves that desolate whole countrysides – to eruptions of earthquakes; to the tyranny & injustice (how naturally the words ran into absurd rhetorical couples which one would be ashamed to feel on one's own lips!) Then, secretly, they had all felt ~~this~~ the same discomfort & depr~~ession~~, at of their own unworthiness, of their own cynicism; & giving their names or time or money to the cause or the fund, each had come away with the same ~~sense of profound unreality.~~ dissatisfaction ~~feeling:~~ ~~conscio~~ they had been deceived

[margin: their ~~interest,~~ their pity, their

hoping that they were separate)]

But, perhaps, thought Mr. Bankes, as he looked at Mr. Tansley, this he is the man. ~~He gav~~

† There was always the chance it them always the benefit of the doubt. At any moment the

† A 142; B 147 (1.305)

sincere man may arise: the man of genius, the great man. ~~Moreover,~~ [leader above "great"]
Probably he will be excessively disagreeable to us old fogies, thought
Mr. Bankes. Unkempt, ill-mannered all of that. ~~And~~
~~But after he had listened to Tansley talking, again the unreality~~
But – here Mr. Bankes came to the usual conclusion; Mr.
Tansley could not tell him ~~nothing that he did~~ what he did not know not know already.
He ~~w~~ abused the Government. Perfectly justly no doubt. But
Mr. Bankes himself could abuse the government. ~~In all the~~
It is not abuse that is wanted, Mr. Bankes felt; thinking of his
plants, & their nervous systems & respiratory organs: In sciences,
there is creation; in art, creation; but in this art, some say the
highest, there is nothing but abuse, ~~nothing but soun high flown~~
words, that mean nothing: intrigue; (he will do well in Parliament
very likely, he thought) & when we ordinary people, who are
quite ready to do what we can to help, come & ~~say tell us,~~
tell us what to do, make us believe you; ~~we get~~ a handful of sand
thrown in our eyes. Yet one must be scrupulously careful,
Mr. Bankes corrected himself; ~~for~~ It is undoubtedly to our
interest ~~to~~ that ~~no reformer should arise.~~ not ~~things should remain as~~
they are.

For [it?] Tansley was describing his [?] success on a tour.

Such thoughts ~~were~~ could lead only in one direction: the
decay of religious belief. And if at Mr. Ramsay's table
one began thinking of the decay of religious belief, one looked,
naturally, at Mr. Ramsay.

~~It is~~ "They are so much worse off" Mrs. Ramsay
~~no~~ began, ~~but so much~~ under the influence of Mr.
Tansley's style that instead of thinking of Betty McNab
& Ellie Kennedy she thought of 'them', the poor,
who were ~~w~~ 'happy' or miserable, in blocks;
but ~~she could not stand~~ there were things she could
not stand. Certain hypocrisies, as they left her lips, stung her.
Here at last ~~were~~ was the

He knew by some curious physical sensation, as of nerves erect, that
an of some attack upon
he was jealous ~~of~~ in ~~some~~ obscure way; ~~afra~~ anxious to
defend his own life work, his science; & therefore not entirely
[openminded
fair to this young man Tansley & his view; for Tansley seemed to
be saying ~~to them all~~ How you have ~~all~~ wasted your lives.
Tansley seemed to be rather a cocksure young man. But ~~of course~~,
Mr. Bankes allowed, he had courage on his side, & youth.
But It is,
~~However the immediate question was~~ Mr. Bankes ~~asked~~ observed to
that is
himself, ~~what~~ the decay of religious belief has been responsible
for much of this (that there is no St. Francis: no ~~gr~~ leader of social
reform) & if at Mr. Ramsays table one began thinking of
the decay of religious belief, one looked, at least, at ~~Mrs.~~
Mr. Ramsay.

~~That the destruction~~ ~~What indeed was he thinking~~? –
~~this~~ Not a combatant himself, Mr. Bankes had faith in
Ramsay, ~~who~~ But at this moment, at this precise moment,
† Mr. Ramsay's face expressed nothing but protest & even horror.
At what catastrophe? ~~Poor~~ Mr. Carmichael had asked
for another plate of soup. Leaning back he had
touched the maids arm, & requested, that his plate should be
[din?]
returned to him, full. And she had ~~given him~~ his plate.
And he was now addressing himself to his second helping
when one, according to Mr. Ramsay, was more than enough
for any human being; when the process of drinking soup
was distressing: when he slobbered it over his whiskers.
when of all things, Mr. Ramsay detested hanging about
waiting for people to finish. This was in his face,
next
~~undisguised~~; & ~~at any~~ moment ~~he might say something:~~
saying it [?] eyes though no
~~But~~ He was capable of it. Like a pair of hounds his
words flew like smoke on top of his emotions. But –
Mrs. Ramsay had told him ~~of~~ that story about begging
eighteen pence to buy tobacco. He should have his
soup in peace then; he should gorge & guzzle to his hearts
content then; but nobody knew – so

† A 143, B 148 (1.309)

Mr. Ramsay seemed to say, ~~clasping his hands~~ together, what anguish this restraint caused him; ~~only his wife~~ only his wife would

† give him credit for it. But if you clap the breaks* on to a wheel that is going, full tilt – that was his sensation: for the rapidity of his mind, & the acuteness of his sensations, over trifles, ~~there~~ then sparks fly; & the whole of his body was a shower of sparks; ~~beautifully~~, perfectly controlled, he considered, looking at his wife to verify this statement, ~~He had not abused poor old Poor old Carmichael might have his soup~~, He remembered her story about Carmichael begging eighteen pence to buy tobacco. He

wd. ~~could~~ not grudge him [his soup for] anything. And sighing ~~profoundly~~ Mr. Ramsay [sharply] enforced his wifes demands that somebody should run up & pull Andrew out of his bath; ~~speaking~~ venting upon his sons his tartness, his irritation, while, consuming soup placidly, Mr. Carmichael sat ~~in~~ there, unmoved, benignant, to all appearances indifferent to this hubbub, to that hubbub, wrapped in content.

It might be true that he had asked his wife for eighteen pence. ~~She was certainly a most disagreeable lady.~~

been up to see them. It might be true that kind Mrs. Ramsay had [paid] ~~visited~~ them [a visit] But ~~that sort of thing did not trouble him.~~ These sort of things made little impression on him. He In the vast & it must be admitted bewildering hailstorm, among those variously flying splinters of matter, things to do, things not to do,

being up to time ~~appointments to keep~~, deciding this, deciding that, ~~he had~~ keeping appointments – & ~~very justly~~ one cannot expect the government of India to provide a man with competence who is unable to turn up at the required hour at the required place, for the government of India is a mighty cog wheel & the in ~~at~~ ability of one cog to grip another cog impairs the efficiency

* VW's misspelling

† A 144

(1.311)

of the whole machine, so he would explain to his dear friend Andrew,
bearing nobody any malice, ~~comp~~ never complaining of injustice,
& interested in his own case as in that of another;
among all their obstacles & impediments he had found only one
sure panacea: to twiddle his [long?] thumbs before replying to a question
"Never ~~speak in a hurry: he~~ let ~~yourself be driven~~ to ~~advised Andrew.~~

the Burmese habit

He had adopted the Burmese habit of twiddling his thumbs;
& ~~that he had found very helpful.~~ & ~~so had never~~ before & this
replying to a question. ~~You could~~ not be forced to say what you
might regret having said ~~la later~~ in reply to a question.
& thus for 3 years to avoid being led into precipitate statements which ~~is~~ one
was apt to regret.* later. ~~There~~ (So with his soup, so with his
acrostics, so with his poetry; he was not precipitate. ~~He~~
let id~~eas simmer, & then crystallise.~~) He met a bear, on a
pass in the Himalayas, where a more hasty man would have
been inclined to action, he ~~remained still, the stationary~~
meeting a bear on a pass in the Himalayas, he had
remained stationary! And so with his acrostics; with his poetry.
He did not hurry himself. He liked the sound of words.
~~He believed that~~ He bade Andrew listen to the sound of words.
He translated Persian into English. ~~What did~~ But here again he
~~waited~~ allowed the words to come of their own accord. He had
been told that people wrote things in a flash. He begged
Andrew not to believe it. The process Often for months at a
time he did nothing. Then it was better to do nothing – But
he had (he confided the secret to Andrew only, who alone
visited him in his sunny room, & was shown the sacred
relics in a little box such as one keeps studs in)

some highly sacred tooths- amulets- silk cords-

~~then~~ he had seasons of inspiration. ~~He wrote~~ They would
come, ~~inconveniently, an~~ especially at Lords, watching the cricket.
They seldom came in winter. They never lasted long.
But, when they came, Mr. Carmichael might have been
seen [ ? ] his large [broad?] head to the sky of St. Johns Wood
in thanksgiving for his inspiration. They would be
published shortly. But he did**

* MS 158 verso (1.313)

** End of volume I. See appendix C for the fragment of 'The Ghost of Sterne' which appears on 156 verso and 157 verso.

to avoid precipitate statements
which she was sure to regret
later.*

* Written in the centre of the back of the last page of the writing book. MS 155. (1.320)

To the Lighthouse.
March 17th 1926

52 Tavistock Square

* Title page, volume 2

is She heroic? lilie?



17 March
1926

If ~~words come,~~ ~~they come~~ of themselves.
There was the story of the bear on the Himalayan pass – ~~Mr.~~
he
~~Carmichael~~ had twiddled his thumbs. So with his acrostics,
with his poetry: he did not hurry himself: if words came
work
they came. What good ~~poe~~ writing has ever been done in a hurry?
he asked Andrew, who alone of all the world was admitted to
Mr. Carmichaels bedroom, & had been shown those sacred
the the silk the
relics ~~a~~ tooth & ~~some dried~~ seeds & ~~some scraps~~ of silk
in a little ~~wood~~ scented box. ~~For~~ Did he not sometimes
wait a whole winter for words to come to him, Mr.
Carmichael proceeded, sinking into his arm chair. (He
translated <u>Persian</u>) & his eyes fixed blandly upon the sky
watch the flight of words
† seemed to ~~gaze~~ await contentedly as a cat will
& one [flies?]
watch the birds by the hour. ~~one~~ at last ~~will fly~~ within
reach. So, ~~disregarding Mr. Ramsays methodical industry~~,
at last a word came his way, & he set it down, completed
at all
~~another of those stanzas which~~ & had no doubt that these
stanzas, which he translated from the Persian, were
long, so infinitely by
destined to endure so ~~many centuries~~ that the ~~lapse of~~ years
he ~~spent in~~ the months he spent making them were mere
in making it
mere drops in the That his own time vanished like a
Yet
drop of rain upon the window. And if there were
other ways of life than this, he saluted them; if there were
men ~~of more active~~ other views, he ~~only~~ prayed them to pass
him by, as slipping upstairs he craved of that
kind lady Mrs. Ramsay that she should not
require him to stop & talk to her, for in such
matters he was inadequate, he knew. As for
wasting his own meagre opportunities (for compared
with many men he knew himself to be of little account)
~~his~~ he was not ~~at all~~ inclined to ~~do~~ it: ~~he~~ was
so that, after a pause, a second helping of soup seemed to
desirable; he would, unconcernedly, ask the maid for it.

[Left margin:]
4 £ 8d
8 160

his

& he catches it;

(for how cd one
write regularly

other ways,

the ~~sun~~ the
of warmth for food;
of the comfort of a
chair; a
little expedition; some
trifling gratification
of the senses.

† A 145, B 150

But he was growing very fat.

† ~~Like all~~ / his ~~daughters~~, Prue & Nancy knew what was passing in ~~their father's mind~~ their father's ~~Mr. Ramsay's~~ mind: felt his irritation; knew the cause of it, but with this difference between them – Prue was eighteen, & therefore already ~~admitted~~ a member of the great ~~that great~~ corporation, grown up people; so that she desired ~~harmony~~ above all things/ Nancy was sixteen; & therefore still ~~detached~~ outside ~~of all~~ groups & societies; ~~lit~~ d~~etached & aloof~~, so ~~that if she~~ so that she desired of all things freedom. & could not restrain herself, seeing her father scowl, seeing Mr. Carmichael tuck his napkin in & spoon up soup, ~~afresh~~, from ~~such a~~ spasm of delight of merriment, of criticism (for why were old people so absurd?) as shook her, & would shake all the children, Mrs. Ramsay knew. ~~They~~ They would all burst out laughing ~~she.~~ ~~So~~ ~~why not light the candles~~?

† ~~Fetch~~ Light the candles, she said promptly, adding how dark it was getting; & Nancy, Roger jumping up simultaneously exploded by the side board, & then, to make up, lit the candles with the greatest assiduity; showing themselves most eager, most indefatigable in this matter; so that

† the eight white candles were soon lit, & their shades adjusted, & after the first stoop of the flames, they stood upright burnt up again & seemed to draw with them up into visibility ~~the whole of~~ the long table, & in particular ~~Ros~~ the ~~dish of fruit in the centre.~~ the pinks the yellows the blues of the fruit in the centre. what ~~How~~ ~~she had arranged it~~ ~~Mrs. Ramsay.~~ had she done with it, Mrs. Ramsay wondered, inspecting ~~the~~ Rose's arrangement; of grapes & pears; – how they were built up about a horny pinklipped shell, so as to

† have the effect of some trophy fetched from the bottom of the sea & ~~Fruits of the sea, Neptune's banquet, the~~ not so much of actual ~~things, but~~ of fruits of the sea, of Neptune's banquet, of the

[Margin notes: "harmony" (beside "things/ Nancy"); "at the / of amazement / at the astonishing / antics of the [~~wo~~?] old" (beside "Carmichael … shook her"); "reminded her" (beside "have the effect")]

† A 144, B 149; A 145; B 150, A 146; B 151

~~of the Bacchus~~ – ~~in short of nothing~~ –
of the bunch that hangs over the shoulder of Bacchus, ~~or is~~ among
~~lion skins~~ leopard skins & torches wavering ~~gol~~ red & gold
It was odd, Mrs. Ramsay thought – her power ~~of~~ with her hands; &
~~Th pr~~ in her pride, she saw how Mr. Carmichaels eyes
feasted like bees upon the sight, plunged themselves into it, & [broke this & that from it]
returned from it laden with gold ~~to his hive~~; to ~~make honey from,~~
~~while she & all~~ For now they were all lit up; [&] – the
faces on either side of the table had [were] all brought nearer
in the candle light; & composed, as they had not been in the
twilight, into a party round a table; while ~~outside~~
† the night ~~was outside~~ [was]; separated off by panes of glass which
far from giving any accurate view of the hedge, or of the
urns, ~~changed them, &~~ rippled them strangely so that it seemed as
† if, safe & dry the company sat at table, surrounded by [in the midst of]
~~wavering~~ water sprinkled with lights. ~~It is~~ [on an island]

It has ~~suddenly~~ become unreal, thought Lily Briscoe,
trying to account for the feeling of exhilaration which had
taken possession of them; & thinking how it was ~~partly~~
like the scene on the tennis lawn ~~over~~ again, ~~& was~~
when they were all so light hearted, & was partly due to the
~~queer lighting~~ – ~~these~~ little candles in the large, sparely [with its pale green walls ✓]
furnished room, & the uncurtained windows; [&] to the transparency [~~soft~~ bright]
of the lights, [all the faces in] when in came – ~~several things~~: First Minta
Doyle; then Janet with a large earthenware pot; then [the candle light,]
Paul Rayley; & then the ~~little~~ Swiss girl, with
more dishes; ~~& Paul Rayley came~~ & sat between her
& Mrs. Ramsay, ~~Minta~~ Doyle, all of which had
to be set down, that is the dishes had to be arranged;
Minta & Paul had to find their places (he between he –
Mrs. Ramsay; she beside Mr. Ramsay) & ~~Minta~~
they were both frightfully nervous.

† "Poor Minta lost her brooch" said
Mrs. Ramsay instantly.

† A 147; B 152; A 148

& he was moved by the ~~odd~~ lamplit love she had, her glow, her untidiness,

"Yes, my grandmother's brooch" said Minta, ~~to~~ with a sound of lament in her voice; & a suffusion of her large brown eyes which ~~in~~ roused all the chivalry in Mr. Ramsays heart; so that he he scolded her ~~for being dryly~~.

† How could she be such a fool? he ~~said~~ asked.
She was by way of being terrified of Mr. Ramsay

She was by way of being terrified of ~~Mr. Ramsay~~. He was so fearfully
clever. ~~In truth, she got on with him beautifully, &~~ He made her
feel so common, she would say; & ~~& she had tried to talk about~~
but
~~George Eliot, whom he mentioned, but nervous of~~ having left
the third volume of Middlemarch in the Tube, ~~could not~~
that
~~a fact which she had never regretted until this moment, could not~~
ran out of literary conversation, ~~& they~~ the very first ~~e~~
But
evening; ~~but~~ Nevertheless got on with him beautifully, & ~~now~~
~~liked him to call her a fool, which he did when he called her~~
~~a fool, he called her a fool, she felt quite at her ease with him~~,
~~only~~ & ~~knew that only a little~~ & ~~determined to not much~~
~~frightened, only enough to make it seem rather daring to~~
~~she felt~~ what Lily Briscoe had never felt in the course of her life –
that ~~every~~ round about her was a golden haze. She could not help it:
she could not alter it. Sometimes she had it; sometimes not; ~~or~~ but
knew that
tonight she had it; she ~~was awfully glad to think that~~ tonight
&
she had it; ~~&~~ Mr. Ramsay felt it; & that when he said
within the
How could you be such a fool? he was under circle
not about George Eliot [of course?]
~~the shell~~ of her ~~g~~ golden haze. She need scarcely speak;
~~or~~ any nonsense that came into her head. Please, what had he
been doing? ~~what right had he to~~ ~~Had he been virtuously~~
~~occupied~~? (for she could chatter to him any nonsense) ~~Reading~~?
† How many pipes had he smoked? It was a fact that
Mr. Ramsay liked talking nonsense ~~better than anything in the world~~
for a time, with a young woman, with a pretty young
not quite
woman, who (but the distinction he made was ~~not by no means~~
off
clear) ~~looked~~ ~~did her hair,~~ "didn't scrape her hair ~~up~~"; which
Minta did not, but Lily Briscoe did; & that included
something flying, something even a little wild &
into
bold & harumscarum into the bargain. There was some
quality, which Mrs. Ramsay herself had not – some lustre, some
richness, some intemperance, which attracted him: solaced
him; & led him to devise curious treats for these

[Left margin:]
it terrified her to be made to talk to him, especially as

so that they had to give [ ? ]

& tonight she felt

somehow so that he spoke with that she curious tone wh.

it did not matter about George Eliot, but

better than anything in the world

† B 154, A 149

favourites; they might cut his hair for him; plait him chains, or
interrupt his work, pulling him ~~up~~ out of his chair to play at
croquet with them;

Mrs. Ramsay knew it. At this very moment she felt it, &
asked herself how then it would have been if he had married one of
them – those girls she meant, with a certain golden-reddishness
about them, like Minta, whom she liked too; indeed she was
not jealous; indeed she was almost grateful to them, for their ~~pulling~~ laughing at
him till he seemed young & fiery & romantic; ~~no longer~~ &
not caustic; not ~~w~~ burdened; not overcome with the greatness of his
labours & the sorrows of the world & the ~~failure, or~~
precise degree of failure or success of his books; but again, as she
had known him, at the beginning of life, ~~with his temper~~
† gallant~~ry & his simplicity~~ simple. For herself, she liked ~~the~~
her boobies – that was her husband's name for young men
like Paul Rayley ~~who were not brilliant~~; ~~but never
pretended to be anything~~ There was, she thought, beckoning
Paul to a seat beside her, something most charming about a
young man of twenty six, ~~& so who is not all nerves, & all~~
He need not be brilliant. ~~She was not brilliant~~ She had
enough of brilliance. And how unfair, & how absurd, & how
~~entirely lacking in commonsense examiners are, she~~
to call him stupid, she thought, as he took his place, awfully
sorry awfully sorry to be so late beside her He would eat –
whatever there was. And he gave ~~her a~~ did she know this flower? A flower we found,
~~It was something common that grows on moors~~; ~~something~~
& he pretended that he wanted her to name it; ~~whereas~~,
~~what had happened was that he~~ though it was quite a common
flower. ~~We picked it for you~~, he said; & so she would
take it & keep it; ~~& put it away among those~~ so it
would remind her; so it became instantly the token of
~~W~~ For ~~what could one say~~? They had agreed
not to say anything, either of them, until they were alone
with Mrs. Ramsay. ~~Yet~~ ~~But he~~ did And yet when he saw
her, he felt he must tell her, & so gave her a flower he had
in his button hole. Which he had meant to keep always.
~~But he instead~~ ~~It was~~ So she took it.

† A 150, B 155

sat<br>
~~how sorry~~ beside her, saying that he was sorry, awfully sorry, that they<br>
[were late,<br>
did not deserve any food, & so on.

But it was<br>
~~No sooner had he sat down than~~ ~~it seemed~~ impossible ~~that~~<br>
that she should not ~~know~~ knew ~~what had happened to him~~; & how,<br>
[since lunch,<br>
~~such a thing had happened~~; ~~he~~ a thing had happened; ~~which~~<br>
& it<br>
he was changed; ~~all~~ was her doing; ~~yet~~ "~~We~~

"~~A flower we found on the cliff~~" he said, ~~taking~~

We ~~had to look go~~ went back to look for Minta's<br>
~~her~~ wh really<br>
~~Minta~~'s brooch" he said, & ~~really~~ ~~that~~ was ~~quite~~ enough: ~~as~~<br>
~~as he said~~ his tremor over<br>
by ~~this way~~ ~~for~~ Mrs. Ramsay ~~to~~ knew then; "we" ~~went back~~; & then<br>
it cost him to say<br>
the little effort the ~~little hesitation~~ in saying Minta; she<br>
~~knew then for certain, & having~~ & by ~~the~~ especially by that<br>
'we' which, she thought ~~will~~ is the first time I have heard him<br>
say it, & it seemed to her extremely moving on his lips "we",<br>
that they were now<br>
when it implied, as she knew it did, ~~a~~ a lifetime together, for life,<br>
& &<br>
impl~~ied~~ his care, his suffering – She knew then ~~by exactly~~ what<br>
speak<br>
had happened, & how he could ~~scarcely~~ ~~keep his eyes off~~<br>
Minta, ~~or~~ & how the ~~table~~ lights glittered in his eyes; & how<br>
how<br>
everybody seemed to him a little unreal; & ~~an immense~~<br>
gratitude filled his heart.

~~But she must help them~~ –<br>
~~But from the~~ A ~~fragrance rose from the great~~<br>
peering into the great<br>
~~brown dish~~; But twist~~ing & steaming~~ an exquisite scent of<br>
olives & oil & juice rose from the great brown dish; &<br>
† ~~she peered into it &~~ & she must help them, [ ? ] that a<br>
special portion should be ~~kep~~ given ~~her~~ to William Bankes;<br>
Nobody would believe how much thought had gone to that dish<br>
It had been stewed for three days & she thought as she peered into the<br>
† ~~It~~ dish, with its shiny walls, & its confusion of savoury brown & yellow<br>
~~sweetness &~~ slabs in ~~which were bayleaves & port,~~ lying at the<br>
bottom, this ~~will celebrate the day, this w is the~~<br>
~~I'm glad we had this for the great day~~, some irresponsibility

† A 151; B 156

curious sense of ~~celebrating an~~ rising in her of ~~all~~ celebrating a festival, tenderly festivity, at once ~~wild &~~ ~~wild &~~ ly freakish ly ~~& tender~~, as if ~~she~~ being a married woman, ~~&~~ a ~~mother she was~~ laughing while she ~~el~~ celebrated, ~~there~~ as if ~~there~~ two emotions collided in her, one profound – for what could be more serious than this – the love of man for woman – what more commanding, & impressive,? ~~& the~~ bearing in it the seeds of death & tragedy: at the same time, ~~something sportive~~ – ~~something~~ lovers, those ~~entering into~~ suffering illusion, those glittering-eyed, whom she would have to pack off together for their walks their talks, & perhaps devote one sitting room entirely to, ~~them~~, ~~these she~~ these & she mocked, & decorated, ~~hung garlands round, a~~s with garlands ~~of laughter;~~ must be

& yet at the same time these lovers these people entering into illusion, must be danced round with mockery & decorated with garlands of ~~flowers~~

"It is a triumph" said William Bankes – It was delicious: it was rich; it was tender; it was ~~thoughtful~~ real cooking with skill & taste in it, not merely serving up lumps of meat up ~~roast~~ browned over. How did she manage these things in the depths of the country? he asked her? She was a wonderful woman – he thought

It ~~was~~ is a French ~~dish~~ receipt", said Mrs. Ramsay. ~~She was~~

† She ~~felt~~ agreed with Mr. Bankes, ~~that~~ what passes for cookery in England is ~~simply~~ an abomination. It is putting cabbage in water. ~~It is Then you throw away the water which~~ ~~It is~~ Stews, ~~rice puddings~~ –: which can be ~~d~~ so delicious in France – all this tastes like leather & sawdust in England. After years & years she had Roasting meat till it like shoe leather. Cutting off the delicious skins of vegetables. ~~Every sin~~ [Stewed?] Boiling, stewing,

† roasting, never anything else: & so wasteful too. ~~so wasteful~~ that a French family ~~could easily~~ can live, on what an English cook throws away. Upon all this they were ~~entirely~~ agreed: so strangely

† A 152; B 157

They ~~agreed. How happy she seemed~~, ~~for been Mrs. Ramsays~~ Her
exaggerations gave a sense of extraordinary ~~happiness.~~ happiness
She was spurred on by some inner exhilaration; ~~one~~ English
"Any little French Inn," she ~~was saying~~ said –
& Lily laughed at her. How childlike, how absurd – yes, Mrs. Ramsay [was
overpowering. ~~Sh~~ always she got her own way ~~Its~~ Lily
& she was perfectly happy. thought she had brought off this now – Paul & Minta were engaged –
~~& it seemed her doing.~~ She put a spell on people. Why Lily
"~~How did Minta~~ felt it – ~~the~~ She felt Paul
Rayley sitting there ~~silent;~~ under that spell; ~~that~~ for it was
Mrs. Ramsay's doing that too – ~~there~~ that deep, that inarticulate,
that ~~glowing~~ terrifying ~~attractive~~ glowing ~~male~~ silence – Mrs. Ramsay
exalted that; worshipped that; & acknowledged that as the
light of life, its & the way he kept looking across at Minta,
~~&~~ his tremor, his abstraction – Mrs. Ramsay sanctioned all
† that, worshipped that, & would ~~in her~~ having achieved
that, ~~proceed~~ somehow laugh to lead her victims, ~~garlanded,~~ to the altar.
But Lily did feel it, ~~herself:~~ she felt it really too much. She
† felt inconspicuous, insignificant, sitting beside Paul Rayley; &
~~like a~~ And she felt it herself. She ~~felt more~~ emotionally,
how inconspicuous she was by his side; he, glowing, burning;
she aloof, satirical; he bound for adventure; she moored to the
banks; he, in some way launched, incautious, given; & she
solitary & unillusioned; left out, ~~unclaimed~~ – she was
ready to implore a share ~~in his~~ if it were disaster
in his disaster & said
"How did Minta lose her brooch?"
She was repaid by the most exquisite smile; veiled
of ~~course Paul Rayley knew:~~ by memory, tinged by dream,
for clearly
~~But~~ I shall be up early & find it

† A 153; B 158

But this was to be kept secret from Minta. So that he lowered his voice, & turned averted his eyes from ~~that~~ where she sat, by Mr. Ramsay.

Lily would have liked to have ~~have taken~~ vowed violently outrageously ~~her~~ that she would help him; ~~only~~ believing hoping that she would be the one, in the early dawn, to light upon the brooch, on the beach, & then be included among the sailors & adventurers, ~~the~~ those who have sacrificed, cast adrift, & ~~gone~~ hoisted their sails.

But what did he reply to her offer? She actually said
† with an emotion she seldom let appear, "~~Do~~ come with let me help you",
~~&~~ He laughed. ~~Perhaps~~ he meant yes or no – either perhaps. But it was an odd chuckle. ~~So~~ entirely regardless of her: ~~so~~ as if he had said Throw yourself over the cliff if you like; as if he had said – ~~Lily found herself veering violently away again in the opposite direction~~ turned the heat of love
† upon her cheek, & scorched her, where she had seen only the lovely ~~brilliant~~ flame: the heat of love, its horror, its cruelty, its treachery, its savagery unscrupulosity. Lily looked at Minta, being charming; ~~be~~ at the other end of the table; in the centre of her ~~golden haze~~ & ~~could see~~ her, ~~shrank for~~ her, trembled for her, exposed to the this heat of love; ~~horror & this savagery~~. ~~For it is awful, love~~; What ~~quite~~ like a deer gashed, or a flower ~~tree~~ felled; & then, seeing the ~~m~~ salt cellar, she remembered with a start, ~~how she was~~ to move the tree in her picture to the right: ~~thank Heaven, she breathed~~, ~~such an &~~ she So escaped, & so so rejoiced, & thanked God that she was need not to marry anybody even Paul Rayley. ~~She had her painting. And the detestable passion, which the unscrupulous, the demented, the~~ but might paint. might escape the floods ~~horror~~ of brutality which this estimable passion lets loose upon the world, its

to h
Such was the complexity of things. For what happened at the Ramsays
[was
simply Lily, (especially) at the Ramsays was to think what she
could not say, Indeed two things at a time, one the opposite of the other,
it
as now; love is the beautiful, but so that I tremble on the verge of it
throwing myself into the flame; but also despicable; it is also the lowest &
vilest of passions, so that a nice young man, with a perfect profile
under its [?]
with a cane — profile is instantly becomes a rough, a bully under its influence
He was like a man who breaks open the doors of timid maiden
the old Kent Road — ladies & bran or swaggers in a suit of cordoroys down some
† backstreet in Whitechapel. Now, Lily thought, Yet Lily knew,
its wreaths, its roses, its — how from the dawn of history odes have been sung to Love,
yet
& garlands wreaths hung round it; & how if you asked nine women out
of ten what they desired they would say; 'love'; yet meaning all
† the time that there was nothing they abominated more, or
tedious,
thought more puerile, & inhumane, like the The truth lies
between the two, she sup As for the truth, What then was the
And the — truth then? Something she supposed between the two – &
she supposed; & luckily there was no compulsion upon her to
always
tell it. All her life she would say one thing & what other
it was
people said. It was safer, simpler, & so frightfully difficult to
For
be quite sure what one meant. For it was Yes, she did
feel moved by Paul, Minta; she could not deny it. liked them
& immensely, both of them –: it was very beautiful.

Mr. "There is, said Mr. Bankes, That liquid the English
said Mr. Bankes
call coffee", – a remark that roused Mrs. Ramsay to
the depths of her heart, & was broug led directly to
the allied but more agust august questions of pure butter &
uncontaminated milk; as her sons & daughters were aware,
for Speaking with emphasis & eloquence, as if she had
never mentioned the subject before, she described the iniquity
of the English dairy, was about to substantiate her argument
when
with charges when yells & peals, the all round
the table, beginning with Andrew, in the middle, like a fire

† which leaping from tuft to tuft of furze, her children laughed; her
                   &         [husband
laughed; she was laughed at, fire-encircled, forced to ~~va~~ veil her
crest, dismount her batteries & only retaliate by displaying the raillery
† ~~am~~ ridicule of the table to Mr. Bankes as ~~the~~ an example of
what one suffered, attacking the prejudices of the British public.

Conveniently, for she had it on her mind that Lily was out of things,
                                 [she
exempted her ~~&~~ from the rest; claimed her an adherent; &
so drew her in. ~~That charming old maid, as Mr. Ramsay called~~
Charming as she was, & exquisite in her own way too, with her
~~sa~~ little puckered up face & Chinese eyes,) She was out of things, Mrs.
Ramsay felt; so was Charles Tansley; both suffered from
comparison with the glow of the other ~~two~~. Both were aware of it,
she felt; ~~while it made~~ Charles Tansley ~~disagreeable, quite~~
~~naturally, it depressed her poor little Brisk, she~~ was all on
         poor fellow
pins & needles. No woman would look at him with Paul Rayley
in the room. ~~there~~. With Lily it was different. She faded; became more ~~&~~
~~more~~ inconspicuous. than ever. Yet, thought Mrs. Ramsay as
she claimed her help, ~~in~~ (for Lily should bear her out that
she had not talked about butter & milk for at least three days;)
† ~~she is~~ of the two Lily will wear better. For there was in
                         a little flare of
Lily a ~~sort of~~ thread of something; an angularity. ~~a ch~~
a ~~quality~~ of character which in ~~her~~ spite of everything Mrs.
Ramsay ~~could not~~ liked, respected; though no man would.
† Obviously not. Unless it were an ~~od~~ older man, like
William Bankes. But then he cared, well, Mrs.
Ramsay thought sometimes that he cared, now that his wife was
dead, more than any one for her.

charming as she was with her little puckered face & Chinese eyes.

Oh but nonsense, she thought. William shall marry Lily.
Foolishly, she had set them opposite each other. That could be
[remedied tomorrow.
Everything seemed possible. Everything seemed right. ~~It seemed so~~
Just now, (this cannot last, she thought) she hovered, like a hawk,
suspended; like a flag ~~flutt~~ floating, in the element of
joy which filled every nerve in her body ~~& without~~
fully & sweetly, ~~&~~ not noisily, ~~& th~~ rather solemnly; for
did it not arise, partly, from ~~the~~ solemn things? love of
† husband, love of children, love of friends? ~~& not~~ which
in this profound stillness (she was ~~h~~ helping William Bankes to one
very small piece more; & peered into the depths of the ea
† earthenware pot) seemed, ~~with~~ for no special reason, ~~without a~~
~~word said~~, or ~~any accident to bring it about~~, in the ordinary
[suddenly — wonderfully] course of things, ∧ to rise up, & ~~become could one imagine such a~~
~~thing — like a peal of silent bells; or the~~ like a smoke, an incense, or
a fume which being ~~invisible &~~ imperceptible to the ordinary
senses ~~one might~~ was for her with her dreading ~~of ins~~ expression as shaded
~~insincerity & words~~ ~~sentimentality~~ & ~~words are always one or~~
~~the other~~ The insincerity, the sentimentality of words, ~~was for her~~
divinely satisfactory; & partook, she felt, carefully helping Mr.
[so solid & entire it seemed] Bankes, of eternity, ~~reminding her~~ was immune, like the past itself,
from change & glowed in the face of ruin ~~&~~ a constant
jewel, so that here tonight was the heaven for such as her;
Yes, she assured him, there was quite enough.
Andrew wanted more. — the still space which
lies — close about the moon; ~~the~~
~~And moving~~ there ~~with the since~~ She could move
or be at rest; could wait a moment, now that they were
† all helped; & then like the hawk which lapses suddenly
from its high ~~station~~ poise, flaunt & sink, on laughter,
easily, reposing her whole weight upon what at the other

† A 158; B 163; A 159

† end of the table her husband was saying about – was it square roots, cubes, the numbers on tickets? ~~And~~

Mrs. Ramsay did not know to this day what ~~that~~ it meant: but her husband did. Her sons did ~~too.~~ She leant on their strength. Cubes & square roots & ~~y~~ x plus y; P Talleyrand & the Princesse de Ligne; Voltaire, Madame de Stael & the French Revolution; ~~how~~ she let it ~~all~~ uphold her, & sustain her, this admirable fabric of ~~beautiful~~ masculine intelligence, which ran up & down, like iron girders ~~which, without~~ crossed this way & that, upheld the world. ~~Until~~ so that she could trust herself to it utterly, & even shut her eyes, & or blink them be lost for a moment, like a child ~~blinking~~ dreaming up from its pillows at the myriad layers of the leaves of a tree; & then, waking, ~~she would~~ there it was be ~~in~~ still being fabricated. For now William Bankes was giving ~~his opinion of the pre~~ praising; Waverley novels; & springing to his feet metaphorically,

equalling something else;

† rejoicing at this chance of asserting his existence, Charles Tansley whose father was a chemist, whose grandfather was a ~~boat~~ fisherman, was ~~denouncing with~~ in his own how if they asked him, ~~had C~~ English literature was denouncing them. Being ~~a~~ the son of a working man ~~he was of course he was he approached literature from a different point of view.~~ Literature is not a mere pastime for idle hours. he said So many people at the table had enjoyed some books occasionally that they felt uncomfortable. If only Prue would be decently kind to him, Mrs. Ramsay thought, he would not say these things. ~~But~~ for though William Bankes would never be ~~rude~~, unkind, she could judge what he was thinking – impertinent puppy, & all the rest of it. And he was not, like that & (for he sending his little sister to a good school, &

~~& still she was perfectly safe~~.

208 William Bankes was praising the Waverley novels. Then
snatched his chance
160 Charles Tansley, like a dog ~~let off the chain~~ at last, denounced
them. As the son of a chemist, the grandson of a fisherman, he
rushed in – all because Prue would not be nice to him; &
denounced them; when ~~anybody~~ ~~it was all~~ when he knew
† nothing about it, nothing whatever, Mrs. Ramsay thought,
~~Like~~ ~~All~~ ~~The world was so divided, she thought~~; observing, rather
than listening, for it was the way people said things, not the
actual things they said, which ~~convinced her.~~ conveyed to her the
~~aptitude or~~ their aptitude or disaptitude & you had only to
to ~~see~~ tell
hear ~~the~~ him laying down the law ~~about the to know how it was~~
~~hopeless forever~~, ~~how he knew nothing, nothing whatever, but~~
~~then in~~ that he ~~did not know, had~~ how he was among
those ~~whose~~ the natural enemies of all ~~painting &~~ arts
~~writing~~, for which she bore him no grudge. No. For
then they were free to do other things; ~~&, if it was unfortunate~~
~~that it~~ young men of his type were ~~necessary~~; & if it was
unfortunate ~~that~~ & ~~did~~ hindered the progress of the world
that they had these limitations ~~yet it was enviable too, & left~~
~~so that she had never known~~ it freed them; & lent him that
that fierceness, that power, ~~which~~ ~~that~~ which ~~issuing as it did~~
which might issue in a love ~~of his~~ mankind, qualified as that
seemed to be inevitably by his hatred of the arts – And
somebody, not Prue, would be kind to him, & then she felt,
~~again~~ he will not say ~~all day long "my~~ one moment
will be
"my dissertation;" the next, "my grandfather" – but ~~would~~
~~well, he would~~ never be in the least like Mr. Carmichael –
For he was chanting somebodies poem, why she did not know

& in her clairvoyant state she saw him denouncing the Waverley novels because his feelings were snubbed, & thus he must protest, how he was the son of a workingman, &

& she could see how it was – he wanted to assert himself, & so it would always be with him until he had ~~was his~~ got his professorship, or married his wife, & then he ~~would be~~ very v~~aluable in some way. she had free to do what~~ ~~but at present he could only say~~ at one moment "my dissertation", ~~but~~ & it was ~~sheer non moonshine all this about~~ nonsense for him to ~~pretend that he~~ to talk about books; when he was thinking of himself as she could tell by the sound of his voice, & his emphasis, & his uneasiness. ~~But he But inevitably the But &~~ In her clearsightedness which seemed ~~to pierce the without effort~~ or ~~bitterness to unveil one after another,~~ to go round the table unveiling each of them without effort, ~~in a tranquil~~ like a light stealing under water so that its ripples, & the reeds in it, & the minnows balancing themselves & the sudden silent trout are all held up in their reality to the ~~view~~ eye to ~~feast on~~ look upon: ~~then glancing~~ she saw & heard them & liked her husband for his annoyance: about the Waverley novels; yet ~~for he was~~ being saddened suddenly & sincerely by this little man's dislike of the Waverley novels – which he knew by heart; ~~then she like for what~~ & then ~~there was Mr. Bankes~~ liked Jane Austen, & ~~& their~~ but whatever they said (~~for instance~~ Mr. had this quality ~~that it~~ as if ~~when she saw~~ what they said & [bends?] was ~~only~~ like the movement of the trout, when the same time the ripple moves, the light ~~changes~~ quivers; & the all is suspended in the same one can see the ripple & the ~~light, & the~~ whole life in the stream & the gravel, & something solemn & dark surrounding that one flash; so that ~~she she now~~ if Mr. Bankes said how much he preferred

& the impression he was making,

Jane Austen to any other writer

so that it passed out of Mrs. Ramsay's mind ~~that she had had any reason for~~ how, naturally, in daily life, she would be
† casting a net over all this, ~~&~~ & forced by the exigencies of behaviour to separate & judge & connect & applaud – Now it was

† A 161, B 166

~~But~~ Now she dwelt on it; with her wings spread;

It was ~~really interesting~~. How long do books last? ~~Then~~, what qualities make them last? ~~Then, Mr. Ramsay~~ She minded [its being said] the fact that Scott was out of date. Mr. Bankes laughed & attached no importance to these changes in fashion. ~~who~~ Who could tell what was ~~go~~ going to last? – who minded? Mr. Ramsay minded very much. He thought constantly of his own fame; Mr. Bankes scarcely ever thought of such things at all. Mr. Tansley was reading Tolstoy. [About that he was quite enthusiastic. Mrs. Ramsay thought that he had given up thinking about himself. He thought War & Peace the greatest ~~book~~ [novel] in the ~~w~~ world. Still, he was thinking of himself a little. He was never as impersonal as Mr. Bankes. What is taste? asked Mr. Bankes. Nothing made him budge from his own view – he did not mind leaving books unread. He read Jane Austen & Scott over & over again. ~~M~~ Paul Rayley liked Trollope. [But] He could think of nothing clever to say.

† ~~however so he~~ Minta said ~~her grea~~ she did not believe that anybody [really] liked ~~reading~~ Shakespeare. ~~At this~~ Mrs. Ramsay ~~liked this very much indeed.~~ ~~And He~~ agreed that very few people liked it as much as they said they did. Andrew thought that this was going too far. ~~But some of it is~~ People might ~~not~~ see that his father was ironical. There is considerable merit in some of it, however, he said. [but he added] Minta supposed he was making fun of her. But she did not mind in the least. He was so vain, so extraordinarily vain, that one need never be frightened of him – perhaps not so much frightened of him as of Mrs. Ramsay, who was not

† A 162, B 167

not vain, so that you could scarcely take her off her guard.
Mrs. Ramsay thought ~~almost~~ almost the same thing of Paul
& perhaps more inscrutable
Rayley – how much nicer, she found stupidity than cleverness.
For the stupid have no ambition to thrust themselves forwards,
& thus instead of always thinking am I being clever, am I
being admired they think whether one is hot or cold, whether
one ~~mu~~ feels the draught, or would like ~~another~~ a pear;
She might sit there forever, & Charles Tansley would never
remember to offer her a pear. But then Paul
Rayley ~~And~~ would; & so, ~~again spr~~ fluttering her
wings over the table & all these odds & ends of speech,
which were like the ~~little~~ darts & dashes of trout, she
felt no ~~grudge against Charles Tansley, any more than~~
~~against that fish, for how there is no The reeds~~ saw
Nancy
at the same time the reeds in the pool, & the
walls of brown water ~~& the night, when~~
† surrounding them; ~~when, having looked at the~~
deciding that after all she did not want a pear, she
& her eyes
suddenly saw Rose's creation, rising up like a
crown or bouquet of flowers on the top of the water;
with its beautiful curves, & its interstices, its hollows &
huge bulges; ~~something the extraordinarily~~
~~beautiful it was she pl~~ she too, like Mr.
Carmichael, went plundering the fruit, ~~n~~
~~trying~~ first looking at the banana, then at the pears,
& putting one colour against another, one curve, one
hollow, without knowing why she did it, but
~~gett~~ each time she ~~saw~~ did it she ~~was~~
became gradually more satisfied, & ~~more until rising~~ she
† ~~saw to~~ & she ~~called~~ looked at Rose & Timothy &
Prue & Andrew all sitting side by side, & thought

† A 163, B 168; B 169, A 164

† Mrs. Ramsay knew all that, & hoped that the talk would soon leave this dangerous subject of ~~book~~ the fame of books. But then Minta said she did not believe that anyone really enjoyed reading Shakespeare. &

But he added, there is considerable merit in some of the plays. & Mrs. Ramsay ~~wondered whether th seeing~~ saw that Minta liked being laughed at & was not frightened; ~~that~~ she realised his extreme vanity, & would take care of him, so that she attended now to ~~Paul Rayley~~ who ~~wished to to show that he had read books~~ to what Paul Rayley was trying to say: how he thought Trollope was better in his way than Dickens. A very stupid remark. Mrs. Ramsay knew that, but then how much nicer stupidity is, she thought, ~~when~~ than cleverness, for when Charles Tansley said that War & Peace knocked out all the Waverley novels & all Jane Austen, what he meant was Tolstoy would have approved ~~as~~ of me, but not of you (that is, not of people who have servants & table napkins) – & ~~that was~~

† ~~really stupider, more stupid~~; he was thinking of himself, but Paul, like all stupid people, never thought am I being clever, am I being admired, never thought about himself, at all, but whether she was hot or cold, whether she felt the draught, whether she wanted a pear. ~~And though~~ She did not want a pear; ~~she wanted him to go on, being wanted nothing~~; ~~Her eyes rested on the dish of fruit~~ She did not want anybody to take any fruit. Her eyes rested on the dish & went in & out of the ~~round~~ apples & the thick ~~bananas into~~ the interstices & hollows, among the grapes & bananas, putting a yellow against a purple, & then a curved ~~ag~~ shape against a round shape,

anxiety about his own books & his own fame,

† A 162, B 167; A 163, B 168

without knowing why she did it, or why ~~she beca~~ as she did it she
† became happier, & then she thought, looking at Rose, who
~~set~~ sat between Timothy & Prue, how ~~t~~ odd, ~~she~~
that one's child should do that!

How odd that they should [to see them sitting there,] sit there in a row, [her children] Timothy
Rose, Prue, Andrew, almost silent, but with some joke
of their own going on, she ~~kn~~ knew, from the twitching of
their lips. ~~What it could be, she~~ It was something
quite apart from ~~what~~ everything else something
they were hoarding up: something ~~that would~~ [that would not end when]
that would ~~serve~~ to carry the world on when her own
ripple was spent. ~~Hoarded behind~~ There ~~was~~ [all that] hoarded
behind those rather set, rather solemn faces; for they did
not yet talk easily ~~though Prue~~ ~~But~~ Prue certainly was
lovely, [tonight] / lovelier than she had ever looked, as if the
glow of Minta opposite, the ~~sense of~~ happiness, the
excitement of the evening, were reflected in her; ~~but~~ it was
the rising of that marvellous sun, ~~man~~ the love of
men & women, which, ~~as it~~ was stealing over the
rim of the tablecloth, & ~~wil~~ entirely without her
knowing it, was ~~giving her that sky that~~ [~~restin~~ in her eyes & making] making her
† glance at Minta now & then, shyly [curiously] happily, so that
Mrs. Ramsay, hovering over one & then over another,
† as they said this & that, ~~you shall have all that~~, [vowed to herself But]
~~much~~ more ~~than all that~~ (for ~~she~~ was ~~her~~ ~~own~~
daughter) one of these days. But you will be
far happier one of these days, because you are
my daughter, she meant, & therefore it was certain
that she would be happier, as they were all, to Mrs.

[Left margin:] the door was shut up in their own room – she wondered what. as if the joke would explode when they were all dead in the future –

† B 169, A 164; B 170; A 165

protected in some odd way, ~~made~~ & raised above the lot of
ordinary people – a fact which was due to her husband, not herself,
that ~~great man,~~ ~~but he~~ & ~~rising~~ she ~~said rose~~ &
& hesitating for a moment she looked to see if they were ready
to leave the dinner table: but he was having some joke with
Minta; ~~a bet about some game, thing~~; about a bet,
she waited; ~~of course~~ how proper Paul Rayley was thinking embroiled in how
marvellous Minta was & William Bankes ~~had really~~ wa
enjoyed himself she knew; & Charles Tansley – she
liked him better for being so annoyed. & Lily ~~seemed to~~
have some ~~private joke of her own – she lik that was~~
Lily's point; & she always had some little affair of her own
† on hand – She waited. This moment partook of eternity; she felt was
~~inm~~ immune from change. ~~A~~ This glowed in the face of
† chaos; & She looked at the window. ~~But the~~
~~but it was~~ now so dark that only the candles were
to be seen in it; dark now with candles wavering in it.
~~Here were the walls of the~~ they were like stream which surrounded
~~them, & then~~ as ~~they were by the walls~~
& it seemed to her as if she ~~were still floating~~
could go in & out here, among the dishes & the glasses,
even as the window glowed with its little candlelights (for
the pane was now dark ~~with~~ as night) & the flames
burnt brighter) ~~glowed~~ & also it was like a
† great cathedral with the sudden bursts of laughter, &
then one voice ~~spea~~ (Minta's) speaking alone; &
~~it~~ like some service in a Roman Catholic Church;
which always ~~seemed to~~ her irreverent & therefore
she waited; her husband was in such spirits that
he was ~~quoting~~ laughing at Carmichael;
old Mr. Carmichael rousing himself was quoting the
words But it would never come h

[Left margin: how aloof she was! how independent of them all!]

[Left margin: a poem a]

† A 158, B 163; A 165, B 171; A 166

& a voice (Mr. Carmichael's) began chanting

Come out & climb the garden path

Luriana Lurilee

The China Rose is all abloom & buzzing with

the yellow bee

& the words sounded they were floating about in

~~but she which~~ sounded as if ~~it~~ came from the darkness outside

& had no connection with any body

I wonder if it seems to you

Luriana Lurilee

That all the lives we ever lived &

all the lives to be

All full of trees & changing leaves*

Nor did she ~~attach much meaning to them~~

know quite what they meant, but like music, they

~~relieved her of th~~e seemed to ~~make~~ to

saying what ~~everybody had been feeling, &~~

she had felt, everybody had felt, but by herself she could never known

~~have thought~~ how to express ~~that deep, strange~~, the feeling,

that had haunted her all the evening ~~but it was not~~

& in addition ~~exactly what the words said, but the~~ sense they gave of

† someone ~~c~~ coming out from his shell, & being natural,

which was very & expressing the longing that was in

the fantasy & the all of them for some other life, & for roses & changing

leaves, their sorrow, ~~their~~ The astonishing desires

hopes which each

now

It was ~~old Mr.~~ Augustus Carmichael.

She waited.

Now surely it was time to ~~leave~~ go.

But ~~Mr. Carmichael went on chanting~~

---

* Charles Elton, 'Luriana Lurilee,' also quoted on MS 194, 214 (2.47)

† B 172

† She got up.

With that little effort which always attends a change of mood,
rising from ~~some~~ the depths where it had not been
got up
necessary to say this is this or that is that, she ~~rose~~ ~~got up~~
~~rose,~~ & perceiving how it was necessary now to carry
~~forward the whole~~ everything on a step further ~~&~~ yet
still
~~why, she thought to herself, can one not~~ with half her
remain
being she seemed ~~still~~ to be there still, in a
† scene which was vanishing as she moved, among
emotions which ~~had been extremely real but~~
hung about her, & yet, even as she moved, & took
changed,
† Mintas arm & left the room, it was ~~over,~~ it
itself it
~~they~~ formed ~~again,~~ differently & became ~~part~~ the past

29th March
1926*

* Written in pencil (2.49)
† A 167; B 173; A 168

To the

* End of volume II

Original MS of

TO THE LIGHTHOUSE

by Virginia Woolf

Part I* Uniform Edition pp 174-191**

* Typed, on blue paper

** Handwritten, probably by Leonard Woolf

& perhaps, feeling, when she went,
how they missed it.

did
† that firm swift ~~secret~~ ~~secret~~ decided way, Not that she ~~was~~ in fact
run or hurry upstairs; She felt, rather, inclined just for a
moment, ~~to shed, as it~~ to stand still, after all that
one
chattering, & pick out ~~whatever it was~~ some single thing:
the fact that Paul & Minta were engaged; to detach it,
separate it off; clean it of all the motions & follies; & so
hold it before her; bring it to the tribunal where, ranged
about in conclave sat the judges she had set up in her to
decide these things. Is it good, bad, right wrong? Am I
justified? Where does this all tend? & so on, righting
herself after the shock of the event; & quite incongruously,
using the branches of the elm trees outside ~~as~~
to stablise her position. All must be in order.
She must get that right, & that right, she thought, ~~as if~~
insensibly approving of the dignity, of the tranquility, &
now again of the very [beautily?] upward fling of the
elm branches, as the ~~wind r~~ wind raised them. So
† For it was windy.

---

* VW's page numbers begin here.
† A 169, B 174; B 175

† It was windy, so that the leaves now & then brushed ~~open~~ ~~clear~~ open a star, ~~& lit it &~~ the stars themselves seemed to be shaking & darting light & trying to flash out ~~irregular~~ between the edges of the leaves. Yes, that was done then; & as ~~over~~ with all

† things done, now one thought of it, clear of chatter & ~~emotion~~ ~~people~~, it ~~one flicked it~~ it seemed that it had always been, & was now shown, & ~~had been thought of in the dawn of things,~~ & ~~was~~ partook of immortality, was as a paving stone in the torrent of ~~the~~ living, a firm place to step on, ~~& looking back one would say~~ to which one they would return. ~~Char would come back to this night then~~ ~~Then They~~ They would come back to this night then. And it pleased her to think how ~~in the~~ all their lives long ~~with~~ in their memories she would be woven, & this, & this, & this, & she went in, noticing with a laughing affection, for she knew their shabbiness & how ~~ch~~ old they were – the table on the landing & the ~~cha~~ rocking chair & the bust of her mother. ~~In this home was~~ all that would be revived again in the lives of Paul & Minta, so she thought, with her hand on the nursery door, feeling that community with other people which emotion gives as if suddenly the walls of partition had became thin ~~as paper,~~ so that her own death would matter rather less, since Paul & Minta [merely inherita?] inherited the things she had accumulated – the table, the rocking chair, & map, & ~~taking them in to the stream of their own lives,~~ would swap them on ~~& on & on~~ ~~And~~ she ~~open~~

map of the Hebrides.

so that practically it was all one stream &

† turned the door handle, ~~&~~ firmly, ~~so as to~~ lest it should squeak, & went in, ~~to the~~ pursing her lips slightly, as if to prevent herself before she had spoken from speaking aloud. But it was not needed. She was annoyed. There was James wide awake, & Mildred ~~in her~~ out of bed.

† A 170; A 170; A 171, B 176

It was the skull again. She had told Mildred to move it, but Mildred, of course, had forgotten; & now there was Cam wide awake in her bed, James wide awake in his, because Cam woke up terrified by ~~the shadows~~ it, & ~~James of course~~ to James it was the apple of his eye. ~~Indeed~~ It was a horrid thing – a ~~wit~~ boar's skull that Edward had ~~shot~~ sent them from India, & foolishly, she had let James have it, ~~na~~ & it had been nailed to the wall, & ~~wh~~ then of course this happened; ~~they little quarrelled~~ ~~So~~ Mrs. Ramsay said could they not take it down? But ~~it was~~ nailed to the wall, Mildred ~~to~~ said. Then Cam must go to sleep & dream of lovely palaces, said Mrs. Ramsay sitting down ~~on her bed~~ by her side. ~~No:~~ ~~because if)~~ she knew it was there she must see it. said Cam † And it was true. Wherever they put the nightlight (& how could Mildred sleep without a light in the room? ~~she was~~ afraid of beetles) ~~one saw the a~~ ~~shadow of the tusks, as Cam said.~~ there was always a shadow somewhere. ~~Poor old pig, said Mrs. Ram~~

What had possessed Edward to send them this horrid boar's skull

The nail was so firm – besides James was so cried if ~~one even touched it~~ she so much as [being?] touched it.

"It was only an old pig" said Mrs. Ramsay, a nice old black pig like the pigs at the farm. Cam liked ~~the~~ pigs" ~~at the farm~~. Cam was terrified; Cam hated shadows; Cam could see the tusks whichever side she lay. She saw the shadow move. She must shut her eyes & think of birds & flowers & beautiful butterflies.

Well, then, said Mrs. Ramsay, ~~it must~~ we will cover it up." & ~~she~~ they all watched her, going to the chest of drawers, & opening ~~first the short drawer, & shutting looking in, & shutting it, & then opening the long drawer & taking~~ out ~~a~~ the little drawers quickly & not seeing what she wanted, & then quickly taking her shawl & winding it round the

† A 172, B 177

skull, & ~~making it sound & comfortable, & [wra?]~~
wrapping it round & round & round, & then she went back to Cam,
& laid her head down almost on the pillow, & said Oh how
lovely it looked – how the fairies would love it. It was like a great
bird's nest now. And it was, rather. Or it was like a great
mountain, ~~with~~ such as Mrs. Ramsay had seen in
Switzerland, with beautiful villages, full of flowers, &
birds singing, & little ~~girls with~~ girls, & little cottages with
smoke going up & ~~What~~ her mother had said was
true; it was like a mountain & a birds nest & a hanging
garden ~~on the side of a cif cliff, & birds~~ & a cloud, &
† And now James had got what he wanted, said Mrs. Ramsay
crossing over to his bed, & he must go to sleep at once.
But he wanted to ~~say~~ ask her something. ~~It was~~ She
suddenly remembered what it was going to be – it was
about the Lighthouse of course. Did she think they would
go to the Lighthouse tomorrow? ~~she~~ he asked
No not
She thought that they would not go tomorrow but she
thought ~~that they would~~ go soon. The very first fine day she said.

Cam looked & saw that

& she promised she would go to sleep & dream of mountains, gardens & beautiful birds "And everything that is ~~lovely~~; & stream, & parrots, & Mrs. Ramsay repeated, slower – slower, more & more mechanically, until Cam's eyes shut,

Feeling for her shawl, & remembering that she had
wrapped it round the boars ~~h~~ skull, she ~~to went~~, got up, &
stopping a moment to see that they had both lain
down ~~that & shut~~ Mildred was in bed, she
once more coming to see
thought that that the window was not wide enough open, –
so ~~crossed~~ & pulling it down another inch or two &
~~hearing the wave~~ so that she heard, more loudly, the
waves falling & got a ~~little~~ breath of the ~~sweet~~
the cold untainted night air she ~~left~~ murmured good
night & left the room, saying to herself, as she shut
the door "that is good Charles running up to his
work" & she only hoped, as she let the tongue of the
† door slowly lengthen itself, that, ~~necess~~ he would not
bump & bang above the nursery, ~~for she thought~~

into the lock

† A 173, B 178; B 179, A 174

going downstairs again, necessary though it is that
he should win his fellowship
& waken the children, who were so easily woken, &

*He did drop things on the floor she thought
making up a little tune of C T*

* Written in pencil

for they neither of them slept well. They were excitable children, & Charles Tansley – she instantly saw him ~~in his~~ & thought that he ~~she had~~ actually had / knocked over a pile of books which were on his little writing table in the window; & he had picked them up ~~undid his collar, yes,~~ for then sat down, at his table ~~rather grimly a poor young~~ man; he had not succeeded in impressing himself upon anybody at dinner, ~~beside his candles,~~ ~~he~~ & ~~said to himself~~ felt very lonely & ~~really~~, if she could have thought of an excuse for going to him she would have done so, but He looked & she would have gone into him, but ~~rem~~ reflecting, with one half of her brain that ~~this was her invention~~ – he had not knocked over his books – ~~she next~~ that it was all her invention – she ~~reproached herself for~~ thought herself silly for exaggerating as usual, reflected that no power on earth could ~~give~~ after all help him to acquire those graces which were so attractive in Paul Rayley, & heaven ~~pro~~ had provided a substitute in moral philosophy or John Stuart Mill so that all things considered it might be better to leave him. Yet she would see that he was better treated tomorrow, yet she would feel relieved when he went, yet he was very good with her husband, yet his manners certainly wanted improving, observing too that now she could see the moon itself ~~, &~~ through the staircase window, – the shadowy ~~dinted~~ much dinted moon – she turned from all this to the very next moment – Prue & Andrew, Paul & Minta, all opening doors & coming out into the hall; muffled.

poor young man to work or read when all the others were enjoying themselves

~~Looking~~ Coming down stairs, looking out of the window, then turning ~~& at once~~ Prue saw her mother & felt at once ~~two things~~ – ~~that~~ how she was a child, again they ~~& she~~ had been feeling extremely old; how that was the crown & grace of life, her mother coming down stairs, & they all

† knew it. Yes; Minta should look at her; Paul should look at her:

* VW numbered two pages 142.

† B 180

For, she felt, in a way which she could not describe, Here is the thing itself – her mother ~~being to her~~ having only to appear to make Prue feel that what they had been playing at was now ~~[?]~~ ordered; their going sanctioned, or if not, condemned, & as nobody else in the kingdom had Mrs. Ramsay for a mother, this was Minta's great chance, & Paul's – And

actually to ennoble it,

her beauty, too, to Prue, always seemed to ~~be saying to them all~~, stamp the moment, & she was a little afraid of her, &

† was her slave, & would never grow up ~~[?]~~ or leave home, with her there, & never wanted to, but only to come out into the hall & see her coming downstairs, & say to her, hear

"We thought of going down to the beach" & ~~see~~ ~~hear~~ her sum up the position instantly ~~had~~ debate it, should they go, or should they not go? & then decide with that mood of revelry & ~~rather~~ which was delicious in her, ~~[?]~~ & made her the soul of any junketing, yes it was quite right to go down to the beach; & why not swim, & why not catch a shark fish . . . saying ~~which she pulled Mintas~~ fastened Minta's cloak about her,

saying

† & ~~then~~ ~~really~~ would have liked to come with them; but no: there was ~~William Bankes; there was her~~ – her husband, she meant; she meant to, she wanted to sit down in a particular chair, under a particular lamp, & taking up her knitting & ~~a book~~ take up her book.

They must really not be late she said.

Had anybody got a watch?

Paul Rayley of course had a beautiful gold watch, which he took out of a little washleather bag; & seeing that bag, Mrs. Ramsay felt how extraordinarily lucky Minta was – to marry a man who kept a watch in a bag; so she went into the drawing room.

Slightly annoyed about Andrew*

---

* Written in pencil

† A 175; B 181

144

because it was so foolish

† The thought, which of course she would not say to anyone, tickled her [in its absurdity] [secretly] & with a smile on her lips she went into the drawing room, where, to her surprise, there was only her husband, reading.

However, he did not want to be interrupted – that was clear, ~~from~~ He was reading – what? something that moved him very much; ~~& why did it move him~~; ~~to a som inter~~ for ~~with he~~ besides being intent he was all the time half smiling, & then as she knew controlling his emotion, & yet all the time he was discriminating & not allowing himself to be unduly influenced, but & weighing one thing with another:

"The Antiquary" – dear old Sir Walter, she thought, smiling & ~~but with~~ ~~no longer~~ no longer irresponsibl~~y anymore~~; & sitting down

† under her lamp, in her chair, opposite, & taking up her knitting. For Charles Tansley (instinctively she listened to hear ~~him~~

of books

bump & bang upon the floor) said he was done for: then her husband thought, "That is what they will say of me"; so he went & [ ? ] got The Antiquary, ~~he~~ wh he loved ~~The Antiquary, but nothing would ever make him tamper with truth~~; ~~he would He might want a thing to be true; but~~ ~~If he found it~~

But

If his reason told him that it was true – Sir Walter was done for – very well then he would accept that fact; Except about himself, he ~~was rational~~ would accept anything. Not liking to think why he was so irrational about himself so that perhaps other people, Lily for instance, had guessed at dinner ~~how~~ why he was so irritable ~~at dinner~~ when they talked about fame & books lasting, not liking ~~to~~ the sense she had sometimes that ~~his~~ the children wondered, a little, she began her knitting, & at the same time all those fine ~~point~~s gravings, as with steel instruments, became drawn again about her lips & forehead, & she became ~~like an image which owing to her beauty~~, ~~like~~ still, & composed, ~~as if all~~ like a tree which has been tossed & quivering & now, when the breeze falls, settles into quiet.

But ~~then~~ How great a mind he has, she thought.

† A 176; B 182, A 177

She could not judge his mind indeed; ~~but~~ Nor was it intellect, exactly;
[it was
† his way with him; his loftiness; His truthfulness, His – & feeling
rise up in her that same feeling which she had had at dinner
which
~~the brooding calm of a~~ soul riding the waves ~~which~~ in a brooding ~~calm~~,
peace, & ~~yet~~ then somebody begins, the China rose is all abloom &
buzzing with the yellow bee, ~~come out~~ & all the lives we ever
she felt herself like a leaf blowing ~~through a~~ in at a window
lived & all the lives to be, come out, come out* – she
~~took~~ looked over her knitting at the books on the little table, &
took one, an anthology of poems, & opened it ~~anywhere~~, laying it
on her knee, ~~And~~ Never reading at all, except in this way,
& always stopping, interrupted,
† ~~she turned leaves~~, turning leaves, climbing from this to that, she
had not any ~~sense of~~ security whatever, or any knowledge even, but
of names, but only ~~how the that the lines about the~~
~~sonnets of Shakespeare~~ felt it a great relief; & ~~at the~~
~~same time had~~ for she loved ~~to get at~~ the repose of the words; &
the the soft flowers
nightingales & the crocus being in the shade;
~~its~~ counterbalancing ~~of this one that she did feel, more & more.~~
~~She read some poetry every night or the Opium Eater.~~
her world being overarched, in the evening, ~~by~~ by this ~~strange poetry~~
[~~world~~
strangeness; And she kept turning over the pages & knitting
† rhythmically, & looking now & then at her husband, who still
did not want to be interrupted, for he was being led on, like a fool, to
must [waste his time.
† He ~~had~~ just to finish the scene in [~~sand~~?] Mucklebackit's cottage.
~~That old~~ ~~They said nobody read it now.~~ ~~And~~ There was no
nastiness, no sex interest. But the life, the power – If they didn't
~~car~~ read it, the greater fools they. ~~But~~ & he could scarcely
& he slapped his thigh. He felt his lips twitch.
muttered
~~Well~~, we shall all be forgotten one of these days, he said aloud.
~~shutting the book~~. ~~rather flushed~~, ~~rather excited~~. ~~& rather~~
~~ashamed of himself.~~ Turning the page, but he did not mind.
It was a splendid chapter; the humour was magnificent. And
if after all, one need not attend to the love making seriously –
fish
it was the old beggar & the old ~~peasant~~ ~~fish~~ wives; he
could not help mouthing the Scotch dialect to himself

* 'Luriana Lurilee,' MS 182, 214
† B 183, A 178; B 184; A 179; B 185

(3.19)

(146)

He felt fortified, & forgot completely the little rubs & digs of the evening; [its
† exasperations & intolerable boredom; feeling now ~~that~~ invigorated by this [man's
strength & sanity & his ~~feeling certainty that~~ belief in the straightforward
simple things, which Mr. Ramsay felt so strongly that, when it came to [~~the~~
poor Steenie's drowning, ~~the~~ he could not choke down his tears, &
but raising the book a little, ~~sat~~ let them fall, & shook his head from
side to side, & forgot completely what he was doing, save for the
sense of his wife there, who must not interrupt him – & was
keeping from him he was obscurely conscious, intolerable bores.

in his sympathy & sorrow for the ~~poor old pa~~ poor old parents

Let them
~~It was done.~~ ~~If they were going to~~ improve upon that, he
thought, ~~finishing~~ as he finished the chapter. ~~And~~ Immediately,
he began thinking, how it was the old beggars & fishwives Scott was
good at; ~~how~~ the lovers were fiddlesticks. The man innocence ~~of the~~
man was ~~incred~~ astonishing. He was contemporary with
Balzac after all. But if it ~~hampered him~~ limited him his
lack of interest in the eternal sex problems was also ~~a source of~~
~~th~~ one reason for his vigour. Mr. Ramsay felt that sex interest was
† hugely overdone. If this sort of thing seemed old fashioned to the
young men, ~~that~~ naturally they did not buy his ~~own~~ books,
Mr. Ramsay thought; & One ought not to complain; ~~Here he~~
~~looked at his wife,~~ if they did not read Scott. Here he looked
at his wife, who was reading & knitting, but, like a person in a
very light sleep, was conscious of the very moment that her
husband shut his book. ~~She was~~ He ~~often jus~~ liked just to look at her.
He liked to think that everyone had taken themselves off, & he & she [were
alone; ~~just~~ for ten minutes or so

Mrs. Ramsay raised her head, but like a person in a
light sleep, seemed to ~~ask~~ say that if he wanted her to wake she
would, otherwise she was sleeping. She was rocking; she was
stretched
~~sa brooding; on the rhythm, in the~~ mesh ~~stretched tight~~ of Shakespeare's
sonnets.

† Well? he said at length. ~~And~~ ~~At once~~ quizzically,
as if he were ridiculing her gently, for being asleep in broad
daylight, ~~but~~ & at the same time hiding the delight of her

† A 180; B 186, A 181; A 182, B 187

her presence & the immeasurable comfort of her beauty, for he thought, it was silly [wrong] to ~~think that he had~~ reproach himself. He Neither of them would have lived differently; ~~her~~ to him, ~~woman she~~ she was more beautiful now; worn & old; worried; teased; driven to death with all these people.

She woke instantly. ~~Could they have lived differently~~? Well, she said, echoing him ~~dr~~ dreamily. She tried to remember all that had happened since she had seen him alone: the dinner, & the engagement, & the children being awake, & Andrew ~~in the hall~~ [& Paul's watch;] Andrew being so ~~stiff w shy~~ [silent] [now] with her: & what else?

† ~~They have gone down to the beach she said~~, ~~She shut he~~ Her book shut itself on her knee. Mr. Ramsay said that he supposed they had hit it off — ~~he divined something of the sort~~ [the engagement he meant.] It all seemed to have happened a long time ago; or it seemed ~~as if~~ to have become part of their own lives, ~~But how explain that feeling? as if Mrs. Ramsay thought~~, It seemed to her that it had already melted in to the ~~great~~ ~~thick~~ ~~trunk of~~ fabric of their lives, ~~&~~ like a stream which eddies ~~round~~ at first & then rushes along in the main current. She felt that there was nothing to be said about it. She felt, especially when she had been reading poetry, ~~that how~~ [[start?] [nothing?]] little could be said, & ~~that~~ not rightly; & she was coming to shrink from talk more & more — not light gossip of course or fun [joking about] (that Paul had a wash leather bag for his watch) but ~~who could say what she felt now?~~ about other things — her relationship with her husband, & the children, & one thing happening & then another thing, & the sense she had that it was all, somehow, right; & yet so ~~profoundly~~ tragic — oh yes: ~~when~~ [why] ever ~~she if~~ anything happened, it ~~was always the tragic~~ — was one's first thought of ~~tragedy? &~~ — always death, somehow, dark somehow; ruin coming.

† Only he would say no. ~~The~~ Through the crepuscular walls of their intimacy, (for they came astonishingly close now & then) she could

† A 183, B 188; A 184, B 189

She could feel him keeping watch on her thoughts, & beginning, directly they turned a way he disliked, to fidget; ~~putting~~ raising his hand quickly to his head. (from his knee to his head)

Very well. If he thought it wrong to be pessimistic, he knew better than she did. But the other thing she found so difficult – † expressing her feelings. ~~N To~~ He was so much simpler, so much ~~more~~ less hesitating than she was; so that it was ~~easy for him~~ it was always he who ~~began,~~ began it; & sometimes he would reproach her. A ~~very hard hearted w~~ heartless woman he would call her. He would say she snubbed him. But it was not so – it was not so. ~~When she thought how~~ Had he not given her everything, ~~so that, intently , on as~~ ~~And was she not stupid & ordinary & rather dull compared with him? &~~ And did it not always seem to her He knew it was not so. ~~Did he know know it? She must write her letters~~ some – ~~She After all,~~ ~~When they~~ Had he no crumbs on his coat? Was there nothing [to?] she could the [?] do, & so on to avoid ~~spea~~ talking? She never could say things she felt. So, getting up She stood at the window, with the reddish brown stocking still knitting, & watching the light from the lighthouse. ~~Now it was so dark that the sea, on either side, seemed like black marble.~~ It came & went; ~~h~~ direct & strange, & over the sea, like a

to tell him that she loved him.

more demonstrative

only she cd. not say He knew it was not so – What she felt.

And she thought felt knew ~~perfectly~~ ~~certain that he~~ was watching her, & she knew that he was thinking what of her, & ~~The~~ more beautiful than ever, & she knew that it would ~~give him exqu great pleasure could she turn & say to him you have made me so perfectly happy; you have~~ but no: she could not do it; was not necessary to say anything; & that it ~~was~~ † enough for her to turn round ~~with her~~ knitting, smiling because she had known he & she turned round, with her knitting, & smiled at him, because – oh of course she was † perfectly right; ~~she~~ he knew what she felt: & she need only say to him "Yes: its going to be wet tomorrow".

she knew that he wished him to tell him how she loved him

† B 190, A 185; B 191; A 186

April 30th
1926

## Part Two.*

### I.

† It grew darker. Clouds covered the moon, & in the early hours of the morning ~~the~~ a light rain drummed on the roof, & starlight moon light, or the lights at sea seemed put out. ~~What~~ Nothing
† could withstand the flood, & the profusion, the downpouring of this immense darkness; which ~~like a flood~~ [crept?] let in at keyholes – ~~crv~~ crevices & stealing round the window blinds, came ~~trickling~~ in at the bedrooms & sitting rooms, & ~~doors of~~ swallowed up here the ~~glint~~ white of china & there the flower the sharp edged furniture. When Everything was confused & confounded, there was scarcely any identity left, either of bodies or of thoughts. ~~& only~~ From the many ~~brains sleeping~~, & bodies lying, either in the rigid attitudes of the old, ~~or in~~ cramped ~~flung~~ almost passively there in the crease of the bed, themselves creased with the habitual ~~be~~ stoopings & movings of many years, ~~there~~ or easily lying, scarcely covered, ~~like children~~ in the first years of life. as if the least cover were too heavy, & the mattress ~~m~~ only ~~upheld them & & cradled them~~, nothing but dreams & confused thoughts & broken lights like the the flash – ~~glitter~~ the bright strange effervescence of bubbles rising
through ~~from~~ deep water, which burst when they reach the surface, keeping, now one ~~hand was~~ a hand was raised, or a as if to clutch at something, or to ward off something, & now the anguish of life, its concealed pain, & the misery which is forbidden to cry out ~~b~~ for comfort, parted the lips of the sleepers; ~~or &~~ now & then, some body one laughed; or ~~in the eager tones of the childlike happiness had talked~~

* See appendix B, an outline of 'Time Passes.'
† A 189, B 195; B 196, A 190

150

or somebody talked with the confidence of a chattering
child, complete nonsense. There might have been ghostly
~~comforters~~ confidantes about, gently pacing from room to room, &
nameless comforters, ~~who would~~ treasure up ~~in their~~ the
to ~~hide conceal in their~~ & engulf in the folds of their cloaks,
what was murmured & cried; or, stooping, to receive gravely,
the odd changes, from torture to calm, from hate to indifference,
which, in the dark bedroom, ~~in the~~ with darkness pouring.
~~In~~ from above & below, ~~the~~ came & went ~~over the all these faces~~
~~Then~~, ~~Pacing & stooping these confidantes, these nameless comforters~~,
their
~~presence of~~ ~~For~~ Otherwise, the sleepers with ~~those~~ extraordinary
&
gestures of hope, ~~their~~ cries of despair, & the chuckles, ~~of~~ like birds, of
senseless merriment, were thus mopping & ~~be~~ mowing ~~to~~ ~~in the~~ to
no one: reached out for nothing, & acted in the depths of the night
a drama unseen Shadows & darkness ~~only~~ alone then
their
received them, unfurled their wings, & gazed from hoods ~~with such eyes as~~
~~may open in the depths of nothingness,~~ & received such
ecstasies as might ~~wak~~ half wake a sleeper when midnight is
past &, dreaming of his joy, he cries out; &

Were there ghostly confidantes about, nameless comforters
&
gently pacing, gravely stooping; to treasure up, to engulf in the
folds of their cloaks, what was murmured & cried, ~~or to~~ &
~~accept behold to~~ & ~~receive the~~ to accept & to understand those
g ~~odd~~ changes from ~~hate to~~ torture to calm from, hate to
indifference which came & went on the sleepers faces?
Had each, in short, ~~ar arriv arrived~~ in sleep ~~at the~~
reached out in sleep & found ~~a hand & taken it &~~ at the foot of the
bed some standing ~~sle~~ silent the ~~shape of~~ counterpart, ~~or~~
the sharer, who hol~~ding in his hands holds the~~ of their
deeds; the sharer? found now, in sleep, ~~the~~ completeness ~~which~~
by day
~~the day~~ denied them, & to him cried, & to him confided, & to him
his waking it
laughed ~~that~~ senseless wild laughter which, had the ~~living~~ heard, ~~they~~
[would
have frightened them? To each a sharer; to each thought, complet~~ion~~; ness
ed
& in this knowledge ~~calm &~~ content; – ~~So~~ it might seem ~~So it~~ it
might be that, ~~in dreams~~ dreaming sleeping each passed from
the house & paced the beach, or walked the hill, or
penetrated ~~fu deeper & deeper into that dar into the~~ cloud.
[?]
passed down the stairs, ~~& peeping into the drawing room~~
like ghosts who will no more put on the cumber &
loneliness
trouble of flesh, & so gained the desire of their hearts, loneliness
~~to be alone.~~ & found in loneliness the consummation,
to escape, ~~to~~ & to be alone, & to cry out & have the
wind ~~echo~~ toss back an answer – ~~that was the~~
find
& to wander & to discover, & ~~to open the door &~~ find
all the flowers, all the ~~sharp edged~~ furniture
gulfed in darkness, & to shed in that darkness,
nose & eyes & the old slips & shifts of the tongue, ~~& to~~
~~all~~

Then they say, ~~after all~~, how there is no soul, ~~&~~ no
or
~~no~~ immortality ~~& no~~ completeness; ~~& that~~ The ~~tables~~
sharpedged furniture is there, they say, & the flower, but it
~~has died before morning~~; & they say the day is
all; & ~~what~~ our duty is to the day; & ~~those who~~

escape is cowardice & the wind nothingness, & the furniture all.
& ~~these chinks & crevices which might tempt anyone of them, in the~~
this immense darkness, & sleep, ~~which might~~ tempting ~~anyone~~ to
~~believe in~~ escape ~~& try~~ it are the cloaks of superstition & deceit.
The covering of the ~~silly brood~~ of ~~timid~~ fear & reverence, ~~terror~~ &, sloth.
The darkness increased, until at last on the beach, when the
waves broke they ~~too~~ seemed like night shaking her head back,
& despairinly* lettin

* VW's misspelling

& raising it & again to There musing with [~~he~~?] a ~~ben~~ a mourning [~~to~~?] so profoundly & benignantly ~~the doubtful a~~ as if she lamented the doom which drowned the earth & extinguished its lights, & of all the ships, ~~the~~ & towns, ~~the houses~~ left nothing. Yet if there is no soul, & the day is all, why should we, escaped from the house, & pacing the beach, imagine robes flowing ~~down~~, & eyes with ~~the~~ lids compassionately lowered, as ~~if the presence regarded~~ as if to behold ~~the~~ our sufferings ~~on earth~~? And why, ~~then~~, imagine, pacing the beach, ~~how the~~ & letting words escape on the wind, how ~~like a~~ the wind answers, & the wind ~~says~~ comforts, & ~~blows back the assurance that~~ the wind too has ~~care thought of us, &~~ comes ~~along the~~ down on a ~~beach~~, & strides across ~~the bay~~, ~~with the~~ warmth ~~of a friend~~? & ~~seizes us on its arm~~ the wind opens its arms? ~~The sea, too, which the flows~~ Or is there any answer in the sea, ~~when we ask it to assure us~~ when we wrap us about in its beauty; & ~~let flow from our~~ shoulders its ~~purple, & dive or does it not suffocate~~ or none, & is it only fearing, trembling, hoping that we spin from our terror the purple robes, then clothing to cover forces ~~which remain ho untamed~~? Did they not all seize & waken

down

If anyone asleep that night, at the Ramsays, – ~~either Mr. Carmichael in his [?] or Paul, or~~ Paul, or Mr. Carmichael for ~~example, had~~ Nothing stirred in ~~bedroom or sitting~~ the drawing room, or in the dining room. ~~Did~~ the tumble & the battering, the ~~[ ? ]~~ drench & darkness of the sea, & the wind & the rain, & the ~~night~~ nobody moved, not

the mindless warfare, the soulless bludgeoning

† Nothing stirred in the drawing room or in the dining room. ~~& i &, what w~~ but owing to the old hinges, & ~~faded~~ shrunken sea moistened woodwork, which ~~warped~~ wet one winter shrank dried in the summer, certain ~~winds~~ airs detached from the main body of the wind, ventured into the house. ~~In the It was not wild, though~~. Almost one might imagine ~~as breath~~ questioning, wondering, as they gently attempted the ~~ti falling~~ hanging wall paper:

† A190

– would it ~~last~~ hang, ~~there~~ would it fall? Then gently brushing the
walls, one ~~might [fairly?]~~ on they passed, as if gently ~~[wi?]~~ seeking to
smo fade obliterate, ~~the to cover~~ to yellow & ~~f~~ the honeysuckles there,
they stirred (gently too, for it was a soft September night)
the torn paper in the basket, as if of all this in the drawing room,
now that ~~they were the~~ people were sleeping, ~~had~~ were open to them,
between
& there was had intercourse with them – & the wind & the wastepaper,
~~Or in the~~ To obstruct its progress, the cook however,
had placed more durable implements; Her ~~bald~~ silvery saucepans
~~were ranged~~ there on the shelf: & on the table, to
duly set out, there were cups & saucers; ~~&~~ china; teapots.
~~Curiously, in &~~ so that it was hardly possible, however,
the chilly air might attempt it, to stain here, or fade, or [disarrange?].
~~Could~~ But among sleepers

And the chairs, & the tables & the books, & the silvery saucepans in rows
the shelf, how long would they endure, & of what nature were they? [on
† & ~~could & given over to us~~ the Were they, too, of the substance of
wind & rain, allies, with whom in the darkness, wind & rain
could commune? But passing among the sleeper, ~~who~~ surely
there must be doubt. [& one must] Everything else can tarnish & perish, is
dissolved again; ~~here remains here~~ but not there. And one
would say to the grey airs of midnight, & the wandering gleams
~~which~~ of moonlight, of light which wavers up the wall &
across the ceiling, phantom soft, how they had no power to
smooth, to ~~obliterate, to destroy~~. touch, or to destroy, upon which,
wearily, ghostlily, as if they had feather-light fingers, &
~~could~~ ~~phantom~~ could disappear & come again, so now, they
would fold their light garments, ~~& sigh~~, & die away, having
looked upon ~~eyes~~ shut eyes, & fingers loosely closed. They would
now betake themselves to the staircase, ~~for exam~~ to the window
for example; they would nose & rub & fumble the pane;
descending, ruffle the ~~light~~ cloaks in the hall, &
then meditate how to chill the apples in the plate on the
dining room table. Grey dew might bead their ~~round~~ redness, –
their roundness crinkle, soften, & be ~~stained~~ turn brown.
~~As for the~~ ~~th~~ ~~If~~ They tried the picture on the easel in
the drawingroom, they brushed the matt. They blew ~~along~~ a
little sand. [along] Reaching the roses, ~~the great~~ in the
white jar, with its swelling sides, & its blue stain, like
the blue of skimmed milk they tried there too – how
to nip petal from petal, how to loose the fibres,
sap the firmness & ~~tak~~ tinge the ~~clear~~ [cloud the colours] pallor, with
~~mud &~~ stain & blotch. ~~Then,~~ Now, gathering into a
~~chorus, where~~ centre as if all this prying & peering
were ~~alien to~~ but the work of spies, detached from

[margin:] & the light persistency of feathers,

† A 191, B 197

army to bring news of the enemies dispositions, where to attack they gathered in the middle of the house, & gave together one of those aimless gusts of lamentation ~~which~~ to which ~~so~~ some ~~a~~ swing door near the kitchen replied, opening, admitting nothing & shutting again. Then they seemed for the moment [ ? ] routed. Then, as if to take up the burden of the nights complaint, to reenforce the failing powers of darkness & destruction, ~~con~~ the ~~sea~~ waves ~~felt~~ beat upon ~~the shore~~. The sullen thunder alone ~~filled the house~~. ~~The night~~ All the world then seemed turned to water, ~~the 1 shores flowing away into water~~, the ~~islands~~ to be little islands in the sea; & the sea beat ~~on~~ on these shrink to islands upon whose shores the waves broke, ~~on to~~ whose earth [out?] crumbled into the sea. A Ruining, & devouring, round ~~the~~ such crags of earth as were still left the ~~waters~~ the dark waters flung themselves, ~~upon 1~~ & pranced, & pawed, & withdrew, to fling & prance & paw. ~~Almost~~ One could hear the ~~world~~ earth washed away at midnight – & the water running This done, having now recovered their strength, ~~ones~~ the old stealhy* patrol of the house was resumed. ~~here~~ by the light airs, by the phantom lights.

* VW's misspelling

a wavery taper
[?]
[?]
boxes & old
clothes

which seemed to come from some wandering taper which is
moved uncertainly by a wavering hand, again moved upstairs, into the
bedroom, & into the attics, & among boxes, & clothes.

For example, the shawl which muffled the ~~wild~~ wild boar's
the those
skull ~~was~~ stirred; ~~those~~ hanging garden, those clouds, & valleys of

like a balloon
pendant over
great precipices

singing birds, ~~were~~ floated to & fro. But again, seeing how
short a time was before them, & how great a resistance even a
shawl offers to a light air, the spies ~~&~~ desisted ~~again~~ from
their attempts to [distingrate?] the hanging shawl. &
~~again~~ Indeed they could scarcely move a loose pane, or stir
the coat of the sleeping dog, or ~~put any impediment in~~ impede
the way of the beetles in the kitchen, sliding from ~~corn~~ dresser to

(2)

† carpet. ~~Moreover, how~~ And Further, what is one night?
A short space, ~~especially in the north~~, especially where the

like a turning
leaf,

darkness dims so ~~so~~ soon, & so soon a bird sings, a cock crows, &
a faint green quickens in the water. ~~All w Light will soon~~
~~return, & the night upon night is needed. Night upon~~
But then night succeeds to night. They lengthen, they darken;
~~the~~ some of them hold aloft clear planets, ~~moons of argent~~ &
plates of brightness. The autumn trees ~~become like take on~~,
take on
ravaged as they are, the splendour of tattered flags,
burning in the gloom ~~of some stone against the wall of the~~
& marble pages

of
cathedral
caves,

church ~~wall~~, where the gold letters describe death in battle, &
bodies buried far away, – ~~or lost, or sunk~~. So they
gleam in the yellow moonlight, the light of harvest moons,
~~which behold the stubble fields, & the cli~~ the light which
tranquilises labour & brings the wave lapping the sand ~~lit~~
with a caress. Then it seems as if, ~~divine goodness~~
touched by human penitence, ~~had~~ divine goodness had
drawn the curtain ~~which~~ & displayed the treasures ~~which~~
we should enjoy always, certainly: the clear sky, the
quiet wave, the hare erect in ~~his form~~, the ~~bird~~
~~[?]~~ cow ~~tranquil, the flowers~~ boat rocking ~~the moon~~
† which did we deserve them we should always own –

† A 192, B 198; A 193, B 199 (3.43)

158

But alas, says divine goodness, twitching the cord again & covering the
~~he~~ a [?] them breaking them up,
treasures, ~~& to~~ with rain & mist, with mud ~~& agitation~~
~~penitent though we may be, temporarily~~, our penitence deserves
only a glimpse; ~~& our h~~ &, looking into our hearts, & finding what is
not pleasing to him there, he corrects us thus. The nights
are now ~~full of wind &~~ rainy & windy: the ~~old~~ trees plunge & bend; &
their dishevelled & dishonoured leaves, ~~sta~~ fly helter skelter until the
they lie
all over the lawn, & up ~~the bank~~, & packed damply in gutters, &
rainpipes, ~~they lie~~ ~~pocked & stamped, &~~ with their pock marks on
them, ~~& their~~ & ~~dissolve~~. ~~The sea, then eq equally too,~~
also, ~~the~~ sea ~~plunges &~~ tosses & breaks itself, until ~~col~~
~~the~~ for ~~colour~~ there is ~~mud~~ black with a
Also the sea tosses & breaks itself ~~As for the~~ ~~Then~~ indeed
when ~~the nig~~ autumn is far advanced, it is again possible
sleeper
to attempt X & should any escaped soul, any ~~dreamer~~, who
fancies that in sleep he has grasped the hand of the sharer,
walk the edge of the sea, no image ~~will readily~~
divinely prompt ~~to tame~~ chain the night & sea to service
will readily come to hand; maps will all survey ruin, &
then damp. discomfort ~~the~~ & fear will drive the
† craven to sleep again & forgetfulness. Then indeed
when autumn is far advanced it is again possible to
attempt.

† A 194, B 200

now again when autumn is far advanced it is possible
to attempt the house again. Moreover, all the beds are
empty; the air, the f gleam now ~~full~~ brush ~~turned~~
~~so~~ bare mattresses, & as they nibble & fan, meet ~~only~~
nothing that opposes them with warmth, ~~or~~ but
only hangings that flap, wood that creaks, ~~&~~ the
bare legs of tables, ~~& the~~ saucepans, book cases.
What people have shed & left – a pair of shoes, a
shooting cap, a few hairpins, & a some old
gloves – those ~~keep~~ alone keep the ~~shape of the~~
human shape & in their empty[ness] way indicate how
once they were filled & animated; how once, a
~~lady~~, ~~[?]~~ ~~put~~ st~~anding~~ before the long looking
~~glass put~~ her hand to her head, & clasped, perhaps, some
~~put hair pins in her hair, or somebody~~ hands were
busy with buttons & hooks; how once this looking glass
which now reflects the washstand ~~held in it~~
~~woman~~, was all moving with women's shapes, dressing, &
reflected children, & the door opening; ~~& almost~~
the incessant shadows & colours of a room full of
change. Now, ~~if th for nig~~ day after day, night after night,
gradually, uninterruptedly, the light gradually changes.
turns, like a flower ~~admiring itself in water,~~
reflecting itself in water; ~~shaking its petals; in~~
a flower absorbed in its own reflection which nothing stirs
only the shadows of the trees [stooping & brandishing] gravely indicated with a
~~shv~~ shiver~~ing~~ shadows a kind of obeisance; ~~or~~ a
† rook makes a ~~shad sha~~ dark spot fly across the
pale green matting on the bedroom floor.
So ~~it proceeds in loveliness~~ So loveliness reigns, &
stillness, & & together compose something which

[Margin notes:]
some faded shirts & trousers in wardrobes

deep like a stage

the ~~dart~~ [dash] of a dog

Now [~~the~~?]

† A 195, B 201

160

wears the quiet of ~~fr~~ shapes from which life has gone, into
which eternity has breathed; ~~like the sands when~~
an empty shell, ~~sand~~ untrodden sand, ~~horizons~~ ~~pools~~
surprised something ~~seen~~ from a train window – a pool, a ~~ch~~ wood –
which is scarcely robbed of its solitude; so soon will it
~~sink ag~~ sink into peace again. ~~It~~ Even the prying
of the wind, the soft jaws of the clammy sea air, fluffing, nosing
do nothing to disturb this ~~solitary~~ solitude, this beauty, this
integrity, for where ~~noth~~ there is nothing to excite, &
no collusion, & no compromise, it seems as if
truth were there, at last, robed in its own

this air of simple integrity, for where there is no strife & collusion
no compromise, it seems as if truth were there, ~~undraped~~,
itself, undraped.

~~So~~ ~~And what~~ ~~As~~ Nothing it seems can break that pure
image; ~~or~~ corrupt that innocence; or disturb the ~~lovely~~ swaying
mantle of silence which ~~day after day~~, week after week &
~~month after month~~ lies upon the house, ~~where save for the~~
ing
~~wandering gusts & the si damp sea air~~, ~~&~~ weaves into
passing
itself the tremb~~ling~~ cry of a rook & the [~~fainter?~~] ~~stranger~~ ~~calls~~ &
out a sea [moves?] out
echoes, which coming ~~far from sea~~, ~~&~~ from the sea, or
the ~~hum far away in the fields of some~~ some hum rising
~~far away in the~~ in ~~the fields~~; ~~whether~~ some throb; ~~some~~
in silence. ~~pulse~~. & then gently ~~mak~~ muffling & folding the house again.
on the landing
Only suddenly & for no perceptible reason, a board creeks; &
then again the wrapping of the shawl loosens itself as
† after ~~of~~ centuries in one second a giant avalanche detaches
itself, ~~& where the wrapping~~ one fold of the
shawl loosens itself, ~~& whether by~~ as if some
insidious jaw concealing its operations had finally bitten
through some tie & loosened the shawls hold upon the
skull. At the same moment, too, – almost more
surprisingly, with a sound like the grating of iron
& the

† A 196, B 202

As she lurched – for she rolled like a ~~a~~ ship at sea, & leered, for
her eyes ~~though seemed~~ fell on nothing directly, but with a sidelong
as if
glance, expressing a whimsical approach, a method perhaps of
of the world
deprecating the scorn or anger which might be [ ? ] upon her –
for — she was not completely mistress of her wits, & yet had did not mind in
~~had~~ & humour
wh [blend?] indeed — ~~enough to laugh at dust & clean~~, ~~or~~ ~~laugh~~ ~~a sort~~ of tolerance
for the sanity of other people, as ~~she rolled thus, smiling~~
sang
~~even in the empty rooms at something she~~ she ~~mused~~
~~the~~ a her voice in ~~a~~ song. ~~which~~ Rubbing the glass of the
~~look~~ long looking glass, & leering sideways at her own
swinging figure, she chanted something ~~about~~ which had
been gay, & ~~surely perhaps~~ on the stage twenty years before,
but now, ~~like a~~ coming from the toothless bonneted old
denuded of all the force of words, of accent, meaning, — caretaking woman ~~had lost its starch~~, ~~become~~ & turned
as ~~far as words can turn~~, ~~into~~ rolled out like the
~~so~~ ~~whimsical~~ the voice of witlessness ~~itself~~ & endurance &
~~long~~ ~~age~~ ~~all~~ humbleness which depressed almost to the
verge of non existence ~~without~~ itself. The voice of the
~~indomitable~~ principle of life, & its power to persist; &
~~its sorrow~~, & its courage, & its ~~side long persist~~ assiduity,
~~for rejected~~ & its determination, denied one entrance, to
seek — ~~try~~ another – & its humour, & its sorrow, so that ~~if~~
seemed
to have turned her old sprightly dance song into — Mrs. McNab ~~had been~~ ~~chanting~~ ~~crooning an~~
an elegy which ~~had~~ long living had robbed of all
&
bitterness, ~~so that~~ ~~which she~~ the burden ~~of her tune~~
~~seemed to be accept~~, if it was (as she
† lurched about dusting, wiping) ~~accept or accept.~~
~~not to fight, but to accept~~; & ~~if~~ this humble creature
could accept, if even her old body had its indomitable
reason for continuing in its humble way ~~persistin~~
persist; And if she in her bonnet thus survived,

† A 197, B 203

~~& wished to survive, surely~~
she survived & wished to survive [with] ~~Yet from the flash of her sidelong~~
~~glance, its queerness~~, ~~& why she seems~~ & her lurch & her smile
And then, the meaningless strain, ~~hummed its elegy too:~~
~~gave expressed some~~ without ~~saying~~ using any word gave off so
such a ~~volume of plaintiveness that sound of plaintiveness,~~
~~such a cry~~ cried out how [~~on?~~] ~~deeply~~ the witless old woman
was weary of it all; how it was [very] not [now] good, not [a very] happy, not a [place] place to
lie & loll in – this world that she had known for seventy years;
~~how~~ & then again – ~~unable to face the~~ with her sidelong leer
which ~~could not~~ must slip & turn aside, even as she
~~sloo~~ stopped dusting & gaped at her own old head in the glass
she seemed to shake the ~~sorrows of her world~~ [it] off her
~~She~~ as if ~~askin well~~ ~~There was after all~~, ~~something or other~~;
& ~~yet~~ & then resumed ~~her work, dusting, singing~~ &
until all / to start again, her old amble & hobble
dusting, singing

Oh yes, there had been beauty here, & life here, &
Beauty ~~was gone~~, & ~~life was ended.~~ & it was gone, & it was ended;
~~Mrs. MacNab~~ yet the living with their mops & their dusters
let issue on the grave of beauty, ~~a~~ this incongruous song of the
twisted the crazed & the thwarted, who, one ~~would think~~ had
no reason to desire life, no gift to bestow, or give to take; & yet
as they lurch & leer, through the lurching & leering, at once
song dirge they
as perform the obsequious sing the ~~elegy &~~ let rise up intertwined
there twined in with it this ~~with the dirge & the elegy~~ itself an incorrigible hope; a
hope founded in the case of Mrs. MacNab, certainly not on
reason, not on
a hope had not founded on reason, not founded surely on satisfaction (for
of the town
she was the butt & outcast) but founded perhaps (~~here~~
~~as her wits were half crazed~~, all conjecture must be
(her cheeks were yellow & old) distorted) on the dumb persistency of the fountain of life, &
on moments (say they came obscurely, here & there, at the
wash tub, in with her children who had gone now to
with
America) of which ~~breathed~~ of illumination, when the
breeze ~~was~~ in the west & the clouds white in the sun, &
~~standing at her & she & it was some the gift of life~~
whatever it may be: she understood ~~what, in moments of high great emotion~~
~~great poets have said~~ whatever it may be that then
appears ~~to sweeten labour, &~~ consolatory, & ~~com~~
& beneficent; it seemed better to live; it seemed as if
a channel were tunnelled in the heart of obscurity, &
the meaning & through the firt they made ~~&~~
to make her lean her heart against the thorn & if she was infinitely mournful, & dirgelike [?] [say?] [set?] ~~in her~~ gave her there issued peace, enough, when the grind & the
grit returned to sweeten that barrenness; for
~~strangely as~~ in her sidelong glance there was,
account for it as one may, the forgiveness of an
~~compl~~ understanding mind

How Mrs. MacNab, of all people, had come to
tolerate & to forgive, who shall say – Mrs. MacNab, the

whose existence was ignored who was nothing but a mat for
kings & kaisers to tread on, who would indeed stand patiently in the
streets *to see the kings go riding by,* & whose sugar & tea were ~~now~~
about to be ~~cut~~ ~~cut down by their passions &~~ reduced at their command,
passes ~~any sort of an~~ ~~that of the~~ understanding. Unless it be granted
that the crazed, & the mystic, & the visionary have access to
† are possessed at long intervals it may be of compensation: the
wind in the West, & the ~~breeze~~ sun upon the clouds. If they
find in them absolute good, an ~~extra~~ lump of sugar more or less
matter nothing. They are warm in the frost, & have
comfort in the desert. Only Mrs. MacNab was not of these;
she had been drunk in her day, & of her six children, two, it was
said, were not by her husband; she had lived, she had loved, in
short, & if consolation came to her it was of some
warmer, subtler kind. Perhaps she had an open heart, a
loving heart, & thus if she asked charity (her caretaking
was given her to help her) ~~rather than~~ she returned it by
thus

* A line from 'Luriana Lurilee,' MS 182, 194 (3.59)
† A 198, B 204

Leaning her bony breast on the hard thorn she crooned out her forgiveness.

Sunday May 9th

3

† Was it, then, that she had her consolations in ~~moments~~ of ~~illumination~~, when with the breeze in the west & the clouds white in the sun she stood at her cottage door; for what reason did there twine about the dirge this incorrigible hope?, & ~~how~~ why, with no gift to bestow & no gift to take, did she yet desire life, & sing as she dusted & leered? ~~how~~ Were there then for Mrs. MacNab, trodden into the mud by civilisation, a mat for kings & kaisers to walk on, moments of illumination – at the washtub, say, with her children? (Yet two of them ~~at~~ had been base-born, & three had deserted her) Some cleavage of the clouds there must have been; some channel cut in the heart of obscurity through which issued light enough to make her grin like that – looking at herself in the long looking glass; & ~~seeing there a wisp of with her [homy~~?] forgive, tolerate, understand.

† The crazed, the mystic, the visionary are possessed at long intervals of comprehension, & find in them some absolute good so that a lump of sugar more or less matters nothing; they are warm in the frost & have comfort in the desert. But Mrs. MacNab was not of these. She was not among the ~~haters of life; not~~ among the skeleton lovers; not among those who voluntarily surrender ~~their~~, make abstract, & ~~find in some~~ reduce ~~th mul~~ the multiplicity of the world to unity & its volume & conflict & anguish to one voice piping clear & ~~single~~ sweet. ~~Th Thus, when all the mysti~~ when the inspired & lofty minded, who had walked on

† A197, B 203; A 198, B 204

walked on the beach & heard, in some lull of the storm, a
voice, seen a vision, & so ~~into~~ mounting the pulpit interpreted the
[senseless?/surely?]
& made public how ~~simple~~ ~~everything is, &~~ it is – to love, to worship,
Mrs. MacNab, continued ~~to muddle~~ ~~things up down below~~.
& drink & gossip ~~down~~ as before. ~~And it seemed~~
as if ~~the true duty of~~ it were in the muddle ~~&~~ of
~~un~~ & inexplicability of things, the struggle & the weariness
tiredness, ~~the search~~ ~~the~~ ~~a~~ that she discovered ~~not~~
those reasons which she never divulged for ~~carryi~~ opening
the windows & dusting the bedrooms; as if her message to a
world now beginning to burst into the ~~in w~~
voluntary / loveliness of spring were somehow transmitted –
the irrepressible
rather by the lurch of the body & the leer of her smile, ~~by her~~
~~than by~~ & in them were the broken syllables of a
revelation more ~~profound~~, ~~but~~ confused, but more profound,
than any accorded to solitary watchers, pacers on the
beach at midnight. ~~anguished~~ preachers &
diviners.

Yet to them, ~~too~~, as the evenings lengthened ~~again,~~
~~there~~ came the strangest intimations, ~~as if the~~
~~su~~ the most authentic beckonings, ~~as if~~, in the sunset &
the sunrise, in the windy evenings, ~~voices a~~ when it
they were
seemed as if some~~thing~~ were hailing them out ~~the~~
of their flesh, ~~to a~~ & that flesh were streaming down the
wind, & they must needs fly with arms stretched to the
wild ~~gleaming~~ shining west, or the dancing
stars or the ~~m~~ merriment of the waves.
It ~~seemed~~ as if the wave were ~~them~~, ~~break~~. so
proudly arching, ~~so~~ splendidly sw~~ee~~ping, & the
in ~~their own~~ themselves~~, as if in all~~ this

broke in them, & the dance of the stars were their joy, &
~~all the all this purity & fierceness,~~ & the tree's strength & the
cliffs nobility & the clouds majesty were so
brought together purposely, to body forth a might ~~which~~
& beauty ~~in~~ which was in them; & now, being expressed
outside of them, ~~must signify more than the simple~~
signified the ~~beaut~~ pattern of the whole: ~~signified~~
~~a design & purpose~~. its purpose, its design.

When the winds brought this together for whole weeks in spring

May 14th

purpose
were so brought together to assemble the scattered parts of the ~~faith~~ of
[the
~~he~~ vision within them. Now displayed ~~outside them~~ ~~it was~~
in sky & wind & what was
in cliff & sea, ~~what they~~ ~~it~~ the thing seemed manifest, outside, & inside,
made
~~miraculously~~ ~~seemed~~ miraculously one.

For a week at the end of May this unity ~~was~~ persisted
~~&~~ The spring without a ~~lea~~ leaf to toss ~~or a bough to~~
wide eyed
watchful
laid out,
very bare & bright presented itself like a virgin fierce in her
chastity contemptuous in her purity; ~~& was there, in~~ the
very ~~& rather~~
fields & on the sea, / pure / heartless & ~~if it were not for~~ the
as if
~~dreams & desires of the beholders, apparently~~ entirely
unconcerned with ~~their~~ ~~what was done or thought or hoped or~~
feared. ~~Beauty, she~~ The ~~with the dreams & desires of the~~
beholders. with what was done or thought, ~~by the beholders.~~ by the
[beholders.
† ~~as if their~~ Nevertheless, ~~thes~~ dreams persisted; &
it was impossible, ~~so str~~ to resist the strange intimation which
&
every gull & flower, ~~the~~ trees – the bright pure earth itself
seemed to declare, but if ~~one~~ questioned ~~them~~ at once to
they triumphs
withdraw, ~~as~~ ~~as to~~ the triumph of good, the [inevitability?] of
happiness; ~~the~~ ~~& again~~ or to resist the extraordinary
us to
stimul~~ation~~, which seemed urg~~ing~~ ~~the one to seek a~~
the
~~people~~ hither & thither as if in search of some good, some
hard crystal it ~~might~~ be, entirely remote from ~~their~~
pleasures
~~n~~ known & familiar ~~pleasures~~ & virtues; something
altogether alien to the processes of domestic life; something
bright & fierce & hard, ~~let f~~ a crystal laid on a sandy
floor, a diamond glittering in the white dust. And then,
suddenly, as it seemed conquered & acquiescent, softened now
& tender, the spring seemed to the watchers & pacers who
the watchers
were seeking a revelation to have knowledge of ~~their~~
tears: ~~to~~ cloudy, to have compassion, ~~& all~~
singing
~~echoing with birds~~ ~~voices~~ & ~~boys who~~ bees humming & the
& instead of seeking this absolute

† A 199, B 205

to have taken on a knowledge of their doubts, of their sufferings,
veiling herself, & ~~sending blue~~ bending her head, & ~~letting~~ her
compassionate gaze fall brooding, in beautiful transient melancholy, in
~~sh~~ flying shadows, in sprinkles of ~~sof~~ small rain,

Now again when spring was far advanced it was possible to
attempt the house ~~again;~~ ~~with allies flies, gnats, spiders, sm who~~
& now
~~for allies, so that~~ when the wind ~~& the~~ began to breathe & the
&
shawls & coats to move ~~a~~ ~~there moved with them a~~
with them round & round
flies buzzed in the sun, & there could be heard tapping at the
tall green
long windows ~~some~~ the leaves of some ~~quickly shooting~~ plant.
Then the ~~light~~ stroke of the lighthouse, which had laid itself
bed &
† with authority upon the ~~mat~~ carpet when the nights were dark,
gliding
~~seen~~ came ~~with the moon~~ mixed with moonlight, gently &
stealthily, as if it laid its caress ~~upon~~ & lingered was ~~came~~
& went, & came lovingly again. But in the midst of this
loving caress, for no reason, – except perhaps that the damp
had loosened it imperceptibly, & the ~~w~~ wind
dislodged it, the shawl burst asunder. Another fold ~~was~~
had fallen. A long streamer now hung from the
boar's skull & was fanned gently, this way & that way,
in those short spring nights, full of ~~sl s m~~ ~~light fre~~
silver from the moon & the lighthouse, & those hot
days, when the ~~grasses~~ scarcely tapped upon the pane, &
only one tortoise shell butterfly dashed from window to
window.

† A 200, B 206

| | | |
|---|---|---|
| 25 | 52 | |
| 8 | 3 | |
| 33 | 156 | |
| | | 33 |
| | | 40 |
| | | 10 |
| | | 83 |
| | | 73 |
| | 10 | |

4.

in the spring
† Now again the wind breathed in the house flies buzzed round in the
weeds
warm yellow spot of sunshine, & ~~there~~ could be heard,
~~weeds~~
tapping the window pane, long ~~grasses~~, stray wild flowers,
which had grown close to the glass in the night.
When darkness fell, the stroke of the lighthouse which had
† laid itself with authority upon the carpet when the nights
were dark came mixed with moonlight gliding gently &

on the empty bed

stealthily as if it laid its caress / & lingered & looked & went &
came lovingly again. ....
The curved tooth on the lower jaw of the skull was ~~unc~~ laid bare;
& then the ~~strea~~ shawl, which now hung down like a streamer,
waved gently this way & that, throughout the short spring
nights ~~& the silver-robed by the moon & the lighthouse~~, &
the long summer days when all the empty rooms seemed
to ~~hum with~~ murmur ~~with the~~ with the echoes of the
fields & the hum of flies, & the ~~the f light so~~
&
sun so barred & striped the rooms ~~th so~~ filled
hazy
them with a ~~liquid~~ yellow that Mrs. MacNab when she
came to dust, looked like a tropical fish, oaring
a
~~her w~~ its way through ~~the~~ sun-lanced ~~water~~ sea.
among
~~up rose the bookcases like~~ rocks: ~~the tables floated~~ ~~like~~ islands;
~~strange~~ corals & crystals. ~~glowed & twinkled on the~~
But slumber though it might without apparent change ~~through~~
~~ran for a~~ so ~~the~~ there came later in the summer ominous
sounds ~~which~~, thuds, rumbles, like ~~regular~~ thunder
regularly repeated, which with their repeated shocks still
further loosened the shawl & ~~distu~~ helped the wind & the
damp sea air ~~at their insidious task~~. [to nibble, to undo, to
dull, ~~&~~ tarnish & slowly eat away ~~the~~ house a]
in this work of ~~disintegration~~. destruction. ~~Once in a~~
Now & again ~~the~~ some glass actually tinkled as if it

like the repeated blow of a ~~heavy~~ hammer on a thick substance, in the cupboard | ~~were a current~~ it vibrated to a current in the air, were pierced by ~~some anguish or joy which~~ [a] thrill. ~~The nature of which was not disclosed.~~ of an unknown nature. Then

joyful or tragic, as if a giant voice had screamed & shrieked so [on even at last?] to reach the cupboard † where the tumblers stood.

again silence; ~~& then~~ [or] nothing but the sound of waves again, & the & then night after night, ~~the~~ & sometimes in plain midday, when the roses were all blooming & the light was turning its ~~shapely~~ shape clearly, seemed to drop a stone in the ~~w~~ even into this silence, ~~& this indifference. And~~ this brilliance, this complete indifference.

& blazing color

Then ~~the escaped~~, indeed those who had gone down to pace the beach & ask of the sea & sky what message ~~it~~ [they] reported or what vision ~~it~~ [they] made [affirmed] manifest, had to consider among the usual & the delightful tokens of divine bounty – such as the sunset on the sea & the colour of the waves & their frolic & their grandeur & the majesty of the cliff – something unexpected. For instance, a murderous looking ship; ~~would appear, or~~, leaden, ashen, sinister; or, a little froth & stain upon the bland surface of the sea, as if ~~beneath~~ something were foaming or & ~~being bitten by sharks be~~ boiling beneath.

the calm moon rising

---

† A 201, B 207

(173)

This intrusion into a scene ~~which was~~ otherwise
calculated to stir the most sublime reflections & lead to the
most comforting conclusions stayed their pacing. If
that snout ~~out in~~ thrusting itself up ~~in the~~ there ~~expressed~~
~~the desire wish to~~ meant death, & starvation, ~~&~~ pain,
it was difficult to abolish its significance, & to continue,
by the sea ~~walking by the sea~~, ~~to adm marvel at the~~ as one walked to
marvel at the ~~completeness, & at the roundness, &~~
rounded completeness of ~~human~~ existence. ~~the the nature~~
† & how nature ~~capped what wa~~s supplemented what man
advanced, & completed what he began, ~~&~~ for Equally benignant &
sublime, she contemplated his misery, she condoned his
remained meanness, she acquiesced in his torture. ~~She was as~~
beautiful ~~beautiful as ever,~~ ~~& yet~~ but how could one ~~forget that~~
still. bring that ugly snout, that lean murderous ship, into the pattern?
~~The black snout interfered with the whole composition.~~
Was there no composition at all then? ~~Was it~~
~~Was it~~ ~~And there~~ Was This dream of harmony & completeness
was but the reflection in a mirror – [& the snout broke the
~~mirror~~, & the mirror was not only ~~such~~ a superficial glassiness
such as forms in a state of quiescence when the nobler powers
are asleep? ~~Anything was nobler than~~ Semblances
~~such as these meant nothing; & so~~, impatiently yet
despairingly – for beauty has her consolation, however
illusory, ~~she may be – it seemed nobler & more necessary now~~
~~to~~ no more beach pacings, no more contemplating was
possible, & for years, ~~for~~ a solitude desolation reigned there;
the mirror was broken.

Night after night, ~~in~~ summer & winter ~~nothing was~~
waves & sun, the torment of storm & the ~~d~~ arrowlike
stillness of fine weather held their court without ~~interve~~
interference. ~~A~~ Listening ~~from the~~ – had there
been anyone to listen – from the upper ~~chambers~~ rooms of the
house, ~~which where the~~ only gigantic chaos could have

† A 202, B 208

lash with their tails & churn with ~~tails lash &~~ their fins ~~churn~~

† been heard tumbling & tossing; the winds & the waves disporting themselves like the amorphous shapes of leviathans whose brows were pierced by no light of reason, whose ~~tal~~ lunged & plunged in the darkness without cause or reason; Now it seemed ~~fiercely~~ battling for no reason, then at peace; now ~~in~~ mounting in lust or conquest one upon another, so that they seemed to until it seemed as if the the universe were ~~filled from~~ earth to sky ~~with~~ was full of shapes mounting one on top of another, battling & tumbling – ~~& the~~ now swiftness, now stagnant, but always in a ~~wild~~ brute ~~commotion~~ confusion. When in spring the flowers ~~all started~~ [?], & ~~again~~ the urns were casually filled with ~~some~~ the trailing ~~geranium, they too seemed~~ elongated petals of some windblown plant, these too seemed clothed in beauty – yes – lovely as ever – ( Mrs. MacNab, stopped & thinking no harm since the family would not come, no one knew when, never again perhaps – it was said the house would be sold, stooped & picked a bunch to take home with her) yet nature's beauty, ~~the~~ her involuntary & irrepressible creation ~~of this~~ of a ~~force which had created the wind too~~, now seemed ~~cold It seemed~~ eyeless, brainless, empty.

And the stillness & the brightness ~~of the day was~~ equally strange, ser~~ene though it~~ ~~might~~ be, ~~the trees still, & the flowers bright~~, with the trees standing there, & the flowers standing there, & ~~Everything quiet & nothing happening, &~~ looking before them & beholding nothing & ~~spe revealing completely~~ yet completely open, & ~~utterly revealed~~, yet eyeless, & ~~terrible in~~ so terrible.

Thinking no harm, for the family would not come, never again, some said, & the house would be sold next year perhaps, Mrs. Macnab stooped & picked a bunch of flowers to take home with her; ~~as she went in to air the rooms~~ laid them on the table ~~when she~~ while she did her dusting. Suppose the house was sold, it would want doing up. For there it had stood all these years without a soul in it; & now, ~~according to one~~ ~~of the young la~~ would Mrs. Macnab see that ~~the~~ everything was straight – for it might be sold, Mrs. Macnab understood, to a gentleman from Edinburgh.

After all these years, the books & things were mouldy for what with the war, & ~~one thing & another,~~ help
† being hard to get, the house had not been cleaned as she could have wished. The books were mouldy; ~~&~~ the plaster had fallen in the hall; ~~& upstairs in~~ the & the damp had come through the ceiling.

~~So she~~ But people should come & see things for themselves. They should send somebody down. For there were clothes in the cupboards – what was she to do with them? Mrs. Ramsay's things – poor lady, she would never ~~not~~ want them again any more; ~~not her~~ that ~~this~~ old grey coat, for instance, which she wore gardening. Mrs. Macnab could see her – ~~with the little~~ as she came up the drive, ~~in the~~ evening, stooping over the her flowers plants, ~~for she would~~ ~~have~~ in that cloak: then these boots, & the brush & comb

† A 204, B 210

left on the dressing table, for all the world as if she expected to
† come back tomorrow. The little dressing table drawers were
full of ~~her things.~~ bits of things – laces, handkerchiefs –
~~Fre~~ Opening the drawers, even after all these years, a
Mrs. Macnab could smell something that brought ~~back – but what~~?
~~A vision – yes~~, something beautiful, but very very distant, as if she
put a glass to her eye, & there appeared ~~at a~~ little coloured figure
at the end, of a lady, in a grey cloak, ~~sto~~ stooping, looking up at her,

Good evening, Mrs. MacNab, ~~the~~ she said –
She had a pleasant way with her. But ah dear, many
things had changed in these years; many families lost their
dearest. So Mrs. Ramsay was dead; & ~~youn~~ Mr. Andrew killed they said
& Miss Prudence, who had married, she had died too, with her
first ~~bady~~ baby they said, but Everyone ~~w~~ had lost someone,
in these years. Prices had gone up shamefully: they didn't come
down either. She was by the flower bed on the drive,
with the children playing about, & ~~ev~~ no one thinking ~~of~~
~~of wars in those days. any no one~~ Mrs. Macnab
well remembered her.

So across the

$$\begin{array}{r} 30 \\ \underline{6} \\ 180 \end{array}$$

A ~~little~~ dim figure, of a lady in a grey cloak, bending ~~down~~ among white
flowers on a summer's ~~night, &~~ evening appeared her[illegible]
& here & here ~~as Mrs. Macnab went,~~ ~~as~~ by the open drawer ~~of~~
by the washstand, by the cupboard as Mrs. Macnab ~~went~~ did
the bedroom – It was ~~more~~ like an image seen through a rather
feeble telescope; ~~it~~ was cut out like that – ~~a lady in a grey cloak~~ –
without ~~any~~ feeling to it much else, save some queer pleasure, rising in
~~Mrs. Macnab's~~ old Maggie's brain to think of herself going up
the drive to have her tea perhaps in the kitchen on a
summer's evening when ~~everything was~~ things were better than they
are now. She sighed – she moaned. The little picture
~~the ghost~~ ~~who~~ which had come back to the bedroom, ~~like a~~
~~for a moment~~ to waver across the wall ~~&~~ like a momentary
sunbeam on a cloudy day vanished. Old Maggie saw nothing ~~at all.~~
Compared with everything else there – the mahogany chest of
drawers – the brass bedstead – the ghost which old
Maggie had
~~Such was the fate of that w ghost.~~

saw only the chest of drawers & the brass bedstead which needed polishing.

They survived. ~~The~~ Pleasant ghosts – & she had had a way
with her, Mrs. Ramsay, & ~~would not~~ could not alter those;
could not stay. It was only by fits & starts one ~~got the~~
thought of them. ~~A la~~ Stooping among her flowers – old
Maggie ~~might~~ could say it ~~herself, but~~ but her old crazed
† wits were flitting off elsewhere; ~~The~~ There was
too much here to do for one ~~person~~ – woman – to do.
too much – too much.

So, when she had gone, ill temperedly banging the doors,
& forgetting her flowers, the house seemed like a
shell deserted of life, & given over to moulder on a sandhill.

† A 206, B 212

Then the long night seemed to have set in; the final triumph
of the little airs, the clammy breath, ~~to be~~ was at hand.
† Soon some thistle would be thrusting its head between the tiles in
& dislodge it:
the larder; & the swallows ~~who had nested yearly in the~~
would come in through the broken window & nest in the drawing room,
a shovelfull of
& the floor would be strewn with straws & ~~the~~ plaster
would fall, & rats carry off this & that behind the wainscot, &
butterflies pass through the rooms at will, & ~~when~~
~~then~~ while outside in the garden ~~poppie~~ wild poppies
would sow themselves among the dahlias, & cornflowers, &
hollows filled & banks raised
the ~~grass would wave~~ & the lawn would ~~be~~ wave
long
with grass, & ~~the tapp~~ ~~hollows~~ beds be grown over,
seats curved across with bramble sprays, sudden
beauty flower in the midst of chaos – a sure rose, or a
fine carnation, ~~&~~ while the gentle tapping of a weed or
wd
two at the window pane now became on winter nights ~~al~~
~~a bull~~ a drumming, a battering from ~~stout~~ ~~thick~~
thorny ~~stout~~ trees that had rooted themselves, or creepers
that had grown thick & clasped the walls.

could prevail the
What power against ~~all~~ ~~this~~ fertility & insensibility
of nature? Old Maggie's dream, her dim telescope vision of a
lady in a ~~grey cloak~~ stooping over her flowers? ~~had~~
But after
flickering about the bedroom for a moment, but vanished.
~~watchers & preachers~~, Though the lighthouse came & went again,
† the sudden scrutiny – its long look & then, sharply following,
its two quick glances, ~~met nothing in that~~
seemed perfectly satisfied with what they saw.
As for the watchers, the preachers, ~~the souls who who~~
~~had~~ those spirits who, in sleep, had left their bodies, & dreamed
of some communion, of grasping the hand of a sharer, &
completing, down on the beach, ~~the~~ from the sky or sea
the cliff, ~~or the~~ the ~~fu~~ fullness that was incomplete, the

† A 207, B 213; A 208, B 214

179

vision that asked for ratification, either they had been
woken from their dreams by that prodigious cannonading which
had made the wine glasses tinkle in the cupboard, or
that intrusion – that black snout – that purple foaming stain –
had so gravely ~~interfered~~ damaged the composition of the picture
that ~~w~~ they had fled. They had gone in despair. They had
dashed the mirror to the ground. They saw nothing more.
They stumbled & strove now, blindly, pulling their feet out of the
mud & stamping them further in. Let the wind blow, let the
poppy seed itself, & the carnation mate with the cabbage.
Let the swallow build ~~on the works of Shakespeare; & the~~
~~butterfly flaunt~~ in the drawing room, & the thistle thrust up the
tiles, up & the butterfly sun itself on the faded chinzy~~es~~ arm chairs.
~~Let the ch broken china be~~ & all ~~beaut~~ civilisation lie
like broken china to be tangled over with ~~the~~
blackberries & grass.

For now had come that moment, that crisis, ~~in the~~ when if a
feather alight in one scale, it will be weighted down – & so if
if a feather had ~~blown~~ alighted the house would have fallen in:
would have become past repair; & ~~out~~ picnickers, would have
boiled their kettles in its ~~e~~ ruined rooms, lovers ~~in~~
sought shelter there, or ~~som~~ the shepherd stored his dinner, &
taken his rest there, with his collie by his side. Then
~~even the~~ the walls would have fallen in, & then ~~coming~~ over
the hill, ~~only the since the tangled garden could~~ ~~what would have~~ nothing would have
remained to one straying into this wilderness, this ruined barn,
(for such it seemed) in a wilderness of ~~old~~ unkempt shrubs,
~~some~~ the only things which would have testified that ~~here~~
people had lived somewhere about here would have been
† the ~~extraordinary~~ apparition of a red hot poker; ~~the~~ a chipped plate.
If the feather had fallen, – if it had plunged the scale into
darkness, – but there was a force working on the other side;
something leering & lurching; ~~something~~ something that was not highly conscious of its
own purpose & certainly not inspired to go about its task with
dignified ritual or solemn chanting. But in old Maggie & her
crony, Mrs. Bast, there was a force: (they came with their
brooms & their pails they moaned: they crooned – they got to work.)
There was a force perhaps in their craziness (~~for without being~~
~~locked~~ in ~~danger of locking up, their minds were blank,~~
or vacancy of mind; which slowly & painfully ~~began~~
stayed the corruption & the rot; rescued from the
pool of time which was fast closing over them now a bed now a
basin now a cupboard; fished up from oblivion ~~the~~
all the Waverley novels, & a tea pot one morning: in the
afternoon restored to the sun & the air a brass fender & a
set of steel pokers & tongs. Some rusted laborious birth
† attended with the creaking hinges & the screeching of bolts &

ask them what
the war had
been about –
did they know?)

† B 215, A 209; A 210, B 216

180
280
1440
360
5040

& the slamming & banging of damp-swollen wood ~~might~~
~~have been~~ ~~been~~ seemed to be taking place, as the old women
slapped & slammed, upstairs now, now in the cellar.
They drank their tea in the bathroom sometimes, sometimes in the
study; contemplating now, the magnificent conquest of the taps &
the freshly painted bath; now their more arduous &
indeed more partial ~~conq~~ ~~triump~~ ~~c~~ triumph over
innumerable volumes of ~~old~~ philosophy which, black in the
beginning were now not only puce coloured ~~& white~~
with white cascades of damp, but bred little mushrooms –
~~seret~~ secreted spiders. ~~Then,~~ suddenly, ~~her~~ as she wiped
~~& ba~~ them, the telescope fitted itself of its own accord to old
Maggie's wandering eyes, & in a momentary stability she saw
the old gentleman, on the lawn. ~~He was~~ as lean as a rake – He
~~was~~ wagging his head. ~~He~~ Was he dead too? ~~Some~~ said [it was] he, Mr. Ramsay
some said ~~she~~ He was standing on the lawn; she could see him now. [margin: it was Mrs. Ramsay]
So for a moment the little ghost, held in the charwoman's eye,
revisited the lawn, wagged its head; & recalled ~~that~~ (who ~~kne~~ by some
devious faith) ~~he~~ a joke of Mildreds in the kitchen. She was
† hot tempered like all red haired women. ~~But~~ She [always] saved ~~her~~
a plate of milk soup for Maggie. Mrs. Ramsay quite thought she
needed it, bringing the wash up the hill every step of the way
herself.

† A211, B 217

Thus they ~~recalled the happiness, the security of those summer days~~; ~~&~~ old Maggie un~~win~~ding [wound] her string of memories, glibly, jovially from the centre ~~there~~ – ~~that~~ [her] kitchen, where Mildred would be ~~her~~ [bustling with] a good natured woman, ~~but fiery like all sandy~~ ~~a red haired girl~~, ~~or woman~~, rather, Mrs. Ramsay in & out of the kitchen, but liked well enough by the maids; ~~or always~~ & always they kept a plate of milk soup for Maggie, why there were sometimes more than twenty in the house – ~~But~~ Mrs. Bast had ~~no such~~ [unfixed] rooted in ~~no~~ such soil, wondered how ~~they had such~~ [they came to have] that beasts skull ~~came~~ there, shot in foreign parts no doubt – & Maggie ~~had ex~~ (the shawl had been folded & put away in the drawer) & Maggie ~~would wanton with the~~ wantoning as with her wandering tales of Eastern gentry coming from the Indies, ~~Mrs. Best~~ ~~all sorts of company coming in those days~~, & She once seeing them, through the door hinge, all at dinner ~~ladies & gentlemen~~, ~~flowers~~. ~~courses,~~ [they would be washing up till midnight,] all in their finery, Mrs. Bast thought it ~~out~~ [said] not in reason that they should [expect to] find the place as they left it, seeing that ~~the a lawn soon grows over if you leave it~~ – ~~&~~ only ~~Mr.~~ old David came, ~~& he with his~~ [out but] & he stopped when his leg got bad after the fall in the cart, & [perhaps] then no one came, – than seeds might be sent but who should say if they were planted?

Margin: [ ? ] the [sunny?] [ ? ] of the safe summer days

Margin: without profit from ~~in~~ its splendour,

Margin: (getting up & [hauling?] looking at the ~~Geo~~ man ~~Fred~~ ~~now~~ with his sythe* in the garden)

† [margin mark beside "leg got bad after the fall in the cart"]

~~B~~ They knew, both of them, some ~~stories~~ things [~~wh~~ the way some things had gone –] – they could ~~say~~ [tell some stories]: ~~but & say them they did leaning in the window sill~~ so they ~~joked~~ hinted, (Mrs. Bast bored enough with the old loose tongued doddering creature, but glad of her weeks work at the house now that ~~the~~ work was scarcer,)

~~George~~ ~~Fred she ha She hailed~~ [&] Fred ~~stopped~~ ~~his~~ looked up at them, staying his ~~sy~~ ~~sy~~ [the] scythe,

* VW's misspelling

† A 212, B 218

which had done very fairly since there was only one square ~~army of~~
of thick waving grass yet to be demolished on the lawn
while the ~~ba~~ behind him the shining grass lay prone; the
the curt stubble was crisp. He ~~brought order &~~
laid low the wilderness with each sweep, & to do him justice was a
steady worker, slow but remorseless, as if each movement were
timed by ~~an accurate sent out by the shock of~~ issued from his heart (a
sucked in & sent out; so that even now he would waste no
words with the women in the window, only grinned & spat, & resumed
again that rhythmic singsong stroke, which ~~was~~
advanced like the sweep of an invincible army over the
~~insugr~~ insurgents rioting ~~before~~ & wary in their tumult ~~b~~ up the
bank & over the lawn & ~~so~~ laid them flat.

(a powerful but ~~not a~~ inarticulate organ)

When, at ~~six~~ in the evening, & the pale green swathes
lay twined with convolvulus ~~or~~ & wild flowers on the lawn,
when the rooks were deliberating, fastidiously, tentatively,
among the tree tops, & from again like some half
heard melody some adumbrated music what whose notes the ear
half catches but lets ~~some~~ notes fall drop so that the harmony is
never completed, now the time assured, but now there are
long pauses & new notes reiterated close together
the sea & the machine, the pigeon, & the boys voice, all
struck far & faint, ~~yet~~ out at sea, deep in the fields, in the [a?] [?]
until it seemed as if harmony were about to triumph &
then suddenly ~~the~~ in would rush the wind
as if now they must unite together: but then in rushed the
wind, & all was dispersed.

a barking dog

at last, ~~there came in the evening, the when George~~ all the labour
~~was~~ banged to,
stopped: ~~cloth~~ dusters were flicked from the window: the windows shut;
keys turned — they locked the doors, George ~~shouldered~~ his ~~syth~~ stopped, ~~a~~
[automatically
still; & then at once, as if the cleaning & the ~~sy sy~~ scything had
~~du dulled~~ the sound, ~~began that half heard melody~~ with the
rooks deliberating fastidiously tentatively among the treetops,
that halfheard melody, that adumbrated music which
the ear half catches but lets fall – cries, shouts, bark, far or close at
[hand –
~~wrapped up in the mesh of summer stillness & suddenly~~
~~h~~ was ~~heard, & lost, & that music began,~~ & then the ~~rooks,~~
was
creaking of the rooks joined with it, rising fully deliberating [regreting?]
above the tree tops, & then the insects cheeped & then the
where it lay
the cut grass started & shivers ~~ran through it~~, but
~~always with notes were dropped, &~~ & Gradually, with the
† sunset, ~~peace~~ sharpness was lost; & like a mist rising,
quiet rose, the rooks settled, the grass settled; ~~At~~
~~ease, & woul loose~~, ~~Freedom & ease, content & peace~~ was the
came sighing
~~lot of the~~ whole world shaking itself down to sleep, darkly
here without a light to it, save what came suffused through leaves,
& palely caught by flowers.

so widely spaced is it, & half close & half faint, half here & half far away,

Then, in the darkness, ~~the one~~ restless spirits who
&
had left their beds to ask what fate meant, what God meant, to
what destiny ~~the ball of the world rolled, could once more~~
they moved, to ~~say~~ feel assured on the beach of
indeed
Then ~~when~~ calm had returned. Peaceful messages breathed from the
waves ~~on the beach, &~~ to the house. Never to break its
sleep again, ~~never to to~~ to lull it rather more calmly, ~~no~~ more
there, in bed, to
sweetly to rest. What ever they dream holily wisely, ~~we~~ confirm,
What else were they murmuring? And behold, – ~~yes~~
~~Indeed,~~ their message, their wisdom, no sooner was it
thought than they wore it a garment of splendour;
~~cast it like a~~ swept it ~~one swirled it, & they~~ the
wave swept up the beach. Then, like a ~~th~~ mind so

† A213, B 219

[*]

sleep in contemplation that its least thought is [just?], & is returning to ~~profundity & merges with the deeps & is again round, fuller this time~~, in the ripple of some profounder meaning they broke again, & ~~they~~ broke [again; & each wave ~~seemed to~~ added, if one walked there, with the light [enough?] only to distinguish the outline of the cliff, & ~~one~~ a few harbour lights, & a ship's lights, assurance upon assurance.

* VW did not number this page.

~~Inscrutable is our thought.~~ ~~Each wave is only~~ the But that ~~its~~ on peace ~~was~~ is a brooding peace, ~~its~~ on beauty a ~~significant~~ ~~beauty,~~ ~~who can look on us & deny~~? tenuous beauty. We lie at your doors wishing you well, ~~&~~

~~To which~~ Who; waking ~~then~~ in the depths of this dark, this ~~to~~ silent, this restful night ~~when~~ where the ~~[high?]~~ darkness was a veil ~~spread over something~~ whose ~~murmur~~ sigh was as ~~the~~ a seemed ~~the like the~~ murmur of secrets & wisdom too deep to be fully uttered, could even now, after chaos, after storm, resist the desire to find out there down on the beach ~~some~~ ~~in~~ on the pale sand, with the waves breaking, & only a light at the harbour, a light on some masthead, a light on the cliff, & piercing its slumbrous bulk, ~~to~~ something more.

the lighthouse looking, now gravely now, stilly now,

And yet, seeing how much we have suffered, how often, when the secret seemed ours, been mocked, ~~now~~ on the whole now ~~we shal~~ it seems better ~~to~~ only to lie here, in the dark; It is indeed a perfect summer's night, & with in these latitudes the light seems only shaded not gone shaded; & ~~it is exquisite & soothing & consoling~~ to wake, & to lie with the windows open, & the voice coming through the windows, too gently for us to catch the words, the voice of the beauty of the world, & to let it sing to us, ~~those old ancient~~ that ancient music ~~which heaven knows no heart can resist,~~ that ~~grow~~ murmured strain which seems to ~~say li~~ bid us ~~lie still~~, lie quiet, all night long, so that ~~when~~ everyone is asleep, it may impart to us, ~~so [surely?]~~ attentive, its message. – how The wave ~~sweep~~ breaks on the shore.

186

~~Surely~~ ~~And the sea held~~ ~~Who could resist the desire~~

But ~~to w hear that message,~~

The voice ~~entreated the sleepers to lie turn again & dream~~ again, or if they would not actually come ~~again~~ to the beach itself to

† listen, at least to lift the blind & look out upon a night so magnificent that it ~~could only~~ must for ever mingle with

the thought of happiness ~~their happiest memories.~~ ~~The blue of night has been the~~ the ~~background of so many scenes of love,~~ the ~~what~~ lay spread beneath, ~~around, abov~~ them; to realize how they stood in ~~the~~ to stand in the presence of th~~is aug~~ a ~~ust~~ God, whose robes were ~~flowing, whose~~ flowed down ~~& whose~~ ~~& he had his~~ whose was head crowned, & ~~who h~~ His hand was on his c sceptre & his eyes ~~wor~~

† a child might look into. ~~But~~ And if the sleeper still faltered & ~~murmured~~ said no; that it was vapour, this splendour of his, & he had no more power than the dew, [the dew was ... ful he] without complaint, ~~without~~ or argument, the voice would resume its song: ~~would~~ Gently the waves would continue. And everything – in the room, ~~the cupboards & the chair,~~ ~~would assume~~ ~~as if they too agreed, the~~ a ~~so~~ freshly ordered, straightly ranged, seemed ~~then to~~ lie under that enchantment, ~~ordered~~ ~~in some more stately way.~~ ~~In the~~ placed more statelily* placed, ~~more gravely conscious.~~

to conscious more gravely of some order ~~in the world~~ & purpose which when the day broke they would fulfil.

Indeed the ~~night~~ voice might resume, as the leaves of the passion flower tapped upon the window & the curious shadowy half leaf half chair lay ~~slid in such apparently~~ slid enlaced interlaced on the floor, had, if he might ~~support this~~ ~~merely continue to exist~~ ~~as a background for the~~ ~~It was enough for him~~ to ~~lie thus~~ ~~reign thus, magnificent~~, he was content with this: this was enough. – to fold the sleepers round & be there, should they choose to look ~~through some chink in~~ the blind ~~at what~~ to be there.

After all then, might ~~one not say~~ they not

* VW's spelling

† B 220; A 214

(3.103)

accept: it they might without ~~failing~~ losing their power, or giving
~~way to his~~ up their scepticism, or sinking once again into the
soft depths of acquiescence, they might, half timid, laughing; or
assuming some expression which could not be mistaken for
mere rapture, lie watchfully awake, & see, now through the
chink of the blind the splendid monarch, hear, through some
the open window the deep voice persuading, & entreating, or
merely chanting to itself; flowed down in purple & blue, &
[sent?] : ~~Go~~ hear the vast sigh of all the seas breaking
in measured [tide?]
round all the islands, but now controlled; &
measured; & [ ? ] & hear the the birds begin; &
the dawn weave their voices into its whiter garment; &
~~then hear the~~ hear the whole begin; & then,
at last forgetting to discriminate between ~~whil~~ wheel &
bird, yielding at last perhaps to that marvellous
night, & the roll of all those seas, & the immensity of the
sky; feeling incapable of more of divising ~~a plan~~ for
making a footstool of beauty, or a handmaiden of nature,
~~So~~ lapse & fall, ~~& on~~ only, before losing consciousness
again, & sleeping once more, ~~the~~ the sleepers in the
house might recognise in themselves, with
delight & astonishment & something like fear, from
~~the cry b st the~~ cry of some bird, it might be, in the
grinding on the road far away of an early wheel –
another emotion half waking them at the moment,
sleepy, & mixing & mighty, & making their hands
† leap, even as they fell over the edge of the cliff into
sleep, with ~~a~~ the stab & stir & wild expectation &
desire of the ~~com~~ coming day.

† B221

(Rodmell)
May 27th
1926

## Part Three

.1.

† "Then what does it mean, what can it / all mean?" Lily Briscoe asked herself, wondering whether, since they had all disappeared, it behoved her to go to the kitchen for another cup of coffee or to wait a here. So ~~inappropriately, by~~ using a catchword picked up from some book or other she tried ~~to contract her myriad emotions,~~ this first morning at the Ramsays ~~again,~~ to contract her myriad emotions; to make some phrase resound where there was nothing, to cover the blankness with [?] of her mind. For really what did one feel? Nothing nothing ~~At this~~ moment, not much. She had arrived ~~rather~~ late ~~the~~ last night; When it was ~~It had been~~ very beautiful, & dark & strange & not real. Now she was awake: sitting in her old place, at the breakfast table ~~at Mr. Ramsay's right hand~~. It was very early – not quite eight. They were going to the Lighthouse – Mr. Ramsay, Cam & James. They shd have had to be off ~~to catch the~~

† ~~tide, early:~~ they had to catch the tide, or something; Cam was not ready ~~& they were late~~. ~~So~~ Mr. Ramsay had lost ~~his temper~~ So James was not ready; Nancy had forgotten the sandwiches, or something. & So Mr.

† Ramsay had lost his temper. There he was marching up & down on the terrace outside. ~~&~~ One could hear doors slamming banging all over the house, & ~~once~~ Nancy had burst in, ~~with all sorts of~~ things [to order & banged out of the room] asking in a ~~that~~ queer half dazed half desperate way ~~she had~~ as if she were forcing herself to do what she had no sort of gift for doing, "What does one send ~~t~~ the men at the lighthouse men?" as if this were some curious piece of knowledge which she might be given anybody might possess just as there one might give her be a hammer in a cupboard, or a pair of scissors ~~but probably was~~ not. For ~~how co~~ who was going to answer her question? ~~On~~ At an ordinary time, Lily could have concentrated her mind & thought of ~~tea~~ tobacco, tea chocolate, newspapers comforters – but ~~it~~ nothing was ordinary, quite. All was frightfully queer. ~~But~~ so ~~that instead of thinking o~~ that a question like that seemed to set doors ~~swinging,~~ banging swinging to & fro in the mind. ~~blown by some rather~~ It was useless to attempt any answer. Anyhow, Nancy had disappeared.

† A 217, B 225; B 226; A 218

Why was one sitting here at all? Where was one? Who was one?

~~That~~ It was all very unpleasant, ~~cold clammy vivid & so vivid, so real~~: & [clere?] & glaring. & yet unrelated; as if she why indeed ~~h~~ did anything happen as it did happen? For she had no attachments or relations it seemed; she was ~~set down here among~~ sitting among clean cups at a long table alone. & for a moment, ~~with extreme~~ vividness, felt cut off from all

† contact with human beings, & able only ~~to frame~~ ask one question after [another, They ~~might~~ all ~~have been~~ seemed strangers to her; ~~she~~ the house, the place, everything seemed strange. ~~The whole~~ She had no attachments, to it she felt,

† no relations. with it & anything might ~~happen~~, & whatever did happen — whether it was ~~Nancy bursting~~ a [maid coming?] in in, or these voices calling, or Mr. Ramsay ~~reciting poetry~~ passing on the terrace ~~had~~ seemed ~~so queer~~ like that — up in the air cut off, ~~As if~~ at last ~~one saw~~ the extraordinary nature of existence, was made plain, ~~& one could~~ ~~some little~~ as if some link had broken. As if some link had broken & at last one realised how extraordinary it was — life. How aimless, how chaotic, how violent, she thought — & really, whatever one might say, almost entirely without feeling, or reason or thought or anything There was Mrs. Ramsay dead; Andrew killed: Prue dead too: Then they all got together & ~~said had breakfast, & Mr. Ramsay~~ like this in a house on a bay ~~& began~~ poured out coffee ~~at eight in the morning~~ by [why?]? But ~~Heaven knows what its all about~~, & she had to keep saying to herself ~~what a tragedy how~~ this is terrible this is, how ~~ter~~ this is tragic awful not to see Mrs. Ramsay sitting there as she used to sit; when really ~~what she felt was~~ ~~that was all forced & put on~~ She did not feel it; she felt nothing: only why? ~~why? why~~? on earth do we do it?

had that quality — it was a question — ~~a~~ something extraordinary

Suddenly Mr. Ramsay looked at her, through the bay window. ~~He was thoroughly out of temper, & so~~ although she had finished her coffee, she pretended to drink, in order to keep ~~that terrible, that~~ him sinister ~~that~~ man at bay. All she had heard from him this morning was scolding — scolding ~~the~~ Nancy, scolding James & Cam. Old Mr. Carmichael had taken his coffee out on to the lawn — ~~It was odd to be able~~ to notice everything with extreme accuracy, &

Whenever anything happened she asked why

† B 227; A 219

~~Yet to feel nothing whatever~~
because it was so peaceful perhaps. ~~But it was uncomfortable rather than painful~~ But it was not painful to her, only extremely uncomfortable, & yet suppose that all one's life ~~one~~ had ~~lived~~ in a dream, & this was true, ~~one could not help being~~ Lily Briscoe thought, putting her empty cup down again, as Mr. Ramsay had passed on. At any rate, she thought, looking ~~about round the~~ at an engraving on the wall opposite, one must take one's chance ~~always~~ of finding out; however unpleasant it is & she figured herself as a rider being thrown up into the air. by the kicks & plunges of an unruly horse, with a back like a ~~sharp~~ knifebow. What is it?" she asked herself again, ~~as if she~~ with an odd feeling that she had very nearly laid hold ~~upon something~~ of ~~the highest importance~~ – or almost actually had grapsed ~~what people~~ call "~~the meaning of life~~" ~~which, once laid hold of,~~ ~~would~~ something that intensity of understanding which relates everything together; ~~so~~ that it was all right – the misery, the scolding – & these eternal questions which, ~~what~~ everything that happened now seemed to set banging & swimming inside her. ~~Oh, Nancy~~ again ~~w~~ ~~hunting for some~~thing in ~~a cupboard~~ Is it in the side the sideboard, & ~~carrying on a~~ conversation with someone inside, about its being there, or being somewhere else.

What does one take to the Lighthouse, indeed? or in the cupboard on the landing? Nancy was saying. on the stairs, & Lily thought, That she said ~~much~~ rather like Mrs. Ramsay" – ~~Why don't I feel more~~? ~~she wondered~~. It was She sat ~~there~~; ~~she was~~ There, in that empty she thought. ~~Now she is dead.~~ But nothing happened. Then it must simply be a game of chance, she said. (~~all~~ she had tags in her mind) but she would use them until she ~~dis~~ formed ~~better~~ shorter words) ~~All~~ We come & go – We ~~just~~ say ~~things~~ "see people": or, sometimes, – (this is very odd she thought) ~~although we know we have only seen~~ we don't "see people" for months. Then they're dead. We don't "see them" –

been

it wd be as well to find out what the truth is –

get something – like a white ~~wav~~ crested wave among ~~green wav~~ the usual green waves

There she sat there she sat there she repeated waiting for her feeling to well up.

And what relation is that – "seeing people"? The hideous callousness, [the entire temporariness, ~~ch~~ & the ramshackle jerrybuilt houses run up, here & there, called friendships, called loves – Mr. Ramsay: Yes: she thought of him: As vain as ever, as touchy, as ~~egotistical~~; absorbed in himself; this man nevertheless, had what we are told (she was holding a dialogue between herself & a china pepper pot) & the pepper pot which she which was 'we', the great voice of public opinion) what the pepperpot, (which she seemed to remember too, ten years ago) tells ~~us is~~ the we are told is the greatest of human calamities – his wife's death, his sons; "killed in battle" & all the rest of it; & ~~his daughter, with~~ Then Prue dead, with her first baby. Still – Mr. Ramsay – well, she did not see what difference it had made to Mr. Ramsay. If one must be honest, he seemed to her only crosser, more exacting,

192

to protect herself, to ~~give give herself a~~ chance of ~~going on~~
~~thinking finding out what it was all about~~, why it was
all so queer, to give her eyes a chance of reading there
large plain letters in which everything seemed now written;
seemed
Everything was a symbol. ~~The anger~~ Nancy bursting in with
her "What does one send to the Lighthouse?", Mr. Ramsay
reciting
~~flinging off.~~ marching up. down. Mr. Carmichael coming in
softly, ~~mu~~ bumblingly, taking his coffee, taking his toast &
making off to eat it in the sun. ~~Its~~ The extraordinary
of it
† unreality was frightening, but fascinating. And her lack of
normal about
any feeling at all – that was so strange, considering ~~that she~~
~~ought to be thinking of Mrs. Ramsay all the time~~, how she had
but it was plain
loved Mrs. Ramsay; & her sense ~~as~~ she sat alone at the
~~long tab~~le of ~~having~~ the truth ~~made visible in~~
was
~~being~~ written up – the staring unmistakable truth – how ~~there is~~
~~nothing~~ (she seemed to be reading this so that until she had
that they were just like that;
said the words) ~~things~~ – ~~it she felt nothing whatever~~
~~& they~~ they were too odd, too unrelated, for one to
~~to~~ be able to ~~use the old sayings~~ anymore so to
catch them, to coop them. ~~N Mrs. Ramsay~~? – who was she?
A dead woman. ~~This was her home & though; &~~ A
~~a presence~~, what was that? A voice on the stairs.
some one passing the window. She felt nothing: yet
~~personal; but was awed; A~~ revelation was taking place.
~~Was there then something they these things made, more~~
some one coming in & going out – ~~She had her hands~~ on ~~some~~ an
extraordinary ~~discovery~~ of life ~~in its~~ naked, pure; unalloyed
with the sentiments & ~~trif~~ wrappings up ~~&~~
~~trivialities~~ of its such it was; ~~& She had her hands~~
but
on some discovery. ~~&~~ – ~~But what which~~ exalted
~~terrible~~, amazing strange.

~~She looked at Mr. Ramsay.~~ Only if Mr.

(we perished each alone*

flinging off

She must collect these symbols.

of everything,

& she was dead;

the truth

she did not know what she was going to say –

extraordinary.
random
& [ ? ],
such was life;
when ✓

* W. Cowper, 'The Castaway,' also quoted on MS 267, 283, 317, 362 (3.115)

† A 220

putting an end to this –
Ramsay caught her eye, he would be all for reducing her exaltation
It was she wanted
as indeed all contact [men?] be ruinous; ~~she desired~~ loneliness &
is else She bethought her – if he she had
something – something else ~~oh she~~ had left her paints in the hall
last night. her paint box. †

something else – her paint.
But
What

~~Getting up, she~~ She hurried off, before Mr. Ramsay should
turn~~r~~ again to get her paint. & ~~So, by standing her easel~~
~~there on the edge of the lawn, & putting her canvas~~
nervously she unstrapped the box. She fetched herself a
with rags, bottle, brushes.
chair. She fussed about, rather unnecessarily ~~to keep off~~
~~Mr. Ramsay~~ Whenever Mr. Ramsay ~~approached~~ turned towards her.
With him ruin approached, chaos approached. She did not
want to talk to him – she did not want to hear him speak as
did last
he might, of Mrs. Ramsay./ Last night he had done it, as
not
when everything was so ~~unreal that~~ muddled up that she had ~~only~~
felt ~~as~~ one thing more than another. But now if he should
† ~~begin~~ – ~~really she could not stand it.~~] "You find things
much altered." Dumb & staring though they had all sat
all these children, six children,
she had felt (knowing them scarcely at all, James, Nancy
† Cam, Roger,) how they raged under it. A house
of England
^ full of unrelated passions – she had felt that when she
went to bed. And on top of this chaos, Mr. Ramsay got up,
& ~~seeming to~~ ignored it all, ~~& not to notice anything.~~ & said
(she had been touched ~~though~~ You will find us much changed."
& ~~the~~ had
† ~~Poor~~ ~~And~~ They/ all sat ~~silent.~~ as if he must be allowed to
~~[ ? ]~~ sum things up as he chose; & still [sit in?] them some
or [shown?]
some ~~restraint, some covering which as their~~ real, some restraint.
But she had noticed James the Sullen, ~~doggedly~~ frowning
a
as if he held ~~some~~ leaf in the garden in ~~the~~ his mind;
vice (it was powerful, she guessed); & Cam the Bad, with a more
beaten expression twiddling her fingers, as if she would
twist it was he
torture whatever ~~she held until~~ this ~~torture~~ ceased to torture
The
her. ~~Then,~~ It was about going to the Lighthouse, &
being up in good time; ~~but~~ & Did they not want to come, to [ ? ]
Mr. Ramsay asked, holding the door, &, had they

stood it
She ~~put it~~ on the edge of the lawn

~~called~~ them the Kings & Queens six the Red, the Good, the Stern, the Sullen, Cam the Bad & so on

at the moment

& there they had sat

† B 229; A 221; B 230; A 222 (3.117)

dared disappoint him, (for clearly he had some wish of his own about it)
would ~~ready~~ to sink & ~~vanish in the~~ disappear & be drawn
tragically under in the bitter waters,
fling himself backwards into the waters of despair. Such a
gift ~~was~~ he had his for gesture. She could remember that. Doggedly
James ~~said~~ said he agreed: Cam stumbled. ~~That~~ was tragedy it seemed to
~~Lily Briscoe~~. Not palls & funerals, dust & the shroud. But
reluctance coerced; & children (Cam was 17, James 16 – both in the
flush of youth) trodden under. She had looked for somebody
who was not there; ~~& Then~~ she had sudden thought of Mrs. Ramsay.
† Then, ~~what with one thing & another, the beauty~~ being tired, &
muddled inexpressibly, & people moving in & out with candles, & some
curious beauty some melody some air such as houses have
after absence folded her round, & she had lost herself in it

to
May 31st † She set her ~~canv~~ clean canvas upon the easel, ~~as a~~ protecti~~on~~ her
~~against~~ from Mr. Ramsay & his exactingness.

Let him be on a terrace, let him not even speak to you, & yet
forget
his presence permeated, pervaded. One could not ~~ignore~~ him,
even at the end of the terrace, with his back turned. He would be
down on her in a moment demanding – She ~~chose~~ rejected one
brush, chose another. ~~Where other people (all women it seemed to her)~~
~~poured out life gave, he did not give. He was sealed, intact; she~~
† ~~porous~~ He did not give. He asked, he demanded. Like a sealed
She like all women
vessel, he kept his virtue in him. ~~She, women, porous~~ gave, gave, gave:
life flowed like blood from a wound. Thus giving Mrs.
Ramsay had died; ~~& left nothing~~ What had Mrs. Ramsay left?
Lily Briscoe, ~~flourish~~ with her brush trembling slightly in her
fingers ~~hand~~ looked at the scene ~~which~~ she was going to paint –
† Nothing, thought Lily Briscoe; ~~th~~ there she had sat, with James,
ten years ago. Now she was gone.
But why repeat ~~these~~ this? Why ~~try to bring up from a~~ be
always trying to bring up some feeling one had not? ~~Why~~
~~among all the feelings which all the rest~~ she felt a
with
perfectly inadmissible irritation ~~against~~ the Ramsays.
~~They had her at their mercy. She ought not to have come~~.
They ought not to ask all this; she ought not to have come. And at
forty four, she thought, one cannot waste weeks ~~on~~ when one is 44.
For she was utterly unable to concentrate her mind on what she was
doing. ~~Nothing so annoyed her as~~ She held a brush; but
like this
it was irritating to hold a brush ~~merely for~~ show; a brush, the
~~instrument of such rapture, to be treat be treated~~ the only
entirely dependable thing, in a world of chaos, a world of
worry, vexation, trivial daily implacable worry: that one
should not trifle with. But he made her. He
was bearing down on her. Women cant paint women
can't write – she remembered Charles Tansley~~s~~ saying that
& ~~if he had been here, she would have said w And why~~
it up
not? Well, thought Lily, ~~giving herself up~~ in despair,
† ~~thinking herself lost~~, ~~putting her l~~ ~~letting her~~ hand fall in

† A 223; B 232; A 224; B 233

desperation, it would be easier to give ~~way~~ way; ~~to~~ really simpler to
~~take on the~~ to attempt ~~that~~ an ~~some~~ imitation at least of that glow, ~~that~~ majesty
which she had seen in the faces of so many women when,
surrendering whatever vestiges of selfishness, of independence
that they possessed, they they had blazed up
with every appearance of genuine exaltation, & a blaze which
was certainly one of the most beautiful things on earth (she
could remember the look on Mrs. Ramsay's face) into complete
sympathy & surrender; & forgetfulness of all else in the world; &
joyousness in the fulfilment of instinct; & delight in
† reward; & some gratification which escaped her, but she
believed to be intense & unspeakable; ~~& said to Mr.~~
Ramsay (~~if it were Mr. Ramsay~~) giving Mr. Ramsay what
Mr. Ramsay wanted: sympathy.

(2)

~~But not from her.~~ He stopped. Among her
many admirable qualities – his wife ~~was~~ had been ~~very~~ fond of her.
Lily did not possess ~~the~~ ~~to his eye.~~ the ~~crowning~~ gift of
~~charm~~ beauty. ~~To~~ She had shrivelled slightly. She was
scarcely likely to marry now, ~~& presumably the affair~~
~~betw~~ Mr. Ramsay thought. She had not Minta's charm.
~~But Peop~~ ~~But there~~ she was, painting one of the ~~those~~ little landscapes of hers,
† & it was only polite to ask her whether she had everything –
~~Yet~~ oh Everything ~~thanks~~ said Lily nervously. ~~No~~, She could not do it.
~~Old maidishness was her dower~~. She knew what he was about to say.
Then he looked out to sea. Their eyes rested on the lighthouse
together. Was it going to be calm enough to land? she asked.
† Never did anybody sigh as he sighed. Without concealment, or
shyness, with the force of some primeval gust,
all he had suffered – ~~his wif~~ the death of wife, of son, of
daughter – ~~filled~~ seemed suddenly to fill him & to issue in
a sigh of such despondency that any woman in the whole
world would have known exactly what to do: any woman,
except myself, thought Lily. I am an outcast, an old
maid; something that has no right to exist, she thought

† A 225; B 234; A 226

197

Yes
He ~~lik~~ wished to go there, said Mr. Ramsay, for in the old days his wife sent them things. ~~The poor~~ There was one poor boy in particular, the
† keeper's son, with a tuberculous hip.

Any woman in the whole world would ~~be feeling pity~~ & ~~thought Lily: & all she felt was~~ know what to say thought Lily yet all she wished was that this enormous flood of grief, this insatiable hunger for sympathy, this great man who ~~was, she felt certain, mysteriously connected with the~~ this nobility this incorruptible integrity should go, should leave her; should not sweep her off her ~~feet~~ in the gale of his sighs. But ~~another came~~.

(he was a great philosopher she told herself)

† ~~They did not mind how~~ Such expeditions ~~exhausted~~ were very painful, were exhausting, said Mr. Ramsay, & exhausting he added, looking towards the house, ~~as if he while he tolerated~~ where, Lily hoped, James & Cam were hastily swallowing breakfast, for she could not sustain this enormous weight of ~~grief &~~ sorrow & regret & ~~something~~ & all the draperies of age (he looked to her extraordinarily old, ~~unke~~ white, tragic) a moment longer.

& shattered. Yes It can [?] her, even this did not awake her pity)

† Wherever he looked, [longing?] as it was ~~he sighed; Mr.~~ even old Mr. Carmichael, benevolently peering at them over the top of a novel, peering but with eyes too ~~mild~~, at a distance too serene & remote to take part in this glut of grief, ~~this only~~ seemed to suggest only some sad ~~reflection~~ – yet. Lily knew, worked [freely?] ~~there would never be a word of this in masculine society~~; could she magically transport the huge old man lying in the wicker
† chair ~~to~~ alongside them, & so dam this effusion which rocked her up & down on its tide; for, ~~she knew~~, no ~~with a man a~~ no man sighed like that to men. All this belonged to the secret chamber, which she so much dreaded, of women's

too discreet

that he was unfortunately strangely incongruously alive still;

† B 235; A 227; B 236; A 228 (3.125)

looked about
† Still she could say nothing; only feel how, as Mr. Ramsay turned
disappointed of help from her, to look for it elsewhere, his
† gaze seemed, ~~like a crape veil~~ to fall, dolefully upon the sunny
envelop contented, drowsy
grass & cast the rubicund, ~~the contented, the half~~ bulk of
Mr. Carmichael ~~into a &~~ in a veil of crape. as if
his existence in a world of woe
as if his colour ~~his content his bulk were~~ unfortunate; incongruous;
provoked to dismal thoughts. Could Mr. Carmichael only be wafted to
Then [them,
† Lily thought: ~~For instance told her~~ this effusion of sighs & lamentations
stanch would cease instantly: ~~no man would~~ ~~men together~~ he would
could man be staunch this ~~lamentable~~ outpouring which as she stood there,
applied to not knowing what in the world to say made her feel the
stanch the inadequacy of her own womanhood. A woman, she provoked this
wounds of [horror:
men she should then as she had seen other women do ~~she she~~ receive it.
~~But all this~~ immense self-~~pity, this~~ But no. His immense
poured
in watery swirls self-pity flowed about him. She stood there nervously grasping her
flowed about her. † paint brush. ~~Heaven could never be sufficiently thanked~~!
She seemed to be Heaven could never be sufficiently thanked! She heard
drawing in her skirts sounds ~~of~~ in the house. James & Cam must be But Mr.
still, or if *Ramsay ~~still~~ (~~so she felt~~) still exerted upon her solitary figure
the immense pressure of ~~all~~ his ~~demands~~ concentrated woe; his
~~loss of wife & son & daughter;~~ his age; his frailty; (~~physically he looked as~~
his wrk usual) his desolation; his devotion; & his solitary pursuit
of objects which (here he noticed his bootlace undone, &
Lily positively breathed more freely as he stooped his
~~from~~ his sombre height ~~beside her, &~~ & placing his foot on a
[stone?] ~~knoll of grass began with~~ to ~~knot &~~ brace & knot a
boot which it suddenly struck her to say, was
† remarkable. She was ashamed of herself. To praise his
her to solace soul
boots, when he ~~had~~ asked ~~for her~~ attention to his ~~miseries~~
when he came like a child fallen on the shingle, to show her
his knees & [raked?], his hands bleeding, that surely deserved
annihilation, was surely her fault. Yet she cld not help it

"What beautiful boots!" she said.

~~And at once~~ – ~~Nothing His boots~~ Yet – so incalculable
his
was Mr. Ramsay – ~~he lifted~~ a face beaming with pleasure.

* MS 250 (3.127)

† A 227, B 235; B 236; A 228; B 237; A 229

199

They
There must ~~be action &~~ have been certain thoughts, occasions in the
past life of Mr. Ramsay which were the ~~just~~ cause of ~~his~~
just self-esteem. It would have appeared so. But no.
Nothing, it seemed ~~roused his~~ so roused his pride &
~~contented his~~ warmed his dependency as the thought ~~of his~~
† camp~~aign in~~ years & years ago in this matter of getting his
boots, made to fit his feet, of pure leather. ~~The most~~
How ~~many attempts he had made~~, what perversity he had
encountered, & finally what triumph he had won – he told her the story.
human perversity that was unbelievable. He raised his left ~~leg~~
foot; then his right foot. And then, [the] ~~having~~ demonstration being
complete, to crown all he showed her, he insisted that she should
instantly understand & practice, his knot. ~~It was one~~
~~of those~~ how [a] marvellously it combined simplicity &
~~effectiveness. Si~~mple a marvellous combination of
complete simplicity & entire efficiency. He ~~tied her~~
† He untied her shoe lace; he tied her shoe lace.

thus he had triumphed over human obstinacy, vanquished the scandalous human

Why then, [of the] ~~at all~~ inappropriate moments, should there come over her,
as he stooped, to ~~show~~ practice Mr. Ramsay's knot, now at this
very moment, as she stooped, ~~an~~ so much sympathy that she was
tying up her shoe, ~~the~~ should she be so tormented with
sympathy for him that, as she stooped, the blood rushed to her face: she
† felt her eyes swell & tingle. ~~This He had this knot in the face~~ of
death. He had no one now to show his boots to. He tied this knot in
solitude. ~~Terribly It was~~ intolerable, ~~to th to her to think of~~
That he Incredibly courageous ~~with the simplicity of a~~
he faced disaster. ~~She saw~~ His figure suddenly
appeared to her ~~like that~~ infinitely venerable; It was those
boots of his. his pride in his boots; ~~it was t the~~ she
She would [give] ~~do ev~~ him ~~whateve~~ everything Now ~~indeed the~~

entirely inappropriate as it was,

was that it?

facing complete disaster with a firm laughing [?]

And Mr. Ramsay
[Ah!] ~~Ah! Here they~~ are! Mr. Ramsay exclaimed.
Cam & James were there, at last; They approached, side by side,
a serious, melancholy couple.
She felt for Mr. R.,*

* Written in pencil
† B 238; A 230; B 239

† *But he noticed that his bootlaces were undone. Remarkable boots they
[were, too,
Lily noticed; substantial, colossal ~~the boots of a~~ yet like everything
† Mr. Ramsay wore from his frayed tie to his half buttoned waistcoat,
~~so moulded &~~ his own indisputably, ~~distinguished, chara delicate,~~
in ~~sol~~ his absence ~~the~~ [drawing?] pathetic or surly as the expressive [core?] may [it?] be
~~distinct,~~ She could see them walking to his room of their own
accord ~~instinct with the inspired by his sur~~ living, ~~on he~~
a part of him. "What beautiful boots!" she exclaimed.
She was ashamed of herself. To praise his boots when he
asked her to solace his soul, when he had shown her, like a child
craving sympathy, his bleeding hands his lacerated knees,
then to say cheerfully, what beautiful boots you wear!
deserved, she knew, annihilation instant & complete
Instead, Mr. Ramsay seemed instantly revived. His pall, his
infirmity
cloak, his draperies, fell ~~off~~ him; & Praising himself, he smiled
~~showed beamed seemed ten years~~ younger, as if this talk of
boots ~~had turned his mind~~ recalled ~~pleas~~ something which was a
pride
real source of ~~gratification~~ to him (yet Lily reflected, he ~~is~~
has every kind of honour) ~~as if he were~~ as if ~~in the welter~~ &
† ~~chaos of life~~ here was a sunny island, where peace dwelt, & sanity
reigned. ~~He had~~ Well might she praise his boots. Boots he explained,
usually
~~are among the usual~~ were, ~~until he went into the question~~ – for
~~himself,~~ among the curses of mankind. ~~But~~ As a young man he
resolved to [?]
had ~~appele applied his brain to the problem~~ He had fought this
accumulated obstinacy, perversity & ~~stul~~ knavery ~~of generations~~:
~~of all th~~ the boot makers. ~~He had prevailed. The results~~
(he made her observe)
At last – he had triumphed. They fitted precisely. They were made of
[the
~~finest~~ of nothing but leather. He raised his left foot; he raised his
Next
right foot. He ~~showed her his knot. Three times he knotted his boots.~~
There was only one method – his own.
Three times ~~in~~ He asked her whether she could tie a knot.
system
He pooh poohed her feeble ~~efforts~~ Three times he knotted his
boots: three times he unknotted them. He tied hers for her.

Why at this [?]

* MS 248–9

† A 228, B 237; A 229; A 230, B 238

(3.131)

202*

† & his own battle to fight with the world, in which no one can help him ~~help him~~, ~~& his~~ ~~She~~ She felt now that sympathy would have been an impertinance; & was really upset when, drawing himself up again, Mr. Ramsay exclaimed something which meant that at last they were ready. James & Cam were there at last. They appeared on the lawn. They approached side by side, lagging, a serious, melancholy couple.

* Page 201 wanting

† B 239

But why th~~at surliness~~? was it like that that they came? She could not help feeling that they might have ~~done more to for him.~~

† come more cheerfully, ~~like & so given him since he had the~~ ~~Her sy~~ He had ~~wakened her sympathy, & now, of course~~ & so given him what now that they were off, she would [have] not be able to give him: ~~Nor~~ [He] did ~~he~~ [not] any longer want it. He ~~preserved~~ was now an ~~independent elderly man [but?] who needed nothing. He~~ now an elderly man, who was quite independent of her. ~~He had become straight, even military~~ ~~Taking his~~ He slung a knapsack round his shoulders, he straightened himself; he had all the appearance of a leader making ready for an expedition. He looked his children over & sent Cam for a ~~ca~~ coat. Then, wheeling about he led the way, with his firm military ~~tramp & those~~ tread ~~&~~ [in] those wonderful boots, down the

† to the gate, his children following him, ~~with a look of~~ as if fate had devoted them to ~~this~~ some stern enterprise, & they went [to it] ~~with suffering, but not without~~ open-eyed, suffering, ~~but~~ with ~~some~~ [a] touch of solemnity. ~~They were still~~ young enough still ~~perhaps~~ to be drawn acquiescent in their father's wake; ~~still~~ ~~unconsciously~~ [but they brooded; they] suffered So they passed the edge of the lawn, ~~&~~ ~~all silent,~~ & it seemed to Lily that she witnessed a procession, ~~flagging, silent, but advancing with that some a~~ ~~strange~~ common feeling which made it, flagging & faltering though it was, to her strangely impressive. Now they were gone. ~~Lost in~~ Deep [Thinking of something intently,] in his own thoughts, Mr. Ramsay never looked at her. Now they were gone.

have the chance of giving him.

but suffering

in complete

moving under the stress of some common

3

† But what a face! she thought. She wondered what he thought of.

† A 231; B 240; A 232

204

(3)

But what a face, she thought, ~~what an extraordinary face~~, &
feeling ~~her~~ ~~emot~~ the sympathy which she had not been asked to give
troubling her to find expression; ~~how~~ What ~~did he~~ had
made it like that? Thinking, ~~mainly;~~ night after night
the reality of — she supposed; about / kitchen tables, she added, remembering the
symbol which in her vagueness, ~~about the nature of phil philosophic~~
~~thought~~ as to what Mr. Ramsay did think about, ~~had~~ Andrew had
given her. Something visionary & austere; ~~&~~ something bare,
hard, not ornamental. ~~For~~ His ~~face~~ There was no colour to
this [it] object, & it was [all edges & angles;] uncompromisingly plain, ~~yet in this~~
† ~~very plainness~~ & / ([Mr.?] Mr. Ramsay had [kept] his eyes fixed always
intently & ~~pi~~ upon this distant object, which upon [this object] it,
distracted — never allowing himself to be ~~deceived,~~ or ~~dis~~ deluded,
~~or holding on~~ until even his face ~~had~~ ~~wore the~~
became worn ~~or~~ too & ascetic, & partook of this
unornamented beauty & ~~impressed itself on her as~~
~~was, now & then~~, which so deeply impressed her. And then,
worries; they had fretted it, not so nobly. ~~Sometimes~~ [for] it seemed to
her that sometimes ~~his~~ he had ~~suspected that there was~~
~~he had~~ had his doubts about this table; whether it was the true one,
perhaps, or the only one, or whether ~~a~~ it was worth the time he gave to [it –
He had had doubts, she felt, & that was what sometimes they
she suspected — talked about – Mr. & Mrs. Ramsay – ^ till late at night, & then
Mrs. Ramsay looked tired, & then she Lily flew into a rage
† with him. And now he had nobody to ~~say~~ tell him
that the table was there & he had found it; so that
he was like a lion seeking whom he could devour, & his
face had that touch of desperation in it, of exaggeration, which
alarmed her, & made her pull her skirts about her, & then
his face had too to crown it. ~~an~~ something very simple, very

† B 241; A 233

205

in [little?] human ordinary things for ~~or~~ whatever happened.

~~something very~~ suddenly, unexpectedly (as when she praised his boots,) a ~~most~~ surprising recovery of sense & interest & [a zest for ~~m~~] humanity; which passed (for he never concealed a feeling) & ~~felt with~~ into that final phase of which ~~she had not noticed in his face before~~ – which he so much ~~moved her~~, [~~su~~] interested her, & indeed made her

† ~~extre~~ irritated with herself for having ~~stoo~~ missed her chance of saying anything: that quiet reasonable ~~stag~~ mood, that mood which ~~without being exalted, was~~ was not exalted or remote or austere any longer but expressed the serenity of a mind ~~that has ceased to worry or~~ which has shed its worries & its vanities, & perhaps lost its ambitions, but is yet drawn on, as she had seen him drawn on, at the head of that little procession to the beach, steadily out of one's range. An extraordinary face it was to watch – Here the gate banged. They were gone.

4

She felt ~~an extraordinary rel~~ [extremely relieved.] The gate, which was never oiled, seemed to cut her short; to prove that, for better or worse, she had lost her chance.

4.

~~It was as~~ if something ~~sn~~ snapped; a bramble flew back in her face;
she was stung, shocked, yet exhilarated. So roughly her
meditations were broken short. & at once, with enormous relief
she saw
~~She looked, for the first time~~, at her canvas. ~~It was~~ as if it
floated up & placed itself for ~~the first time~~, white & uncompromising,
~~facing her, confronting her,~~ before her, It certainly seemed to
rebuking — rebuke her; ~~saying~~ with its ~~imper~~ cold stare, to ~~say intimate~~
drastically recalling her;
~~that~~ for all this hurry & agitation of feeling; ~~to dry up her~~
out it
to spread — & ~~at the same time to spread like the~~ through her mind ~~an~~
as
[~~pe~~?] [~~&~~?] first an emptiness, ~~when~~ as her disorderly sensations
† ~~tr~~ trooped off the field; ~~&~~ then, peace. She looked blankly at the
~~can~~ canvas; then at the garden. [In her hurry, she had pitched her
picture she wished to paint
white washed wall, — easel anyhow; without considering the ~~angle~~ nature of the
a picture
composition.] It was one she had attempted before — the wall, the
edge of the house, the line of the ~~head~~ hedge; ~~made For some~~
cutting across, [falling thus down?] — ~~reason~~, There was something in the ~~heights~~ & relations of those lines, in
[their
& the mass, of the hedge which ~~still~~ had ~~always~~ stayed in her mind
& all its softness & brilliancy of colour a contrast, a [contradiction?] — all these years. ~~She had~~ It had ~~set her always seemed to her~~ that
~~there was something there~~ — ~~Now & then~~, Her picture originated
in such deposits of line & colours, ~~which when of ex~~
problem
as that — stayed there like a ~~puzzle~~ ~~coming to her mind~~
which came to mind ~~when she was~~ from time to time,
automatically — ~~London, or~~ the Brompton Road, or before her
looking glass, when she was pretending to comb her hair. ~~Now,~~
But there was all the difference in the world between this
† involuntary making of pictures in her minds eye, & actually
laying her brush on them. Now was the disaster, the danger.

She had taken the wrong brush in her agitation, & also
pitched her easel wrongly. She now ~~adjusted the~~ fixed the little
spikes firmly & precisely into the ground; & taking her stand,
which ing
~~began~~ raised her brush — ~~a~~ trembl~~ed~~ in a painful yet ~~extremely~~
exhilarating — ecstasy ~~like a For the brush~~ How to do it — that

† B 243; A 235

205*

Even even
† the question. For one line placed on the canvas immediately committed to her to ~~a~~ a conflict, ~~a~~ to innumerable risks, ~~f~~ & the need of constant & irrevocable decisions. All that, in idea, ~~was~~ had seemed simple, became in practice immediately complex,

& — the waves / the / flat from the cliff
~~seen from~~ the cliff, ~~not a~~ waves are all symmetrical; but to the
er
swimm~~ing, how vast clefts divide them; & they have~~ are divided by steep gulfs, & have towering crests. ~~Urged~~ the leap must be taken; & the risk ~~which~~ run. She ~~made her~~ Her preparations were made; her palate spread; & now

~~driving~~ remorseless spirit behind that driving ~~sensation~~ her, [coming?] in & out †

shoved ahead
with a curious physical sensation of ~~leaping~~, being urged on, &
to the
trying her ~~utmost~~ to control her leap, she ~~laid the t~~ made the first quick decisive stroke. It flickered brown over the pure
with a second firm
† white canvas. It & without pause, ~~exc~~ attaining by degrees, a ~~dancing~~ rhythmical ~~sensitive~~ movement, as if the

~~[?]~~ be tremulous as flesh, but also firm,

one
brush itself were ~~a~~ sensitive ~~proboscis of instrument of some~~ some sensitive weapon ~~in the~~ ~~inspired~~ with nerves ~~of its own~~
scored
She ~~scribbled~~ her canvas ~~over with~~ with light brown
which
~~sl~~ lines ~~wavering~~, ~~whose~~ ~~extreme~~ sensibility froze into

for all their

~~whose~~ sensibility ~~enclosed~~ ~~described~~ ~~the~~ at once settled into something ~~formidable~~ permanent. She had committed herself to that now. The statement was made.

---

* VW repeated numbers 205 and 206. (3.143)

† B 244; A 236

206

June 21st 1926

There was the next wave rising up on top of her. Those lines enclosed
† a formidable ~~space~~ shape For what is more formidable than a ~~space~~ shape bulk matter,?
~~How it bulges, which, as Lily saw it, is~~ enclosed between two lines enclosed between two
lines / this this bulk, matter, this impersonal tremendously impressive
obtrusive object? Lily felt ~~it~~ Here she was again in it — the presence of that old
enemy of hers, that ~~sh~~ problem ~~shape~~ shape;, form; ~~that~~ which
exercised upon her a sway which she never could explain. A
white lampshade ~~is not in itself anything whatsoever,~~ yet
~~th~~ as ~~she sat reading, or talking she~~ would ~~find~~ draw her eye ~~drawn~~ to it
with a fascination which was, (if she thought about it) reprehensible.
It protruded; it ~~existed; it was~~ impended. Its solidity was
~~the~~ Nothing could exceed ~~the space there between the hedge & the house~~ its
~~in~~ reality: nothing could be more present, more compelling, more
like the presence of ~~the stark~~ what~~ever~~ it is that rules the
~~world & compels our allegiance; or exacts our submission~~

blending in

~~of some~~ apparition ~~behind~~ of truth behind appearances, the
the hidden apparition of truth; compelling; & calming too.
She saw her old enemy, her old problem; she ~~recognized~~
admitted its tyranny over ~~us~~ her, as if she had
& the peculiar nature of this relationship, — which differed from
any other, ~~being an~~ in that it called ~~he~~ upon her perpetually to
fight to make efforts: it was intolerant of acquiescence. This
God — shape, form, mass bulk — unlike other Gods,
~~said~~ roused her to perpetual combat; & here she would be
at it engaged in vain warfare for the rest of her days.
Summoned forth ~~from all her~~, called beyond the comforts &
† She liked it; she rejoiced in it; but still to exchange
the fluidity of life for the concentration of painting / was always
[~~fling?~~] was always ~~like~~ a surprise & an effort & [more?]
that is more drastic than it had been the time before; &
more prolific of terrifying doubts and dependencies, &
questions; as for instance, What do I do it for? And
have I the right, & am I fitted, & am I not appearing
selfish, & all the rest; among which would boom

† B 245; A 237

but now more faintly, the echo of all that flagellation which
~~any~~ woman must ~~bear from stand fro~~ suffer from the whips of men
men like little Mr. Tansley she remembered, as she contemplated her
† next stroke. Women cant ~~w~~ paint, ~~women~~ cant write ~~women~~
cant create she murmured over to herself, anxiously considering
to what her plan of attack should be. Suddenly
And then, as if some juice necessary to the lubrication of her
among the blue, the umber, the saffron, faculties were [?] spontaneously secreted she began ~~quit~~
instinctively to ~~p m tak~~ move her brush about falling in
again with some rhythm, which if she suggested it,
† seemed too capable of bearing her along with it.
~~Oh Ch~~ Christopher – no Charles Tansley, she mused, crooning
like a kettle on the hob, ~~the~~ & recalling the little
arid man whom she had last seen in this garden, very
bristly, ~~very~~ ten years ago. He was dead – no: on the contrary
he was married; &

† B 246; A 238

for

the old divine anxious pleasure ~~was at work, which while~~ it
stimulated her to ~~think~~ even as she stood absorbed to bring back
~~the little such~~ the figures as ~~that~~ this — people who had ceased to influence her
one way or another, ~~He had married, & f The little~~ She had
last seen the bristly energetic ~~man, here~~; little man

to conjure up

of people like that; the figures of people who had ceased to influence her;
but had been part of her once; ~~So he had, too. In those old days~~ been [~~&~~
when she stayed with the Ramsays, coming up behind her
he had stood (a thing she detested) smoking bad tobacco, couldn't
afford good tobacco — ~~(then~~ He paraded his poverty; His principles
stuck out of him. He got on all their nerves. ~~And He sneered at~~
† He stalked about with books under his arm. He 'worked', ~~when~~
ostentatiously, on the middle of the lawn; ~~&~~ he 'worked' after dinner.
~~Then he said informed her of~~ He ~~attacked~~ her; now~~, as she could see,~~
fastened on to her & ~~talk explained his views & discoursed~~
they agreed: ~~about~~ sometimes Mrs. Ramsay had to interfere.
~~Angry arguments that were the~~ ~~Then~~ Now, he married, &
became to Lily ~~considered~~ one of those figures one meets in
newspapers, "Charles Tansley" — ~~a She met his~~
~~He wrote letters, articles, & Charles This Charles Tansley~~ &
~~signed letters, was one of those~~ He wrote letters: &

then had got his job; had married; was one

perhaps spoke at meetings. & she had an idea ~~that he lived~~
~~at Hampstead~~ & had three or four children, & that all daughters too,
whom he brought up to ~~consider themselves inferior~~; &
she supposed with complex [~~feel~~?] dry justice & disapproval; &
~~never into had he~~ she would be inclined to think that
he had never enjoyed a moments happiness in his entire life,
~~but Mrs. Ramsay threw rather a different view light on him.~~ saw
~~But how~~? By laughing at him on a picnic about an
umbrella. ~~Suddenly Then for a moment,~~ That showed
~~a different side~~ — & he then becoming — ~~oh~~ as most people
do at times — perfectly natural.

they wd be daughters

[ ? ] angularity;

if it were not for

And why not thought Lily. crooning like a kettle on the hob.
~~Why A very~~ Daily it seemed to her she became less able

† B 247

~~to~~
whats it mean, this putting on & shoving off, when we all of us
fundamentally ~~are nothing but simplicity? n~~ so simple? &
all ~~the~~ of it – ~~Charles Tansley's temper~~ & ~~won~~ all this network of
temper, ~~all~~ these angers & arguments, seemed to her quite
incomprehensible; & her own annoyance ~~that he s~~ when he

almost incredibly simple – like a coat one throws on when it is raining.

stood by her side smiling, & her depressions & miseries – at
not being more beautiful, or a better painter – ~~what did~~
~~they all amount~~ all, all now seemed like a little ~~rash,~~
† Mrs. Ramsay came round the rock & made them look at the sea.
Was that a lobster pot, a chest, or a seal? she asked. But it was
not the question. it was ~~the~~ the thing in her which

So every

~~It was in her nature.~~ ~~One~~ of the things one liked her for. A kind of
childlikeness. Perhaps then she was not clever? Did
she ever take part in an argument? Did she not often
get up & leave the room at the crucial moment? But
~~then she had s~~he had shown Charles Tansley then, in
differently. She sat on the beach & wrote a letter. She
left her spectacles on the rock. She seemed to say
And this 'Charles Tansley' who wrote able letters to the papers
sat down by her side & began playing ducks & drakes.
said [?]
Was it a lobster pot? she kept asking. And he kept
choosing the flattest stone he could find & making
them skip along the waves. And she looked up
now & then & laughed.

Why did this stay in her mind as the happiest most
profound scene she had ever been at; why
And ~~she had by~~ sitting there sketching she had been
as if all were ordered & appointed; as if ~~from~~
~~one~~ human life too were susceptible, like a picture, to
~~moments of~~ arrangement & order; & now & then whether
by freak or some superlative merit ~~in~~ of character
some transcendent beauty, the

† A 239

```
   200
    280
   ────
   1600
   400
  ─────
 56,000
```

(210)

Lily stepped back & screwed up her eyes;
Committed to this particular adventure, she was now sternly set, [out] – & was becoming momentarily more & more indifferent to her own fortunes, ~~as a~~ to ~~her own person~~ & arms & legs & hair & complexion
† & whether it were time for this or time for that, & if she was liked or disliked or ~~who she was~~ [who she was & what she was] & all the rest of it affected one as a work of art she thought ~~That was perhaps an~~ (~~for at forty four~~ ~~always~~ [The] cloudlike ~~crossed the mind, now & again~~ [question which shadowed] [~~explanation~~: about human relationships & death & art & life: – ~~sometimes~~ grew dark / like a cloud about to burst & one thought This is the answer. That ~~among us there are~~ [there are] creators among us & Mrs. Ramsay was one of them; {They say to life "Stand still there"} was true perhaps she thought. ~~And~~ They say to life "Stand ~~still there," & they enforce it~~; bringing together the wall, the sky, the hedge – ~~but it was~~ the whatever it might be, herself, Charles Tansley, the breaking waves: They ~~elicit~~ [draw] from each its element –
~~An artist, a creator~~ –

~~Sure enough, thinking~~ And [en]~~c~~ircling ~~like a~~ Charles Tansley again, running over him, as she ~~stopp~~ chose another brush, she thought how it was not necessarily angular & [sensibly?] sandy haired & repulsive, his home & his children; but on a summer evening they would sit together on a terrace, talking; & again she would be perfectly simple, herself, a as on the beach, when Mrs. Ramsay did it, by looking over her spectacles & saying "Is that a lobster pot?"
† All was silence. ~~in~~ Nobody even yet seemed to be stirring in the house. ~~It was still early of course; & perhaps they were not even up yet~~ – She looked ~~at it, be~~fore ~~placing her~~ ~~going on, looked~~ at the ~~peaceful~~ house, sleeping there in the early sunlight with its windows green & blue with the reflected leaves; &
And now indeed she was thinking of Mrs. Ramsay. She was feeling strangely, remotely with this extreme unreality

[Margin notes:]
for the densely & oppressive hovering feeling the cloudlike [feeling?] † of the question which stood over above her

that

– one or two people, they are rare, –

like anybody else, just talking,

† A 240; B 249; A 241, B 250

~~which seemed to her so much more real than~~

Not the Mrs. Ramsay of flesh & blood; but this other, the who was hidden ~~& this~~ a ~~spirit~~ laugh, ~~& this~~ an essence, something gone [remote & completely [into a?] substance, yet stealing back & modifying & moulding one's thoughts. ~~Who~~ It was all Mrs. Ramsays doing still – that she thought tenderly of Charles. Still she prevailed – Faintly almost imperceptivly* she made herself felt. She had put off the robe of flesh & taken on another. For Lily never saw her now. ~~She~~ only sometimes she thought of her.

The ~~white~~ still house seemed in consonance with this; & the thin smoke; & the clear fine early morning air.

~~She wished to share her~~ ~~Little as it was~~ It was unreal, it was faint, it was astonishingly pure & exciting & she hoped no body would open the windows, ~~nobo~~ & dy come out of the house, but that she might go on painting now.

For now ~~it was~~ terrific the problem horror was on her again: the question of colour. But one moment – as if impelled by some curiosity which she must gratify, or driven by some discomfort which she must assuage she turned ~~to look at the bay. It struck her that she would be able~~ to look whether she could to see their boat, down below, in the bay. Would they have had time to get to the beach?

* VW's spelling

212

one moment.
But ~~she stopped~~. As if impelled by some curiosity which she must gratify or driven by some discomfort which she must assuage, she went a pace or two to the end of the lawn, ~~whence she could~~ to see whether down there, ~~where~~ the ~~sea spread, & one~~
in the harbour
~~beach spread~~ she could see the boat, ~~&~~ [Would they have had time to ~~reach the sea~~? get there?] & the little company starting for the [lighthouse
Ramsays starting

in the shining blue hollow of the bay
Down there among the little boats ~~to anchored~~ which floated
in the calm
some with their sails furled, ~~others~~ some slowly (for it was very
† calm) moving away, she chose one, ~~with~~ where the sail was even now being hoisted; ~~to~~ & decided that there, in that
little boat — very distant, & ~~to her~~ ~~en~~tirely silent ~~craf wa wa seated~~
Mr. Ramsay was sitting & Cam & James. Now they had the sail
for they all seemed † up & now — after a little flagging & hesitation, ~~she saw~~
shrouded in profound the sails were filled a puff of air ~~filled the~~ caught the sails,
silence & moved ~~si~~ with deliberation
filled them, & ~~taking its way~~ the boat ~~sailed away~~ took its way
moving past
~~out making; she saw, among~~ the other boats, out to sea.

2*

The sail flapped over Cam's head. The water chuckled & slapped ~~the~~ & for some time the boat rocked a little this way & that, with the sails slack & creased. & it seemed as if they would never s~~tart. They~~ move. Then [Macalister's ~~b~~ boy got out his oars,] & the~~y started~~, Mr. Ramsay, who detested hanging about, said something ~~to~~ rather impatient, & Macalister's boy got out his oars, & ~~they~~ began rowing. But her father would never settle down until they were flying along, he would keep looking for a breeze & watching the sail. Nor would they look at him, nor would they smile. For he had said that she
† was to sit there, & James was to steer; & ~~he had~~ He had made them come. They would neither look at him, nor speak to him; nor forget this intolerable injury to the end of their days.

* VW may have numbered this '2' because it is the first change of scene from the lawn to the boat. She had already numbered an earlier section '2'. See MS 246. (3.157)

† A 242; B 251; A 243

213

rise
† & in her anger she hoped that the breeze would never ~~come,~~
so that he might be thwarted, since he had forced them to come
against their wills. ~~They~~ All the way down to the beach she had
with James ~~they~~ ~~she~~ had lagged behind. ~~They knew each others minds~~. Without
speaking they knew each others minds; & how each felt
as if their heads were bent down
the same ~~dull~~ sullen rage; like trees pressed down by a remorseless gale.
Speak to him they could not ~~Speak to him they could~~ not. They must come, they must follow.
the
~~And then~~ And ~~then~~, there were these intolerable parcels – Nancy had
&
to produce them: ~~she~~ was scolded too; things one took to the
~~Light~~ lighthouse: ~~& sighed over~~, sacred ~~relics~~, tokens, wrapped up in
an &
that odious mixture, ~~of gloom, of falsity: & Since~~
~~he~~ of gloom & sorrow which ~~there was~~ no ~~being frank~~ about.
a sanctified, an odious mixture ~~one could not undo~~ ~~The One~~ ~~Now the~~ So there
they would sit James steering, ~~with his father beside him~~,
Cam curled up in the bow; & they would not say anything; but
they would look at him, now & then, where he sat with his
~~long~~ legs wriggled round each other, waiting impatiently for a
breeze. They would both ~~hoped that the~~ Heaven & themselves
~~would~~ And they hoped it would be calm. They hoped they
might ~~be~~ put back again. They ~~hoped~~

† But now when Macalisters boy had rowed a little way
they caught the breeze; they the sails swung round; &
& the boat quickened itself, & lay flattened on the water &
uncurled his legs &
shot off. ~~as~~ There upon, Mr. Ramsay relaxed his tension, took out
† his pouch & he ~~shared it with Mac~~ he handed it to Macalister, &
they
now in spite of all their suffering & boredom, he was happy; quite happy
James & Cam knew. He

~~She gave it up.~~ Now they would sail on for hours like this.
Mr. Ramsay would ask old ~~John~~ Macalister, ~~the~~ a question;
~~usual sorts~~ of questions. "Then she comes round the point –
& old John would answer it. Then they would smoke together.
[Macalister
would take a cord in his hand; he would loosen a rope, or knot a rope;
he ~~would~~ the boy would fish; & James would be forced to
keep his eye all the time on the sail. For if he forgot, then

† B 252; A 244; B 253

the sail puckered & ~~creased~~ shivered & the boat ~~stop~~ slackened &
Mr. Ramsay & old John ~~crd~~ cried out to him to do this or that. Look out [look out
She comes [driving] round the point ~~like a bird~~ old Macalister said;
~~describing telling his~~ giving his account of [that] some famous [~~ship~~ [?]] event; &
Mr. Ramsay, [first] ~~adopting~~ [too hearty] ~~a manner~~, ~~which was later dropping it, &~~
~~said~~ tossed his head, & looked [across the line of] where old Macalister's finger pointing
slowly round the bay. They [could see the] men ~~had been driven up the~~ clinging to
masts. ~~He had seen~~ And ~~the~~ we shoved her off, & ~~she came~~
round the point," – so Macalister went on, [shoving & gesticulating] describing
how, that bleak winter's night, they had launched the life boat, & it
† & he called her "her" & Mr. Ramsay somehow brought his voice into
tone with the old man's voice, & ~~his~~ held his pipe, as the old
fisherman held his; & ~~yet~~ ~~there~~ [there] was nothing insincere about [all] ~~t~~hat.
His eyes sparkled. He threw his head back as if he were
down there pulling with the other men on the beach. Only his
hand as it flung itself out was, they noticed, ~~a~~ so white, ~~so~~ &
chiselled & shaped, compared with the brown thick mass of
Macalister's hand; & ~~there~~ on his little finger he wore a ring.
But he was thinking ~~how they launched the life boat.~~ He was
thinking (they could read him like a book) how he too would
~~have lent a hand; &~~ launched the life boat.
They looked at each other, past the bay & Macalister & Mr. Ramsay.
They looked at each other steadily. ~~& with~~

[Left margin: giving his account of the [great] storm in which ten fishing boats had foundered, / here & there / the / [was] at his [ ? ]]

† A 245; B 254

25
17 "the stagnant [part?/past?]"
42

215

the
& liked the thought ~~of it; liked~~ the storm & the dark night & the ~~men~~
fishermen striving there. [So they could tell from the closeness
with which he followed Macalister's story;] he liked disaster.
He liked the bareness & nakedness of things, ~~effort,~~ terse language;
that men should labour & sweat on the windy beach at night
pitting their muscle & brain against the howling wind. ~~& the~~
he liked that the wind should howl; he liked to shed all trash & dross &
simple
superfluity. ~~&~~ he liked working men; & ~~good~~ women, & keeping house
anxiously
at home. ~~while the~~ ~~storm~~ with their children sleeping.
So they could tell from the closeness with which he followed ~~the~~
Macalisters story of the eleven ships driven in for shelter,
that stormy night. Three had sunk.

& to bare himself & brace himself

& that the wind should be wild; the seasons fierce that the waves should rage;

James & Cam looked at each other, past the boy & Macalister &
Mr. Ramsay.

† Still their grievance weighed them down: they had been forced; they
had been bidden: ~~&~~ he had borne them down with his gloom & his
~~sorrow.~~ bidding them subdue themselves once more to the
~~ceremoni~~ ceremonies ~~in~~ which he ~~found so awful a~~
satisfaction. ~~It was part of some strange ritual~~ –
bend
take part in his rituals; bow themselves to his ~~atti~~
prostrations before that grim ~~&~~ altar which they approached
reluctantly, hating their own solemnity, but ~~awed.~~
drawn on ~~irriv~~ irresistibly. Yes, the
breeze was freshening. The boat was leaning; the ~~water~~
~~waves~~ ~~water raced &~~ sea was sliced all green &
quivering on either side – Cam could look over into the
&
clear quick water, the deep, ~~the~~ brilliant; & James,
one
~~with loosening~~ with his hand on the tiller, one on the sheet,
had his
~~steered~~ ~~grimly joy~~. steered grimly; & ~~there began~~
~~to rise in them that~~ ~~from~~ the movement & the effort began to
stir in them, bound as they were in servitude to ~~an~~ a
the knowledge the
tyrant, some ~~profound~~ joy. They would escape & be gone. They

authority

judged necessary (on ~~this~~ on a September morning, to take parcels ~~chocolate~~ to the Lighthouse)

racing green

† A 246, B 255

216

~~sail, past the stagnant, the tepid, the enclosed; & find~~

† They would be free & alone. They would pass on & beyond – But, the movement ^ breeding in him too some strange exaltation, Mr. Ramsay ~~lost supp~~ ~~filling~~ filled his pipe again chanted ~~beau~~ sombrely, in his ~~beautiful~~ deep & ~~beautiful~~ sonorous voice, "We perished, each alone,"* ~~& hearing him they both felt~~ & stopped himself, ~~& repented,~~ & & with that usual spasm of repentance ~~&~~ or shyness at having violated the ~~priva~~ decency & reticence of life, & ~~desiring to~~ bury ~~his~~ ~~said~~ covered his outburst instantly with a cry & a wave of the hand.

in the ~~stor~~ Macalister's story,

** "See ~~our~~ the little ~~island~~ house" he said ~~pointing~~ gesticulating, ~~as~~ as if he wished Cam to look; ~~at~~ yet he was not thinking of her she knew or of the house; ~~until in her~~ But she raised herself, ~~& looked b~~ from looking at the sea racing green on ~~either side~~ & looked back at the land, & tried to make out which was their house. Houses were scattered about on the hillside so strangely. ~~The There was the whole town,~~ that she could not make out ~~the way~~ which was which. ~~But~~ And it all looked composed & peaceful, & as if in the dawn of time; ~~men~~ human beings had lodged themselves precariously there, with the hills behind them, facing the sea. & had made peaceful community, & ~~sleep was~~ peace rested on them now, & But as for their house, which was it? ~~That~~ Perhaps it was the little white block rather to the right – ~~only~~ No, for their house had trees.

* 'The Castaway,' MS 242, 283, 317, 362

** MS 267–77 are reworked on MS 283–301.

† A 247, B 256

The whole world wore ~~a dreamlike~~ a f~~aint, a far away look~~k:
a refined an unreal look: ~~already~~: the little distance they had sailed
had already put them far from it; & given it the ~~com~~ composed
~~finished~~ look of something which recedes ~~from & is now~~
any longer
~~which having~~ in which one has no part. It was beautiful; it was
melancholy.

She ~~sat~~ ~~tried to make out which of all the little white houses~~
~~was their house~~. She could not be sure which of the houses
was their house.

5*

† "It is that boat with the brown sails" Lily decided; ~~For &~~
watching it catch the breeze & start; & ~~she~~ turned back, ~~having~~
to her easel.

space
† There was her ~~space~~ ~~shape~~ confronting her: ~~pl~~ &
~~the further problem of the colour which was to the her~~
~~remores~~ that remorseless ~~plain~~ ~~fact~~ problem; that ~~us~~
austere ~~ex~~ presence; which ~~was t~~ which ~~was~~
~~which s~~. ~~Now that she had quitted herself of her duty~~,
demanding her ~~presence~~, now that she had quitted herself of her duty –
for such she felt it – her duty towards Mr. Ramsay. She followed
him with ~~sy~~ sympathy: she tried to send after him the sympathy
~~he had rejected~~ which had come too late. But ~~this was more~~
space, the looming bodies, the crude, the tangible, the fact the
presence – the thing she felt pressing out upon her &
out of the visible world, this messenger who seemed ~~to & for~~
to wait starkly & calmly & then in one seemed to assert its
rights & recall her from her strayings into a world that was more
terrible & more intense than the ~~w~~ world of affections –
human intercourse, into a world where failures were
is not personal, more terribly punished but success, ~~of~~ & she dreamed
nor fleeting, but always of success was not evanescent, but ~~rock~~ hard
rock – & ~~reca~~ called her back to it. She
had her momentary indecision. She took her brush. She
said to herself, like a child repeating a lesson mechanically

* Section 4 began on MS 254, 255. Section 2 (MS 263) should have been numbered section 5. Cf MS 291 for a reworking of this passage. (3.167)

† A 253, B 262; A 255, B 264

how Mrs. Ramsay sitting on the beach

200

280

1600

~~4400~~

56,000

8 ~~20~~ 60.

now she must note down ~~the discovery about permanence~~ this –

† *"Stand still here" some people say to life stand still here;
for instance, Mrs. Ramsay. And she began making blues &
umbers combine, ~~the little heaps on~~ mixing the little heaps on her
palette, quickly seizing ~~the~~ a rose or a ~~ro~~ yellow, &
imbuing them in the mixture, wh~~ich absorbed her.~~ &
which she then applied ~~lightly, dexterously~~: ~~It was beginning~~
to ~~glow~~, ~~The canvas was now almost beginning~~
~~to shine~~ ~~Colour was beginning to flower come out on the canvas.~~
& ~~then~~ again, like a dancer precariously treading through the figures of a
dance, her brush seemed to be moving in some methodical
yet dangerous measure, & ~~he~~ ~~pos~~ her mind again began
throwing up to the surface ~~now this figure~~ now ~~that for instance~~
things she had done, people she had seen, old words; little ~~scenes~~; –
~~gr~~ groups ~~or~~ but strange, mysteriously, on ~~the~~ one thread:
time stand still here.

For ~~surely~~ that was an odd power to have,
~~odd indeed to~~ And why now have Mrs. Ramsay sitting on the
beach, compelled there.

A

* MS 294 (3.169)

† A 240, B 249

219

Sometimes ~~th a~~ the pages blew away over the sand.
For she filled many pages with her little round writing that was impossible
to read. A network of communication was kept up.
it was
It was part of her system of life. And perhaps, like so many things she did,
[done
instinctively., fulfilled some need. ~~The But did it not~~. And ~~so~~
~~right it seemed,~~ whatever she did, ~~that, far from~~ seemed so
right that, if it had been ten times odder, or ~~more repre~~
more questionable, one would not have questioned it. And so she came
back always to this – not saying it, but feeling it: Mrs. Ramsay knew. ~~the~~
which
~~that~~ implied a secret. something hidden; profound. ~~That implied, Lily~~
~~thought~~, a ~~And oddly enough~~, With Mrs. Ramsay – whatever she might
[be
doing, & she was for the most part doing something – writing, knitting,
one was quite frequently aware of ~~secrets~~ ~~something hidden,~~
secrets; secrets ~~never to be made plain~~. ~~that she knew~~. Secrets
which would make stable the race of life, & deepen its shallowness.
† For ~~the lovely moment is trebled~~ in Yet never was anyone less
communicative; or more satisfied to rest in the joy of the moment.
A dish well cooked: ~~gave her infinite satisfaction.~~ ~~pleasure~~.
† a flower made to grow; – ~~Then~~ [ And now, putting on the pale
wreath, she had gone with her quick step, ~~to~~ – (She figured her
advancing through the fields of ~~asphodel~~. She took her way through the
fields of asphoc~~del~~. that image was mixed up with all thoughts of her)
~~But~~ ~~Now~~, when she
a ~~marriage~~. or, again, Lily remembered, smiling, ~~at the thought~~
it was a marriage.
*They did not always turn out well, by any means.
For instance, Minta Doyle & Paul Rayley. Minta, as Mr.
lamented
† Bankes ~~pointed out,~~ had holes in her stockings. ~~There was~~
large holes ~~in stockings~~ which showed too, when she strode
about ~~as~~ taking great steps; jumping, kicking. ~~A~~
† ~~These~~ holes might be accidental; or might on the other
run through an entire life, spread ruin, disorder. ~~After her~~
the first
~~marriage with Paul~~, ~~some~~ years were quite successful;

* MS 297–9 (3.171)
† A 256, B 264; B 278, A 269; A 256, B 265; A 257, B 266

of that marriage were quite successful, or seemed so. There were ~~the~~ two little boys, & But, by degrees perhaps on both sides, ~~the holes began~~ things worked loose. ~~He~~ They came home at [at such] ~~too~~ different hours; ~~to share a bedroom.~~ ~~for some reason~~, Lily imagined them meeting on the stairs, Paul in Pyjamas, Minta garish, extravagant, artifically wreathed & tinted about three o'clock in the morning. To finish the picture, Paul must be ~~surprised~~ carrying a poker, ~~to wa~~ in case of burglars; Minta [eating] ~~cramming~~ sandwiches. ~~So they~~ What did they say? meeting there in the cadaverous morning light on a staircase ~~which~~ had holes in its carpet, Paul, ~~who kept his exquisite profile grew~~ had grown withered. His aquiline beauty was ~~was~~ not ~~perhaps~~ of ~~the kind~~ [could have] to improve[d] [with] unless sober ideals, family happiness, domesticity: ~~But how~~ let him sit up ~~all night, or act the part~~ of sitting reading. then yawning; & going to bed. But not with this life – [it had coarsened, though] for he wandered off.

† He played chess in taverns: [debated & was solitary] coffee houses; ~~He~~ [For] ~~And~~ the visitor ~~thought~~ felt ~~how~~ that though there was still an air of joviality about the place, ~~a~~ Minta would object to any ~~very ser~~ private conversation between you & Paul a would object to his, for example, showing one the cucumbers (at the little cottage near Rickmansworth) at great length, ~~for then he might be~~ in case he said anything: so

† she would join them, throwing her arm round his ~~ne~~ shoulder. [But lately] ~~Still they~~ remained fond. ~~They did not part~~; she thought ~~had~~ they were settling [perhaps] into another phase together: ~~& as so many did~~, after all. She thought Mrs. Ramsay would have been forced to allow [that] much more was possible,

She rather suspected that Paul, playing – whatever it might be – in a coffee house, had there met somebody sympathetic; & this, far from breaking the marriage, had righted it. ~~For Mrs. Ramsay was really too primitive~~, But what would Mrs. Ramsay have said? Mrs. Ramsay would have said it was utterly & entirely unthinkable.

her sorrow
for Mrs.
Ramsay –
gone –
utterly*

[Left margin notes:]

There were scenes, at first –

which had holes, dust about & no beauty.
was
sordid. (the

(she went to see them sometimes perhaps he too had his faults

a perfectly different kind of girl,

* Written in pencil

† A 258, B 267; B 268

† But the dead, thought Lily, encountering some obstacle to her design, so that her thought ran slower, ~~are~~ are ~~entirely~~ at our mercy. ~~Though~~ She [~~would have hated her?~~] has faded & gone. ~~Nothing is~~ We can override her wishes; we can improve away her limited, her old fashioned ideas. She recedes further & further from us.

less than

For though ~~only ten years have passed, each has shoved us a little~~

mockingly

And / she seemed to see her, ~~mockingly~~ there at the end of the corridor of [years,

~~with her~~ impotent, unable to exact or to assert anymore; ~~the~~

& for a moment, as ~~if she were~~ ~~the~~ Lily Briscoe exalted in her own escape from death, in the triumph which ~~she~~ her views, her ideas, he

able to stand there, able to paint

ways of life enjoyed. ~~Why~~, ~~she could paint~~. And then, taking her little step away & leaning her head ~~to~~ one side, she considered the problem of ~~the house~~, more generously she reflected upon the strange fate of death; ~~& how~~ which in a moment stayed the hand & glazed the eye; & thought how perhaps if Mrs. Ramsay had lived, & she could not forbear pitying Mrs. Ramsay for not knowing how easily & happily

that far away figure

~~she~~ the Rayleys managed, – she managed, though ~~they~~ their lives

of what

~~lived in~~ the very opposite way that Mrs. Ramsay advised. or admired.

were the

if

† *Why, ~~she had never married; &~~ Mrs. Ramsay ~~wished~~ ~~had lived, she would have insisted upon marrying~~ Lily must have married William Bankes.

Already that autumn he was "the kindest of men" – He was Poor William Bankes – I wish he had someone to look after him" –

had

& she ~~was~~ "~~scientific~~ a scientific head – ~~so that~~ they were sent walks together to find flowers. What was this mania for marriage ? Lily wondered, stepping to & from her easel.

their

Why did ~~they~~ in ~~those days~~ believe in sepulchral union – ~~believed~~ in locking people up in the catacombs & turning the key on them for ever? Relentless, remorseless, ~~Mrs. Ramsay~~ pressed on, giving in ~~marriage, &~~ it seemed to her now. And she remembered how William Bankes

* MS 298–300 (3.175)

† A 260, B 269; A 261, B 270

222

had comforted her that evening, when Charles Tansley had been
listened to
† gulling her; had taken her gently, seriously, with his wise, child's eyes; &
how she had explained to him that a ~~shadow~~ figure may ~~be needed~~
as part of a picture; & ~~how sh it shocked him at first~~. ~~For~~
was
~~She had left~~ the faces ~~blank~~ can be left blank; & it ~~is~~ not
through any lack of respect for motherhood or childhood
that she used Mrs. Ramsay & James as a triangular shape,
~~holding the two sides of the picture together.~~
† necessary to the picture. With his scientific mind, he had
did not necessarily
understood. But ~~really must~~ understanding lead to marriage?
It had not. She still saw him. ~~She was even now painting a~~
~~picture for his~~ ~~dining room.~~ ~~But~~ They
† kept up a most satisfactory intercourse together. They went to
plenty of
Hampton Court, & he always left her perfect gentleman that he
was, time to wash her hands while he took a stroll by the
strolled through the courtyard
river. Then they admired the buildings. His knowledge ~~was~~
astonished her. & ~~it was never &~~ yet it was never dry, for
~~if he could tell her when this was built or that altered,~~
he would always be stopping to admire either a plant or a
child (~~one~~ it had been his greatest grief not to have a daughter)
vague the
in the / half ~~absent minded way which~~ abstract, the aloof way
which was natural to one who spent so much time in
laboratories that when he came out he walked slowly
lifted his hand as to screen his eyes ~~sometimes~~
paused & with his stick pointing at some flower or
other, merely to enjoy life. It was one of the
consolations of her life – her friendship with
Mr. Bankes.
† And it is much better than marriage.
So she addressed the drawing room steps. for
there Mrs. Ramsay had sat so often, knitting, writing,
sometimes with a book on her knee, often a
child

a [ ? ] of feeling
towards her*

---

* Written in pencil (3.177)

† A 262, B 271; B 272; A 263; A 264, B 273

This
~~But~~ she owed ~~this~~ to Mrs. Ramsay; ~~however,~~ & she looked at the steps [where Mrs.
Ramsay used to sit ~~with~~ knitting, writing ~~often~~ sometimes with a
Had she [this much?]
book on her knee, often with a child. ~~The wraith~~ which she had
[now?]
dismissed a moment before, the impotent, the excluded, now
~~shaped itself in a won an aspect of beauty became a~~
~~wore had its beauty wore an aspect of beauty.~~ became
one
swam up from its faraway distances, ~~&~~ seemed for a moment kindled, real.
And Lily turning against her own callousness, implored this ghost
to ~~take her ap accept her~~ to be~~lieve her when she~~
~~humbly said that she was grateful~~ – accept her thanks; but
~~the ghost no.~~ She was misled, she was tormented by the
it
but too beautiful, too sorrowful, too noble. Mrs. Ramsay
was not like that. She did not sit with folded hands & flowing
robes; her eyes downcast ~~& the~~ or gravely ~~meeting fire looking~~
expectant; ~~Beauty which came at the lightest call, dimmed~~
ed
~~her~~. Beauty dimmed her. Beauty flow~~ing~~ round her like the
white light of candles obscured her. ~~She was gone; she was lost.~~
She sou~~ght something~~ She wore an old shooting cap, Lily remembered.
She ~~threw a shawl round her~~. She clapped it casually on her head.
It seemed as if a lustre rested there, on the step; as if the thought of her
~~were~~ composed ~~like a dream~~ itself at once into ~~a statuesque~~
shape that mourned; a grieving he had been so beautiful; &
this beauty now seemed to ~~heighten her~~, to
She wore an old shooting cap, ~~Her~~ Where was
that woman gone?
And sure enough, something swam up there on the ~~s~~ drawingroom
steps: the shape of a woman, beautiful, silent with downcast eyes.
She was extremely beautiful – She ~~said~~ was musing, pondering.
~~She was like a the figure of~~ She
~~about her,~~ But what did she mourn? Why was she grieving?
Why
~~What~~ had death given her the part to play that was none of hers
in life? Yet, the longer she looked, the more
plainly Lily could see before her that astonishing beauty; & it

Now of all
things she wished it

as she implored it it
to take her thanks,
forgive, to accept,
her ~~her~~ gratitude
And sure [enough?]
something
sure
but the next
she was [?]

Yet her image
gave off beauty

that composed & mournful attitude. She must one day have seen it,
as she had seen so many ~~changes &~~ things. ~~Now~~ they ~~eye brought~~ came
[back;
~~But then too there was the~~ ~~But not~~ so ~~still~~; not so exalted. ~~When was~~
But
For where was the shooting cap she clapped to her head; where the
[galoshes, in
~~which she would~~ But now it rested there, apart & alone; ~~or~~
now it was a
& Lily felt ~~tears again~~ This is beautiful & it is solemn, but it is not
~~the~~ & ~~She felt~~ ~~I never~~ how the bounds of her knowledge ~~used~~
She felt ~~This then is to continue my acquired~~
real; this is what I have ~~maid~~ made

it has its
inequity
beauty Lily thought,
wishing to peel it
off & roll it up
& throw it
away.

[ ? ] on her ~~feet~~
She pulled on, sitting on the chair in the hall, when she wanted to
run through the wet grass after – what?
Mrs. Ramsay was always running. ~~She had it seemed~~
~~an eye that reach~~ It was a joke that she could see ~~slugs eggs at~~
slugs ~~all~~ across the garden.

~~How~~ But ~~neither the~~ ~~And yet how beautiful; &~~

And that was part of the charm at least – the discrepancy. For
there it remained, dominant, on the drawing room steps, the
composed the magnificent figure, robed in beauty, abstracted.
~~She wa~~

~~Mr. Carmichael~~

But what was the look she had when she clapped the deer stalkers
† hat on her head, or ran across the lawn in galoshes to find slugs?
Who could tell her, who could help her? Mr. Carmichael?

† He lay on his chair with his hands clasped above his paunch
flowing down
his beard with the yellow stain resting upon his breast. He was no
longer reading, but had the appearance of some vast brute which is now
The
~~remembering &~~ has gorged itself & is now ruminating. ~~His~~ book,
that which ~~she took to be the had supplied he~~ was his ~~sour~~ source of
nourishment, lay fallen on the grass: Lily ~~had a sense of the~~
as if the
words ~~overpowering~~ ~~some~~ felt that it gave off the incense of poetry,
there
lay smoking on the grass; & the fumes of words ~~rose~~ permeated
~~rose slow~~ & ~~ascend~~ ~~through~~ the old man's ~~being brain~~, being,
[ceiling?] of his mind the stresses
coloured the walls ~~hung~~ [reassured?] & [?] him, as opium
had, she supposed (it was only Andrew's story) given his body its
bulk, its lethargy, & his eyes their ~~sno~~ smoky look, as if
the mind burnt ~~behind a~~ deeply behind a clouded window pane.
Thus he would lie by the hour, she remembered, &
she could still see him slouching past the window, where Mrs.
Ramsay sat, furtively, ~~&~~ clumsily as if he wished to escape
detection, but she always stopped him. She could not
feel unhappy
endure that anyone should ~~feel out of things~~. She tried to draw
him in. But somehow she was never successful. She
& knew that anyone
resented, Lily suspected, anyone ~~who had no need of her~~.
not
have no need of her should ~~be wld~~ ~~independent~~ of her: that any man should: &
Mr. Carmichael ~~was the exception among men: he~~
~~did not depend on her.~~ was oddly aloof: he had no needs, Lily
thought; He shared that unpleasant peculiarity with her.
For she had no needs either. She painted; he wrote.
But Mrs. Ramsay ~~was~~ – that one who ex ~~put~~
~~pulled up the weeds, or~~ searched out slugs (her
children said she could see a slugs egg half across the
garden) & pried with her spectacles ~~on~~ into dishes,
when she was ~~broiling~~ dropping laurel or sherry;
shred by shred, drop by drop, to concoct some
~~amazing~~ triumph of cookery, ~~wanted~~ so ~~was only~~
infinitely preferred
so ~~much preferred~~ life. *Could she have stood painting.

* MS 334
† B 274; A 265

(3.183)

† could she have lain reading a whole morning in the garden?
It was unthinkable. She disappeared. Without saying a word
the only token of her errand ~~being~~ a basket on her arm
She went off, to the town, to the poor, to the stuffy ~~little~~ rooms, the
little
the close, the sordid rooms, where ~~old~~ suffering women,
men crushed by ~~some~~ accident in the prime of life, languished,
died with the torture before them of children left or wives left;
to live There she came. And ~~once~~, Laugh who would
own
~~[In?]~~ Among her friends the ~~futility of~~ acts such as these
were to be
was known to be futile; ~~the~~ easy benevolences, luxuries that
so
drew off the flood of pity, & ~~sati fi~~ & satisfied the giver that
gave neither
~~more~~ action & thought were not needed. Perhaps it was Mrs.
Ramsay's beauty. Anyhow, Lily could not help it: ~~she~~
~~thought~~ followed her often going to the town with her
† basket, silently: she noted her return. She thought
eyes that are closing in pain & despair have looked on you. She
thought, ~~your~~ beauty has been with them. She adored
that goodness. ~~from the bottom of her heart.~~

† A 291, B 300; B 301

227

~~But t~~ But bulk & mass, the line of the house ~~central~~ going so, the line of
going imposed themselves on her [the
hedge / so ~~made it the imposed their laws on her~~.
stared ~~out~~ at her. We are your ~~sl~~ masters; ~~Your allegiance is to us,~~
seemed to say
they said. And so she could only watch Mrs. Ramsay going, watch
&
Mrs. Ramsay coming back, figure to herself, ~~wonderingly~~, the
how she ~~was led to ca these journeys instinctively~~ the kind of
instinct within, ~~of her~~, how ~~she was inspired to~~
† there was within her a natural instinct like the swallows for the
south; like the artichoke for the sun – Lily could find no
image for that natural instinct, ~~which~~ turning her to the
~~sufferings &~~ human race, making her seek her nest in its heart.
Could she have stood painting with a woman dying? a woman
needing sheets, ~~or~~ to her bed, or food? There was always a woman
dying. Misery pervailed* Such foothold as they had won (herself &
Mrs. Ramsay) was only a bare standing place, ~~& all round~~
~~them~~ Lily herself stood painting. ~~Mrs. Ramsay crossed the~~
what she did to
that was ~~her method of~~ help~~ing~~ the dying woman, she
reflected; she had painted twenty dozen pictures, most of which
were scraped, cut up, painted over, given away, shamefacedly, or
hung in the servants bedroom. ~~Still it was her only an~~
too
~~offering that too~~; obedience to an instinct ~~which commanded her~~
~~to bring out the~~ a commanding, an overwhelming instinct
~~Who could tell which was best~~? or
Never mind. It was in obedience to an instinct, a commanding, an
overwhelming instinct. It is not we that have made ourselves –
some such thought as that fortified her ~~against~~ One had no choice.
Moreover, explain it who could, she believed that ~~she~~
~~reached the same point by painting~~ these sincere pictures of hers
that were stacked beneath sofas or occasionally came
in for a word of praise, not for the right qualities,
from critics, were ~~be her best~~ somehow an attempt to
solve the problem. ~~an effort~~ to reduce ~~chao~~ chaos to order, to

* VW's misspelling

† A 292

(3.187)

to solve the problem –

it was
How profound a problem ~~faced~~ her; ~~The wall, the hedge,~~ the
~~house; co~~uld she have mad~~e that~~ Could she have painted that
picture, she would have done more to help the dying woman –
~~no~~ neither
~~the eternal~~ dying ~~woman, who had not food nor clothing~~,
than, by giving her food & clothing, shelter & sympathy.
~~For how~~ could ~~they~~ A picture that ~~did what, in flashes,~~
to be
she saw ~~was possible, which~~ made the wall so so, the
hedge so & the house so, ~~which clothed that~~ & clothed
~~them in the fitly did was the only~~ helped it that was the expression.
~~But~~ But it was not the expression, she thought, (having applied
herself fiercely to the exacting hedge, for half an hour)
[~~Them?~~] There is something better than helping dying women.
Something, heaven be praised, beyond human relations altogether, in all
this talk of you & me, & me & you, & ~~for~~ one loving another, & one
not loving another, all this little trivial baseness of
about which we made so incessant a to do of marrying &
giving in marriage, pales beside it is irrelevant beside it.
Yet so terrible a doctrine could not be confessed. Tansley
would have shot her. Mrs. Ramsay would never have
spoken to her again. understood. ~~Inhuman Yet somehow~~ Pictures are more
it
important than people – ~~That~~ had a dreadful sound to it.
~~But let us put it like this then~~: But the way to put it
~~was more like~~ this – Yet a ~~world st~~ which
Yet ~~a society which makes no provision~~ for the
the soul, ~~turns away~~ it must be confessed, she thought,
a
that the mind ~~turns~~ has ~~its bias~~ towards ~~other~~ things
than ~~art the abstract, & the~~ lines of houses & hedges; ~~&~~
swings its way out of the turmoil here; & has a sense of
reaching some more acute reality where it can rest.

That reality seemed now ~~all al~~ all
round her. Some line had gone happily, or it
might be, the friction of work had heated her mind

(229)

to such a heat [?] of illusion that its fire light glowed
upon the landscape & made her see ~~the wh~~ the drawingroom
steps & the wall & the hedge in some ~~a~~ illusory, yet apparently
~~such~~ Everlasting & undeniable ~~rel~~ relationship
~~where they themselves were~~ openly & freely ~~a~~ ~~expressed~~.
As the [mouth drew?] ~~Her mind~~ How could she doubt it?
† She was extended, & freed; ~~&~~ she ~~became all fire herself.~~
~~She had passed~~ ~~It the~~ she was cut loose from the
ties of life; she enjoyed that intensity & freedom of life
which, for a few seconds after the death of the body, one
imagines the souls of the dead to enjoy: one imagines then
that they have gathered themselves together & ~~can~~
~~they become~~, ~~for those moments, how infinitely inten~~
& complete & forcible with the force of an organism
which is now at last able to unite all its powers.

~~Some mystic idea~~ ~~Excursions~~ It was attended, too,
with an emotion, which could be compared only with the
gratification of ~~hum~~ bodily human love. So,
unhesitatingly, without fear or reserve, at some moment
of culmina~~ting~~ ion when all separation is over, except that
~~final~~ delight of separation – that it ~~can be~~ which is has
consciousness of mixing – ~~the two people~~ bodies unite;
the human love has its gratification. But that, even,
was less complete than this; for who can deny it?
Even while the arms are locked, or the sentence married in the
air with complete understanding, a cloud moves across
the sky; & ~~in~~ each lover knows, but cannot confess,
his knowledge of the transience of ~~all~~ love: the
mutability of love: how tomorrow comes; ~~how~~ they they
words & other kisses. ~~But~~ & they are only
tossed together & nothing survives.

But here, since the lover was the ~~horrible~~
formidable enemy – space – their union, could it be achieved,
was immortal. No cloud moved, in that landscape; no
death came ~~nowhere~~, between them. It was an awful
marriage; forever.

† A 265, B 275

For somehow the sympathy which had come too late, made her feel she must follow him, & keep him in mind; ~~send~~ his image was stamped [ that ~~Strange man~~, ~~There he would sit~~ He would be sitting in the boat there with his [[in her?] strange light eyes fixed upon nothingness. ~~He would be~~ thinking Now & again presumably he would think with satisfaction of his boots. Then again of that kitchen table. then of his fame. ~~For still~~ He was enormously ~~interested in~~ vain. It told against her that she had

† never praised him. It reduced their relationship to something neutral; ~~this new~~ without that element of sex which was ~~cli~~ made his manner to Minta Doyle, she remembered, so gallant, almost gay. ~~For Minta~~ He would pick a flower, for her ~~or make a joke~~. ~~&~~ she borrowed his books; but how could Minta read them? She dragged them about the garden, putting in leaves to ~~mak~~ mark her place. ~~Yet~~ But it was this attitude he required; & enjoyed & perhaps. for all his ~~severity~~ acuteness, ~~he did~~ accepted ~~literally~~ blindly; ~~He had so extreme a desire for~~ At ~~any rate~~ ~~he gave her~~ ~~He had so extreme~~ a ~~desire for sympathy~~. He gave her books. He accepted her floundering blundering helter skelter praise. Lily had always looked away ~~from there~~ in a kind of shame. How could he be so blind. so vain?

And now he must do without, she supposed. Now he must suffer; for he gave her the impression of having [schooled?] himself: ~~he certain~~ ~~certain not~~ ~~behave now more~~ for instance, there was the [?] of Cam Cam's coat. ~~She recollected~~ ~~of~~ The morning had provided her with a thousand such impressions. They clung to her like some pungent flavour. Do what she would to obey the command her picture laid on her, she kept thinking, he did this, he looked like that. And how mechanically & ~~w~~ severely the children came down the path! ~~Have~~ ~~The~~ It ~~was~~ all flared in her face, with a double effect of reality & unreality due, she supposed, to her return after all these years, so that whatever happened had did not seem a natural process of living, but symbolical of life. ~~It was~~ as ~~if~~ ~~And then, as~~ She thought, too, of things that had happened; of ~~Ta~~ Charles Tansley; of Minta, as if their lives ~~were~~ had suddenly been stamped & struck off, ~~&~~ So one

† A 254, B 263

came to little rises in the ground, when the landscape had a an air of being seen in its final truth.

felt
~~She had said~~ ~~that a moment ago abo~~ut The thought connected itself with ~~some~~ another,

*~~A few of the thoughts that have~~

2 I will lay before you some of the thoughts that have come to me on such an occasion as this: But you will notice that there is a note of interrogation at the end of my title. ~~For~~ It is true that ~~though~~ one may think about reading as much as one chooses, but it is

impossible ~~abominable~~ to lay down any sort of law about it. Here, in this room, we breathe the air of freedom. There are no laws, no ~~inequal~~ law givers. Each man & woman has to make up his mind for himself.

27 Perhaps it is the better & more important point. To get the shock in strongly & ~~clearly~~ firmly ~~as possible~~ [~~unified?~~] ~~as as~~ – as ~~much~~ personally as possible is perhaps the ~~better~~ the most necessary of all things. Without that private – peculiar feeling, we ~~cannot build or~~ all reading is dust & ashes. But once received, there comes the much more curious task of discriminating, sorting out & judging.

* Passages from 'How Should One Read a Book?' follow. See appendix C for another segment of this essay. (3.195)

Monks House
Rodmell
4th August
1926.

To the Lighthouse

(type page 202)*

Uniform Edition pp 255–320**

† ***Strange & faint & far away it looked. ~~Ye~~ Yet there, somewhere, was their house. & the garden with all those paths & lawns, & their [so intense, so acute were all left there] ~~seemed as if they had also left~~ their thoughts & feelings there; ~~but now they were~~ cut off, & ~~existed~~ ~~They were cut off~~. [& here] ~~They~~ were ended. ~~They were small &~~ infinitely remote. ~~And~~ ~~For~~ [she] now ~~here~~

† she was, in this boat, with her father & ~~James~~ & the Macalisters & James.

became diminished, cut off & left behind

The compact between them held;

the [chuckling?] the rushing: here life formed itself round in the little circle.

For this was now real; the boat; the sea; her father, & the Macalisters & James. ~~Only, again, what was~~ this ~~new experience~~ – was ~~strange, this was new: this was extremely exciting.~~ And in this lay the light of something so new that it is strange; & unreal; & infinitely exciting; she looked at James.

Their compact held; to resist [& tyranny with] coercion to the death. But he was changed. Steering, with his eyes fixed on the sail, frowning slightly, he looked as if he too ~~were had been were now~~, & isolated, & ~~lifted~~ cut off from the things they both knew; so that they were no longer the 'children', who had overslept & been scolded: ~~no longer~~ [but] something had come between them & separated them & made them strange to each other. ~~She would drag her fingers through the waves.~~

But I beneath a rougher sea"★ said Mr. Ramsay – ~~& whelmed in~~

~~His~~ for ~~though~~ having looked at the shore & located with his keen longsighted eyes the position of the house, ~~he was made to feel,~~ felt again come over him a sense of some~~thing~~ wrong, some harm, some perfidy offered him which threw him for redress upon the sympathy of the world. If the whole world had occupied itself solely in weeping his sorrow? that tribute would not have been

† too great. ~~He needed~~ The whole world should have been composed

* For a discussion of the pagination, cf introduction. (3.197)

** Probably added by Leonard Woolf

*** MS 283–301 are a reworking of MS 267–77.

★ 'The Castaway,' MS 242, 267, 317, 362

† A 247, B 256; A 249, B 257; A 248

solely of women, & they should have listened to him, lamented with him, pitied him; given him that divine sensation which of all he coveted most ~~fixedly~~ of endless inexhaustible sympathy – sympathy in which he could bathe, to which he could return – For who had [perished?] & been more tortured than he – ~~who~~ his son, his daughter – his wife all gone; & he left alone, worn, aged, broken hearted – the words came to his lips in a curious ambling singsong; ~~&~~ aged & broken hearted, he would murmur, & feel nothing but the exquisite delight of the sympathy which the world he was imagining would give him – so that sometimes ~~in a queer dramas~~ minutes fled in these queer dramas in which he beheld himself, ~~the stake~~ like the lonely stake, the beaten poll (& here he looked at his hands which were lean enough to confirm the dream) & then ~~again~~ beheld the divine faces of comforters looking up at him & offering him the solace of innumerable sighs; imploring him to tell them what he suffered; & ~~then~~ which he would recite, in words which & get again the divine ~~im~~ relief of sympathy & grief succeeding each other ~~spoken together;~~ & ~~so this~~ this would go on ~~until a~~ repeated & repeated, & failing & being renewed, until it would seem to him suddenly all so vivid, [he?] all so clearly heard, that ~~nothing could until~~ it became like a play in which he could be the actor, & also the audience, & [who?] ~~yet~~ suddenly with a great start, he ~~would stop.~~ stopped.

~~Was there Cam: James.~~ old Macalister. The Lighthouse.

Look at the house! he repeated.

And now James turned his head to look over his shoulder

[*]

as his father bade him.

For now again, woken from this drama of the lean form crucified & the women endlessly pitying, he must make them – the children – happy; friendly; must see that they grow up admiring, loving, courageous; must fortify them with memories implant in them some help against the battle ~~of life~~ before them. Had Cam looked?

He ~~asked her~~ waved his hand so that they should both look; & ~~began telling them both~~ how

But Cam could not see the house. She was shortsighted, like her mother. She could see nothing clearly. And ~~this~~ since he had the long steady gaze of a leader, of an explorer, used to judging distances & keeping landmarks in view, ~~this~~ he could see [clearly, [everything?]. infirmity of his child's annoyed him.

† There was the house he said. Pointing his finger, he made her look along [it], leaning against them.

"There!"

But James knew that Cam would never be able to see any~~thing~~ [or] at that distance. She was shortsighted. & she did not want to see [the house] ~~either.~~ She was obstinate as a mule. She ~~James~~ Another impression was added to the enormous store which he held already in his head.

* VW did not number this page.

† A 249, B 258

But Cam could not see the house. She was shortsighted; like ~~her mother.~~ {Also} She looked in the wrong direction. This annoyed Mr. Ramsay ~~Mr. Ramsay~~ {he} wished her to see the exact spot where the house was. {see the house; it annoyed him that she could not;} because {particularly about places} he liked accuracy; because, ~~too,~~ after his outburst, ~~he~~ whose the extravagance ~~of which~~ he ~~always regretted, he wished that to was distasteful~~ to him he wished to recover himself by an ~~emo~~ {extra} additional sanity: because, finally, consistent, inviolable, powerful beyond any other emotion, was his desire to anchor his childrens minds, in the waste & turmoil of life upon some rock. ~~It was distressing that his~~ Yet ~~daughter~~ {Cam} did not know the points of the compass.

Laughing, {[they?]} {&} teasing; {&} scolding, {&} ~~urging~~ {[?]} he discovered that she did not know at all: was that west, was that north?

Cam did not know, James ~~thought~~, was sure of that. She did not care, either. [At anyrate she was not going to ~~own up to him.~~ ~~show~~ {own} either that she knew or that she cared.] Her bright vague eyes gazed & ~~ag~~ gazed – & at last Mr. Ramsay dropped

† his hand, & ~~faced the problem which~~ {thought} what should he say to her? How should ~~he approach her~~? How should he control ~~this~~ his hand & his voice & his face, & all the obedient [~~Now~~?] quickly ~~forming~~ shaping ~~obediently~~ gesticulating forms who had been with him these seventy years now? ~~How should he dodge that making him~~ ~~In a~~ In a world where the only desirable thing was truth, {He} ~~it humiliated him to be so easily put out of the truth way of truth. They judged him.~~ made to gesticulate. ~~He They judged him~~ was humiliating ~~But~~ he was old, worn, tired: true. Ah, he would not gesticulate. He would ~~find something to say.~~,

~~How~~ was the puppy unhappy, left alone". Who was going to take it out today?" he asked her. & James

thought pitilessly, now she will give way. Now I shall be left alone to carry out ~~my~~ the vow – ~~which was to~~ He had sworn it in the garden when he was a child: to resist

† B 259, A 250

206

tyranny to the death. Decked in a thousand brilliant colours
this vice came among men. [They were effective; & they conquered]
People always went under to ~~them:~~ the tyrants; women ~~did~~ in
particular; ~~but~~ the loathsome vice ~~always~~ showed through
~~it all~~. He might charm, he might preach; he might be
a great man for anything James knew;
They charmed. They wheedled. Now he was wheedling Cam, about
this puppy; & she would give way; & the compact would be left to him
carry out. to resist tyranny to the death.
~~But she did not answer~~.

Sometimes ~~a over~~ upon a hill that has been green & bright &
sunny, a cloud falls; gravity descends; there, among all
the miles of surrounding brightness, alone is gloom &
sadness; for a moment, for a space. So now & if one can
fancy thought among hills & high places, it would seem as
if they must ponder the fate of the clouded & darkened; so
Cam was ~~sudd~~ overcast now, with the cloud that rested on her,
of the whole burden & battle & disaster of life; & how
impossible of solution; & how her father's voice asking who
was to take the puppy out, ~~was~~ cleft her, ~~for she~~
was the & question like that addressed to her by people who wished to
forerunner of all questions of all the desolate, the
abandoned, the criminals, who when the gates shut on
them, repent their crime, & beg for forgiveness; but there is
always a lawgiver, stern & just, who forbids forgiveness, &
† rightly too; a lawgiver who has somehow laid open
upon his knees the tablets of eternal wisdom; & says no, & rightly
of all human qualities she revered justice most, she
thought; her brother was most godlike; only an
existence like this, she thought, still gazing at the
shore, whose points were unknown to her, with one will

† A 251, B 260

enfolding another, python-like, forever & ever, & ~~the~~
~~&~~ making peace impossible, is a torture & a distress for which she
thought, there is no cure, no end.

Jaspers ~~taking the puppy out,~~ she said.

persisted.
And what was she going to call him, Mr. Ramsay asked.
And she said ~~she didn't know~~. she ~~didn't~~ couldn't think; & Mr. Ramsay
said Spot, Frisk, Pink? ~~Po~~ & ~~James steered grimly,~~ & she said,
~~not~~ not
nothing, & James thought "She will ^ give way ~~not~~ like that;
but quite suddenly, & he waited for ~~he~~ look to come in her face
She will look.
which he remembered. They ~~turn~~ their down, he thought; they
pretend to be thinking, or considering. ~~Then suddenly~~ they look up:
(For ~~in his own mind the dead his mother,~~ he called his mother 'they'; it
was of her he was thinking; ~~so~~ she would be knitting; his father
would be standing there, saying Spot, Frisk, Pink? like that
& she would be angry; & suddenly, vanquished, overcome, she would
look up!

James thought,
~~Suddenly, as if she gave up the struggle, her eyes would~~ a flash of blue, he could remember; & then tyranny had triumphed. ~~He called his mother 'they'~~; & the conqueror, for so he always saw his father, demanding, taking, making off again, content, marched off content.

from eyes suddenly raised ~~&~~ laughingly;

He watched her critically; gazing back at the shore ~~at the shore; & her father waited~~; ~~& He~~ She would give way, as they all did, he ~~judged. But she went on looking back; tragically~~; But ~~not quite in their way.~~ Not as they had done; ~~His mother~~ – For ~~with~~ Cam being, for one thing, ~~so~~ ignorant, & like them all ~~at the beginning of a~~ how should he put it – what one word could single out from ~~describe~~ the † infinite series of impressions which time had laid down, leaf upon leaf, fold upon fold, ~~on his~~ in his brain – impressions ~~of sights & sounds, of scents, & wh voices, of dresses rustling, of bracelets tingling, & the white underside of leaves, of the wash & hush of the waves~~ – ~~all of which had he done their part in making them as~~ how should he single out from all this, ~~& the~~ impressions which had fallen on him, ~~on h~~ & on her too, he supposed, from childhood – scents, & sounds, & voices passing, & the tap of broom overhead & the wash & hush of the sea at night, which accumulating, seemed to wash round ~~& something~~ the monuments composed out of such ~~frivolities, batt~~ great figures, like pyramids or kings statues, ~~dominating~~ a desert, standing sentinel in their lives, the his mother, his ~~father, & the fig~~ures of friends too, like old Mr. Carmich~~ael, like~~ Minta Doyle & Paul Rayley; symbols of humanity, giant shapes in which were hid where treats were hid & the myriad myriad tiny people; varieties of the race; & all this experience, which they had shared, had made them different; ~~made them different now~~: ~~gave~~ them ~~a softness~~, a ~~solidity~~; something that turned the edge of the blade; & where they ~~the old~~ would have looked down & up, & [ ? ] she, Cam, sat dappling her fingers in the water, & staring back. ~~That they~~ at the shore.

† A 252, B 261

(209)

Well, if Cam would not speak to him, he would not bother her, ~~no more~~ thought Mr. Ramsay.

But she would speak to him, if she could think of anything, firm & fierce, & disinterested, loyal to the compact, yet just to ~~the~~ his demand ~~he made; & yet~~ his integrity, his truthfulness – for, she thought, looking steathily* at her brother, who kept his eyes dispassionately on a certain spot in the ~~su~~ curve of the sail, now, & then looked aside at the grey ~~tower~~ of the lighthouse ~~you're are~~ free; ~~from his~~ you're not exposed to a pressure which ~~she felt~~ it – to this curious pressure, she meant; this

For all his attraction bea~~ten~~ as he y

† extraordinary temptation; ~~She could~~ For nothing no one ~~could be more~~ attracted her more than this strange old man. His hands were beautiful; & his ~~strong,~~ shapely feet. His voice was beautiful, & his words. ~~He~~ Above all, his haste & his fervour; his oddity; his ridiculousness; his burning extreme energy; & his remoteness; ~~& his~~ But what remained intolerable, & would forever indicate as with the suddenly raising, unknown to himself, of an arm, upright, & monitory, & enough to quell the stormiest passions of her heart, ~~was~~ was his intolerable ~~arrogance, his irra~~ demand upon her, upon James, upon the whole world perhaps; Submit to [me.

he was beautiful; he was e

So she would not say

* VW's misspelling

† A 253, B 262

(3.211)

Give me what I want, because my need is so enormous; that was his demand. But his need was not greater than ~~other peoples.~~ Her's ~~was enormous~~: [even] ~~James's too.~~

~~She~~ So she said nothing; ~~for she would never submit; but~~ but looked, [doggedly] ~~still, sullenly~~, & sadly, at the shore, which wore a [vaunting] [an air] ~~look~~ of exquisite peace, as if the people there had fallen asleep, she thought, as if or had felt [fall down on them] descend on them a mantle of perfect calm.

went about lightly, easily, free to do what they wanted. wrapped in a mantle

5

*Yes, that is their boat, Lily Briscoe decided, watching the boat
† with the brown sails flatten itself upon the water & ~~pass~~ shoot off. There he sits with his strange light eyes fixed upon nothingness. And are they still silent, she ~~th~~ wondered, sitting Thinking how they had followed him down the path; ~~are~~ & how ~~they~~ [staring [so?]]. ~~had struck her like a procession, &~~ it had seemed to her that th~~ey had taken on the~~ [they were like a procession.] air of a procession were [doomed] drawn somewhere, the children against their will; but why [were they] ~~so savage~~ she asked herself turning back to her easel? For ~~her~~ the sympathy she had not given him weighed on her. [It was always the same.] She had never been able, ~~all the years she h~~ when she stayed there, to praise him. She had always left that to people like Minta Doyle. That was a pity perhaps. It reduced their relationship to something neutral, without that element of sex which had made his manner to Minta Doyle so gallant, almost gay. He would pick a flower for her; she borrowed his books. But how could Minta read them? She dragged them about the garden, sticking in leaves to mark her place.

across the bay

† Heaven be praised for it, she thought; taking up her brush again. ~~There was~~ The problem of space faced her. She had made, with

* MS 268 (3.213)

† A 254, B 263; A 255, B 264

~~canv~~ ~~out~~ ~~outlined~~ Her flickering brown line ~~had left on in the middle of~~ [~~her~~
~~canvas a shape~~, a solid, shapeless, mass; an iceberg; looming, imminent
prominent ~~right~~ unrelated, right there in the middle of the canvas.
~~How~~ It was to be seized upon & animated, & given its due weight
& poise, somehow; ~~made to live~~ there, in the centre, with all the other
weights & colours somehow depending on it – ~~she saw her picture~~
~~like a cathedral~~, ~~whose walls~~: ~~The were all all held together with~~
~~shoring it~~ up, until the whole structure, ~~became~~ was perfectly beautifully poised,
for all its ~~in~~ weight, ~~had a glowed &~~ ~~light~~ Beautiful & bright
~~with~~ on the surface ~~one w~~ ~~it was to be~~ ~~within~~ so that it
looked as if a breath would ~~blow~~ ruffle the ~~int~~ ~~colours~~ yellows & golds & [blues
it was to be clamped together with bolts of iron
the little pleasures & comforts & anxieties of the real world fell from her.
~~Here success was not personal, nor fleeting~~: all was done in solitude
with effort ~~& here directly she took her brush in her hand~~ she
felt face & [colour?] & limbs fall from her shrivelled up; she
~~verly~~ very likely she would be scorched alive, & nothing left of her –
that was her feeling. It was an awful effort & risk; &
~~& all the~~ no one to know either, if she failed, or survived: judges
there were none; yet, inevitably, she herself would read her
fate, much more clearly here than; would measure herself
against a rule whose wishes were marked indelibly.
So, with her brush laden she began to read the precarious
maze, the dance of line & colour, which, as it went daringly
sensitively ~~with acute~~ over the canvas, call up more
intensely than at other times figures, groups, scenes: went
~~fetched~~ flickered an illumination across the sky, even
as if her ~~brain con~~ the invisible words suddenly became plain.

[Left margin:]
touching it at once
supporting it –
depending on
it

a [ ? ]
colour [ ? ]
[ ? ]
[haze?]

Directly
she took her
brush in
her hand

Nancy saying "What does one send to the Lighthouse?"; the greenish light on the engraving; the children lagging down the path; Mr. Ramsay sending Cam back for her cloak: his hand raised as he passed her – all this seemed she thought not like the natural process of living, but symbolical of life. So that had she been able to give her whole mind to it, she would have seemed to start up like all these things seemed to her symbols – & still still; to be full of meaning which All seem as if, A thousand waves follow each other, smooth – small, & then one lifts itself; high. above the rest. Such was the method adopted All these moments were high waves. And these moments; these sayings were high waves. flashes of torches light lit in the lighting up the dark cave in a dark cave. A thousand waves follow each other, small & smooth & unregarded; then one lifts / it self, & the whole is visible. Life is lived Monday Tuesday Wednesday, day after day; & breakfast & dinner; & getting up & going to bed; & saying this & saying that; & putting on & taking off all done mutely dumbly with the docility of a sheep & the blankness of a fish: so the time passes, she thought: & her time had passed like that for her; in & then, why no one can say or what is worse than this smooth slipping away this drip & or again, higgledy piggledy, a flash what is perhaps what is there except flash & jerk; this & that; or again it was different; & things happened from that only too quickly, in flashes & jerks, & in flashes & jerks – lights were pressed in yo one's eyes; & th things flashed & jerked; what was Either way one was the slave of life & or [ ? ] it was all jerk & dash & dazzle & confusion. Rather timid, rather easily agitated, she could think of [ ? ] when this happened & then that happened – for no rhyme or *reason, things were jerked & flashed in her eyes: [Rather timid, she found it easy to lose power over] which was worse?

~~But now & then~~ ~~People might~~

Very well. And then, someone, or something, – Mrs. Ramsay, she

† remembered used to have that power – said, in effect, Life stand still here; & the disorder was orderly; & the flash & race controlled.] so that ~~if one were asked to~~ in truth, one was conscious, increasingly conscious with the lapse of years, of the enormous conglomeration, & depth & meaning; one was not an adventurer bound harum scarum upon a chaotic dance; but rather was called upon to consider endlessly of the meaning of what was shown one. By ~~some~~

disorderly elements were reduced ~~the~~ all things at once came together – like an organic compound – which has been

the & composure at once fell. There was one of those moments. And it could be held in the fingers, looked up & round; & never lost its endlessness, or its ~~ele mystery~~. ~~So tha~~ Threw out like radium its ~~store~~ meaning. ~~mad~~ so that ~~life~~ was after all, she thought, separated: or the And this one could hold in ones fingers, look at, look round; stick in a jar, if need be, & keep there, throwing out light heat colour. ~~It was not all meaningless then; or race~~

By this means, ~~far from being~~, as ~~was said by~~ people said, possibly one might in the course of time work ones way to a system, philosophy, or understanding of life: the first step being that she at the age of forty four, grasped ~~the~~ hold of the fact that there was an order, a succession of stepping stones, or, did one choose to put it so, of flowers, ~~tigh~~ perfectly composed, & of moments when Nancy said what does one send to the Lighthouse, ~~of moments~~ when

† sights & memories of scenes which had the power of radium & the power of ~~life~~ creative so to accumulate & shed light.

* MS 269 (3.219)

† A 240, B 249; A 240, A 256, B 250, B 265

† Why, after all these years had that survived, ~~ringed~~ ringed round, lit up,
visible to the last ~~degree of~~ detail, ~~y~~ ~~yet set in a~~ with all before it
blank & all after it blank for miles?
She sat on the beach writing one of those innumerable letters, which
the wind sometimes blew away across the sand. 'There was the old
cork dipping & bobbing in the sea; Charles Tansley throwing stones;
a wave breaking; racing almost up to the rock where Mrs. Ramsay
sat, writing, writing, in that little round rapid hand that was so illegible.
† "Is it a boat, is it a cork?" Mrs. Ramsay would say looking up,
with one hand on her paper, & Lily herself ~~would be asking~~
(while she watched Charles, ~~so~~ suddenly become transformed).
~~h~~ & would be imagining, half lulled asleep, yet living with enormous
some opened
acuteness, how now at this moment the doors ~~were thrown,~~ noiselessly.
wide ~~open,~~ & one entered in, & stood silently ~~a~~ gazing about, in a
things
high dark cathedral like place, with flags hanging, & ~~dimly~~ shaking
statues gleaming, & that cold solemn air such places have,
steamer
& ~~this was~~ shouts came far away; a boat vanished in a stalk of smoke
on the horizon. ~~There~~, for an appreciable time, she moved,
much ~~at her ease, while~~ Charles threw the stones, & ~~they~~ sent them
~~went~~ skipping ~~over the~~ Did Mrs. Ramsay know it? Did
Probably not. She was glad, Lily thought, to rest in silence,
† incommunicative; ~~to rest~~ ~~to let things to be taken for granted,~~
to rest in the extreme obscurity of human relationships; Who
knows what we are, or what we feel? Aren't things spoilt by
silently
saying them? Dont we communicate better ~~without words?~~
Aren't we (at any rate women) ~~better~~ more expressive silently
gliding high together, side by side, in the curious dumbness,
ones
which is so much to ~~their~~ taste than speech, with the kingdoms
of the world displayed down beneath; ~~not~~ asking no share in
them? ~~Some such fee~~ It was something like that, that she

† A 254, B 263; A 255, B 264; A 256, B 265

215

felt, sitting beside Mrs. Ramsay, digging a little hole in the sand; & it was
due to her own intensity of feeling that the moment had filled itself with
light, had glowed there all these years; ~~so that~~ ~~Suppose she wanted~~
It ~~supplied~~ It was like a candle burning. She went back to it, stuck a
match in, & ~~cast the~~ looked round. lit up ~~the~~ this & that. ~~What would she have~~
~~thought of them~~? Charles Tansley. Minta & Paul. Marriage The War.
What would she have thought, ~~say,~~ about it? ~~the War, & about~~
~~Lily Briscoe stepped back~~ to such questions as that.
Lily Briscoe stepped back to get her canvas ~~in~~ at a due distance.

*The light of the moment shook at random, ~~over~~ as she dipped ~~took up~~ her brush again, hither & thither, lighting first ~~th~~ a stretch of road ~~& two~~ Minta Doyle's ~~walking~~ back; & Then, ~~having seen the thing~~, (it was thus her memory worked) she heard voices; then she recalled ~~the whole~~ how once, she had walked up from the beach with William Bankes; behind Minta who had a hole in her stocking. Now ~~his eyes~~ ~~kept~~ it seemed to flaunt itself before them – how he deplored it – without,

all he most detested;

† as far as she could remember, saying anything! ~~And as she strode in front of them~~ It meant to him ~~ruin~~ dirt disorder; a home with servants leaving ~~&~~ beds not made at midday – ~~all things that~~ bills, ~~perhaps~~, unpaid – all things he abhored. ~~As~~ Perhaps it ~~In fact,~~ ~~was true.~~ she believed, ~~the marriage had been at first quite~~ There was some truth in that vision of the stocking on the sandy path going up from the beach all those years ago – ~~The marriage~~ at first had been successful ~~at~~ first. There were two little boys. Then things worked loose – They came home at ~~such~~ different hours, from different places. Lily imagined them meeting on the stairs – Minta garish, wreathed & tinted, about three o'clock in the morning. ~~To finish the pi~~cture Paul carrying a poker, in case of burglars, Minta eating a sandwich, in the cadaverous early morning light on a staircase with holes in the carpet, dusty, ~~she~~ ~~wore~~ littered. What did they say? Something violent. He was withered, drawn; she flamboyant careless. She ate her sandwich while he spoke – in a mutter, so as not to wake the children.

† That was the sort of thing had happened, she supposed, painting; That is what we call 'knowing' people, she thought. This is what we

call

is 'thinking' about them.

~~Then again:~~ Another incident ~~struck her,~~ came to mind – Paul saying that he "played chess in coffee houses". She always remembered it. ~~For~~ He wandered off: he was solitary. It is

* MS 270–1

† A 257, B 266; A 258, B 267

(3.225)

217

He should have sat at home after dinner, reading his books; should have been domestic; His perfect ~~nose~~ profile hardened & stiffened; for he played chess in coffee houses; & then came home; ~~& then~~ ~~there was th~~ to find Minta out; & then there was that scene on the stairs at dawn. When she went sometimes to spend a ~~summ~~ day with them in the summer at their cottage near Rickmansworth, Minta would object to his showing her, for example the cucumber frame, or the place where he bred [Belgian] hares, in case he should say anything: She came after them, singing & put her bare arm round his shoulder; but she was bored by hares.

Things were strained.

† Lately though ~~(so she~~ here was another scene) they were doing something with the motor car: & from his manner & hers, Lily knew, as if they had told her everything, & both were reticent, that ~~something had happened~~. It was all right now. They had entered on another phase. Paul playing whatever it was – chess, dominoes, in a coffee house – had met somebody utterly ~~different~~ – a pale serious girl, a strong kind girl – a girl anyhow, & this ~~fr~~ far from breaking the marriage had ~~ended it.~~ righted it. They were [perfectly] happy: ~~But~~ [who] what would Mrs. Ramsay have said [of it] to that?

then again with the children

a girl who shared his interest in the taxation of land values – witness the way they talked about

† The dead, thought Lily, encountering some obstacle to her design, which made her ponder, ~~steppe~~ stepping back a little distance Oh the dead! One brushed them aside, somehow, [with ~~a kind~~ sort of pity, a tinge even of [haste?]] They are at our mercy. She has faded & gone.

. . . .

*saying of all incongruous things. "Marriage – marriage", ~~al~~ & all her beauty, all her being, became at once a little ~~pointless~~ dusty old fashioned. What can be done for them, then, she? For a moment she exulted.

Who persisted so obstinately – one could never, even in thought, wrench her round, in saying ~~mar~~ My ~~dear,~~ why dont you marry William Bankes?

* MS 272–3 (3.227)

† A 259, B 268; A 260, B 269

† (Suddenly, suffused with reddish light, she saw again Paul Rayley sitting down by Mrs. Ramsay at dinner. The reddish light ~~was~~ covered him; Minta was all a haze of gold. ~~So they had painted themselves upon~~ her ~~mind, There they sat, like lamps, like torches. burning upon her mind sending~~ a flare up into the ~~sky — such a sight~~ as lasted a lifetime, like the ~~twisted flame~~ of som~~e~~ of a flame of a signal fire ~~on a desert island~~. [She in her little boat saw it; ~~at the same time she had bee~~n It was memorable, symbolical, one of those occasions when a monument is raised by the combined force of myriads of put up by nameless people ~~as a~~ in token of some ~~unknown~~ vast celebration. She heard the roar & the crackle. The whole ~~landscape~~ sea for miles around was ~~cove~~ ran red & gold. Some winy smell must have ~~been~~ mixed with it, & intoxicated her for she remembered her own impulse headlong desire to throw herself over the ~~led or~~ cliff, ~~to~~ & be drowned. (She had offered to go & look for a brooch.) At the same time, ~~even in the height of the~~ at roar & the crackle ~~frighten~~ repelled her with fear, with disgust. with ~~horror at~~ the devouring ~~egotistical~~ force; as ~~this~~ at one moment a blaze is nothing but splendour & light, & at another, seems ~~to b~~ ~~feed~~ feeding laps up unscrupulous on all the treasure of the house. But for a sight, † for a great effort glory flung up (by that quite ~~effort~~ flaming from ordinary young man, too, sitting at dinner, opposite her with a plate of figs between them) it ~~out~~ sur passed everything in her experience; remained, a signal fire burning on a desert island at the edge of the sea; & ~~so would always burn. making the water run red & gold.~~

~~But~~ Odd to think that the parents of this splendour were now ~~just~~ Paul & Minta Rayley.)

~~But~~ But

~~Anyhow, But~~ This diversion ~~apart~~ over, / whatever Mrs. Ramsay certainly ~~would have~~ meant by marriage, & it was probable that

The light was like a flare.

(as so often, among the extremes of emotion

feeds voraciously [unmercifully?]

† A 261, B 270; A 262, B 271

(219)

She meant locking them up in the catacombs & turning the key on them. She would have married them had she been able. She had

She remembered how she had made a note about moving a tree in her picture, in a state of exaltation one night, after talking to William Bankes, & It had flashed upon her that she need not marry.

& the relief of one's escape from her)

(That was a tribute to the effect that Mrs. Ramsay had upon people He had listened to her with his wise child's eyes when he had told her that a figure might be part of a design He had been shocked at her neglect of the neglect of the human significance of mother & son; but he It was not the irreverence that used them, on this occasion, as a shadow. She did not intend any disparagement of a subject, which she agreed with him Raphael had treated divinely. She was not cynical. Thanks to his scientific mind, he understood; w & she The understanding was so rare that she was grateful

he did not lecture, or laugh; or

a triumph of

His disinterested intelligence wh had comforted her enormously. Indeed

† his friendship was one of the pleasures of her life – But why to be able to talk about painting dispassionately. But why marriage, she asked herself?

† It was the penalty of beauty – it Beauty It stilled the life, froze formalised it. It was easier froze it. One forgot the little agitation that was always at work: the breeze that disordered the hair; the flush, tha the paleness; here a remarkable shadow, there now then ugliness. some [sun?] some distortion. Looking b It was simpler to smooth it all out under that mask of faces, beauty which was,

what was the look she had when she

Lily painted.

Having written her Having written her letter Mrs. Ramsay would stuff [the paper with enormous decision in [an?] envelope;

† A 263, B 272; A 264, B 273

220

† Against her will, she had come to the surface & found herself ~~in the~~ half out of her picture, a ~~little daz~~ed, on the lawn. looking a little dazed. at Mr. Carmichael? He lay on his chair with his hands clasped above his paunch, his beard with the yellow stain on it flowing upon his breast. He was no longer reading. He was gorged & ruminating. His book had fallen on the grass. It lay there, giving off a fume of words, of poetry; he seemed ~~to lie there breathing in the incense, torpid, half asleep.~~ & he seemed drugged, drowsy.

She wanted to go straight up to him & say

"Mr. Carmichael!"

Then he would look up benevolently. "About Mrs. Ramsay – about life – about death – about everything in the whole world! But you couldn't say that to Mr. Carmichael. You could say nothing to anybody. The urgency of the moment always missed its mark. ~~One saw children struggling to~~ Words fluttered sideways & struck the object inches too low. Then one gave it up; then the idea sunk back again; then one became, like most middle aged people, cautious, furtive, with wrinkles between the eyes, & a look of perpetual apprehension.

† She looked at the drawing room steps, ~~empty~~, They were empty. It ~~That~~ came over her ~~violent~~ powerfully, for the first time. ~~that~~ Some one was not sitting there. The frill of a chair in the room ~~st~~ ~~st~~ moved a little in the breeze. ~~The extreme unpleasantness,~~ ~~It was extremely unpleasant.~~ ~~it~~ Like all strong feelings, the † physical sensation was ~~acute~~ To want & not to have, sent all up her body a ~~cur~~ starkness, a hollowness, a strain. ~~And it~~ ~~But the physical sensation merged in the~~ how they hurt the mind And then to want & not to have – to want & want! Oh Mrs. Ramsay she called out silently, as if she could curse her for having gone & thus ~~have~~ disturbed her painting. & tormented her with this anguish. ~~Why had she come all this way, to be made~~ why should she have done it? Ghost, air, nothingness – for months Lily went without thinking of her now. Now it seemed as if Mrs. Ramsay had ~~one~~ only been letting one run a little to suit her own purposes. She wanted one back. One came back. She was only that. Suddenly ~~she became the only desirable pe thing~~ in [life Then suddenly she asserted herself again, & the empty drawing room [steps & the frill moving & the puppy tumbling on the terrace all seemed to like hollow phantoms curves & arabesques curvetting, spouting, ~~round~~ a ~~terrible.~~ something; ~~infinitely~~ infinite ~~desirable~~, ~~be~~ desirable: ~~bee~~ that had gone round complete emptiness.

that went with extremely unpleasant.

how they wrung her heart, left it like the skin of an empty orange.

† B 275; A 266

well then
~~What is your opinion of life on the~~ whole, Mr. Carmichael?" she would
trying to But
† say; so she thought look~~ing~~ at her canvas. She was actually crying – that
[is
to say ~~tears~~ both her eyes were full of some ~~rath~~ hot liquid which without
disturbing the firmness of her lips, rolled down her cheeks. But she had
perfect control of herself in every other way. But,, most ridiculously &
annoyingly it was impossible for the moment to paint.
we it
Why did ~~they~~ acquiesce in ~~this monstrous state of things~~?
or
Why don't we do something about it? Are we fish, ~~are we~~ coal – are
we things that can be packed in barrels & rattled across the world
† without protest? She had a wild idea that if she & Mr.
Carmichael ~~toget~~ got up & made some violent display,
the hollow space which the step & the chair & the puppy indicated
would be vanquished. If they shouted loud enough, Mrs.
Ramsay would come back.

It was a degrading state to be in, no doubt. ~~Of~~ All extreme states were
that. Of the pain of childbirth a woman had told her that it was
demoralising. No. So this was demoralising – to wish for
anyone so strongly that one's only notion was to stand up &
† shout. Stop pain, stop pain, stop pain! ~~And~~ It was not
meanwhile
love ~~either~~; for her feeling towards Mrs. Ramsay / was ~~almost~~
~~hatred~~ – bitter – it

*~~Only at last~~, one ~~can so f~~ could so separate into parts this
this bitterness of wanting & this resentment of being made to want (just
[as
she was painting too, & marvelling that she did not care a
straw for Mrs. Ramsay being dead) & ~~half that yes~~ party – yes.
it dawned upon her that her feeling has already finding an antidote
(as they used to say dock leaves grew beside nettles) in a a
a sense, first purely physical, but very lively, of the
&
whole ~~beauty of that~~ ~~Mrs. Ramsays~~ of beauty, ~~of~~ her serenity, of
the majesty with which taking her way among the dead she
had raised & fitted to her forehead ~~a~~ white flowers in a
crown.
She had never heard how she had died: only 'Suddenly'. But

but later embracing the whole character & being & world,

* MS 305 (3.237)

† A 267, B 276–7; A 268; A 269, B 278

† ~~She had~~ but for days afterwards she had seen her, from some trick of a painters eye perhaps raising to her forehead a wreath of white [flowers, & stepping with her usual quickness ~~ac~~ across the fields, among whose folds, for they were distant & the flowers very dim, she had vanished. Now Prue & Andrew went with her. Inevitably wherever she happened to be, were it London or country, her eye then, ~~clos~~ half closing sought in the real world some counterpart, something to help out her imagination; & found it in Piccadilly, in Bond Street, in the moon too, in all hills that were were dying out in the evening. ~~So~~ ~~The se~~ So now ~~she looked at~~ the sea. ~~But no.~~ ~~At the~~ All these states fade suddenly But it was always the same. ~~Nothing real is very~~ Real things ~~scarcely~~ They ~~are always disturbing~~ Dont dream, dont see, reality checked her, recalling her by some unexpected dint or shade. something she could not domesticate within her mind. ~~Thus~~ ~~Now it was the thought of~~ a little sail boat, half way across the bay. Mr.

a suggestion of the fields of death.

in

† Ramsay, recalled by a boat. She thought, that is their boat, I ~~suppose~~. It is now in the middle of the bay. They had been gone an hour & a half. And again – the weight of her sympathy made her try to call up the seats & the coil of rope, Cam's skirt, James' tie, Mr. Ramsays beautiful boots.

† A 270, B 279; A 271, B 280

224

† No one had seen her ~~surrender~~, step off her firm strip of board into the
bitter waters which are there, threatening annihilation.
*And now slowly the ~~pan~~ pain & the anger ~~of wanting, of~~
to be recalled
~~slack~~ ~~lessened,~~ (just as she was pluming herself upon having escaped
sorrow for Mrs. Ramsay ~~she was~~ recalled) lessened; ~~were created~~
~~it seems~~ of this anguish left, as ~~anditot~~ antidote, ~~as a vision~~ a not only
a
but a ~~sense of~~ calm, ~~of~~ relief from pain ~~which~~ a ~~sense of the presence of the~~
assembled
a sense of some one there, ~~in their~~ ~~consoling, whole~~, ~~escaped~~; ~~come back~~,
the
~~consoling,~~ relieved of ~~some~~ weight that the world had put on ~~them~~ her
~~consoling, & yet not~~ staying a moment, lightly & consolingly beside her,
& then (for this was Mrs. Ramsay herself, in all her beauty) raising to her
† forehead a wreath of white flowers, & ~~so disappearing~~ with which she
[went.
[For days after she had heard of her death, Lily had seen her, from
some trick of the painters eye, raising to her forehead]
† She stepped with her usual quickness across fields among whose
folds, purplish & soft, among whose flowers, ~~they~~ hyacinths, lilies,
she ~~had~~ vanished. It was some trick of the painter's eye. For days
going
after she had heard of her death, Lily had seen her thus, ~~stepping~~, with
Sights phrases they their
her wreath, the Bride of Death. ~~It~~ had ~~its~~ power to console.
Wherever she happened to be, if it were in London, or in the country,
her eyes, half closing, sought ~~in the real world~~ something to
base her vision on, she looked down the ~~lane of the~~ railway carriage,
at the windows opposite, if it were London; or in the country, at the
curve of the road, at the mass of the hill. But it always ended
in one way. ~~There~~ Something forced itself on her which she could not
~~brin~~ make submit. It burst through. It snubbed her. dont dream
dont see. It required & ~~always~~ got in the end an effort of
attention so that now, having ~~walk~~ gone to the edge of the lawn.
looked down
thinking of the white figure crossing the field, & ~~fastened~~ gazed at the sea, thinking of the fields of death, & making
† the bars of blue on the waves ~~hill~~ little hills, she was roused
by an obstinate brown spot. It was a boat. It was their
boat. It was half across the bay now. In it sat Mr.
† Ramsay, to whom she had refused her sympathy: & he had
beautiful boots, wonderful boots.

* MS 303 (3.241)
† A 269, B 278; B 279; A 270; B 280, A 271

The boat with the brown sails was now half way across the bay.
So fine was the morning ~~that~~ except for a streak of wind here & there, the
the sea & sky looked ~~as if they met without any~~ [all one,] were one ~~thin~~ substance.
~~& in~~ ~~clear blue substance~~; as if sails were stuck high up ~~in the sky~~; ~~& the~~
in the ~~clear blue substance which might b~~e sky or might be sea.
A steamer on the outskirts of the bay had ~~left a~~ drawn in the air
a great scroll of smoke, curving & circling decoratively, which
remained there, ~~far for miles~~, hanging ~~as if the~~ [in the] air were ~~gauzy~~
~~&~~ a gauze which caught things & kept them; ~~only & gently~~
~~in a gentle dreamy trance~~, in a And ~~what was~~ as happens
sometimes, when the weather is very ~~clear~~ & fine, & still the
~~high cliffs of the shore seemed to be in~~ the cliffs ~~had a~~
look[ed] as if they were conscious of the ships — & the ships ~~was~~ looked as if
conscious of the shore; ~~as if without care for human concerns,~~
~~this as if they the~~ [had] they communication together.

[Left margin: or ~~dropp~~ clouds had ~~fa~~ dropped down into the sea]

[Left margin: letting them sway a little,]

[Left margin: Aug. 17th]

Aug 17th

. . . 6 . . .

† It was awfully monotonous, & very hot too, ~~so fl~~ flapping about, waiting breeze, miles from shore, & miles from the ~~Lig~~ lighthouse, Sometimes [for a] ~~for~~ the sails sagged all entirely, & ~~at once~~ you could hear ~~the waves~~ little waves, though they were right out to sea, ~~brea~~ lapping against the [side of the boat; &] Everything in the whole world seemed to stand still [as if they were anchored in the ~~a~~ harbour.] The sun beat down. The boat became full [of odd little] of squeaks & creaks. Macalister's fishing line went plumb down into the sea. & everybody seemed very close together & ~~quite indifferent to each other,~~ terribly depressed. [The lighthouse stood still, & the hills on ~~the~~ in the distance] Then, almost before [there came a [?] dark line up the sea] [the] † sails filled, the boat would seem to ~~be~~ make an effort, ~~to~~ as if she were bracing herself together, & sure enough, [almost before] the moment after she ~~would stretch herself out & lie,~~ creak & groan & begin to move, half consciously, as if in her sleep, ~~acr~~ through the water. The fishing lines (Cam held one too) would pull aslant again, & the far away hills & the lighthouse would begin bobbing up & down ~~again~~ as before. ~~But nobody had Everyone~~ They all felt much happier, but ~~again,~~ ~~nobody said anything.~~ ~~it was ever so long since anybody had spoken.~~

Suppose that anybody had spoken, half an hour ago, James would have ~~almost certainly~~ have felt as if a little stick, something finicky & obtrusive, had been stuck into a stream which was running full tilt at top speed all one way ~~But nobody had spoken~~. His father, who was † reading, had turned ~~the~~ ~~one~~ two or three a page. That was enough. to give the stream a vicious curve. For it was all about his father; the or rather, for his father ~~having ceased had long physically had~~ long ceased to influence his thought, it was ~~about his~~ & the & when his father turned a page, it seemed ~~a very~~ sharp as if he turned it self assertive ~~way of turning a page,~~ an insolent; or insolently, or with a desire to interfere; or with his usual love of making himself ~~conspicuou~~ out an object of pity. Had he, ~~as well~~ in addition to turning a page spoken surely at last something would have happened. ~~James~~ He always had at the back of his mind an idea of a dagger which he would plunge into his father's heart.

~~But this was half an hour ago.~~ He had always*

* Cancelled in pencil; final phrase written in pencil (3.245)

† A 272, B 281; A 279, B 288; A 273, B 282

| |
|---:|
| 16 |
| 10 |
| 7 |
| £35 |

He had always had that idea of ~~plunging something it~~ striking his father, killing something violently. Powerless as he was, to strike, to kill was his [only means of ~~defying tyranny~~ breaking a ~~hole in the suffocating barricade~~ his way out to ~~the~~ freedom. ~~Yet~~ That there was something irrational in this ~~recourse, violent desire, he~~ terror, in this demand, he knew now; He knew now, even at this moment, when he sat with his hand on the tiller, looking fiercely at his father, ~~who did nothing sat absorbed in his book~~, that the thing he ~~would kill was~~ wanted to kill was not that man ~~there, but~~ the old distinguished man who was – strangely – completely ignorant of any ~~such~~ vice on his part, or any anger on his

† son's part. ~~It~~ It was a thing that descended on him: an ~~aug august devil~~, if ~~that of~~ without his knowing it. A thing that had always descended on him; that had perched on his shoulders & pecked at them all when they were children. ~~His fear was~~ And now that he was growing up, there were times when he could see ~~himself~~ his father ~~like a good~~ like a man haunted by a devil, ~~He knew~~ But now that the man himself, who walked about, quite unconscious of it, was burdened with this vulture ~~of was not~~ a thing that descended on him without his knowledge. He was There was ~~n~~ something consoling in the thought. His vices were not ~~himself~~, And ~~wh~~ at the same time that he felt this, The vulture might fly off. might leave him.

~~There was~~ And then they were bound But ~~none the less~~ when he grew up he meant to go for it; meant to track it down wherever he found it. It was a terrible vice – making people do things when they did not want to do them – interfering with free speech – for how could they say, I don't want to do this? No one dared say that. ~~Yet if t~~ The great black vulture whom he felt as a little boy pecking at his bare legs would have clouted them over the ~~wings~~ head with his wings. No doubt his fright was irrational. He was a

† gentle old man, very simple, very austere. Anyone could speak to him. Look at him reading there. Anybody would say, he has no such thought in his mind. But, James replied, ~~as he was~~ swept along by this hot current, ~~nobody who~~ if he says do that, one had to do it once feel that tyranny & you can never forget it. For he tried to ~~exe~~ make excuses, as he

† B 283; A 274

steered for the ~~violence of his own~~ feelings – ~~why, when~~ this. As he grew older he made a very queer kind of excuse. ~~He said~~ & this he felt more & more, ~~it is not him I hate, but how he~~ for he was more & more like that sin-haunted man, that man with the vulture on his shoulder; he was like him in all save that: in bareness & austerity ~~&~~ in some fanatical quality, in some ~~def giv~~ intolerance, & insight: [~~he~~ only no vulture should be

There were only two footprints on a blank space: his own & his fathers.

† allowed to perch on him.] Further, & this puzzled him more & more, ~~there~~ the vulture] Often, he felt, no two people in the world had set foot precisely there, where he came & his father came, together. But further, & this [turned?] his clearness, & puzzled him always a little, ~~what~~ he hated that man not for what he had done this morning, or last week, but for some curious terror which he had suffered at his hands years & years ago. Suppose that as a child his perambulator had been stood in a field where there was a bull; ~~for ever after suppose~~ no but that was not quite it. Suppose as a child he had seen a waggon crush a childs foot – ~~for ever after one would~~ go in ~~fear of waggons, & crushing:~~ that was more like it. A waggon man who crushed peoples feet, yet never knew ~~it. A~~ that he was doing it, & himself sitting ~~lit~~ helpless in a perambulator watching – that was

a little

~~something~~ nearer the ~~explan~~ nature of his anger & terror & the sense of helplessness that overcame him, even now, when his father came striding along the passage, knocking them up, early in the morning, to go [to the Lighthouse.

† But whose foot did he crush? ~~Where was~~ that ~~waggon~~ going What field? (What truth was there in ~~all~~ at the back of all this? (There was ~~that~~ – & here there came before ~~him~~ There was that garden. ~~A~~ that miraculous garden, where

† ~~everything to begin with~~ where before the ~~f~~ fall of the world (& he did really divide time into the space before catastrophe, & the space after) ~~all the~~ if it was not actual fine weather, at any rate nobody was gloomy like this: where there were ever so many people in & out all day long; where there was no dont & do, but simply commonsense prevailing, & freedom. where – how; he did not [know, all the colours were ~~of a kind~~ of deep. glowing kind: blue bowls; jars of great burning red – all in confusion, yet order: windows open, blinds

† A 275, B 284; B 285; A 276

flapping & in those days yellow awnings had to be spread over the doors [to prevent the paint blistering: bowls held ~~b~~ gold fish: ~~an air~~ through the warm summer air voices eagerly talking could be heard: shouts of laughter: ~~& that~~ & then, when night came, it was like a very thin veil drawn over the ~~light of the sun, still like more very soothingly~~ the ~~windows~~ daylight: it hushed & soothed; ~~peopl~~ it covered up what would be glowing there the day after.

~~But~~ But the waggon wheel must have gone over a foot there; even then: Presumably, if he were quite honest, he meant his mother.
A waggon that goes over a foot without its being anbodies* fault, yet, if [you see it done, sitting up in your perambulator, helpless, ~~the~~ it is ~~exc pain~~ torture: it is excruciating pain: ~~Very well. He was now matching it~~
It went over her once or twice.

* VW's misspelling

230

~~opening & shutting.~~ There it was, noiselessly opening & shutting
with the light of the lighthouse coming through, silently, ~~steadily all ni~~ght
~~It had been to him a symbol.~~ opening its eye, ~~of~~ shutting it, ~~in time~~ ~~until~~, [long.
~~Unfortunately~~, rhythm, until listening, seeing, the waves, the light, one [in a kind of
~~fell asleep.~~ ~~nu~~ one fell asleep, but so lightly that all the time one heard
~~through curtains thin as vine leaves~~, the waves, saw the light came & went,
~~Whose foot could he crush there?~~ At the same time, these feelings ~~were~~ [through a thin /~~th~~ cool hat, which seemed ~~to lie over~~ to cover ones the eyes
must be purely nonsensical; for there was the Lighthouse itself:
a stark grey funnel on a rock, something like an extinguisher: ~~there it was~~
~~actually;~~ There was a gulf of some sort between the world before the
catastrophe & the world after it: It was impossible to make the two [things into one.
~~Even there~~, thinking about the world before the catastrophe, he would It became more & more difficult
almost forget why he had begun to think of it.
Or, something ~~so~~ catas
He had perhaps an inkling of this ~~in & it had come to h of the~~
discrepancy ~~between the two~~ & it had come to him through his father –
[the wheel did go over one's foot even in that world.] in that world: [even
though his father's voice, manner, gesture, through something arid &
~~dry~~ & angular, which kept flourishing over one's head & telling the truth.
~~which kept~~ banging & doors; It descend~~ing~~ from the clouds & said
It would rain ~~he said~~, & it did rain. For suppose that world
~~was not~~ Perhaps that was the wheel that went over one's foot.
It rained, of course, if he said so. But the curious thing was this:
This was the ~~aston in~~ intolerable thing: this was what one
hardly felt in the world before its ruin, & always afterwards.
~~He A love of darkness.~~ ~~Truth was always on the side of~~ Rain was truth.
The ~~rain & the How he loved such things as rain~~. So deep
the difference went that it ~~became~~ seemed almost to change the
physical qualities of things. ~~All then was~~ ~~From~~ He could
~~sketch his~~ That voice descended there, in the midst of that ~~perfe~~ctly
easy ~~out~~ down right world; making it shiver & contract. leaving an
indelible trace. For it was not merely that his

Yes it was there: held him

There was really not

For it rained of course if he said so; but what was ~~w~~ worse, what was
was this ~~lasting~~ turn he gave to the whole nature of things, [setting?] {[lasting,}
so that for ever after they showed the wrong side, the grey side.
The Lighthouse had turned grey & stark. And this being the ~~noble~~
nature of truth, it was not to be gainsaid. The world before the rain {was founded on colours; &}
was founded on queer things which one could never seize again.
It ~~was~~ yet those things ~~p~~ kept ringing, ~~suddenly~~ chiming. Confusion
seemed inevitable: slash, conflict. ~~Always in~~ They would be sitting
And if it ~~was the~~ What he ~~pointed out to~~ ~~And if~~ But still
that by no means exhausted what was in his mind about this
† wheel going over a persons foot. When he said "a person" it was
always a sign to himself that he was drawing near that ~~cur~~
~~extraordinary~~ that awful [ ? ], that thing he never wanted to think about
really, since it was devastating & unnerving & ~~[ ? ]~~ terrible, terrible
to think of her – his mother, he meant; but sheered off as quick as he {[could,}
~~calling her~~ refusing to visualise her as clearly as, unfortunately, he was {[able}
† For she could be seen again, unfortunately, by going into certain {little things wh he cd not always resist doing.}
rooms, taking hold of certain little ~~box la~~ painted boxes ~~which~~ or {opening the wardrobe where her clothes used to hang.}
used to stand on her table. She could be seen by half listening sometimes
when Rose talked, in her way, coming down on <u>this</u> word, on <u>that</u>
word; & ending a laugh, with three 'ahs' which always seemed to
~~express the essence of joy, like a birds~~ last drops of some
~~ex~~ perfect happiness wrung out one by one like that – ah, ah, ah. {of [people?]}
Now somehow that wheel ~~had~~ (~~&~~ he looked so ferociously at his
father reading, hunched up, in the middle of the boat: Cam, ~~first~~
~~though she h~~ looked up from her line & noticed it) had {But it is much easier for you than for me, she thought.}
gone over ~~that persons~~ her foot, too; She was sitting by the
window. ~~She became quite~~ stiff all over. There he was {She}
standing over her, roaring, bellowing: no one He was
~~quite~~ certain that she felt the same horror that ~~they did, that~~
he & Cam did. ~~There was that horrible~~ It was some horror
that afflicted them all in the same way: ugliness: noise; violence: but
truth. And then, when he would have plunged a dagger in his
father's heart, she seemed, after sitting puzzled, for a few minutes, to
have made up her mind. She ~~would~~ snubbed him fearfully once.

† A 277, B 286; A 278, B 287

But his mother somehow got up & went away into the distance, leaving [him,

ridiculously; grasping a paper knife, impotently ~~impotent to do anything~~ & ~~he could not follow her, even now~~ & where she went & what she felt he could not, even [now,

imagine. She [tapered off?] ~~became sudd~~enly remote, & majestic; majestically into the distance.

Not a breath of wind blew. The boat was ~~like a very lazy old animal, stretching,~~ sleep~~py~~ stretched itself for a moment & then relaxed

alert, [drastic?] slackened. ~~James felt that his father~~ At any moment Mr. Ramsay might wake up in a ~~state~~ of ~~great~~ ~~an~~ annoyed, ance; &

a thought which made James think all the more intently &

rigidly ~~w~~ about his mother, as though he were stealing down stairs in bare feet, afraid of waking a watch dog, with a creaking board.

~~what happened when she left him, why she had done it, & what was she~~ [~~l~~ike;

what was she like then? ~~He knew now that the~~

There was that phantom; ~~but~~ whose approach was all set about with anguish & tears; so that, speaking soberly one must shut that ~~off~~, ~~if one wanted to~~ all off, for ~~the~~ he wished to be very exact. [When she ~~went away~~, why then ~~sh~~ did she marry him? If they were alone, what did they talk about?] He wanted to follow her from room to [room, as she went about unsuspectingly, & at last to find himself alone with her: & then to put to her question after question. He wanted to

all that colour & sun in the garden ~~master~~ encircle & master ~~the~~ this extraordinary, miraculous garden: where he kept finding himself, ~~which kept coming back~~ rather unwittingly. ~~yet so seductively~~ What, then, if she were there now, ~~would~~ one feel? And could one speak to her?

But what could one say having followed her into some little private room?

† at last, one would be able to speak the truth;

to speak the truth at last – to have done with these intolerable evasions. these lies, these subterfuges. ~~Nobody~~ ~~Someb~~

He could never be told the truth. The truth was the simplest of all things. It might be very unpleasant. "Yes, but your books are not first rate. You are not a great philosopher." Also it was amazing. Old Carmichael was, really, a figure of fun.

Also very amusing; very easy, very satisfying. To her alone, one could say it that was the source of her everlasting attraction for [him –

† B 288

234

Why she had remained all these years, in the background there, like the answer to some question, which nagged at one. What was the use now of asking it? He thought how they lived surrounded by mists & vapours. All the figures of their landscape were bulging or dwindling like figures in a crazy looking glass at a fair Ask a simple question, But why did she marry him? why, if his books were bad, could she not say so? & then, these distorted figures (he had in mind Professors & old women) ~~gave their~~ began their mopping & mowing, twisted this way & that way, until to blunder into the drawing room of a Sunday afternoon was to feel ~~ashamed~~ an insult to them all; to them both; for he had that fibre in him too: And all this, whatever they might say of her beauty & her goodness, she would not have tolerated for an instant.

And ~~he~~ the house grew steadily darker, with things that could not be [thrown away.
~~Little shrines seemed to~~ & there were shrines on in corners where
sacred objects accumulated; & ~~in~~ with their associations thick upon them,
Then there were lectures; nights of early dinners, & long
dreary drives in the heart of winter to tabernacles in the
city where his father, standing up very stiff & upright straight, proved
conclusively (but James could never keep his attention fixed)
how that ~~Go~~ there is no God; ~~but~~ & rows & rows of the ugliest
in a chill green hall people in the world sat in rows ~~sat~~ gaped ~~gaping~~ up at him. James tried to imagine his
there; she he could only see her: ~~would~~ have twitched her cloak round her, feeling the [mother cold.
What would she have done about it? But she was dead by that time. The war was beginning. Andrew was
killed. Prue died. Still his father preached. Even when his
audiences ~~had~~ did not half fill the hall, & were mostly elderly
women whose heads rose & fell, like hens sipping, as they listened, &
wrote, & then listened & wrote, still he ~~p~~ lectured. He liked some ~~one~~ of his
children to go with him. They had to say something in the cab going
back about it, or he was angry. But they had none of them anything
~~gift for paying compliments~~. to say They writhed in their agony. till
~~Then~~ Rose said in a voice ~~of anguish that it was a great success~~.
that ~~was~~ stiff with misery ~~discomfort~~. A great success. But that
did not satisfy him & the evening ended in an ~~mort~~
conflict of emotions – Often they ~~argued the matter among themselves~~
quarrelled about it among themselves: Rose ought to have
she ought have gone thought of something better to say. But why had they got to go to these
lectures when they did not want to? And then Jasper or
Cam would muddle it all up by being extremely sorry
for him.

~~Here James would~~ ~~stick to his point about~~ ~~inveriably get his back~~ despotism.

~~So was James in a sense~~. But James felt always,
~~if a person talks~~ She never talked about her feelings.
You cannot feel, if you talk as he does. about your feelings. At the same time he felt,
& ~~the~~ he felt it more & more as the audiences grew smaller,
& the war went on, & there seemed no good in anything,
~~a the~~ a respect for his father doggedly sticking it out about God &
morals. Nobody could possibly deny that he had an

a brai

an extraordinary mind. He found Jasper reading one of his books.
& they argued ~~about~~ what it was all about.
But as his father treated him ~~always~~ as if he were a bumpkin & a
booby he was not going to let on that he had ~~any sort of~~ ~~interest in it.~~

any interest whatever in it.

And ~~the type of creature who came about~~ – the atheists, the socialists, [the
The ~~pacifist the conscientious objector was~~
Besides they were detestable – the people ~~he liked~~ – the atheists the
socialists, the pacifists. There was a creature they ~~once~~ had
to stay with them, called Charles Tansley.

who liked that sort of thing

237

† Sitting perfectly still in the sun, with the boat rocking, fearing every [moment
that his father would look up, he was powerless to flick off ~~these those~~
~~this~~ these grains of misery: settling on his mind one after another.
~~And the sense of coercion would increase:~~ a band seemed to tie him there,
& his father had knotted it, & he could only escape by taking a knife &
plunging it – ~~Cam, he thought~~, At that very moment, ~~the boat~~
~~shivered~~, & the sail swung round & filled, & the boat ~~seemed~~
~~to~~ pull[ed] herself together, & ~~to creak & groan,~~ & to move ~~off~~ off
half consciously, as if in her sleep, through the water. & then lay on her [side & shot off
~~Half~~ His father, without ~~waking, raised~~ being quite aware of what was
happening ~~raised~~ raised his hand, & let it fall on his knee.
~~Instead of~~ ~~Sudden~~ly — they all seemed to ~~have lost that~~ be at a
distance again, & the fishing lines [pulled tight & began to] lay back aslant across the boat.
in ~~the wa waves~~ which began slipping quickly past them.
whelmed & Cam thought said to herself "~~wel~~ in deeper gulfs than thee",* as if she
were ~~adding up~~ [finishing something] an importunate, ~~sum, pull~~ adding it up, ending it.
Sitting upright, ~~instead of drooping~~, she said [over to herself] the whole poem as far as she
knew it

> ~~We perished each alone,~~
> But I beneath a rougher sea
> And whelmed in deeper gulfs than thee.

† She said to herself; looking at the shore, which faced her, in a sort of [amazement
~~& feeling~~ (Behind their island was another island, ~~&~~ She
was now seeing what she had never seen in her life) ~~she was~~
~~Now if anybody~~ Nothing could have excited her more.
~~Knowing~~ But it seemed to her infinitely strange. ~~Her~~ [The] island which she
idolised ~~did~~ she did not quite know why, privately, – she thought
about it in London, ~~again~~ constantly: she resented other peoples
talking about it – she was furious when people talked about
going there casually, – this place which was theirs, or
really hers, ~~had an~~ was like that. It was only that she was
seeing it from a new angle. She was seeing it for the first time
It lay like that in the sea, did it; ~~& it had~~ at ~~that moment~~
Her fishing line ~~went~~ flew out between her fingers. ~~The~~ It seemed to

* 'The Castaway,' MS 242, 267, 283, 362 (3.255)
† A 279; A 280, B 289

238

now that the boat moving quickly that she held a hold of something thrilling with life, a quivering sharp thread, which ~~connected her with all~~ went down in & the word* both in the sky & down there in the water was astonishingly queerly oddly alive & strange – unreal, this queer morning, when one saw the island for the first time.

* For 'world'? See MS 322.

He saw Cam looking who had been sunk in a kind of lethargy,
now look up, ~~rather~~ look surprised. She had forgotten all about the
thought, [contract, he

~~Her~~ This her
~~This~~ island, ~~their~~ island, the island she idolised privately so that it
enraged her when people said they had been to it, was like that then she
It lay like that on the sea, did it. It had that great boss out [thought.
flowed in
there, & then, the sea came ~~round~~ there, ~~& It looked completely~~
~~different from what~~ & went on for miles in a broad ~~glittering~~ sweep passage to the sky.
~~sweep, glittering in~~ the sun, as she had never seen it. ~~It went on~~;
on & on, out there. Where then did it go? It was a very small
† island, stuck in a vast spread of sea. ~~It seemed to her that they~~ were
adventurers, pirates, people ~~saved~~ from a wreck, & in obedience to
an
~~some queer~~ instinct which ~~lig~~ ~~could~~ ~~made~~ the ~~mo~~ made things
go quickly & gave them an interest, she supposed that they were survivors
disaster, & all depended upon her catching a fish; But [of a
automatically she began to tell herself that they were adventurers, they were a
crew, they had to live on the fish they caught. ~~She~~ [shipwrecked
But at the same time she was aware ~~of that it was an extrao~~
how this
~~even if she chose to play games, it was~~ an extraordinary occasion.
~~A~~ The island looked like that; & She did not know the points of the
But she recalled herself with a jerk. He had been annoyed with her [compass
for not knowing the points of the compass. But that was
But as if the sea were in her mind, & things fell on the top & were
whirled away, so her father's anger, & ~~his~~ her ~~ang~~ unhappiness,
at
about not knowing what to say to him & ~~James be~~ keeping
the compact with James had slipped away in that broad glittering
~~path~~, surface; & now a completely ~~fresh t view had~~ come.
It had changed again. When would it stop changing?
~~Nobody It was like an~~ There was one surprise after another.
Whether painful or pleasant, she scarcely knew. But to be
alive & to be forced, ~~for no~~ from no will of ones own – to be
cruelly, sitting in the boat looking at that island was an
astonishing fact, & her line seemed to flick with an intense
excitement, jerking & vibrating in her fingers, & increasing ~~the~~ her feeling

† B 290

240

That she was ~~somehow suspended, between alive~~ a ~~lump of matter~~ [being] which
with extraordinary capacities for feeling everything here & now – so that
disagreements & quarrels scarcely mattered – & with a future which it
was ~~almost~~ dazzling to contemplate. All this rushed upon her
when she looked up & saw how the island was shaped: how the sea
went spreading widely over there; & then when this glittering
fountain had spurted up with its insensate joy, she seemed
† to catch the falling drops & ~~to~~ with ~~re~~ new zest to apply herself to
all those ~~unsolv~~ familiar half ~~f~~ solved questions which, it
she took up at odd intervals & carried a little further; left to
~~wait on her~~ alone, & then again explored; how ~~the~~ world had come
into existence; about the ancient civilisations of Egyptians; Greeks & [Romans;
the Byzantine Empire; the ~~& then~~ whoever it might be
Shakespeare, or ~~the~~ traffic of camels & tribes marching about the
world; their conglomerations in cities, like Athens, Rome, London: &
how, du~~ring the~~se ages, ~~there stood up in the midst~~ of ~~them~~
the ~~wilds~~ Then the great men; & then the future; & then her
~~father & then~~ instinctively she submitted all the questions
wild, rapid ~~amb~~ heterogeneous [questions] which such thoughts ~~su~~
stirred in her to his judgment. Silently, of course, without
~~being able~~ ~~sayin~~ asking him about anything; for
that would have been impossible; but she had often listened to him
talking with old men, like Mr. Carmichael or Mr. Bankes, had
† ~~coll~~ made a collection of little odds & ends ~~which~~ they had said
but her father in particular which seemed to her, not ~~so~~
only ~~fo~~ in themselves, but from the way they were said,
said incontrovertible: It was his handling of things. ~~Wild~~
& ~~grotesque~~ So ~~she felt~~ order was made to come – He walked among
all the incoherent, the wild & tumultuous ideas that come to her
with a firm half serious tread, neatly brushing them into heaps here &
there, allowing no disorder, & ~~then~~ doing it tidely easily
with complete mastery. ~~A~~ ~~Then, too, he was~~
While he did this, half seriously, often with that ~~curt~~
sarcasm which sometimes made her blood boil / but sometimes
seemed to laugh at her own strangeness ~~la~~ rightly, lightly, trimly,
sagaciously, ~~there was~~ he had always about him some

[Left margin:]
which the shape of the island seemed to start flowing

half submerged half prominent territories in her mind

how one thing followed another;

saying things briefly between puffs of pipe smoke

fragments of immortal knowledge

with rage, at their rawness, their intent to hurt;

† A 281; B 291

of a piece with his grey clothes, & the pipe which he held in the air & put [to his lips
with fine clean gestures something level & grey & quiet: so that it seemed
~~to her~~ to go to him, to sit by him & collect there ~~qu~~ little sayings of his,
was to go into a [?] level ~~daylit~~ daylight: to see the whole of her
tumultuous thoughts lit up, steadily & quietly, with a peculiar
sober light – ~~the sight~~ the light that was light itself: & in that,
neither † ~~all~~ satire & harshness ~~did~~ existed, nor temper, nor annoyance, nor
his extraordinary vanity, nor his peremptoriness, nor his tyranny
(she verified each of these qualities by looking at him) but he was
as he was now (she ~~st~~ gazed at him reading that little slippery
book in the ~~mottled~~ cover ~~mo~~ mottled like a plovers egg)

† A 282

X She did not want his ~~opinion~~ particular approval of any ~~particular approval;~~ ~~thing~~ she [wanted but his general approval.

not if it had his approval, in a ~~general way~~. For she would never be able to tell him I'm thinking about the Dunes, or the stars, or the moon. end of the word,* or the stars ~~He would not share her thoughts.~~ or whatever it might be. ~~If what she thought~~ But she liked to go on with whatever was in her mind in his presence; for he ~~made the~~ what with his grey clothes & his slow definite movements & his turning over the page, or neatly ~~finishing~~ the his ~~regular~~ finishing what he was writing ( sometimes she moved about the room while he wrote & ~~the~~ other old gentleman, sat hunched in the other arm chair) ~~pleased~~ pleased her & she felt herself ~~the inhabitant of~~ to be a very exalted world; ~~even th~~ a more exalted than the ~~world~~ of the picking up odds & ends they said, ~~or not even that~~ – ~~picking up attitudes & gestures; & a~~ an atmosphere ~~of mixed~~ of tobacco & some ~~peculiar~~ smell peculiar to the room, ~~which seemed to~~ itself her a grey quiet harmonious exalted atmosphere / in which she liked to ~~pla~~ let what she was thinking about expand, ~~f~~ ~~though of course~~ like a leaf in water, & if it did well there, in his presence, while in this atmosphere of tobacco & writing & reading The Times & saying very brief things to the other old gentlemen then ~~she~~ it was all right. ~~It might be~~

It was impossible to get it quite clear. It was one of those slim slippery ideas which were always just vanishing over the rim of things. leaving a tinge of odd feeling sensation behind them; ~~& so making up~~ unpleasant, pleasant It was was it? Certainly very exciting. But of course it was against James's opinion: how he was a sarcastic brute: so vain he always brought the talk round to himself; & what was unforgivable, a tyrant. Looking at the island, with its hump & the sea beyond, she ~~visu~~ fixed in her mind, ~~as if to~~ an answer th~~ese charg~~es, ~~upon the room study where he~~ her father reading, her [father writing, ~~her father~~ Then, as if to verify ~~a memory which was~~

† ~~quite~~ that ~~thing at which came~~ feeling she looked at James; & looking at

[Left margin:] & putting a piece of blotting paper over it, & beginning another,

[Left margin:] "If it did well there" – but she ~~knew who~~

[Left margin:] being alone in the room with him.

* For 'world'? See MS 318.

† B 292

(3.265)

she remembered at once a scene of the most
terrible kind – when James stood there with his sums &
argued, & her father argued & they once dashed about the room & she
could only ~~laugh~~, drawing aside into the window, & look at the peaceful
lawn, the grass, the flowers & ~~contrast that peace~~ think of that
happiness & this entire complete misery; ~~Still, she was certain~~
~~that there~~ But then he would be very unhappy. Then he would
~~do it again. Then he would be unhappy~~: but only, James said, & she
~~did~~ agreed, not unhappy for them. ~~He was~~
~~They were all doomed to misery then. Prue died. Andrew died.~~
~~And~~ Afterwards he was unhappy but not unhappy on their account,
It ~~seemed as if~~ [But] ~~And~~ ~~then the~~ door shut, & he was alone with [James said,] the other
old ~~men, & again~~ she continued, when the door shut &
then he would be
And to help herself to an argument which told in her favour –
that he was very different with the other old man, smoking:
she glanced at him now. ~~He was~~ reading the usual little
book with covers mottled like a plover's egg.

that quiet [sublime?]

There is happiness. contrasting it with the misery here.

† What [was] ~~might be~~ in it, she did not know. It was small, & the
little pages, which were ~~a little~~ yellow seemed ~~to Cam~~ closely
written over; ~~with~~ but not with English words; &
And ~~she~~ looked up, ~~it was only~~ as a person who is ~~climbing~~
~~running, or r~~iding ~~looks u~~p who is ~~doing~~ so much absorbed in
in what he is doing that he can only ~~assure himsel~~f sp
who is absorbed in doing something ~~with his~~ now ~~then he~~
& then has to looks ~~at the~~ to keep his feet on the stairs, not to be
knocked over by an omnibus: but all their mind is on the
special thing they which feeds them – fills them with an
extraordinary indifference to everything else; & wondering what he
was reading, ~~but~~ & feeling ~~come over~~ again that ~~no~~ if
she ~~happened~~ to she would like him to approve of her thoughts,
but not to know them, she liked this so much, she felt exalted, – she
felt again the tobacco & the peculiar smell of the study, & heard
him say, between ~~his~~ puffs of his pipe she looked back over the sea.
to the other old gentleman – & thought how, ~~of~~ Macalister ~~was say~~
that the third ship, sank there. With the men "[scarcely in the rigging?]'
[It had gone down into] those blue grey waters.

& it vexes them, & escape then. – they chase it, & they

| | | |
|---|---|---|
| 250 | 21 | ~~221~~ |
| 280 | 7 | 236 |
| 2000 | 14 | 221 |
| 440 | | 15 |
| 64,000 | | |

234*

She had her doubts. She thought that he was sorry, if not precisely them, then for – everything; the poor, the working people. He ~~would~~ [for way of shuffling money into beggars hands; half shutting his eyes ~~as he~~ [had a ~~& then she felt~~, as if it were useless; ~~as if no~~thing could be done; or not [~~did~~ it; that still – And then he would be more than usually irritable, but not [like ~~with~~ ~~on his~~ own account; on account of ~~the whole world~~, everything, ~~And then~~, ~~Often she~~ felt him ~~withdrawn~~

he knew that.

their account or on his acount

For instance, didnt they once feed a dog on cake? That annoyed him

But he ~~had no feeling for~~ ~~was~~ never saw what anyone was feeling ~~That could not be denied~~. Yet That was mostly true.

But the he was infinitely old. ~~h~~ ~~He~~ ~~wa~~ It was inconceivable how old he how much he had left behind which they knew nothing of. [was;

of course James always revered a peculiar quality in his father – what he never derided or criticised: the thing they had in common.

* Reference to typescript page number? Ink same as text. (3.269)

26th August

7.

on it;
† The sea with scarcely a stain, thought Lily Briscoe; the sea ~~like a great spread~~ stretched like green blue silk: the sea summing up, completely
& [calming
taking to her indifferent heart ~~the city, the~~ shore, ~~all~~ strife, all turmoil,
~~& So one made phrases~~ ~~But directly one was conscious of making a phrase, it ceased to have any meaning~~.
So one made phrases; but directly one she thought, turning away from
[the view
over the bay. Yes, she thought, considering how irrational most of our
an
feelings are, & how inevitably even she, ~~elderly~~ spinster [~~shed~~?] of 44, ~~mad~~ was at the mercy of phrases, [& could not extricate herself from their dominion] ~~of waves of feeling~~, ~~very likely~~ that is their boat. ~~Even with the little wind there~~ is, presumably they will reach the Lighthouse by lunch time. But ~~that did not what~~ impressed
† her as ~~she stood looking~~ down into the Bay, was that having gone on this little expedition, ~~his~~ he became at once ~~(as an~~ (~~all~~ the weight of her sympathy still made her mind rest on Mr. Ramsay)
~~set~~ ~~rounded~~ & completed, & part of the eternal nature of things.
Mrs. Ramsay was that now.
[She turned to her easel with a sigh.]
~~As~~ Mr. Carmichael clawed up his book from the ~~grasp,~~ grass, with a gasping grunt which ~~susg~~ suggested infinite contentment

from sid

all the strife, & all the

& how directly one became conscious of making them they burst, having gone

"Stretch out a hand & theres a book" he seemed to say.
And there was a book; & he ~~settled into it~~. But ~~no,~~
& he [snuggle?]
~~as for her~~ he ~~spread it~~ out & settled into it. Otherwise, ~~there was~~ no ~~movement, no sound or sign of life whatever~~. It was all very
they must
† quiet. They must be up, out of bed; but nobody appeared at the
[window.
They used to make off, directly a meal was done, to their own devices. But it was all right, like that; all in keeping with the unreal early morning hour. ~~One only said~~ "unreal" because, ~~as if~~ people were not speaking; were not running violently into each other, ~~with~~ & making all those odd violent noises which after such collisions they do make. Images came to her,

And he stretched out

† A 284, B 293; B 294; A 285

& say oh good morning – What a fine day! Are you going to be so bold as to sit in the sun? Jaspers hidden the chairs! Those wretched children! Still [ ? ]!" Instead of that ✓

~~looking again at the B bay~~, of Mercifully, things were [like this]
[sometimes:
completely unreal: very exciting. Mercifully one was not always
[knocking ones
† head violently against some solid old lady – One glided on ~~between,~~
~~took the~~ shook one's sails ~~out~~ (~~she too w~~ she was looking at the
bay where there was a good deal of movement : little fishing boats
starting: a steamer ~~had was~~ majestically circling the bay)
out
shook ones sails, & took ones way ~~out~~ into that no-man's
that
territory; ~~the this~~ empt~~iness that was after all~~ land;
empty it was not; but full to the brim. Here & now, it was full to the
brim; ~~& one wanted time & loneliness to shake ones sails out in this~~
She seemed to be standing up to the lips ~~in the most~~
in ~~sensation, in thought~~; in ~~up to the stood i~~ was ~~swimming~~
~~moving in th~~at ~~astonishing intoxicating~~ shining air
~~which~~ it; to move & float; to sink; – yes, for these waters were
all
† unfathomable; naturally, since time had spilled into them, & ~~lives~~ –
many many lives – In them was all that beauty of hers. ~~&~~ a
all those children of hers: her attitudes & thoughts; his too;
~~all~~ of the old washer woman & her basket; waifs & strays of ~~ro~~ sounds &
[colour
miraculously caught up; ~~& colour~~; & ~~florid fiery~~ red eyes
hot pokers: ~~the~~ a ~~grey green leaf: &~~ the purple of a clematis:
In this was ~~no w~~ the air & breath of life: its
an air that was finer than any other; a sharper passion; &
where she stood, ~~slaped~~ & whether one
& what was to stop one, on either side?
& it was inexhaustible, this world they ~~had left~~, ~~them~~
~~fired with more~~ & whether she went this way or that way
~~there met her lips & this stinging~~ it stung her & encompassed her, &
~~it seemed to her~~ that she could pass from ~~one~~ end of the world to
~~another~~, ~~down corridors of time~~, ~~past,~~ or & & quickened her eyes into a
~~peculiar~~ brightness & ~~f~~ stung her lips ~~into a~~ with a peculiar sharpness.
And one could ~~g~~ pass thus over & round & here & there.
the
~~And perhaps~~ It was some inkling of this which ten years ago,
standing almost on this very spot, had made her ~~so treasure the~~
~~suddenly aware. Suddenly~~ she had said she thought she must be in
love with the place. Love, they said, ~~was the~~ moved the stars & the

† B 295; A 286

Love did all sorts of queer things probably.
To the lover, ~~not~~ to ~~whom it is not granted to be~~
might be the
So there might be lovers, differing from the sexual lovers; who,
standing, for ~~example,~~ painting, ~~or~~ might, as lovers are said to do,
might be the power, to select, ~~from~~ might be the power
to choose here & there, in obedience to an instinct, of course,
old woman, leaf, ~~chi~~ child at the window, & endowing
them with a ~~[ ? ]~~ wholeness not theirs in life,
objects of love, & centre,
† make of them ~~a~~ one of those globed, ~~th~~ centres of thought,
crystals of emotion over which for ever & ever
thought loves to play.

† B 296

chair 35/–

paint 5.9
[nt. gw?] 12
" 12

nation 8
[Cam?] 12
[Brooks?] 16
———
36

2.10

248

~~The~~ Her eyes were still on the brown sail of Mr. Ramsay's boat. Insensibly however, she they left that ~~minute~~ particular speck, & ~~rested~~ began as she watched the horizon to see how the sky was changing, & the sea changing, so that a [slightly, view which a moment before had seemed ~~trans~~fixed in pure calm was now vaguely unsatisfactory. The wind had blown the ~~steam~~ trail of steam ~~all~~ about; & there was something wrong in the spacing of the ships.

~~That, too, needed to be taken into the mind & left to~~

Rolled about in

In the depths of winter in the Brompton Road she would see it as it [should be seen, ~~no doubt~~. again rightly. ~~Drop Dropped into~~ her mind, she ~~wo~~ she would, unconsciously, ~~separate & separate~~ arrange, it ~~&~~ order it, & clean it of superfluities.

~~The~~ ~~So with But the~~ which indeed was what one did with all life ~~this~~ too. (So that it was only in absence, after some time had passed, & one had recovered from the horrid shock dealt one by ~~facts~~ what she thought turning towards the house again, & seeing ~~at~~ close to her feet Mr. Carmichael reading; & then her canvas; So far It annoyed her that she had done so little work.

one cleaned it of superfluities later in the Brompton Road perhaps. But here at the moment things were too confusing.

~~This crud~~ The morning had been full of interruptions: She could not rid herself of this concern about Mr. Ramsay She kept looking over her shoulder & wondering where they got to, what they were doing. ~~Yet~~

She must return to that ~~endeavour; though it needed a great~~ screwing up of her faculties. She must

the two forces.

† She could not achieve that razor edge of balance between the ~~two great forces~~ ~~force of~~ what was happening here, on the lawn; & ~~there~~ Those two forms of life which

~~She wanted nothing that she could~~ She looked at her picture. There was something wrong in the picture, too. ~~A line, a~~ The line of the wall wanted breaking there? ~~a~~ was the mass of the tree too heavy there? She felt obscurely distressed, disordered in some part of her own balance; so that from experience she knew ~~that it would be~~

† A 287

how there was nothing for it but to shut one's eye to that picture for a [time;
wait; ~~miserable~~ in such patience as she could command: trying to
understand what her problem was.
*What was her problem then? She was trying to get hold of something
which evaded her. It evaded her when she thought of the
~~view~~ picture, & when she thought of Mrs. Ramsay.
† Phrases came. Visions came. But what she wanted to get hold of
was that very jar on the nerves, the thing itself before it has been
made anything: the germ, in painting, in knowing, of all art &
affection. Get that again, & start afresh, was all the advice
† she could give herself. But one got nothing by soliciting
urgently. One got only a glare in the eye from looking at the
line of the wall, or thinking Mrs. Ramsay often wore
velvet shoes, & a ~~shawl.~~ green shawl if the weather was raining.
A † Miserable inefficient machine the human apparatus, ~~for~~ painting & caring
she thought, ~~always~~ always breaking down at the critical
moment ~~capricious incalculable~~. The whole machine
gave out: & then where was one?
† Well here on the lawn, she thought, kneeling to squeeze out a
a little more grass green, though she did not intend to
~~paint any~~ paint – only to do a ~~litt~~ little donkey work at
the corner of the canvas. Kneeling on the lawn, which, she
made herself observe, was rather hard, for it had been on the
whole a dry summer. There were colonies of plantain spotting it
about which ought to be killed. [One of the children used to be sent
round with a] The rooks were ~~roll~~ flying about in a
~~way which suggested autumn~~. decoratively making black crescents.
with their wings; scimitars ~~in~~ with the air
And ~~then there was Mr~~.
† she would have liked to attract Mr. Carmichaels notice
somehow; ~~or even~~ to have rifled his stock of ideas, or
started one of those aimless ~~pu~~ pointless pleasant
conversations ~~which~~ all about nothing.

* MS 332 (3.279)
† B 297; A 288; A 287; A 288; B 298

~~But~~ The old man had become rather famous lately. ~~His name~~ ~~verge~~ His name ~~was~~ appeared ~~in papers~~ girt about with some romance in [newspapers. People were beginning to say that Mr. Carmichael who had always been known to a few enthusiasts, as ~~one~~ ~~among~~ one ~~of~~ the finest translators ~~of~~ in our [literature time: & so on. ~~He had written also a~~ few essays & ~~some~~ a book of his travels was going to be re-printed. & in view of this

† ~~But~~ he looked just the same, heavy & slow & benignant.

It was said that a book he wrote in the 70s about traveling in Burma was a masterpiece

But she ~~wo~~ could believe it — ~~she had liked his leisurelyness; his~~ independence; & ~~the his one great~~ He had that quality; & ~~She knew one curious little~~ was true fact about him: also this: that he "had been heart broken at Andrew Ramsays death". The phrase had come to her casually from some~~one~~body who knew him. ~~They s~~ in his home. ~~They said~~ he thought all the world of Andrew of him: She had a picture of him marching through Trafalgar Square the day ~~the news~~ Andrew's name was among the killed, grasping a stick ~~with his old hat pulled over his eyes.~~ But he was almost entirely silent; ~~or only said n out~~ probably never said anything to any~~one, but let~~ certainly never had never ~~said a word of the least~~ importance to her. ~~Yet~~ People handed things round, like this, about him now. No one had ever heard him say then.

~~And~~ Yet this was one of the most important friendships of her life — ~~They had never He They had never spoken to each other, but~~ Perhaps they never would say anything.

† They would go on eternally passing each other with a sort of mumble on stairs, sitting side by side on lawns exchanging views about the train service & the boat service & the weather. She had never even read his translation, except a line or two in quotations; & then she had recognised the quality she had always felt ~~when he~~ something very impersonal & extremely moving, about a Camel & the desert: something it was apparently very simple. but if she had known anything about writing she would have been sure that this was the thing that lasted for ever. something simple but everlastingly strange.

† A 289; B 299

~~251~~

But ~~owing~~ to the extraordinary composition of the human brain; she was
~~Yet in some way~~ these ~~friends~~
The little ~~that one knew of people, could be extremely~~
She had a phrase – she had a picture. But both were extremely fertile.
He had the quality of ~~which~~ belongs to those who during a life
of being ~~a ver~~ hospitable to ideas. What one thought about him
[germinated. Thus, he was a
figure of some humour. ~~One~~ Took opium, never knew the day of the
[week; &
superficially the prey – the gentle unworldly prey of landladies: gave his
socks to his hostess to wash: had ~~litt~~ the simplest ideas of ~~social~~
[AH] & drifted about the world, lodging

251

† *~~What was the problem~~?

~~to~~

its ~~own~~
& trust that in ~~its some~~ inscrutable way, the brain would ~~find offer~~ solve
[the problem
spontaneously ~~some~~ if ~~it~~ one ~~forgot all about it~~ did not ask it

A miserable & inefficient machine, she thought, ~~this our~~ the human
at the
apparatus for painting, or feeling; it was always breaking down; critical
moment.
~~at the the The whole machine~~ gave out; one could neither think
was
† nor feel, & then where is one?

Here on the lawn, she thought, kneeling on the hard dry turf, &
squeezing ~~out~~ some olive green which could ~~safely~~ be applied
back of the
safely in one corner of her picture. Here on the ^world, ~~am I sitting~~
a Ma
~~Lily Briscoe~~, ~~spinster~~, aged 44. [~~How many~~ million & million
such creatures ~~was~~ the world was carrying round & round on its
back at that moment? There were several little colonies of
plantains, she observed; & the rooks were swerving about
making black crescents & scimitars ~~& in the air~~. with their
wings in the air.

As for old Mr. Carmichael, lying there with his feet on a
campstool, she ~~wondered about him~~ liked to be in his company on
this exalted station (for she could not shake herself free from the
sense that everything ~~was hap~~ this morning was happening
for the first time & the last time; as a traveller, even
out of
† though he is half asleep, knows, looking ~~from~~ the train window
& even rubbing a clear space in the clouded glass so to look,
must look now
that he ~~will nev~~ is now ~~seeing some town or h mountain~~
~~for the only time in his life~~, for he will never see that
particular town or mountain again.

She would never see ~~it again~~, Mr. Carmichael again, perhaps.
He was growing old. He was growing famous, she remembered, ~~for~~
smile
with a ~~little~~ amusement (perceiving how his slipper hung from
his foot) for his translations; & a book which he had written about

* MS 329 (3.285)

† A 287, B 297; A 288; B 298

252

† his travels in Persia forty years ago. And somebody had said that when he heard of Andrew Ramsay's death he had lost all interest in [life. Perhaps he had walked about the streets ~~holding~~ grasping a large stick. He had walked ~~about~~ up & down the room, he had ~~drop~~ let his pipe fall, he had gaped & opened a book, & ~~one by one,~~ the leaves had turned over, by themselves? ~~He had always been~~ ~~But he was almost entirely silent.~~ [She did not know. They seldom spoke, except about the train service, & the ~~weather~~ boat [services, & the weather. She had only read scraps of his poetry quoted in reviews. ~~For~~ But ~~owing to~~ without reading it she knew how it ~~must of course be~~ it went, slowly & sonorously; ~~with~~ it would have ~~great~~ his ~~that~~ quality ~~which she respected felt in him, something~~ be seasoned, & mellow; as it ~~all~~ ~~sn~~ it would be mature. ~~like~~ An enormous deal of thinking would have gone to the making & be completely free from

† ~~pettiness or prettiness.~~ There might indeed be ~~something st~~ clumsy ~~about it.~~ Had he not always lurched rather awkwardly past the drawing room window, with a newspaper under his arm, trying to avoid Mrs. Ramsay, whom, for some reason he did not much like? She would always try to make him stop & talk. He would bow to her. He would halt unwittingly & bow profoundly.

Annoyed that he ~~did~~ ~~had~~ want her ~~did not like her,~~ Mrs. Ramsay would offer all sorts of things: ~~ask questions: was he~~ coats, rugs, newspapers.

† ~~But it was no good.~~ There was some quality in her which ~~evidently repelled him.~~ he did not like. He did not like, perhaps, her masterfulness. She was so authoritative, so direct; ~~&~~

A ~~slight~~ noise drew her attention to the drawing room window – the squeak of the ~~window~~ hinge, as the light breeze played on the window.

There must have been people who disliked her very much, Lily thought. There must have been people who thought her

† A 289; A 290, B 299; B 300

too sure of herself – too drastic. Then she had no religious beliefs. Then [she
† was reserved. *And (to go back to Mr. Carmichael) one could not imagine her ~~painting~~ standing painting, sitting reading a whole morning on the lawn. It was unthinkable. Without saying a word to anyone, the only token of her errand a basket on her arm, she went off, to the town, to the poor, ~~took to some taking a flowers food. flowers clothes~~ There to sit, in some ~~st~~ sordid little bedroom; – Often & often Lily had seen her go
† silently off with her basket; she had noted her return.) She had thought eyes that are closing in pain & despair have looked
† upon you. It was an instinct, like the swallows for the south, the artichokes for the sun, ~~makin~~ turning her ~~often~~ infallibly to the human race, making her seek her nest ~~there~~ in its heart. Oh ~~no~~, she could ~~ha~~ not have stood painting with a woman dying. And there was always a woman dying.

(unconscious as she & always was of her own appearance)

She thought Beauty has been with them there.

And this was perhaps a little distressing to Mr. Carmichael. & to herself, too, ~~of~~ secretly. ~~To stand painting~~ – ~~to sit reading~~ while a woman dies a mile off in want –
~~They both distrusted action? No~~: ~~They would~~ Some notion was in both of them about the ineffectiveness of action; the supremacy of thought. Her going was a reproach to them; yet they felt, the care of the world was more truly theirs than hers: or they felt, distress at their own impotence to help; or the usual everlasting sorrow ~~which dogged the~~ of the safe at the predicament of the insecure. ~~In that~~
on the edge of that blue sea, in the breast of this moorland, there is the eternal woman dying in rags. But Tansley's contribution to the problem was futile in the extreme. Except for that brief moment when he threw ducks & drakes, & ~~seemed like other people~~, ~~what could~~ & Mrs. Ramsay wrote letters, what could be more insufferable ~~than~~? The one word 'I'' – he repeated it over & over again. As for his opinions to her dying day she would not foget that he paid 2d for his

* MS 276

† A 291; B 301; A 292

(3.289)

tobacco. Increasingly grubby (she had heard him at a meeting) he was no doubt the most high principled of them all: slept out ~~d~~ of doors all the year round; had no maids. Incapable of telling a lie, ~~he~~ Her own pictures she believed were more to the good of the race than his preaching – though if they were not painted over, they were given away shamefacedly, hung in the servants bedroom.

10
20
12
---
42

[336 is a fragment of VW's essay 'De Quincey's Autobiography.' See appendix C.]

256

1st Sept

suddenly

And he had made her realise the ~~hatred which people have for each other~~. profound hatred which separates man from man. (But she ~~would~~ lost this, walking home along the Strand.)

† Then, ~~by, a~~ suddenly the old cork or whatever it was began bobbing up & down among the waves: & this strident arid ~~rauco ra~~ red faced man on the platform became an angular boy who with all his faults put by out ~~of a scholarship~~ his earnings enough to educate a little sister. Enormously to his credit, said Mrs. Ramsay, looking for her spectacle case among the pebbles. Oh dear, what a nuisance, lost again! – ~~Mr. Tansley~~ ~~A thousand thanks~~

And he put his chin back against his collar & smiled

Don't bother, Mr. Tanley.* I lose thousands every summer." And he let the exaggeration pass. One must suppose that, on ~~som~~ walking back to the house again, or ~~one~~ on one of those expeditions which took a whole day to some far away spot on the hills ~~where a bonfire had to be lit to boil a~~

† ~~kettle, &~~ he had confided in her – The extreme egotism of young men assured her. She was singularly tolerant. Why, here was Lily helping herself to Mrs. Ramsay's tolerance to rectify her own warped & ~~prejudi~~ narrowed vision. ~~For he had~~ after all this time! For of course nobody was in the least like ~~what~~ the her

Her idea of Charles Tanly.* He was a grotesque – a scarecrow. ~~Could one embody~~ served ~~in her mind~~ the purpose of a whipping boy. She found herself ~~flagg~~ flagellating his lean sides with sarcasm when she was out of temper. But in time he became unrecognisable for a man at all. He became a mere forkshaped ~~ru~~ root. ~~Th~~ a symbol – a ~~whereas,~~ Indeed, people tended so to shrivel in one's mind; unless one were always at pains to freshen them up, or ~~to~~ made use of some third pair of eyes. to ~~gi to~~ give ~~them a~~ see the other side with depth. Even so – well, it was shameful, considering the extreme

* VW's misspelling

† A 293, B 302; B 303

(3.295)

vividness of ~~ones own~~

She stopped. She recognised that the current of feeling was ~~being~~ flowing in her veins again after its lapse – ~~her~~ ~~the solution of her~~ her [~~turned~~ problem [The extreme vividness, she murmured, &] might at any moment occur, if she kept on ~~steadily~~ steadily working at the background. ~~She dipped her br~~ush in green paint again. in the background

& fertilising

might solve itself

The vividness of her own sensations, standing there looking at the wall, ~~the window, the sky~~, was enough: but then, she reflected, one knew very little about other peoples sensations. ~~The fatal barrier~~ There were [barriers between herself & Charles Tansly* was this: fatal barrier: that he hated [pictures, never looked at a thing. ~~She~~ ~~She never was no good at thinking~~ – Race, religion, ~~co~~ rank, ~~whatever~~ any other obstacle was soluble; but how could one grope about in the mind of a person who neither saw nothing; or had ~~no~~ h any inkling ~~of the~~ ~~that there~~ exists of the whole structure which rises on top of a sight like that – (the wall & the window & the sky) or ~~has any guesses~~ what it implies what it asserts. Her love of painting had with its commands, its prohibitions, its assertions, its ~~grip of the mind~~? The antagonism was eternal – ~~this~~ they were would threaten her world. So he From that sprang his "Women cant paint", & her derision of the pushing shoving self-assertiveness of the male. ~~Passing~~ & they squabbled whenever they met. – presumably they had each a liking for the other, & some desire for the others good opinion. And she did

it was too much perhaps It became [ ? ] , standing in this glare, to resume

mutually destructive.

* VW's misspelling

She did not deny ~~for a moment~~ that he had a brain.

¶ ~~Paul Rayley had none~~.

~~How be sure, she wondered, of anybody~~?

And then the ~~interpretations one~~ wild leaps one made, the

~~re~~-meaning one attached to some negligible gesture –

a pause, a tone of voice; some little phrase which was spoken without

any consciousness that ~~it was the very lifted a curtain &~~

~~it was it was an extraordinary revelation: & then~~ the

of the uses it would be put to

it would be treasured & used & kept perpetually: the glimpses one

had; & the hours of barrenness; & the moments of dissatisfaction;

& the compulsion – none the less ~~to be forever in some relation~~,

to keep close to ones kind; the stress that was laid on them ~~all to be~~ all

~~forever~~ striving after something, ~~were it a sinless state, a~~ perfection

some ~~at~~ act that was

~~republic, or a picture such as she imag~~ined; but what? Here a

republic without ~~war or~~ crime: ~~here the~~ abolition of capital

punishment; a philosophy; & their attempts at union

& their flying apart again; ~~& then~~ it was all queer enough

& ~~the same sometimes of~~

~~come to think of it~~ & & the wonder, which with years grew rather

~~than diminished at~~ the

& the extraordinary silence in which the day went by, the rare, the life passed

diminishing, silence ~~surroun~~ separating one from another,

& the ignorance & the narrow bounds that ~~were~~

& the twist, given, rightly or wrongly, to the whole fabric

& ~~how in an instant one divined~~ what

& the glimpses one had – ~~oh it was wonderful enough~~, whatever

ones fortune, to be set down, ~~here or in the midst~~

it was ~~w~~ enough to be set

~~here, & even in the solitude of her~~ in the midst of all this; &

even in her ~~spec~~ solitude she could call back

258*

† So perhaps, when she thought of Mrs. Ramsay she [was?] was out there, too.
~~Beauty was a~~ To ~~see~~ know her one needed twenty dozen pairs of eyes
at least. ~~Even so, how~~ or ~~perhaps it would be better to shut ones~~
One wanted some secret ~~ins~~ sense, ~~very sensitive~~, fine as air, ~~[?]~~
which ~~stealing~~ stole in through ~~the~~ keyholes; some long tongue of infinite
~~elasticity & sensibility which could elasti~~
~~which to~~ where surround her as she sat knitting or reading with
† an atmosphere which took into itself & imparted ~~all~~ the
imaginations; all that went through her mind: what the wall
meant to her, & the colour & the window: the sound of the
waves breaking. What ~~b~~ solitary beach did they not
break upon in her consciousness? And then to know
what stirred & trembled when the children cried, cricketing,
How's that? How's that?", to feel the first
tremor of laughter, & find its origin; & to be sure what
~~cliffs of cut cliffs, or boundaries~~, be aware, seriously
~~& con~~ how the whole vista of her mind had in it certain
~~marks or~~ & what those grave outlines were, which
presumably stood sentinel over the come & go of her
~~sensations~~ mind at work? ~~All that she thought in solitude~~
~~Why did she, after all~~, And then ~~how was one to~~
~~re capture anything when he~~ Mr. Ramsay passed.
What a trail of curious feeling went through the whole of her,
& sometimes seemed to rock her in profound agitation
upon its breast; ~~when he spoke~~, ~~severely to James~~; He had only to speak one word, or once or
said nothing even; as if now & again the presence of her
† husband was enough to to stoop & give her his hand up out of a
chair & suddenly, Lily thought, she understood, ~~with~~
how ~~they had~~ once when they were both young, she had
thought to herself (adored & courted as she must have been) surely

[Left margin: so that it would pass through / caught up gathered up into its texture the glittering particles – (Lily had seen her look up ~~on~~ once to it) / She could remember]

* VW numbered two pages 258.

† A 294; B 304; A 295

Theres that yes:

trusty strange man; & it had come over her, as she took his hand to get out of the boat & land on the island where they were picnicking at some summer party, that she would say ~~for the sat~~

† the word now, which she had hesitated to say. It would ~~[ ? ]~~ be said quite simply without demonstration ~~of feeling~~ on her side. ~~But the devotion, the trust the~~ And he would row her back; & lose his temper with the lock man; ~~& then, & then~~ ~~But Mrs. Ram~~ ~~But she would~~ ~~And~~ And as she had & ~~it did not matter: &~~ one supposed time after time, in secret, the same thrill – something peculiar ~~with~~ to them both – had passed between them: obviously it had, for in the rough & tumble of daily life, there was always the sense of ~~which so much added to the richness,~~ these little repeated blows: one thing falling there where another had been; which ~~pe~~ ~~made one feel~~ making their relationship fuller, ~~& richer.~~ deeper. ~~B~~ Sad, serious, at any rate, it must have been too.

which gave such a thickness an ~~at~~ air to the atmosphere such a quality *like an echo*

* Written in pencil

† B 305

260

One had to guess at all that had been ~~between~~ them by realising ~~to the full scenes like that~~. such things – looks & gestures; a his smile at her; sitting at the other end of the table, when one of the ~~did~~ something & the silences ~~severe or resentful~~ which sometimes fell [children [between them.

said

It was not a marriage in wh. † For one could scarcely simplify life out into an eternity of bliss. Weaving & grinding it must have been: ~~eight children~~ to bear bring up educate: eight children. Certainly something always seemed to be on the point of There was no ~~usual~~

He ~~was always about to find~~ Oh no. About eight in the morning ~~he would slam his bedroom~~ door. might slam: Or there would be something in the Times. or a A letter might explode on his plate. There ~~And~~ all through the house there would be a sense of of doors slamming & blinds ~~fult~~ fluttering as if a gusty wind were blowing & people scudded about trying in a hasty way to fasten catches & make things shipshape. firm; ~~with an expression of~~ looking ~~very m~~ deeply concerned; ~~on their faces as if they~~ with ~~serious faces which~~ & yet a of ~~mock~~ ~~solemnity for there was~~ yet only arrived & she collided with Paul Rayley in the passage once & they laughed & laughed! ~~A~~ The scenes were absurd. ~~For instance, a~~ because it was so fantastic, so absurd; ~~that a~~ a great man ~~could not tolerate a earwig in his porridge, but sent the plate~~ sending his plate flying through the air into the rhododendron bushes. ~~Some thought that~~ There was a earwig in the [somebody?] milk. ~~Meeting them in the passage, he had~~ A earwig in Mr. Ramsays milk. Other people might have centipedes, & But he had built up around him a fabric of such majesty that a earwigs the very ~~was a~~ were monsters: H~~e had made himse~~lf ~~awful as a~~ He had swelled, ~~he had~~ stiffened, he ~~had become~~ a was no longer ~~Then~~ he met them outside his study door, & ~~to atone for a display~~ & ~~he was charming~~. ~~very very simple~~; taking them in showed them his book of of birds; or his immense map of the Hebrides. or ~~his~~ some curious instrument which he kept in his study & never allowed anyone

no one knew why.

Then

but [unevenly?] †

And in his sense of the outrage done him, scowling, gesticulat- [ing he was sublime.

† A 296; B 306

to touch for ~~measuring~~

But it tired her ~~wor~~ cowed her, a little, / – the plates whizzing, & the doors slamming. And there would fall between them sometimes long ~~tense~~ rigid silences. when, in a state of mind which Lily resented for her, half plaintive, half resentful, she seemed unable to surmount the tempest ~~with her usual dig~~nity, or to laugh, as they laughed; but perhaps concealed something. ~~There~~ might be she could not brave another plate in the air, or fist on the table, ~~but m & so let it slide — the~~ hid the letter, or ~~said the le bill,~~ said nothing about or the unpleasant fact – (~~The wind had ripped the lead off the roof & a~~ So ~~the earwigs grew in size,~~ & he ~~& so then at last, becoming aware of the & then~~ But at last, ~~often very late at night~~, he would ~~break through with his~~ demand ~~(being very puzzled genuinely, & so~~ an explanation. He would hang ~~about~~ stealthily about the places where she was – roaming under the window where she might be ~~buy~~ busy

† writing letters or reading aloud; ~~(&~~ & she would pretend ~~to~~ not to see him; ~~until~~ & he would ~~become cra~~ turn crafty & & ~~wary & sly~~, ~~completely master of his temper & his moods yet be~~ completely master of his own temper, & try to win her so; & turn ~~crafty &~~

† still she would hold off, now asserting some of those prides ~~& airs of dignity a~~ & airs ~~of consciousness~~ which generally she was utterly without, due to her of beauty, of sex, to her charm, & ~~would~~ was not to be found alone, but had always some Paul Rayley or William Bankes or Minta Doyle at her side; & at length, standing outside the group, ~~like~~ the very figure of a lean watch dog, a ~~hungry & passionate wolf which sees~~ a famished ~~but~~ wolf, he would say her name, once, only ~~in a t~~ for all the world like a wolf barking ~~in the snow, but with~~ still she held back a in the snow; & he would ~~ba~~ say it once more, ~~but~~ & this time with something of menace in the tone, which would arouse ~~the~~ some deep instinct in her, making her drop her trivialities at once; but

[Margin: (in a ~~tacity~~ tacit despair)]

[Margin: the difficulty,]

[Margin: turn crafty – watchful;]

† A 297; B 307

~~still~~

& then they would have it out presumably:

But in what attitudes & what words? Such an enormous dignity was naturally theirs, in this relationship, that turning away with Minta or Paul, ~~she wo~~ they would ~~no mor~~ hide their curiosity, even their alarm (for there was a greatness in the relationship between the Ramsays which made all these glimpses of it, naked, alarming) picking flowers, ~~playi~~ throwing balls, chattering gossip, ~~while~~ until – well, it was time for dinner, & there they were, he at one end of the table, she at the other, just as usual.

5
300
~~50~~
20
15
~~3~~

† So they would talk as usual. All would be as usual, save only
for some quiver of gaiety? tenderness? in the air which ~~kept~~ went & came
between them as if the usual sight of the family dinner table
had ~~freshened~~ itself in their eyes after that hour among the pears &
~~the~~ plums. Especially, Lily thought, Mrs. Ramsay kept glancing at her
eldest daughter, Prue,. She sat in the middle between brothers & sisters,
always occupied, it seemed, even when she ~~did nothing,~~ was still & silent in seeing that
nothing ~~suddenly~~ happened wrongly. ~~She Prue~~ She must have blamed herself
terribly for that earwig in the milk, Lily thought. She went
quite white. She hated scenes. And now, her mother seemed to be
~~chiding her~~, making it up to her; ~~&~~ ~~to~~ assuring her that everything was
well ~~ag~~ again; ~~& from the~~ to be promising her that same
happiness — She had enjoyed it for less than a year
however. She had let the flowers fall from the basket —

taken on a meaning

(Oh Lord, oh Lord, how did any woman ever paint a picture then she thought.)

all right now

For that was how she went, Lily thought, screwing up her eyes
& standing back to ~~get~~ look once more at that picture; & ~~her mind~~
with all her faculties in a trance; feeling very still, & helpless; & yet her stillness had an intense speed in it
Another ~~ph~~ vision that; forming the instant she heard of Prue's
† death. She dropped all her flowers, scattered them & tumbled
them / , & ~~&~~ reluctantly & hesitatingly, ~~but~~ — How could one
wish to die at ~~twety~~ twenty-five? — but ~~gathering her~~
unquestioningly — had she not the faculty of obedience, ~~that~~
~~in~~ to perfection, dignified not submissive? — ~~Prue~~ She went;
Andrew went. [In what fields did they walk now?
For ~~all~~ they were young. One didn't imagine that they]
They went. ~~But it seemed to her~~ Down fields, across valleys;
white, flower strewn. That was how she would have painted it.
She imagined the austere hills; & the hoarse waves:
The window at which she was looking was whitened by some
dress behind it; oh & shoved open! — a re-arrangement which
did not greatly matter: & now ~~someone w was trailing down, so~~ over
~~the steps~~ There was some one there.

in the sun

† A 298, B 308; A 299, B 309

264

It might be Rose; it might be Nancy; it might be that old woman, whats [her name, finishing her novel;

Whoever it might be, for Heavens sake let them sit still for & not come floundering out & talk to her. Mercifully, whoever it was had settled down inside; had settled down, by some stroke of luck, so as to throw a shadow there which might be useful. A shadow was precisely what she wanted, as it happened. It began to look rather as

It drew things together

† though the problem might solve itself: she could one only keep on; looking, looking, without for a second relaxing this still intensity of emotion, this determination not to be hoodwinked bamboozled not be put off with this or that, but not to accept what the vile nature of the world proffered; lies & corruption, & the could one only seek intensely enough could one Then distortion, & insincerity; & all that flummery which divides us,

Was she not thinking of now almost now in their presence? She did not need to assure herself that here she [ ? ] wished, more quite clearly than ever before; between the between was knew what was before her, & could with a sweep of her mind master every detail tell the time of day: read the letters on the back of the book even: she was not confused She was Its not confusing ed not at all, she assured herself; she was quite on a

† level with ordinary experience; only,

In the presence of whom? of what? reality: not indeed quite: something still evaded her; but something troubled her It was that perhaps: it was And letting her brush fall to her side, she stared wide eyed at the drawingroom window where for a moment a white dress so marvellously imitated the figure she had seen there ten years ago, that she could scarcely seen there, ten years ago. And He must see it, he must share it. She turned hastily to look for the boat.

† A 300, A 299; A 300, B 310

The white shape moved in the window. She let her ~~brush~~ arm fall to her [side.
If it was that, & it seemed to her that it was, somehow, Mrs. Ramsay [herself,
where then was he?
could one press straight on.
† could one [it in] ~~hold~~ the scene in a vice; ~~without so that steadily~~,
& let nothing ~~harmful~~ from outside enter in. One wanted to be quite on
† level with ordinary experience. ~~One wanted to~~ feel thats the chair; & [a
thats the table: ~~And yet~~ yes: but ~~also~~ so to seize them that
~~the extraordinary fact was made clear~~ for the
~~they're~~ themselves as they ~~have never~~ exist
& yet to feel, its a miracle, its ~~a thing that has never happened before.~~
a ~~vision. a~~ its an ~~ess~~ ecstasy. Oh but then ~~most~~
~~what~~ unhappily; ~~for she did not what was this?~~ [~~something~~ The white thing] ~~A movement~~
s~~ome trick~~ flaunt or ~~moved~~. ~~She must~~ moved – the air
~~just~~ lifted some flounce: ~~so that~~ her heart leapt out at her
seized her & again tortured her: ~~with that~~ Oh Mrs. Ramsay! she
cried out, letting her brush fall. It ~~seemed as if she were~~
~~actually there again~~ ~~It was the devil, it was the devil to be~~
~~thus sucked under, when one had got clear of the whole~~
~~horror & terror; to feel the old~~
There she was again; in all her force, ~~drag~~ making one
stop, ~~even now~~; ~~seizing one, & letting~~ & yet
making one feel again the old triumphant ~~invincible~~ power:
~~&~~ how one had loved her; ~~& she~~ ~~And she had gone.~~ ~~There were~~
~~But And for a moment it seemed as if all as that had~~
~~been her were there;~~
~~And Yet she would never actually come.~~ ~~Over her lay that~~
~~They were shut off separated from each other. A~~

But what was strange was that this familiar horror — to want & want & one cd just not to have, then ceased. It was as if like the chair, there, Mrs. Ramsay [— too had asked to be be put on a the level of ordinary experience; & so enjoy [her. Quiet, at her ease, there she sat; & her (it the sh white shape was extremely like chair as it happened was exactly as she used to sit in it) & she knitted without any acute taste, Lily thought, in the colour of wools: flicking her wrist so, & so; & the whole room was filled with that quiet & she smiled, & she seemed to & so looking at her, there came of the thought of her became slowly lit up, ordinary thought it was, with the It became a miracle, it became an ecstasy: — that she should exist. that she had lived, And only where It stayed there this before her, while she painted (for she began again quietly) & grew in until at last, she began to feel herself impelled again, by some instinct beyond her to look for what was it, to be conscious of some for something — or was it some one?

she sat there, quiet & at her ease,

like the thought of the chair,

It was Mr. Ramsay she sought, [going to the edge of the lawn, where (Mr. Carmichael actually nodded benevolently) to her as she passed, feeling in some confusion that she must somehow get him into communication with him & tell him, she went past Mr. Carmichael, who nodded benevolently to the edge of the lawn, & looked out over the sea.

6th Sept

8[1].

† *The Lighthouse was now quite close. One could see the windows in the tower, & what ~~seemed to be~~ a [green in the crevices of the rock] little garden. A man had ~~appeared on~~ [come out & gone in again] the rock. (The breeze had freshened, & now it was a little rougher than it should have been. A white splinter of broken waves showed up against the rock. [It was extraordinary to be able to see all these things.] After having seen it so many thousand times, dim across the bay, it was like clapping a telescope to one's eye. so straight & prominent it seemed, glaring white & yellow. (A man had come out, & looked at them, & gone in again.

(Cam thought; but he had

~~James was excited, he frowned;~~ he ^ looked the image of incorruptible

† ~~guiding~~ as if his hand grasping the tiller directed human destiny; [justice;] & his eyes fixed on the sail, unflinchingly surveyed the end ~~on which~~ to which drove; ~~& yet he was excited~~. James sat steering. He was ~~very~~ excited; [they] he ~~frowned~~; he would not let them see that he was excited. He frowned, but

He had shown that

† ~~Cam knew that he~~ ~~He~~ [but his eyes had an odd blue sparkle in them.] knew how to handle a boat. [~~the~~ ~~He had kept her before the wind~~ & Macalister had hardly had to tell him ~~anything~~ a thing. They were flying along now

They were coming to the Lighthouse at last. ~~Why it meant so~~

† ~~much to him~~ yes, after all these years; ~~& but none of them knew~~ why [None of them knew why it mattered so much to him.]

† And it was like that. He The starkness & straightness of the tower planted there on a solitary rock miles from the land

† ~~satisfied him~~. & seemed to him to ~~be~~ [right – what it should be.] on his side in the war against tyranny. & It seemed to him that ~~they~~ one was now about to start on things for oneself. One had sixty, perhaps seventy years of living before one. One might do anything, go to any part of the world, & fight this demon, he thought, this devil. ~~The devil was~~ It was in his father most; but it was in Cam too. ~~Look now~~. For example – yes – that was very like her. She was

---

* MS 351

† A 301, B 311; A 306, B 316; A 303, B 313; A 301; B 311; A 302, B 312

(3.319)

was wildly excited. She had ~~caught b~~ felt a bite. She ~~drew the line~~ pulled the line in. There it ~~was~~ a ~~gr~~ silver green flash in the water. She hauled a mackerel on board. She looked beside herself with excitement. And then, because ~~his father~~ Macalisters boy ~~pulled the~~ jerked the hook out & her father saw it & shut his eyes in a spasm of horror, Cam all together shut up; ~~&~~ She would not bait the hook again.

fixed the jaw open &

But it was never the thing itself, that she felt but ~~what~~ why she felt it, & what some one else thought about her feeling it – all ~~this was~~ what Cam ~~thought~~ about: ~~never &~~ ~~so~~ did ~~his father too~~. They were fundamentally insincere; One or two people speak the truth, he thought. Rose did. ~~Prue~~ did. Andrew did his mother did. But a fatal streak had got into the family. They were

But was the devil still there? His father had been reading for ever so long. Now he had shut his book; but he was thinking about it. His half shut. He seemed to fill his mind as full as it would hold; ~~&~~ then ~~he seemed~~ to spread it out before him. He was

He was a great thinker. At any rate,

But his father was already immensely old. ~~He was shrunken~~. ~~It was all over for him, &~~ He would have to

8.

† *They were very close to the lighthouse now. There it loomed up, stark
glaring white & black
straight, ~~on its rock~~, & one could see the waves, for the wind had [&
~~at the bare [centre?]~~ rock
freshened, breaking in white splinters. One could see the windows in the
tower, & a little bit of green on the rock. A man had come out &
looked at them through a glass & gone in again: It was
extraordinary to be able to make out one detail after another
when one had seen the Lighthouse looking the same all these years
across the bay. It was like that then, James thought. Behind
the Lighthouse stretching away in a vast grey sweep was the open sea.
It was like that then, James thought. It ~~was as if he~~ had hoped
seemed to
† It satisfied him – it confirm~~ed him in~~ some ~~suspicion.~~
~~What he had expected~~ – him in some idea, in some preconception,
to be
~~th~~ & it was – ~~But why She It was extraordinarily what~~ one
would have wished. in harmony with something or other.
with
But what? ~~was that something~~? he wondered; ~~steering~~
I~~t was~~ with something ~~that he~~ in himself ~~& in his father too~~
& it was in his father too held Yes it was the thing
they shared; ~~togeth only in~~ In him either it had been overlaid with
marriage & ~~children &~~ all the rest The stark
lighthouse & the waste of sea, running God knows where.
which shrugged the whole business of domesticity &
[manners?] off his shoulders.
at the back of his mind
with some idea of life ~~that suited him~~ which lay dormant in him.
He ~~could underst~~and It was what he had in common with his
father:

That old man stood up ~~in~~ a ghastly green-grey hall &
went on telling people to be good. And he believed

* MS 349
† A 301, B 311; A 302, B 312

that they were all sinking in a waste of waters. He liked to think so. ~~Sometimes for a mom~~ent James felt that he alone understood the ~~irritation & the~~ why he was so moody & so ~~ira~~ despondent – it was because the world ~~had~~ was like this – running wild seas round stark rocks, & people went on saying no: it is sweet & cloudy & soft. [But it was hard, & it was bitter, & it was wild; & for his own part, he thanked goodness he had sixty or seventy years before him in which to do battle with it. He would uproot that devil –] [So he went about in those dismal places, & stood up, very straight, & condemned vice & frivolity. But he genuinely beli~~eved.~~ ~~And that was what he admired in his~~ father ~~f~~ said no.: & his father believed that they were all sinking in a waste of waters. He was like some old ~~co~~ sea bird hunched upon a rock. There he sat reading his book with his legs curled round, ~~He was~~ aloof from them all, & ~~sometimes James~~ felt that his ~~quite conten~~t. He didnot want pity or affection or care, or any of the things he seemed to want, he wanted to be left alone on his rock, & then he would sail out into the air, & then he would plunge, like a stone. And he should never have And then nobody would not have hated him, ~~as James had hated~~ him, & yet, he ~~thought, he had never hated his father~~ What he had hated had been the For he did not hate him now. He understood quite well now – that he wanted to be left in peace to read ~~his~~ book. ~~What was his book~~? Aristotle, Plato, Greek was it?

But his

They should have left him alone.

It was Greek, Cam thought; some foreign language anyhow. Greek or Latin probably. ~~It was a~~ little book with a mottled cover which he always slipped into his pocket when he travelled. He always read when they travelled. Hours & hours seemed to have passed. Nobody had spoken for an age. She had been staring up into the sky ~~until~~ She had been trying to imagine – what was the world. really like then? ~~Outside~~ In the house were all sorts of things she knew heart; out here nothing but the sky. What was the meaning of things?

The breeze had freshened a bit too much, Macalister said. It was going [to be Landing a ticklish business. They ~~were~~ must keep her head up well to the North. ~~Then they must~~ James kept her well to the North. He had ~~a~~ the

Did his father hear it

† makings of a fine sailor Macalister said

~~Why didnot~~ But his father ~~listen~~ to that? did not hear it: James looked ~~In time~~ one got to know ev ~~qui~~ quickly to see. No: he was reading.

In time one got to know every shake & sound in the boat,

† Cam thought. She had played every sort of game, she had imagined that they were shipwrecked ~~that~~ ~~how~~ the mackerel what the mackerel felt, drawn up there to die: she had thought of her own bait sweeping white through the waves; how ~~the fish passed it~~. & the drowned men whirling down to the sand; & the sand itself; & the roots of the coast, & how the plunged fathoms deep & then tufted with trees & houses on top: Yes, & she had thought about the compact: ~~tyranny was to be~~ But was & about tyranny; & ~~ho~~ for what reason the crime was unforgivable. ~~It was~~ For this reason:

One

There was nothing in the world except this – a little finger would do to represent it – & ~~the~~ her father said "~~You shan't move~~ it." No. you shant. & one had to hold it still. And The blind ungovernable rage had possessed her. ~~She loo~~ For if his father had heard him praised anything it would have pleased him more than if his father had

* Page number omitted by Berg Collection

† A 303, B 313, B 314; A 304

[*]

Sept. 12th

some obscure sense ~~that he~~ of his own character;

this suspicion as to the true nature of things

† It was like that then, James thought. The sight confirmed him in some
notion of his, some latent idea ~~which it pleased him to have~~
& the nature of things
about himself, about the world, which it pleased him to find come true.–
He had then, been right then in ~~supposing that the~~
~~yet what could it be?~~ ~~That he had~~ The
~~There was a vast sweep of waters, & here & there a solitary rock.~~
He alone, he thought, ~~had tha~~ of all of them shared this
this nature, this belief, with his father. The old ladies ~~said,~~
went chivying the sun about on the lawn; Mrs. Beckwith
~~wa~~ for example; & they said how charming & how sweet & how nice & all
that: & D'ya remember your mother? Whereas, as a matter of fact,
thought James, the world is like this: ~~wild & desolate;~~ ~~That was~~
~~what his father knew too.~~ ~~He looked at~~ the lighthouse,
~~standing black & white on its rock, with the sea spreading endlessly~~
~~beyond~~ it. That ~~wha~~ was what his father knew too.
The sea goes away endlessly over there; it is grey, ~~even~~ in spite
of the sun even; He looked at the Lighthouse & the sea beyond;
~~but only His father knew it too. It was the~~
His father ~~went further.~~ He thought "We are driving before a gale – We are
He looked at reading He read steadily.
~~doo~~ bound to sink. His father ~~read, with his legs curled round each~~
other.

The book ~~That he w~~
~~It~~ was Greek, Cam thought, Latin or Greek. He always read
that book on a journey. And he seemed to have been reading for
hours & hours now. Nobody had spoken for an age.
She had looked up into the sky; One cloud moved very slowly.
She had gazed down into the sea. Little bits of black cork
floated past. She had imagined ~~them~~ dying, like these fish,
beating their tails up & down in a pool of water on the
bottom of the boat; She had imagined the drowning

* VW omitted page numbers from this point on. (3.327)

† A 301–2, B 311–12

men swirling round & round; & the roots of the shore, ~~incessantly washed incessantly, & ris~~ miles beneath, & then rising into clumps of trees, houses, gardens, flowers, above. She ~~the~~ had thought about tyranny & the compact to resist tyranny to the death [too
Wagging her little finger to & fro in the gunwale she acted the effort of [had thought of the mind]
mind to be free; ~~& then~~ [she had] the tyrant – strangling its freedom – she had [her
grasped her little finger tight ~~w~~ with her whole hand: she had thought of
~~That was what he did to~~ them. He said "I shall expect you to be [her father say
ready ~~at~~ [to start] eight o'clock to come to the Lighthouse.
~~Yes, but what was he reading, she wondered~~?
He read on, without moving. ~~He was imperturbable.~~ He submitted to scrutiny. He would unconscious of it. ~~He was~~ It was thus that he [their
escaped, ~~for~~ she thought, by reason of his great nose, & his great forehead, & the little mottled book he held, in his hand with the signet ring. He escaped her. You had your hands on him.
And then, like a bird, he spread his wings, & floated serenely off to settle, out of your reach, on a desolate stump.
The breeze had freshened a bit too much, Macalister said.
~~It was~~ They must keep he head well up to the North he said;
† ~~But James~~ [It] was doing very well, he was doing very nicely indeed. It was [keeping he very steady, he said]
But did his father hear that, James wondered?
For though he could never remember a time when he had not felt,
For goodness sake don't stop (suppose his father were walking up – down the terrace, for instance, & he were playing on the step)
he had always felt too ~~that~~ All the same, I know
that too; It ~~was something to do with~~ [It – ~~what he had felt just now about~~] the sea & the lighthouse:
~~some So that it suppose his father~~
in virtue of which knowledge, hi~~s father's praise, or~~ if his father had him, or even heard Macalister praising him, he would have been [praised

(it was something to he had felt it ~~wh~~ just now, about the sea & the lighthouse)

† A 303, B 313

pleased. But damn it all, he read.

He escaped always, Cam thought. ~~She~~ {One} might be blind with rage: (she [held her little finger tight to recall the agony, the suffocation, of his tyranny: Do this: do that. I won't have this. Obey me instantly: & so on) & ~~suddenly, it seemed he co just as ones hands closed~~ & then, at ~~the crisis~~, ready to strike him dead as one was, ~~off he~~ it was impossible. ~~Turning~~ ~~She remembered~~ ~~once a his coming into the room~~ He stooped, she remembered, {he} picked a yellow flower. And her [mother, taking it with an odd little cry stuck it in her dress; ~~intently~~ She ~~had~~ let him go, ~~too~~ {then}. Yet it was the same sort of ~~scene~~ thing [precisely: He ~~escaped her: always even then~~ It was the same even then. He had his little perch, out at sea, she thought, smiling, as she did, ~~son~~ when sometimes, she ~~came close~~, imagined herself ~~his very~~ like her mother:

~~Her cry was mixed as she remembered it~~ – ~~as if she~~
~~She could not grapple with the~~
It was made ~~up~~ of ~~so~~ amusement & some ~~grief~~ thing like despair, ~~that~~ the little cry ~~that~~
Cam remembered But it ended with three ~~little~~ drops of ~~pure pleasure~~ pleasure – [as
~~She~~ also remembered, & the ~~two~~ Ah – ah ah. That she remembered.
~~She also remembered &~~ often the two ~~memories~~ for ~~the~~ pure pleasure in
~~That~~ The memory would ~~join the~~ attach itself to another, ~~about~~ [the sound of this. of
something blue, pendant, swinging: ~~from which [ ? ]~~
~~but both together seemed pa to make that part of the~~ forest-world,
which ~~[cli?]~~ ~~with~~ having no particular reason or meaning or [strain?] would
float off & become part of ~~that vast, that~~ the landscape, the forest
~~thick with trees, alive~~ with ~~blue &~~ distant, that forest, that
inexhaustible reservoir, ~~from which one~~ which, massed there, in the
background, gave ~~so~~ such a depth to this here. Her finger was
wagging of itself on the gunwale; ~~&~~ & Her finger was almost capable now
~~destroying the~~ of blotting out the entire island. It was
~~It was~~ a forest which contained everything in the most extraordinary
richness & confusion; so that one was always ~~dis~~ bringing
forward something or other to place against this: her finger wagging
It ~~was never plain sailing, quite she thought~~. She saw the finger
~~wa over~~ against the sharp little rock over there into
which the island had shrunk. It was sharp & thin &
~~fragil~~, something like ~~the~~ a ~~leaf~~ dead leaf stood on end.
Yet in its frailty, she thought, was that vast depth, blue, thickly
populated; & that censer swinging, – & her mother taking the
yellow flower, & ~~& all those figures, her mothers~~,
these people. passing up & down, passing in & out
He would scarcely notice if the mast fell on his head, ~~thoug~~ James
thought, ~~seeing how~~, watching how ~~he brushed~~ his father
brushed aside the sail, when, in tacking, it ~~knocked~~
the brim of his hat. His hands seemed to be appointed

like a censer swinging [ ? ] out calm & [ ? ] something very adventurous & queer [ ? ] calm rather low [sorrowful sound?]

seemed to be an [ ? ] harbourage for all sorts of things.

starting out of it as out of an inexhaustible fount,

That extraordinary intricacy;

without any consciousness on the part of the brain, ~~to brush aside~~ to see that nothing attacked him. Yes. The hat was a nuisance. The left hand ~~put it on~~ snatched it off. There he sat, bareheaded,
† with the wind blowing his hair about, & his head against the brown ~~sail — a head which looked~~ of the sail. ~~A very, very~~ He looked immensely [old James thought. He looked as if ~~as if he had~~ done with all this.
James ~~rememb~~ considered how he ~~was~~ had forty or fifty or even sixty years of life before him: ~~how he would land,~~ & it seemed to him that he would ~~Ja~~ land in the Lighthouse & go on, but his father would [land, & it would It was all done unconsciously automatically.
He looked as though nothing could reach him, or touch him; as though [he had ~~embodied now that~~ become the very thing that had lain on the outskirts [of that view of life: James's mind since he was a child; had become the that waste of sea, ~~wast~~ running out to the horizon which ~~is~~ had become one with the ~~had ec escaped them all. But,~~ ~~He was~~ "~~There was~~ nothing between them [as he?] ~~but~~ & America" & he would begin then to chant & cry to swing his stick until they thought
~~Wasn't~~ He used ~~that what he~~ used to say that, sitting on a rock, swinging his legs over the sea. ~~That~~ He liked that. But that wasn't quite right either. (For, ~~now he was~~ the sea alone ~~made him~~ looking at his father) for now he had & yet, he looked a little different from that; he looked as if he had had a sight of something. Could there be land there? He ~~read~~ went on reading. He turned the page – everything he did was full of signs of his temper – swiftly now. It looked as if He was eager, ~~it too~~ to get to the end of ~~the section~~; it. ~~He read~~ His mind seemed to be speeding ~~a~~ up & down, up & down, first this page then that.

† Suddenly he shut the book with a bang, as if to say Thats done it well. ~~A sort~~ He was exalted – He was [satisfied?]

"~~Come, my dears, he~~ Luncheon said briskly: Sandwiches. ~~I want my luncheon.~~"

† A 301, B 311; A 303, B 313

~~Cam~~ They looked at him. James looked at him. ~~His~~ After this immensely [long silence the change startled them.

"~~Come my dears" he said~~ dear

He had forgotten them completely they felt. He was for a moment, ~~speeding away very fast, into the~~ setting some conclusion He wanted He did not want them, ~~he did not want anything, unless it was~~ to gather [up, very quickly a few ~~odds & ends;~~ ~~When he had done~~ Then this, he roused himself & said,

something that remained ~~unsolved~~ over things that went on running in his mind. He did it. He

He sat quite still

Come my dears.

~~It was time they ate their sandwiches for luncheon.~~

He looked content

~~But, they wondered~~ They would where were they to come? What did he want ~~them to do~~ They both now? For a moment it seemed as if he were asking them They were to follow him on an extraordinary [expedition, they both felt: he was leading them, like an old general in a shot torn [cloak – ~~&~~ at the same time they knew that ~~it behoved them to be perfectly calm.~~ He only meant that ~~it was time they ate their sandwiches.~~ this was absurd. They must lunch. ~~They must cut their sandwiches~~ They were almost at the Lighthouse. So

but

~~They were tied with thread~~, They must eat their sandwiches – That was what he meant. He gave to each of them a packet tied up with ordinary sewing cotton, Cam noticed. for she felt that she ~~was so excited~~ the sewing cotton was odd: [any?] was odd; that she would notice everything now: ~~every~~ because it ~~was so strange~~; They were far far out at sea, ~~almost in a~~ they were excited; it was unreal, but perfectly natural. ~~They opened their packets of sandwiches~~. It was ordinary sewing cotton; & inside were little ham sandwiches, very lean & neat.

out at sea, near the lighthouse.

Once | When he was a boy he said

When he was a boy, he said, he had been walking in the heart of the country when he had seen a hansom cab, ~~suddenly~~ appearing in the lane. ~~They had to~~ ~~He had never forgotten meeting~~ It was common in those [days for ~~pe~~ country people to give one milk for nothing: ~~All that has~~ vanished he said. ~~Once he had~~ But they wd be angry in some parts of England if You would have to offer money wherever you went now, ~~he~~ said. ~~Then~~ Now there were hotels instead of lodging houses; & ~~the old people all talked English.~~ Macalister, how old [are you? he asked. ~~All~~ But he said the same, ~~he said,~~ But he was an old man. These were an old man's views. How old was Macalister? Only just past 50 – & the others? Macalisters boy (they sat round eating together) spoke for the first time – He was eighteen. And Cam was 17 & James was 16. They were all infants said Mr. Ramsay, compared with him. ~~Strange~~ times ~~were coming he said.~~ he said & [little of?] For a moment he seemed to to be going to fall into that boding anxious mood when he was ~~apt to~~ say began ~~shou~~ ~~re~~ ~~quoting~~ reciting poetr~~y; bu~~t But no. He ~~was qu~~ ~~The old wizard~~ They ~~were~~ He said that ~~He could remember the man who built that lighthouse he said.~~ He

he said

† He said suddenly that the best dinner in the world was bread & cheese. Oh, but he couldn't cut it himself now, he said. People degenerated as they grew older. They became fussy, they had fancies. When was young one could sleep in the open – shake ones coat like a dog & get up fresh as a lark next morning. He would like to come back again after a hundred years, he said, to see what they'd made of it. "They'll have enough ~~of it~~ on their hands," he ~~said to Macalister;~~ ~~if~~ & they grinned at each other; ~~James~~ & James felt ~~this is~~ ~~It may be~~ ~~true what he says.~~ ~~One of the~~ He ~~is~~ likes fishermen better ~~than~~ ~~anyone~~ ~~most~~ anybody ~~He~~ What he likes best is to ~~smoke~~ eat bread & cheese with Macalister.

that their ~~crust~~ A slice of bread & cheese was what he liked.

(looking at what Macalister was cutting)

---

† A 304, B 314

stand about in the harbour & spit:

He would have liked to live in a cottage & eat bread & cheese; & And they liked him; And he would lie awake at night thinking of the boats, if there were a storm. He ~~was~~ would mope about, if it were a bad year for the fishing boats. And Cam thought that this was what she meant about liking to be ~~the old men in~~ the study with the old men who smoked & read the Times & said very briefly something about Napoleon. Only ~~when~~ now ~~he was~~ it was not quite the same as that now. She felt now, ~~yea~~ about her father, that he was ~~amusing them on~~ as ~~if he were~~ knew perfectly well what he was doing; he ~~was feeling~~, that he had known everything; & that he had back come to ~~think that~~ back to ~~some~~ after all that boiling & moiling, with his book & being a great man, & minding not being a great man, to [his had thrown it off him; & was now telling them stories round a camp fire. No, no, she checked herself. He was saying ~~being very polite~~. He had such beautiful manners; she thought; when he [talked like this.

the old wizard (he knew everything) had put off his magic; he was

† And, she thought, ~~dabbling her finger~~ throwing the hard crust over board, surreptitiously, so that he would not see her. wasting good food, he ~~is~~ this is one must not do anything to distract him. She did not want to be interrupted. What he was saying was so [him extraordinarily important – ~~And again, what she~~ so important, if you were thinking about the Elizabethans, or the stars; so ~~consolatory~~ suitable? What did she mean? She wanted

† A 305, B 315

& that though he was saying whatever came in to his head, it was very [important; not what he said, but – again she felt; as she used to in his study,
~~This is all~~ ~~very comfortable~~ – ~~right~~. ~~Everything is all right, so long as he~~ [~~goes on~~
Thats all right – thats all right; ~~as if~~ & she could go on thinking; The
& he would see that none of them got lost, or fell down precipices, or
tumbled into the sea; ~~a feeling which seized~~ ~~And of the~~
~~blue wall~~ ~~That was very important.~~
& at the same time, he would be very

They ~~Well~~ yes, they'll would have enough on their hands, he was saying to Macalister [as to their children he meant,
~~Macalister said that~~ as if he were ~~amused~~ content to be quit of it all.
And yet ~~he did not~~ far from seeming tired or
& he talked as if ~~he was~~ ~~even going to~~ ~~it were no concern~~ of his now;
yet far from seeming ~~to~~ tired, or angry, or out of temper.
he seemed quite content, a little amused. He ~~seem~~ laughed indeed,

This was were* she sunk, said Angus sullenly, thinking [looking at James.
as if that they would like to know the exact spot where the schooner with
eleven ~~three~~ men aboard had sunk last winter.
~~Ah~~, said ~~Mr. Ramsay only nodded~~ his head.
James & Cam both framed the words

But I beneath a rougher sea,** expecting to hear him ~~burst~~
muttering & murmuring, as he did, so often, & made them
nervous & ill at ease.

† But he said only Ah – as if he thought to himself, naturally: there is nothing to say about that. Drowning is a perfectly simple, straightforward affair; & we all come to it; & the depths of the sea, he looked over the side, out of politeness rather than anything, ~~have no terror for me.~~ are after all only water. We need make no fuss about that, he seemed to say. And having finished his ~~h~~ meal

(3.343)

* VW's misspelling
** 'The Castaway,' MS 242, 267, 283, 317
† B 316, A 306

he looked at his watch. He made some calculations. He said "Well
nobody in particular,
~~And Addressed~~ to ~~the whole lot~~ of them, though it might be, James [done".
that ~~this was his~~ Possibly he [thought
suddenly
Macalister was clapping his hands on his thighs: ~~And indeed none of~~
~~had any right to the remark thought James~~ [them It was almost
impossible that they should even speak directly to each other.
But there was the praise at last! ~~spoken~~
That was James's praise. That belonged entirely to him, Cam said to
[herself.
The blood mounted steadily over James's face; he looked like a little boy
ten. ~~He looked~~ rather sulky, saying to himself that he would not show [of
that he was pleased; he would make out that he was angry.
And now he had a chance of showing his metal. They were sailing
swiftly buoyantly on long rocking waves which ~~seemed to~~
† ~~carried the~~ handed them in from one to another with an
indescribable swing & exhilaration beside the reef;
on the left, ~~all~~ a long row of rocks showed the brown
† through the green water; & on one higher than the rest the waves ~~spurted~~
broke & spurted. The drops went up in a column; one
could hear the slap of the water & the patter of the falling drops, &
a kind of hushing & ~~hiss seeme~~ hissing sound ~~w~~ from the
rolling waves, ~~& the~~ flowing & falling in a kind of gamol* &
that was perfectly free ~~& ye~~ wild & had gone on like this for
ever.

Two men were out on the Lighthouse again, looking at them,
making sure it seemed that the boat was bound for the
lighthouse, before they made some preparations. One could
see their faces & something glittering on a coat. They decided apparently that the boat was coming to them.
Mr. Ramsay ~~still~~ seemed to be calculating the time. He had his
watch in his hand. He looked at the Lighthouse, & then at the watch.

* For 'gambol'?
† B 317; A 307

He seemed Cam thought to ~~be saying~~ have made some bet; about the [time it would take them. He measured the space still left to sail with his eye. And then, he shut his watch; put it back into his pocket, & looked ~~to~~ at the island, searchingly, sadly.

With his watch still in his hand, he looked at the island. He sought with ~~I keen long sighted eyes~~ for the dwindled leaf like shape which ~~Cam~~ [his ~~had her eyes on too~~. now appeared far away on a golden plate in the middle of the sea. What was he thinking now? she wondered. What What was it he sought so fixedly, so intently that ~~she~~ it was painful to [could ~~look~~ see at him? ~~She~~ They felt both of them, ~~we we~~ Let us give you everything — ~~As Only~~ ask us. They both felt, Let us help you. But he looked at the blue frail shape, which seemed to ~~made of some vapour burning~~ & thing that had burnt itself to vapour. & ~~soon~~ it was quite clear, they did not know what he No; he did not want anything. He did not ask anything. He He would never tell anyone what he looked for, or what, perhaps, as he between them, with his hat off & his head exposed, he saw there. [sat

† starring ~~wat~~ & starring? ~~Dont~~ let us ask, they We thought: dont ask — we cant ask, He Starring & starring he with his hat off & his watch in his hand.

~~There are~~ The parcels, he reminded them, speaking so quietly that it seemed as if he ~~only s spoke so~~ were thinking aloud. ~~The things~~ Parcels for the Lighthouse men" he said, & stooping ~~&~~ he filled his arms with brown paper parcels; & stood in the the bow of the boat, very straight & tall, for all the world, thought James as if he were saying "There is no God", & Cam thought, "As if he were leading us ~~upon some there onto~~ that rock" & & they both rose to follow him as he sprang, holding his parcels, on to the rock.

† B 318, A 308

(15th Sept)

9.

"He must be have reached it" said Lily Briscoe, feeling extraordinarily [tired.
But she ~~felt assuaged of her~~ was relieved, assuaged. & ~~her~~ for the [lighthouse
~~seemed~~, ~~owing~~ in ~~to~~ the blue haze, ~~very far away~~, almost invisible – ~~it had~~
& the ~~phy effort~~ of & ~~it needed a great effort to imagine the~~
† & the effort of looking ~~for~~ at it ~~seemed to increase~~ at the same time ~~she was~~
~~making an enormous~~ thinking of him landing seemed to melt in to each [other.
But she was assuaged, she was relieved; ~~she had~~ Whatever she had
† been wishing to give him, ~~that sympathy, which had~~ she had given, at [last.
"He has landed" she said to herself, & sank back, as if it ~~were~~ she need
stretch her mind no further ~~after him~~ into ~~a quiet~~ the rest which
~~succeeds an effort~~;

had become

together to stretch her eyes to stretch her mind farther & farther.

~~It was~~ finished, she felt. It was finished.

Surging up, ~~like a~~ f~~rom weeds, reeds & mud~~, like a river God, ^from weeds & mud he [seemed so
~~shaggy, so huge, & so benevolent~~, old Mr. Carmichael stood ~~by her side~~.
beside her.

"They ~~will have landed~~" he said.

The image stuck to him. ~~H~~ Like an old Pagan god, shaggy with the weeds ~~of the~~ in his hair, & his hand grasping a staff (but it was only ~~his~~ a French novel) he rose on the edge of the lawn, ~~sw~~ swaying a little in his bulk ~~& his benevolence, &~~ & said, raising his hand over his eyes,

They will have landed.

He was enormously tolerant ~~of human weakness~~, she felt, ~~&~~
He spread his hand over all their ~~weaknesses~~ weakness ~~infirmities~~ & sufferings. He had let knowledge ooze into him, drop by drop, till he was steeped in it There he stood, she felt, crowning the occasion ~~without~~ ~~so that~~ ~~as if he had~~ with his silence, as if she had seen him let fall ~~some~~ from his great height a [~~b~~?] wreath of violets, of poppies, which ~~fell &~~ fluttered gently to the earth.

~~Now, she thought~~, as ~~the~~ He he paused there, she turn~~ing~~ed to her canvas, with

† B 319; A 309

eagerly, as if something had moved in her absence

as if ~~the probably,~~ ~~she~~

something had moved while she ~~was~~ had been turned ~~away~~ aside:; & she must

~~to see what as it, or, perhaps, she had there had~~ an idea had come [look to her.

It was ~~one of those pictures~~ It was only a sketch that would be hung in the bedrooms, & then

† the attics; or it would be destroyed. Very likely, she thought, but it did [in not

matter – what was the expression two pins? Two straws? –

She ~~stepped~~ took up her brush. She looked at her sketch, ~~which was~~

looked at the window going so, & the wall; ~~at~~ & saw, as she had

known that she would see, precisely what was needed.

~~That was it.~~ ~~A~~ ~~It was~~ That (she drew a line) which solved her

problem.

Mr. Carmichael was standing at her elbow.

He looked at the canvas – He looked at the step.

He watched her make the ~~line~~ mark which noted for her own eye the

solution of the problem.

But what did it matter? ~~She looked at the canvas~~. She looked at the

The white shape stayed perfectly still.

step. /She drew a line, [?] there, in the centre. She had solved her of the canvas.

problem. ~~Now~~ ~~Mr. Carmichael stood, letting his~~

It was ~~finished~~ over, that vision. Mr. Carmichael, looking over her shoulder, [at the

~~canvas~~, at the Ah, it ~~was~~ Thank Heaven, over! But she had had her

There! ~~It was done~~. It was over. But she had had her vision.

---

† A 310, B 320

# Appendices

## A 'Notes for Writing'

These notes for *To the Lighthouse* are in a small writing book which Virginia Woolf labelled 'Notes for Writing' on the cover and 'Reading and Writing' on the spine. The first page has two dates on it, March 1922 and March 1925. The notes for *To the Lighthouse* are on pages 11, 12, and 13, which are the last ones in the book to be used (with the exception of the final page, where Virginia Woolf, having inverted the book, wrote '10th Feb 1932'. The pages preceding the notes for *To the Lighthouse* contain newspaper clippings, Virginia Woolf's copies of several poems from Robert Herrick's 'Hesperides,' notes for her essay 'Reading' (dated 6 December 1922), and, on pages 7–10, notes for stories, some of which have since been published in *A Haunted House and Other Short Stories* and in *Mrs. Dalloway's Party*. I am including a transcription of the notes on these four pages because one can see at several points the 'germs,' as Henry James called them, of ideas she would develop in *To the Lighthouse.*

1925

Notes for stories – e.

March 6th 1925

The woman ~~who~~ who had bought the wrong dress.

Prof. Brierly on Milton.

~~E~~ Sterne's Eliza

Somebody quite unknown.

The New Dress

& other stories

This book will consist of the stories of people at Mrs. D's party. States of mind. Each separate from the other.

1. The new dress. 2. Happiness (The man who looks at a speck of dust on his trouser [ie?] 3. The picture – I think of the sea – 4. Professor Brierley

My idea is that these sketches will be a corridor ~~from~~ leading from Mrs.

March 14th Dalloway to a new book. What I expect to
happen is that ~~half~~ some two figures
will detach themselves from the party
& go off independently into another
volume; but I have no notion of this
at present. The book of stories ought
to be complete in itself. It must
have some unity, though I want to
publish each character separately.
One of the characters is to be a
pair of candlesticks, or a vase of
flowers. another the picture.
another a long conversation.
These could be done this summer.

5 The girl who had written an essay on
the character of Bolingbroke talking
to the young man who destroys a
fly as he speaks.

The Past founded on [images?] ancestor worship,
what it amounts to, & means.
Some middle aged woman
of distinguished parents; her
feelings for her father & mother –
[ancient?]

One about people looking out of a window & realising
the planets, or some quite other world.
being recalled to this one.

✓1. The New dress.
✓2. Happiness.
✓3. Ancestors.
✓4. The Introduction
5. The man who ~~thinks that~~ wishes to burst into tears at the sight of all this: has unaccountable feelings: chiefly of discomfort;
6. The picture
7. Professor Brierly
✓8. one must be an exciting conversation all, or almost all, in dialogue.

It strikes me that it might all end with a picture.
These stories about people would fill
half the book; & then the other thing would
loom up; & we should step into quite a
different place & people ? But what?*

* Virginia Woolf's last question seems to be answered by the notes for *To the Lighthouse* which begin on the next page.

# To the Lighthouse

All character – not a view of the world.

Two blocks joined by a corridor

Topics that may come in:

How her beauty is to be conveyed by the impression that she makes on all these people. One after another feeling it without knowing exactly what she does to them, to charge her words.

Episode of taking Tansley to call on the poor.

How they see her.

The great cleavages in to which the human race is split, through the Ramsays not liking Mr. Tansley.

But they liked Mr. Carmichael.

Her reverence for learning and painting.

Inhibited, not very personal.

The look of the room – [fiddle?] and sand [shoes?] –

Great photographs covering bare patches.

The beauty is to be revealed the 2nd time
Mr. R stops
discourse on sentimentality.
He was quoting The Charge of the Light Brigade
& then impressed upon it was this picture
of mother and child.

How much more important divisions between
people are than between countries.
~~Ev~~ The source of all evil.
She was lapsing into pure sensation –
seeing things in the garden.✱ *
The waves breaking. Tapping of cricket balls.
The bark "How's that?"

They did not speak to each other.
Tansley shed
Tansley the product of universities had to
assert the power of his intellect.

* The asterisks on page 12 and page 13 and the phrase 'The bark "How's that?"' appear to have been added later.

*She feels the glow of sensation – & how they are
made up of all different things – (what
she has just done) & wishes for some bell to
strike & say this is it. It does strike.
She guards her moment.

## B Outline of 'Time Passes'*

This outline is written on unlined notebook paper. It has been placed inside the cover of volume 1 and numbered by the Berg Collection as the first page. I have put it in an appendix since its relation to the rest of the manuscript cannot be determined.

---

To the Lighthouse

[~~Tie~~?] Ten Chapters

Now the question of the ten years.

[~~Tie~~?]

The Seasons.

The Skull

The gradual dissolution of everything

This is to be contrasted with the permanence of — what?

Sun, moon & stars.

Hopeless gulfs of misery.

Cruelty.

The War.

Change. Oblivion. Human vitality. Old woman

Cleaning up. The bobbed up, valorous, as of a principle

of human life projected

We are handed on by our children ?

Shawls & shooting caps. A green handled brush.

The devouringness of nature.

But all the time, this passes, accumulates.

Darkness.

The welter of winds & waves

What then is the medium through wh. we regard human beings?

Tears. [di?]

~~Sleep th~~ Slept through life.

---

* 'Time Passes' begins on MS 198.

# C Essay fragments

Portions of the early drafts of four essays are contained in the manuscript of *To the Lighthouse*. These are:

'Robinson Crusoe' MS 41–2, published in *The Nation and Athenaeum*, 6 February 1926, and in *The Common Reader: Second Series*, 1932.

'How Should One Read a Book?" MS 43–4, 282. This is a lecture delivered at Hayes Common on 30 January 1926 (*Letters* III, p 211) and published in the *Yale Review* in October of 1926 and in *The Common Reader: Second Series.* The fragment which appears on MS 282 takes up only a portion of that page and it has not been included in the appendix.

'The Ghost of Sterne' MS 156 verso and 157 verso. The writing book was inverted, and this fragment was written on what then became the second and third pages. Published, as 'Sterne's Ghost,' in *The Nation and Athenaeum*, 7 November 1925, and in *The Moment and Other Essays,* 1947.

'De Quincey's Autobiography' MS 336. Published in *The Common Reader: Second Series*.

The transcriptions of these fragments follow.

Robinson Crusoe.

Every stick & stone in the island has its own weight & shape. Nothing moves out ~~of the~~ of its sphere for a single moment. The ~~ci~~ artist ~~art by which Defoe explored the truth of the of the story the plo pl shape everything Defoe takes~~ the most stringent ~~careful & art artful~~ precautions ~~to to~~ & uses the most artful devices used so that we shall fall ~~completely into the belief~~ into complete & perfect ~~trust.~~ belief Now it is sometimes a little slip ~~is derived to~~ lend heightens the sense of reality . . . ~~Sometimes~~ So a man would ~~add~~ speak ~~if he were really~~ telling a story. Or ~~we ha~~ve extreme particularity heightens it, ~~or the whole effect bein~~g to The result is that we not only believe every word he says, & ~~come by an extraordina to~~ find all our senses of what is true miraculously renewed freshened & sharpened, so that we are the custom like children ~~again~~ taking ~~natural objects with~~ enjoying life literally, in practical ways ~~engaged~~ in making boats, baking, building, ~~intently with all our faculties~~ intent absorbed, but ~~from~~ this perfect seriousness ~~something~~ a ~~beauty,~~ & a ~~rises, & a~~ arise that rouses in us a sense of ~~excitement~~ &, of romance. ~~of Stevenson~~ with all his art ~~craft~~ never wrote None of Stevenson's romances has the same power; ~~to stir no~~ because though ~~every device of art has been employ~~ed, they lack ~~this the power~~ to ~~convince.~~ Seriousness & the conviction of truth to which Defoe holds with ~~the~~ literal & ferocious simplicity. ~~That~~ the in the vociferously that nothing in very middle of the foreground stands a plain earthenware pot & to realize that everything – God, man, nature, must give way. One thing ~~being~~ is realised with perfect truth – & all the others therefore fall into perfect perspective. Nor does there seem to be any reason why the perspective wh an earthenware pot entails is not as satisfying, once it is perceived ~~as that~~ ~~surrounded~~

man himself, gloomy & angered, with a broken &

tumultuous

panorama of clouds

~~stars~~ & alps & stars

[Left margin notes:]

every payment is

a state of

~~They are~~ held severly within very re- ~~the~~ light morseless of truth.

for whom custom has made no [dirty word?]

adventure

We are exalted by it to [?] [?] [?]

seen against a [craggy?] &

the full value of facts

to &

Therefore

w

The result is that we believe implicitly, & ~~do seek from belief all~~ & imbibe without any shadow of doubt. ~~w All Our~~ first sense of ~~the f~~ the ~~ple~~ importance of facts ~~is~~ miraculously renewed, so that ~~we are like children, taking literally~~ ~~the all the with a renewed sense of boats, baking, building;~~ & ~~then~~ building baking hunting cooking; ~~Then the~~

all

the delight

in the atmosphere so vivid &

& then the astonishment of incidents – like the wild cat or the goat or the foot prints, seems to expand to its full; & the story moves on not to ~~with all~~ a kind of regular unexaggerated normal ~~step~~, march not to catastrophe, ~~but~~ but inevitably to prosperity, ~~but gathering~~ as it goes, from its perfect seriousness, a ~~true~~ certain grandeur.

all the

savour

& the

[ ? ]

taking

Writers who live at the same moment ~~yet~~ use

[ ? ]

into the soul

Any vagueness about God ~~for example~~, any introspection ~~into the soul~~ any ~~aeth a~~ feeling for the beauty of nature would have weakened the massive effect of ~~what~~ fact.

~~tunnelled.~~

do we mean when we talk about

And again we ask ourselves, what is reality?



(1.85)

But why is it so difficult? Because nobody can teach it.
to your geography teacher
Now if you say Rome is the capital of France, your
teacher can say Nonsense: If you say ~~Henry the Eighth~~
King John had 8 wives; your teacher can say: Nonsense
These are facts
Henry the 8th had 8 wives. ~~These are facts.~~

can say that it is, or that it is not.

But if you say, Robinson Crusoe is a bad book, nobody
can prove ~~that~~ you right ~~or prove that~~ you are wrong.
~~One has to~~ ~~No one can teach you to~~
Yet books ~~do I think contain every sort of good &~~

Reading ~~therefore~~

~~Books~~ cannot be taught. One has to teach oneself
how to read. And that is why it is so extremely
difficult & also so extremely ~~dif~~ interesting:

For let us ~~see n~~ stop a moment & consider what these three girls – Mary & Elizabeth & Helen – have learnt about reading ~~novels.~~ books

They have learnt that a ~~novelist may be trying to do~~ there may be many different kinds of novel. A novel may be a plain story of adventure like Robinson Crusoe; it may be

father & daughter in a drawing room

a ~~comedy of character~~ like Pride & Prejudice; ~~it may be~~ a ~~novel of~~ or it may be about a shepherd & his thoughts when he is alone at night. it may be a book in which fate or nature plays as large a part as human character, like ~~Far~~ The Return of the Native. ~~Besides this,~~ They will have learnt ~~that that no~~ to be on ~~the watch for of a novelist~~ is w~~riting one kind of book~~ perpetually on the watch to see what kind of book is being shaped by the novelist; they will have noticed what ~~kind of~~ language he is using, whether it is plain & ~~easy,~~ direct, or full of images & allusions. They will ~~and~~ have understood ~~what he is~~ why he is ~~putting an emphasis~~ making a great deal of one incident & passing completely over another. In short they will be doing what I think a reader ought to do – they will be taking the writer's sentences, one after another, & building them up in the shape he intended.

The Ghost of Sterne.

She was better, Eliza said, because an idea had occurred to her, which she counted on her friends' help to carry out.
First she wished [before her husband came back,] ~~to be propped in bed~~, ~~in~~ order, she said "to be able to look at us both while she revealed her project."
~~And Mr Mc~~ Charles Mathews returned; ~~The~~ [her] project was ~~reveal soon revealed directly~~ [when] Charles Mathews returned.
Sitting up in bed & looking ~~at them both, Eliza announced~~
she [astonished?] [rent] ~~& their hearts by saying what they~~
the project was revealed. Sitting up in bed, looking at them both, often forced to pause for breath, she ~~eve reveal~~ explained ~~the design which~~ how she knew she must die, how the thought of her husbands loneliness distressed her,
328 & more the thought that he would marry again a woman who would not understand him~~;~~ Were her wits wandering, the couple wondered, as she paused exhausted.
Next ~~Then~~ she proceeded, ~~the~~ Amo[eli]~~rilas~~ own state worried her, [weighed upon her mind.] ~~so~~ with
her ~~young, so inexperienced~~, youth & inexperience. ~~Her~~ ~~surely they would~~ ~~Realising this~~, surely [she] they would grant her the last request she would ever make, &, taking her husbands hand, she kissed it, & ~~kissing~~ taking Amerllis she kissed
it too, ~~hand too~~ "in a solemn manner which I remember made me tremble all over" [&] [pled?] then proceeded to [frame] her terrible ~~n~~ ~~a~~ [[?]] request. Would they pledge themselves to marry when she was dead?

Charles was thoroughly annoyed. Amelia ~~sobbed with ag~~ burst into tears. ~~Never, never, she cried could she feel~~ ~~It was impossible she cried~~
Never she cried; it was unthinkable. Her only feeling for Mr Mathew was friendship & admiration.
The idea was painful, the scene distressing; only delirium could excuse it; & for months a coldness was between them.

Mr Mathew fairly scolded the invalid for putting them in such a [position?] However –

~~However~~, Then, each had a vision: Eliza visited them

at the same moment, far apart, as they were, in their sleep.
In short, the marriage took place about twelve months later.

But what conclusions are we to come to

~~Th~~ Sterne's ghost, we might therefore ~~deduce,~~ conclude was
fundamentally a kind hearted ~~spirit, who~~ creature
who if he ~~presided~~ ~~wa~~ saw one over the disaster of one marriage,
~~saw~~ presided over the to it that a second, more propitious, should succeed.
~~For so one might interpret the~~ Charles told the story
of the Stonegate ghost ~~for~~ a hundred times in the green room,
& no one could ~~acc~~ account for it ~~his coming, or for his going.~~ ~~Again he told the story~~ when suddenly an old widow lady, & this time an old
widow lady, ~~M~~ cried out "Why that was my dear
Billy Leng!" – And then she informed them, how her
dear Billy had been bedridden for years; how, they lodged
next door to the Mathews in Stonegate; how
as his infirmities increased, so did his fears; ~~how~~ he
battered on the wall in search of robbers; how
being the most methodical of men he did this
every night as York Minster struck twelve –
In short ~~Billy Leng was~~ Sterne's ghost was
bedridden Billy Leng.

once he has succeeded (& the condition is indispensable for all writers)

in

that human beings should [exist] be there, but [at a distance;] should not come close; that

~~over everything~~ that everything should be ~~vanish~~ expand & vanish

His sight was difficult & strange. [a]

to dwindle & — that landscapes should spread & vanish away in billowing waves

of ~~soft~~ vastness: that facts should have the same power to recede into the

softness of elasticity. Nothing must press; nothing must hurry. [dim

He requires a subject that allows him to soliloquise & loiter;

here to pick up some trifle & ~~exploit its~~ bestow upon it all the

powers of an extremely subtle & penetrating mind, now to ~~allow~~ brush

the ~~prop~~ [whole] prospect to taper off in mist & ambiguity. [over

circulate & sweep his brush over the whole

~~of all subjects~~ ~~Autobiography~~ ~~The st~~ The story of his own life the

~~expo~~ was his ~~own~~ most congenial subject, ~~for there~~ &

if the Opium Eater is his masterpeice, the Autobiographic sketches

which survey a large stretch of his experience, run it very close.

For here, he ~~It is natural that~~ All this makes it natural

that he should be at his best in reminiscences; & should

find ~~the~~ his most congenial subject in the story of his own life.

40
90

40
32.3*

* Written in pencil (3.293)

# D Chronology

In the following chronology of the writing of *To the Lighthouse*, I have collated the dates on the manuscript with relevant dates in the *Diary* (volume III) and from Virginia Woolf's *Letters* (volume III). Manuscript dates are in italics. Chapter numbers refer to the chapters in the first editions.

PLANNING

| | |
|---|---|
| **1925** | |
| *25 March* | Notes in 'Notes for Writing' |
| 14 May | |
| 14 June | |
| 27 June | Early thoughts about TL. |
| 20 July | |
| 30 July | |

WRITING

| | |
|---|---|
| *6 August* | MS 1. Date on title page after 'begun.' |
| | MS 2. Outline. |
| *3 September* | MS 30. Chapter 4. 'Sophie' becomes 'Lily.' |
| **1926** | |
| [9 January] | Letter to Vita Sackville-West (hereafter VSW). In bed with the flu. '... I was to begin that wretched novel today, and now bed and toast and the usual insipidity.' |
| [15 January] | Letter to VSW. Will begin her novel tomorrow. |
| *15 January* | MS 3. '... the idea has grown in the interval.' |
| *18 January* | MS 1. Second date on title page after 'begun.' |
| | MS 46. Chapter 4. Lily and Mr Bankes look at the bay. |
| 19 January | Feels the invigoration of beginning her novel again. |
| *21 January* | MS 53. Chapter 5. Mrs Ramsay knits and thinks of Lily and Mr Bankes. |
| *24 January* | MS 60. Opening of chapter 6. |
| 26 January | Letter to VSW. Has written twenty pages. 'I have never written so fast.' |
| *31 January* | MS 71. Opening of chapter 7. |
| 31 January | Letter to VSW. Had to stop writing TL to write lecture for girls' school. |
| 8 February | 'Never never have I written so easily, imagined so profusely.' |
| 17 February | Letter to VSW. Wrapped up in her novel; '... it may well be a mirage.' |

| | |
|---|---|
| *18 February* | MS 97. Opening of chapter 14. |
| *22 February* | MS 104. Ending of chapter 10, opening of chapter 11. |
| 23 February | In high spirits over her novel. |
| 24 February | Thinks of people reading TL and recognizing her parents in it. |
| 27 February | Starts new convention of beginning each day on a new page. |
| 2 March | Letter to VSW. Thinking of how she can manage the passage of ten years, up in the Hebrides. |
| *5 March* | MS 129. Chapter 15. |
| *9 March* | MS 3. Notes how loosely and quickly she is writing. |
| 16 March | Letter to VSW. Cannot write for lack of the right rhythm. Today began a new writting book, 'having filled the old and written close on 40,000 words in two months.' |
| *17 March* | MS 159. Title page of new writing book (volume 2). MS 160. Chapter 17, Mr Carmichael at dinner. |
| 27 March | Trying to finish the dinner scene. |
| *29 March* | MS 184. End of volume 2; end of chapter 17. |
| 30 April | Finishes part I, begins part II. |
| 30 April | MS 198. Opening of part II (volume 3). |
| *9 May* | MS 215. Chapter 5. Mrs McNab. |
| *14 May* | MS 218. Chapter 6. Spring. |
| [15 May] | Letter to Edward Sackville-West. 'I am all over the place trying to do a difficult thing in my novel ... ' |
| 25 May | Finishes part II. |
| *27 May* | MS 238. Opening of part III. |
| *31 May* | MS 245. Chapter 1. Lily prepares to begin painting. |
| 9 June | Has had flu. Cannot 'conceive what The Lighthouse is all about.' |
| 18 June | Letter to VSW. Complains that she has been 'slogging through a cursed article' and now sees her novel 'glowing like the Island of the Blessed far far away over dismal wastes, and cant reach land.' |
| *21 June* | MS 257. Chapter 3. Mr Ramsay, Cam, and James have gone; Lily has made her first stroke on the canvas. |
| 22 July | Has put TL aside until Rodmell. |
| 31 July | A 'whole nervous breakdown in miniature' leaves her feeling 'no desire to cast scenes in my book.' |
| *4 August* | MS 283. Chapter 4. In the boat. |
| *17 August* | MS 306 and 307. Opening of chapter 8. |
| *26 August* | MS 325. Opening of chapter 11. |
| *1 September* | MS 337. Chapter 11. Lily recalls being with Mrs Ramsay and Charles Tansley on the beach. |

| | |
|---|---|
| 3 and 5 September | Puzzles over the ending of the novel; thinks it undramatic. |
| *6 September* | MS 349. Opening of chapter 12. |
| *12 September* | MS 354. Chapter 12. James's thoughts as they near the lighthouse. |
| 13 September | Nears completion of the novel. |
| 15 September | 'A State of Mind.' 'Failure failure.' |
| *15 September* | MS 365. Opening of chapter 13. |
| [?16 September] | Letter to Vanessa Bell: 'I'm getting on quicker with my book.' (This letter was probably written earlier in September.) |
| 28 September | TL 'finished, provisionally, Sept. 16th.' |

REVISING

| | |
|---|---|
| 3 October | Letter to Gerald Brennan. Finished a novel ten days ago and already regards it with indifference. (VW probably measures the time loosely here.) |
| 25 October | (diary entry for 14 January 1927) Begins revising and retyping. |
| 30 October | Revising TL. |
| 23 November | Redoing six pages daily. |
| 11 December | Made up a passage for TL. |
| 29 December | Letter to Vanessa Bell. In a hideous rush putting the last touches to her novel. Asks about the cover. |
| **1927** | |
| 14 January | Records the end of TL. |
| 23 January | Leonard calls it a masterpiece. |
| 12 February | Will read TL straight through in print tomorrow for the first time. |
| 18–21 February | Letter to VSW. Correcting two sets of proofs, 'in a state of marmoreal despair.' |
| 14 March | Recalls making up TL one afternoon. |
| *16 March* | MS 1. Date given on title page after 'finished.' |
| 21 March | Pleased with some parts of it. |
| 1 May | Wonders if it is good. |

PUBLICATION

| | |
|---|---|
| 5 May | The book is out. |
| 8 May | Letter to Vanessa Bell. Hopes she will like it. |
| 11 May | Records reactions to TL. |

| | |
|---|---|
| 13 May | Letter to VSW. Thought she would not like it. Thinks the dinner party the best thing she ever wrote. |
| 15 May | Letter to Ottoline Morrell. 'Time Passes' gave her more trouble than the rest of the book put together. |
| 16 May | Records more reactions to TL. |
| 25 May | Letter to Vanessa Bell. There is much of Vanessa in Mrs Ramsay. |

BLOOMSBURY STUDIES
General Editor: S.P. Rosenbaum

*The Bloomsbury Group: A Collection of Memoirs, Commentary, and Criticism* edited by S.P. Rosenbaum

Virginia Woolf *'The Waves': The Two Holograph Drafts* transcribed and edited by J.W. Graham

*Keynes, Cambridge, and the General Theory* edited by Don Patinkin and J. Clark Leith

*E.M. Forster: Centenary Revaluations* edited by Judith Scherer Herz and Robert K. Martin

Virginia Woolf *'To the Lighthouse': The Original Holograph Draft* transcribed and edited by Susan Dick

This book

was designed by

LAURIE LEWIS

and was typeset by

IMPRINT TYPESETTING

and was printed by

UNIVERSITY OF TORONTO PRESS

and was bound by

T.H. BEST PRINTING COMPANY LIMITED

1982